TERMINATED

A REVIVALIST NOVEL

Rachel Caine

A ROC BOOK

ROC
Published by the Penguin Group
Penguin Group (USA) Inc., 375 Hudson Street,
New York, New York 10014, USA

USA | Canada | UK | Ireland | Australia | New Zealand | India | South Africa | China

Penguin Books Ltd., Registered Offices: 80 Strand, London WC2R 0RL, England
For more information about the Penguin Group visit penguin.com.

First published by Roc, an imprint of New American Library,
a division of Penguin Group (USA) Inc.

First Printing, August 2013

ROC REGISTERED TRADEMARK—MARCA REGISTRADA

ISBN 978-0-451-46515-3

Printed in the United States of America
10 9 8 7 6 5 4 3 2 1

PUBLISHER'S NOTE
This is a work of fiction. Names, characters, places, and incidents either are the
product of the author's imagination or are used fictitiously, and any resemblance
to actual persons, living or dead, business establishments, events, or locales is
entirely coincidental.
   The publisher does not have any control over and does not assume any responsibility for author or third-party Web sites or their content.

ALWAYS LEARNING   PEARSON

PRAISE FOR THE REVIVALIST NOVELS

Two Weeks' Notice

"Caine's second series entry continues to raise the bar for urban fantasy.... It deals realistically and compassionately with both the undead and the dead and achieves depth in the process."
—*Library Journal*

"*Two Weeks' Notice* is good, fast-paced fun, and dives headlong into the action and high stakes one comes to expect from a Rachel Caine novel. The writing is brisk and competent, and as with the first book, I'm continually impressed with the fascinating take on 'zombies' in this series.... Bryn is a heroine [who] earns a place in a reader's heart." —The Book Smugglers

"[Caine] captures the sinister side of corporate America in this unique mix of urban fantasy and conspiracy thriller.... It was action-packed, full of twisty plot turns and surprises and a few 'I didn't see that coming' moments. *Two Weeks' Notice* would make an awesome TV series. If you enjoy conspiracy thrillers with a touch of urban fantasy, you are in for a treat."
—Badass Book Reviews

"Caine has succeeded in adding a different twist to a tired genre and created an increasingly complex series populated by strong characters pitted against übervillains.... The fast pace and sinister story line carry readers deep into the underbelly of greed, government control, and a lust for power. This is a series worth watching." —Monsters and Critics

"An entirely fresh take on zombies.... Layered characters and well-interspersed action scenes make the story exhilarating and engrossing." —*RT Book Reviews*

"Bryn is a fantastic character—a strong, independent woman with a soft side for her family and friends.... With even more suspense and chills than before, this sequel is an impressive blend of sci-fi zombie horror with the feel of a dark urban fantasy. *Two Weeks' Notice* is an extremely fast-paced, action-packed adventure that holds on and doesn't let go." —SciFiChick.com

continued . . .

Working Stiff

"One hell of a first novel in what looks to be a must-buy urban fantasy series. From world-building and plotting perspectives, *Working Stiff* completely rocks." —The Book Smugglers

"Caine's imaginative new series starts with a bang as she puts a frightening new twist to corporate greed and zombies. Fast-paced and full of surprises, this is one exciting thrill ride packed with both the best and worst of human behavior."
—Monsters and Critics

"A fun, thrilling new series. . . . Bryn is a capable and multifaceted heroine . . . a great new take on the popular 'zombie' subgenre. Even more interesting, perhaps, is the way Caine has her characters show respect for the dead—something that's missing from nearly every zombie book I've ever read. Well done, indeed." —SFRevu

"Completely engaging and impossible to put down. This unusual, macabre tale will attract both urban fantasy and zombie fans alike." —SciFiChick.com

"An utterly fascinating and unique plot in the urban fantasy arena . . . it will draw you in and not let you go until the very last page." —Bitten by Books

"*Working Stiff* has an interesting story line and there isn't a brain-eating zombie in sight. Conspiracy upon conspiracy made for a good read." —Night Owl Reviews

"[Caine] gives us another strong leading female character who has the right balance of emotion [and] kick-ass to make her come off of the pages as real to the reader. . . . *Working Stiff* has a steady pulse, pulling the reader from beginning to end to see how it all turns out." —Fresh Fiction

"From page one, *Working Stiff* was a wonderful surprise. . . . Bryn's careful, quiet personality is so winning and fierce, I was captivated." —All Things Urban Fantasy

"A smart zombie novel that goes beyond the typical reanimation explorations and delves into the world of big pharma and corporate takeover. . . . This series is shaping up to be a very rewarding and interesting new addition to the urban fantasy genre."   —Alpha Reader

"An intriguing new twist on the zombie mythology. . . . If you're looking for a twisty, fast-paced, escapist read, hop on the Revivalist train and settle down with *Working Stiff*. You can say, 'I was a fan from the start,' because if Caine can keep the suspense flowing in future books, this story has HBO series written all over it."   —*Fort Worth Weekly*

PRAISE FOR THE WEATHER WARDEN SERIES

"The forecast calls for . . . a fun read. . . . You'll never watch the Weather Channel the same way again."
                    —Jim Butcher, *New York Times* bestselling author of
                                                        the Dresden Files

"With chick lit dialogue and rocket-propelled pacing, Rachel Caine takes the Weather Wardens to places the Weather Channel never imagined!"   —Mary Jo Putney

"A fast-paced thrill ride [that] brings new meaning to stormy weather."   —*Locus*

"The Weather Warden books are an addictive force of nature that will suck you in." —*News and Sentinel* (Parkersburg, WV)

"Chaos has never been so intriguing as when Rachel Caine shapes it into the setting of a story. Each book in this series has built-in intensity and fascination."   —Huntress Book Reviews

"Rachel Caine is still going strong, throwing one curveball after another as she continues to shake up the status quo. She successfully maintains a sense of impending doom and escalating tension as the stakes get ever higher. . . . I really like this series, because it's urban fantasy that . . . tell[s] something exciting and original and ever changing."   —SF Site

BOOKS BY RACHEL CAINE

ACKNOWLEDGMENTS

This book wouldn't exist without the incredible patience of my editor, Anne Sowards, and the constant and awesome support of my assistant, Sarah Weiss. LOVE!

Chapter 1

The real problem with becoming a monster, Bryn thought, was that you didn't know whom to trust.

Bryn Davis, monster, paced the floor in silence, surrounded by her friends and allies, and she didn't dare trust a single one of them. Not fully, not now. Only one of them knew the truth of what she'd become . . . and even though Riley Block already shared the secret, and the curse, Bryn didn't know whether she could, or should, trust her.

As for the rest of them, they would be torn between horror and fury and pity, but someone would make it a mission to see her dead, and someone else would defend her, and it would tear everything, and everyone, apart.

Some secrets just had to be kept in utter silence.

"Bryn?" her lover, Patrick McCallister, said in the kind of voice one uses when the first few tries don't break through the haze. She stopped and looked up to focus on his face. *He's tired,* she thought, and despite how conflicted she was about her own situation, she wanted to comfort him. She loved him. It came from someplace deep inside, a wellspring she couldn't block even when she tried. "Bryn, did you get anything from the Pharmadene lab to tell us what they were working on in there?"

She felt a wild urge to laugh, but it was the same self-destructive impulse one might feel standing on the edge of a cliff. *Tell them,* something mad in her whispered. *Tell them, jump, just let it all go.*

Because she certainly had something: proof. The problem was it was coursing through her veins, twisting her into something that was even further from human than she'd been before. It was a far cry from being a dead woman, revived with a miracle nanotechnology drug and dependent on it for daily survival, to whatever she was now. Because her little life-mimicking machines had new programming.

Military programming.

Can't tell him that, she thought, and shook her head instead. "Didn't have time to do much exploring, since they were trying extremely hard to kill us," she said. "It looked like what I saw at the nursing home—they were using innocent people for nanotech incubators. Breeding more of the nanites. This was probably some kind of . . . factory farm." Not a lie, not quite. The nanotech was real, and they had been breeding it in the unconscious, drugged bodies. It was just the *type* of nanotech she was silent about.

"Riley—" McCallister turned toward the FBI agent sitting silently with her back to the wall of the small room. Bryn had rescued Riley Block from a hospital bed in that terrible lab, and as different as the two of them were, as fundamentally antagonistic in many ways, they had this secret in common. Riley didn't look up, but then, there were people in the way. Too many people. It felt terribly, oppressively crowded—this cheap motel room they'd rented as their temporary safe house was meant for a sweaty couple with no interest in anything save the bed.

Bryn felt constantly short of breath, on the verge of violence and screams. She wondered whether Riley felt the same.

Riley finally raised her head, and beneath the signature black bob, she seemed far away. Thinking, just as Bryn was, about her circumstances.

Patrick wasn't done trying to elicit information, and he pounced on the opportunity. "Riley, did *you* get anything from the lab?"

"No," the woman said, which was an outright lie. "No idea what they were doing, but Bryn's probably got it right. I was unconscious most of the time." She lied beautifully, Bryn thought, with just the right amount of flat indifference and just the right amount of eye contact. "How long do we have to stay here?"

McCallister shot a glance toward his old friend Joe Fideli, who was stationed at the window, looking through the quarter-inch slit between the glass and the curtain without disturbing the fabric. Those two men, Bryn reflected, had never lost their Army Ranger alertness, even though they'd cashed out years back—but then, Joe made his living guarding people. Fideli shrugged. "No way to know," he said. "We're still good for now."

Meaning it appeared that their enemies hadn't traced them here. Yet. It had been a hell of an escape from Pharmadene, the government-run drug company, and the chaos had worked to their advantage, but that didn't mean that their enemies wouldn't be on the case and tracking them down. Oddly, that probably wasn't the government itself—only a rogue body inside of it. So they weren't totally screwed yet.

Then again . . . it was impossible to know, but Bryn suspected that the nanites coursing through her body— Version 2.0, these tiny life-supporting machines—were *fully* trackable if the Pharmadene team still had the tech online to do it. Riley had the same issue. They'd done plenty of damage there, but had it been to the right equipment?

Despite the risk of discovery, she wasn't sure how much they dared tell her friends and allies . . . but she needn't have worried, because Manny Glickman, their burly mad-scientist-for-hire, was on it already. How in the world Patrick had first met the man was a mystery to Bryn, but one thing was certain: Manny had skills.

He also had a big backpack of stuff, and he'd unzipped it and handed his girlfriend, Pansy Taylor, a syringe from its depths. "Better safe than sorry," he said. "That's a frequency blocker for the nanites. Bryn, you and Riley had better take it. I'm not sure they can lock on you anymore, but I'd rather assume they were smart and we are smarter."

Of all the people Bryn didn't want knowing about her involuntary nanite upgrade, Manny was at the top of the list. Manny was brilliant, but he was also paranoid as hell, and although she wasn't sure he could kill her by himself, he'd damn well try, and he'd have something hidden in that bag that would be a nasty, premeditated surprise. Manny didn't like being at anyone's mercy and he didn't trust anyone, except possibly Pansy and Patrick McCallister.

Pansy herself was a bit of a puzzle, because she seemed so . . . damn normal. Forthright, sweet, and yet fully capable of handling herself in a fight if necessary. She eased past Patrick and Joe, and stepped around Riley's outstretched legs to crouch next to the woman and give her an apologetic smile. "Large-gauge needle," she said. "You'll feel it—sorry."

"I wish that was the worst thing that's happened to me today," Riley said, and rolled up her sleeve. Pansy administered the shot into Riley's bicep, then safety-capped the needle and approached Bryn with the same needle—no point in worrying about infection with the nanites on the job. Bryn took it without comment. It did sting, and then it burned, but as Riley had said, it wasn't the worst thing in her day. Not by a long shot.

"Excuse me, but can we discuss our resources?" That question, diffidently offered, came from the tall older man, Liam, standing near the bathroom ... and Bryn realized she had no context for Liam now. Before today, she'd known him as the urbane administrator/butler at Patrick's family estate—an Alfred to Patrick's uncostumed Batman, in a way. But since she'd seen him firing an automatic weapon while coming to her rescue, and looking as calm doing that as greeting guests at the front door, she wasn't sure she had any handle on him at all.

"Go ahead, Liam," Patrick said. "Let's get all the bad news out now."

"I can get us funds from the black account, but they'll cut us off soon enough. I initiated transfers to dump cash into various offshore accounts before I joined you today. They'll find some of it, of course, but not all. I estimate we may be able to count on a few million, no more—at least until this is resolved."

That sounded like a lot of money to Bryn, who'd grown up poorer than most, but she guessed that when you were expected to support a group of this size of fugitives on the run, and fight along the way, what seemed like a fortune might dwindle quickly. But then, Patrick's family had been insanely wealthy, in a way that made most of the legendary one percent look comfortably middle class. Oddly, Patrick didn't control the cash; his parents had put it all into a foundation administered by Liam. For being disinherited with prejudice, though, Patrick still did well for himself. Thankfully. The only thing worse than running for your life was doing it flat broke.

Bryn's sister Annalie had been uncharacteristically silent, huddled in the corner near Liam, but now she said, "Where are we going to go? Where *can* we go? They're going to find us, aren't they?" She sounded scared, but more together than Bryn would have expected her to be. Annie had never been tough—she was the flighty, impractical sister, the kindhearted one who constantly picked up good causes and dropped them in favor of even better causes. Never quite doing the right thing but trying for the right reasons.

And also, she was terrible with money. Terrible.

But none of that mattered anymore, because Annie, like Bryn—and Riley—was effectively Dead Girl Walking. The nanites—originally developed as a pharmaceutical called Returné, with the ambitious aim of reviving the recently dead on the battlefield—did their programmed job and kept them all breathing and talking and having a simulation of life, but something in their bodies was . . . broken. What kept them going wasn't resuscitation; it was life support. Annie still needed daily shots of the drug to keep going.

And Bryn and Riley had needed them, too . . . until the newly upgraded nanites had taken over back in the Pharmadene secret lab. Before they'd gotten away, Riley had claimed that these new, improved bugs powered, repaired, and reproduced themselves without any supporting shots at all.

She'd also said they were infectious. And Bryn supposed she had firsthand proof of that, because God only knew, someone had infected *her* with the stuff.

Now she had about thirty days to find a way to stop it or she'd pass on the nanites to some other poor bastard who was susceptible, once they'd matured within her. She'd infect someone. Spread the . . . the disease. Increase the army of nearly invincible soldiers for their enemies—at least, that was supposed to be the goal of the whole twisted program.

The implications of her condition were only just beginning to take hold . . . and the dangers. *I need to tell them,* she thought, and looked at Riley.

Riley was looking at her, too. As if she knew what Bryn was thinking. She gave Bryn a small shake of her head. *Don't.*

"I need—" Bryn said, but Riley spoke at the same time, louder.

"We need some food," she said, and that was true; it woke an instant and uncomfortable surge of hunger inside of Bryn that shocked and horrified her. Because what she craved wasn't just *food*. The nanites powering her now—these nanites needed protein. Meat. A lot of it. And they weren't picky about its source. The scientists had been hideously practical in their design of the little monsters . . . because one thing you could always find on a battlefield was *meat*.

"We'll eat once we're safe," Joe Fideli said, still staring out the window. "Can't exactly call out for pizza right now."

The prospect of having to wait to satisfy that craving was, frankly, terrifying. Bryn tried to ignore the hunger clawing at her, but she knew what it signified: the nanites needed power. And sooner or later, the nanites would take her conscious decision making out of the equation and simply find food—and look, there was a whole room of meat on the bone right here. Between her and Riley, it could be a bloodbath.

"Bathroom," Bryn said, and lunged for the door. She slammed and locked it, and dry-heaved into the sink, then raised her head and looked at her chalk-pale face. Her mouth felt dry, and she drank a few handfuls of water from the sink. Cold and fresh. It wasn't much, but it might help. She sank down on the toilet seat and put her head in her hands, shaking now. Trying not to think too hard about what her life had become.

Dead Girl Walking. That had described her before. But what was she now? A supercharged, meat-craving freak capable of passing on her sickness.

Say it.

Okay, then.

She was now a fucking *zombie*.

The worst thing about it was that she couldn't even really make a choice to end her own threat; the nanites that had kept her together before had made her mostly invulnerable, but these—these were military grade. She couldn't even count on killing herself if things got worse.

She was pretty sure the nanites wouldn't let her.

And she was pretty sure it would definitely get worse.

There was a soft knock on the door, and Patrick's voice. "Bryn? You okay?"

"Sure," she said. She wiped her face, although she was sure she hadn't shed any tears, took a deep breath, and stood up to unlock the door. He blocked the exit for a second, studying her, and she met his gaze without flinching. "I'm just exhausted."

"Do you need a shot? You look pale."

"I'm okay for now," she said. God, the shots. If she didn't own up to her new condition, she'd have to figure out how to explain to him about the shots. "It's just been—a lot to handle."

"I know," he said, and stepped in to give her a hug. "I'm sorry."

He felt so good, so warm, so solid . . . and she felt herself relax against him, just a little. He smelled good, too, as unbelievable as that might have been, after the day's fighting. He smelled like . . .

Blood.

Meat.

He smelled like food.

Bryn broke free and stepped back, suddenly cold again, and said, "Sorry, I need a minute." She slammed the door on him and locked it again, and took another look around the bathroom. *I can't do this. I can't handle this. I can't be around people I like, people I love . . .*

Because it wasn't safe.

The bathroom had a small frosted-glass window, but there were bars on the outside. The motel hadn't heard of fire regulations, evidently, because there was no quick-release on the bars, either.

It didn't matter.

Bryn smashed the window, pushed the bars out from

their moorings with one hard shove, and slithered out through the narrow opening. Her hips fit, though the concrete bricks scraped them raw, and the rest was easy enough. She thumped to the weedy, trash-strewn ground, took a second to get her bearings, and then headed for the eight-foot concrete wall a few strides away. A single leap took her to the top, right about the time she heard the door breaking down inside the motel room. She looked back in time to see Patrick at the broken window. He looked stunned.

Then he looked worried.

"Bryn, don't!" he called. "What are you doing? Don't!"

"I have to," she said. "I'm sorry. I can't explain right now, but please. Just let me go."

She dropped down on the other side, into a four-foot ditch below the wall's level, and then scrambled up and across the road. Not a lot out here in the country, but the road did have relatively brisk traffic with lots of long-haul trucks. Most truckers were wise enough not to stop for hitchhikers, but that wasn't what she was looking for.

She started jogging along the gravel edge, picking up speed to a flat-out run—and then, as the front of an eighteen-wheeler passed her, she leaped sideways.

Her timing was *almost* perfect. She landed on the hydraulic connectors for the trailer behind the cab and immediately slipped off, having miscalculated her momentum—then caught herself just before she slid underneath the wheels.

Bryn scrambled to a balance point and braced her back against the cold corrugated metal of the trailer, then settled herself against the bumps. It wouldn't be necessary to stay with the truck for long—in fact, it might be counterproductive, since Patrick would be dedicated in his search. She tried not to think about what might happen if her perch shook her loose—it probably wouldn't kill her, but it'd be unpleasant for sure.

When the truck slowed down at a crossroads twenty

minutes later, she jumped, landed and rolled into the low ditch next to the pavement, then stalked another truck and did the same jump-on maneuver. This one was easier, or she'd perfected the maneuver; either way, she settled in comfortably for a fifty-mile ride west. No particular destination in mind, because she had no idea what her plan was going to be, but putting space between herself and Patrick seemed like the only thing she could think about. She needed to know herself better before she took the risk of hurting him, or Annie, or any of the others.

But what about Riley? Isn't she just as dangerous? That worryingly practical part of her brain nudged at her, but the truth was, she didn't think Riley was as much of a threat. For one thing, Riley seemed to thoroughly understand her new condition, and she'd learned how to manage it. She'd been dealing with it longer and had made some kind of mental accommodation.

But Bryn didn't trust herself. Not yet.

Not when she was hungry.

She hopped off when the truck paused at a rest stop, one of the big complexes that catered to long-haulers; the luck of it was that it was like a shopping mall, full of clothes to replace the stained things she was wearing, and after she'd showered in the bathroom facilities and changed, she took the rest of her limited bankroll to the restaurant.

"What's your biggest steak?" she asked the waitress— a faded American beauty rose with gray streaks in her blond hair and a friendly smile.

"Well, that'd be the Big Tex, seventy-two ounces, but it's a stunt, honey; we serve it to those big-boy truckers and drunk frat boys, free if they finish it, which they hardly ever do. Otherwise, it's a cool forty bucks. Most don't even make it to the parking lot before they throw it all up. Maybe something like a porterhouse. How does that sound?"

"No," Bryn said. "I'll take the Big Tex. Rare as you can make it and not get closed down by the health department."

The waitress waited for the punch line. When Bryn didn't deliver one, she shook her head and wrote it down on her order pad. "Your ambulance ride, honey. Want any sides with it?"

"Just water," Bryn said. She tried for a charming smile, but the waitress had probably seen it all, and tilted a skeptical eyebrow before heading for the kitchen window. She and the cook had a conversation, and a balding man in stained whites leaned out to give Bryn a look. He, too, shook his head, but in a couple of minutes she heard the steak sizzling, and the hunger she'd tried to leash began to snarl with real ferocity.

Bryn squeezed her eyes shut. *Just wait. Wait. It's coming.*

She didn't know how long she sat there, struggling for control, but it snapped when a plate landed with a thump on the table in front of her—and there it was, seventy-two ounces of pure meat, drenched in watery blood. Just cooked enough to be legal, as she'd ordered. The waitress put down a glass of ice water and stepped back. "Okay, now, when you start feeling full, you just tell me and—"

Bryn didn't even use the knife and fork.

She grabbed the steak off the plate and held it in both hands, and bit into it. The waitress made a startled sound and took a bigger step back, but that hardly registered at all, because Bryn gnawed at the beef, tore at it, chewed and swallowed without even registering the taste except as blood and salt and flesh, and she didn't pause until she'd teethed the last threads of gristle from the bone. Then she broke the bone open with her hands and sucked out the marrow.

Something in her brain registered then—that refueling had been accomplished—and she dropped the fragments to the plate, sat back, wiped her mouth and chin with the napkin, and drank the entire glass of water in one long, convulsive gulp.

The silence got to her in the next few seconds, and she looked up to see the waitress standing ten feet away, back pressed to a wall, mouth open. The cook was leaning out the window with an identically shocked expression. Other diners were completely still, and every set of eyes in the place was fixed on Bryn.

One kid had his cell phone out and was recording. He stopped, put it down, and slow-clapped. "That was *awesome*."

"I—" Bryn swallowed, tried again. "I really love a good steak."

Someone laughed. But not the cook, and not the waitress. They'd seen a steady parade of tough guys in here trying to eat this steak, and Bryn imagined that most of them had left half on the plate.

And nobody had ever swallowed it in five minutes flat, ripping into it like a wild dog.

Bryn threw a generous tip on the table, and got out fast. She stopped again in the restroom to clean herself up. In the harsh lights, she looked—surprisingly fine. She wiped off the remaining grease and splatters of juice, but she felt good. Better than good. She felt . . . *great*.

I can do this, she told her reflection. A steak a day. Or any kind of meat, as long as it isn't . . . alive. It's strange, but I can do it. There's a way to deal with this. I don't have to be a monster.

But she couldn't shake the expression she'd seen on the waitress, either. Her definition of *in control* might be someone else's of *insane*. Either way, it was going to be hard to masquerade in normal life now, when hunger drove her to these kinds of extremes. And how often would it do that? How much would she have to eat? She'd have to ask some hard questions of Riley to find out, but she suspected that the amount of fuel she took on would have quite a lot to do with how much effort she put out.

And considering they were right now on the unprepared, unarmed side of a war ... effort would probably be considerable.

You can't run away from it, Bryn. This is what you are. Deal with it, because it isn't going away.

She went to the pay phones outside in the hallway—ancient things, but still working, thankfully—and phoned back to the motel. She asked for the room where they'd been staying, and was put through, and there was only half a ring before the call connected and Riley Block said, "What the hell do you think you're doing, Bryn?"

"You knew it'd be me."

"Of course I knew—I'm not an idiot. Where are you?"

"At a truck stop off Route 70," Bryn said. "I ate an entire seventy-two ounce steak in five minutes. I think I set the new record."

Riley was quiet for a moment. "Are you sure that was smart?"

"Almost certainly wasn't. But I couldn't—I wasn't sure I could control it, Riley. Around Patrick. Around Joe. And I can't stand that. I needed to eat, and waiting around for a trail bar and OJ wasn't going to cut it. You understand."

"You think it's safer out there? You're going to attract attention ordering those kinds of meals; you know that."

"I know," Bryn said. "But I had to have a little bit of time to myself. Just to test myself. To know—know if I can really control myself."

"I can see that. But you can't be out there on your own; you're going to get hurt."

"I know," she said. "That's why I'm calling."

"We're ready to leave here now," Riley said. "We'll pick you up. Stay in plain sight in the restaurant, and we'll find you. Have some pie. Live a little. It's not like you have to worry about your weight. No matter what you eat, it'll burn right off."

"Bright side to everything, then."

"Damn right," Riley said, and hung up.

Bryn went back to the restaurant, took her seat again, and ordered a piece of apple pie à la mode. Because Riley was right about the calories, this time her body was perfectly capable of enjoying the taste of a good pie. And it was good. Extraordinary. Or maybe that was just all her newly upgraded senses coming online.

She was tempted to order a second piece, but saw a large black van pulling into the parking lot. It flashed its lights twice, and she started to get out of her booth.

The waitress blocked her path. She was flanked by a tall, skinny man in a flannel shirt and jeans with a camera. "Just a sec, hon. We need to get your picture for the wall. This is Matt. He's the manager here."

Bryn was able to get her hand up just in time to block the flash, and shoved forward, knocking the waitress and the manager—who was still angling for a shot—out of her path as she headed for the door. "Wait!" the manager yelled. "It's part of the deal. We have to get a picture of anybody who eats the steak. Wait—"

She didn't. She was out the front doors, across the parking lot, and moving without pause into the black van, whose sliding door had opened for her. Bryn slammed it shut and said, "Drive," and Joe Fideli, behind the wheel, put the van in gear and accelerated smoothly away onto the access road.

There was a moment of silence, and Bryn looked around. Everyone—absolutely everyone, even Joe, in the rearview mirror—was studying her.

"Enjoy your meal?" Manny asked.

Riley was watching her, too, and after a bare second, she gave an almost imperceptible nod.

Bryn sighed. "I have to tell you something. You're not going to like it."

She was certainly right about that last part.

*   *   *

Bryn chose her words carefully, because she knew what she said next would change everything, forever. And she also knew that Riley was using her as a stalking horse . . . and that whatever she said about her own condition, she couldn't implicate Riley.

Not yet.

"You know that the version of Returné I originally was given needed daily shots," she began. "Manny improved the formula and edited out some of the programming to get past the less fun aspects, like being a slave operated by remote control. But the best he could do was extend the amount of time needed between shots."

Manny said, "You say that like someone else has done better."

"They have," she said. "Back there at Pharmadene. But it's a little bit more complicated. You know they were engineering the drug originally for the military, and the military had a problem with the shot-a-day barrier, which—along with the chancy conversion rate—was why they canceled their support. What we didn't know was that the project was still under way by a rogue department working for outside contractors, and that was what I stumbled into at that nursing home . . . a farm for advanced nanites, incubated in the unconscious bodies of people who didn't have anyone to look out for them." She still had hideous flashbacks of that place—of the quiet horrors that went on there.

"We know all that," Manny said. "What does this have to do with you running out for a fucking steak dinner?"

Riley turned her head toward Bryn, very slightly, but didn't make eye contact. Didn't give any kind of a signal.

"When Annie and I went to Pharmadene for safety, we found out they'd made headway on the military priorities," Bryn said. "We found out . . . the hard way. I'm infected with the upgrades now. I don't need shots anymore. What I do need—desperately—is high protein

meals. So you can't just stash me in a motel with a gra-
nola bar from now on. Sorry, but it's a . . . medical condition."

There was a frozen, electric moment of silence.

"Upgrades," Manny finally repeated. "That's why you
survived that fight at Pharmadene. But what do you
mean, you don't need shots?"

She took a deep breath, and took the plunge. "They're
self-replicating, the upgraded nanites. When they mature, they'll reproduce, and that colony will need to migrate to a new host."

Silence again, heavy this time, and finally, Pansy Taylor was the one who spoke up. "Okay, if nobody else
wants to, I'll say it. What you mean is that you're infected,
and you're going to be infectious. And when you say you
need protein, you mean you need meat."

"Jesus Christ," Joe Fideli said. He sounded grim, and
he looked it, too. "Fucking eggheads. The Defense Advanced Research Project Agency engineered the same
tech into their robot battle dog. Official press release
says that it could power itself from available proteins,
but nobody who looked it over was fooled. It eats
corpses. Or, theoretically, live prey, if it can bring it down.
That's what you're afraid of. You're craving meat, because that's how the nanites are powered. You're afraid
you're going to . . . what, eat us?"

"I—" She couldn't lie. "Yes. Maybe. I don't know. But
I needed food, and I couldn't take the risk of staying with
you. Manny, the incubation period is thirty days, so I
think I've got until then to figure out how to stop this
thing. I don't want to spread it. I promise—I don't. But
I'm going to need your help."

"Yeah," he said, "you damn sure do."

And he drew his gun and shot her in the head.

Bryn saw the flash, but she never heard the sound; it
was far too late.

The world blacked out.

When it came back, it did so in a thick, red rush of pain—a cascading signal that swept through her brain and out through every part of her body. The machine, coming back online, and bringing with it twists of agony that curled through her like whip-cracks.

She was aware she was convulsing—and then it was over, and she sucked in a cold breath of air and tried to sit up. She failed, but only because someone was holding her down. There was a smell of burned hair and blood and gunpowder, and voices shouting.

Violence in the air. The van had stopped moving.

"No," she said, or thought she did; she managed to fight the hands trying to hold her down. "No! Stop!"

It would have come as no shock to anybody in the van that she could return from a shot in the head, but still, it made them pause long enough for her to struggle up to a sitting position. "Don't hurt him," she said. Somehow, the words came out right, which was a surprise; she hadn't thought she'd be capable of stringing a sentence together, around the massive, wretched headache. The bullet must have gone straight through and not bounced, she guessed. That would have been a much bigger mess that would have taken time to heal, but even so, she'd have some explaining to do about the blood all over her brand-new clothes. "It's not his fault. He's responding to what he sees as a real threat."

Manny had been tackled, she saw, and Liam was zip-tying his hands behind his back. Pansy had surrendered, but her face was tense and her eyes glittered with fury. Riley Block was holding a gun on her, and paying attention to everyone else in the van as well.

"You know I'm not wrong," Manny said. "Bryn needs to be eliminated, and we need to get the hell away from her. Far away. Did you hear her? She's *infectious*."

"Then so is her blood, Manny," Patrick said. He was holding her, Bryn realized; she was now propped against his shoulder, and his arm was around her, holding her up.

"Everybody touched by blood spatter could be infected now. Including you."

"It doesn't work like that," Bryn said. She felt sick and weary now, and throbbing with pain that wasn't entirely physical. "Can't infect just anybody. Has to be one of the already Revived, according to what I heard back at Pharmadene. Otherwise, normal human immune systems will just kill the nanites."

It wasn't like Manny to react quite that violently, but they were dealing now not with the rational, brilliant scientist, but the man who'd once been buried six feet under in a coffin—buried alive. The same man, but one at the mercy of all his paranoid fears and phobias . . . and Bryn had run headlong into that wall of razors. So had Patrick, because all his observation accomplished was to provoke panicked yelling and thrashing from Manny, until Liam put him in a compression hold and sent him unconscious.

"That won't last long," Liam said. "He needs a sedative."

"Drug him and I'll kill you," Pansy said in a low, level voice. "Promise."

"Would you rather I continue to choke him out? Because I'm fairly sure that risks brain damage," Liam snapped, and Pansy, still smoldering, looked away. "Agent Block, the sedatives, please."

Riley reached down for a backpack leaning nearby, and rummaged through it to find a small zipped case. In it was a syringe and several vials of drugs. She prepared a shot and handed it to him. Liam slid it home and injected Manny just as the other man started to come to, and Manny subsided into unconsciousness again with a soft sigh.

"What about her?" Liam asked Patrick. Patrick studied Pansy for a moment, then shook his head.

"No. Pansy understands that Manny can be dangerous to himself as much as anybody else when he's in this mood. She knows that this is for his own protection."

"Fuck you, McCallister. He's your *friend*."

"He just shot my girlfriend in the head. I think I'm displaying some amazing restraint, Pansy, and you need to understand that we're up against the wall now. No room for bullshit and personal problems, all right? Those bastards at Pharmadene bought out part of the *FBI*, which is generally not known for its ability to be bribed or coerced. So *think*, and stop blindly reacting. We need a safe haven, one where we can test what's going on with Bryn and see what we're really up against. And we need to get off the grid, because sure as hell's on fire, my ex-wife, Jane, is coming for us and she's bringing an army with her." Patrick had never sounded so intense and certain, Bryn thought. And he was right. What they needed right now, more than anything else, was a safe place to plan.

Jane. She was their enemies' frontline general — one who really loved getting her hands dirty. Bryn shuddered. The smiling, cheerfully pathological face of the woman — no, the *monster* — loomed in her mind at the best of times now; she'd endured terrible things at Jane's hands, and the idea of ending up in that situation again was definitely not appealing.

That wasn't helped by the fact that Jane was Patrick's ex — something that, frankly, Bryn still couldn't think about without a stabbing jolt of betrayal.

She pushed the issue of Jane aside. Moving as a team meant getting Manny on their side ... or at least Pansy. Pansy could manage Manny, if she had to do it.

Pansy glared back for a long, long moment, then said, "Manny's never going to trust any of you again; you know that."

Patrick shook his head. "Manny can stuff it for all I care, because once again, he just *shot my girlfriend in the head*. You see the problem? I can't trust *Manny*, either. So we're even. But Manny's safe houses are the only shot we've got at staying alive at this point. Even if you both walked away, they'd find you eventually. He can't earn

money if he can't work, and he can't work if these assholes are on his trail and the world's falling apart. So you
have to do this, Pansy, out of pure self-interest. We have
to win. There's no other option."

She was silent for a long, long moment, and then she
nodded and took a deep breath. "I may just have broken
up with Manny, but I have to admit, you've got a point,"
she said. "Okay. Where are we, exactly? Geographically,
not metaphorically."

Joe Fideli—who Bryn realized was still in the driver's
seat, but turned to face them since he'd stopped the
van—lowered a gun that he'd been keeping ready, and
said, "Exactly? You want GPS coordinates?"

"Highway and nearest town."

He gave it to her, and she nodded and spewed back
directions, which Bryn couldn't follow, because her headache was literally blinding her. *Hold on,* she told herself,
as her stomach roiled in protest. *It'll pass. It'll pass.* It
didn't feel like that. It felt like dying, not healing.

She missed the moments that agreements were reached
and plans made, so the next thing she was directly aware
of was the van whipping a U-turn and speeding back the
way they'd come, which did not seem like so much progress to her, but she was willing to give up control to the
powers that be at the moment, and just rest. *Bullet in the
head still takes it out of me,* she thought, and was briefly,
painfully amused. *God, I need a shower. I reek of death.
Again.*

Oddly enough, though, she didn't feel hungry. Not yet.
So maybe the seventy-two ounce steak had actually done
some good.

They drove for what seemed like hours—steady, fast
speed, curves that must have been freeway changes. By
the time Bryn's lingering headache had vanished, Joe Fideli was pulling the van onto an off-ramp and slowing
down. "Almost there," he said. "Haven't seen any pursuit.
I think we're good so far."

"Either that, or they're just surveilling us and waiting for us to go to ground," Patrick said. "Easier and neater to take us out once we're in an area that can be controlled. So keep your eyes open, Joe."

"Don't I always?" For normally cheerful Joe, that was positively grumpy. "Keep your drawers on. Ten minutes."

It was a long, tense ten minutes; none of them believed they were going to make it, Bryn realized, and so it was an immense relief when the van slowed and stopped. "Pansy, we're at a gate," Joe said. "Looks like a pretty serious gate, actually."

"That's my cue," she said, and climbed over them to the sliding door. She slammed it shut behind her and about fifteen seconds later, the van moved on. The daylight outside the tinted windows darkened to shadow, and then went away completely as the angle of the van's progress changed to a downward slope. It took another two minutes for Joe to pull it to a halt, and then Pansy pulled the van's door open from outside and gave them a tight, wary smile.

"Welcome to the Batcave," she said.

She wasn't kidding.

Chapter 2

The Batcave — Bryn presumed that wasn't the actual name of the place, but she couldn't be too certain of it — looked impressive even from the parking area. It was big enough to park several eighteen-wheelers in a pinch, with high ceilings, and used an impressive amount of steel and concrete. There were major industrial buildings that couldn't boast this fine of an underground parking structure.

It had three exits she identified automatically — up the ramp, of course, but the ramp was blocked by a take-no-prisoners steel gate that wouldn't have been out of place guarding the CIA headquarters in Langley. A red sign announced there was an exit at the back, but it was almost certainly locked, too, at least biometrically. She wouldn't expect anything less from Manny Glickman. The man regularly elevated paranoia to an art form.

The third way out was the elevator, which Pansy had already summoned with the pressure of her hand on a palm scanner. It was a big industrial affair that they could have driven into in a pinch, and it held all of them without crowding. Patrick had the unconscious Manny over his shoulder in a fireman's carry.

Bryn expected the elevator to go up, but instead, it

went down. Down for at least a minute. She sent Pansy a look, and Pansy nodded to reassure her. "This place was a Cold War missile base. One of the few Titan bases they ever built—only about a dozen in the whole country. Manny got it in a sweetheart deal the second it went up for public auction about ten years ago, and he spent years building it out. One of the most secure spots in the country, until you want to go to war against another Titan base."

"I assume they took the missiles."

"Sadly true," she said. "But there's a half mile of tunnels, and more than forty thousand feet of storage and living space. This is where the serious work gets done around here. And I think we're serious now, right? Plus, if you need a secure base of operations, there isn't a better spot. We have hardened communications, a deepwater well system, our own generators, protected airflow, and enough food, drinks, and entertainment stocked to weather a nuclear winter."

The elevator lurched to a stop, and as the doors opened, Pansy gave them a warmer smile and led the way out. "Like I said, welcome to the Batcave. The guest rooms aren't fancy, but we at least have plenty of them. Kitchen and main housing is here in the center. Communications room doubles as the entertainment room, because what's the apocalypse without Xbox? Feel free to explore—oh, wait. Before you do, let me enter your data in the computer. Everything's security controlled."

They followed her to a small anteroom, which required another palm scan from Pansy to open; it had thick bullet-resistant windows and a view into hallways on two sides, with a second door at the other end. The curved console in it featured a state-of-the-art monitor and keyboard, and various equipment whose purpose wasn't immediately obvious. Pansy slid into the operator's seat, and fired up the computer.

It took a surprisingly small time to process each of

them through the security system—a palm scan, an ocular scan, and reading a short phrase into a microphone. Pansy was efficient and calm about it, though she was obviously bone-tired; she handed them each ID cards with clips when the process was done. "We've got extra clothing, too," she said, no doubt because Bryn's were messily ruined. "There's a wardrobe room on level two. Pretty much like a store, sorted by men's, women's, and children's wear, into sizes. Plain stuff, but it ought to work. Raid it as you need it."

She took a pair of wire cutters out of a drawer and snapped the plastic zip-ties securing Manny where he'd been deposited on a plastic chair, and then walked to the other door. Another palm scan to open it. "This way to the mansion," she said. "Oh, and wear your ID cards at all times. You can open the doors with palm scans or eye scans, but you need the ID card on you or the facility goes into lockdown. You don't want to be in the shower when that happens, by the way. I speak from experience. Um ... Patrick, could you ... ?" She gestured to Manny, and Patrick picked him up and carried him through the door. Bryn followed ... and realized that Pansy had been dead-on descriptive in calling this the mansion.

Either Manny or Pansy or both had taken a forbidding room and turned it into a beautiful, soaring living space—the floors were treated, subtly colored concrete, covered with expensive rugs and groupings of lush sofas and chairs. It was modern but comfortable, and vast impressionist and abstract canvases—almost certainly all real, and all insanely expensive—were mounted on the walls. The plasma screen TV was a vast size, but it looked small in the space, comparatively.

And they had books. Lots of books, with shelves that stretched up two stories—a library with its own system of movable wooden ladders.

"Wow," Riley said. "I guess being a mad scientist for

hire pays pretty well. Because I guarantee you he didn't earn this working at the FBI lab all those years."

Pansy gave her a cool, unreadable look, and said, "Thanks, Patrick, you can put him down here on the couch. Maybe you should all go get yourselves some rooms, showers, whatever. Just take the hallways going either right or left. Guest rooms have signs. You can write your names on the boards on the doors."

"Pansy—" Bryn wanted to hug her, but she knew it wasn't the time, and besides, she felt sticky and filthy. "Thank you. Thank you for doing this for us."

"You're probably worth the risk," Pansy said, and gave her a fleeting wink. "Manny's going to be a grumpy, angry bear, and I mean grizzly angry, but he'll come around eventually. Just . . . let me handle it. Oh, and guys? Weapons stay here in this room, with us. All of them. For our safety."

They all exchanged looks, especially Joe and Patrick; they didn't like disarming, but there was no threat here, especially nothing they could shoot their way out of. So with a shrug, Joe put down his converted AR-15, unholstered his handgun, and removed a couple of combat knives. Patrick added to the pile. Each of them did in turn. When the last person disarmed, Pansy nodded her thanks. "You'll get it all back," she promised. "We have an armory on level two. It takes a special code, which Manny and I have. Once he's sure you're all okay, he'll probably share it with you, but it's not for me to do. I've done enough already. Oh, I almost forgot, one more thing. Arm, Bryn. You too, Riley."

She produced two syringes. Riley frowned and shook her head. "We don't need that. The upgrade means no daily shots."

"I know," Pansy said. "The shot I gave you earlier canceled out the tracking frequencies for your nanites, but these will deactivate the tracking functionality altogether. Otherwise, they'll be colonizing bones and making you a living GPS, and we can't keep giving you the neutralizer shots. So be quiet and take your medicine, ladies."

Bryn couldn't object, and neither did Riley; they knew the risks, and also knew how big a gift they'd been given.

Although Manny might end up stuffing them back in the van and out the gate just as quickly. She supposed that she ought to get a shower, new clothes, and as much rest as possible before he woke up, so after the burn of the shot that Pansy administered had subsided, she joined Patrick as he left the main living area and took the door into the hallway to the right. "I can't quite believe this," Bryn said, and ran her fingers over the smooth, cool concrete of the walls as they walked. "How the *hell* does he afford all this?"

"You really want to know?" Patrick asked.

"Sure."

"He holds the patent on at least three major lifestyle drugs developed in the past fifteen years, and he does independent consulting work for dozens of research labs—that's his clean income. He gets much more from sources that aren't quite as . . . aboveboard. Insanely rich people wanting a special drug developed for their own use, for instance—a safe, special, legal high. Private forensic work for corporations that don't necessarily want to involve law enforcement. That sort of thing. He holds a lot of secrets, Manny does, and all that just feeds his native paranoid tendencies. Add to that a certain agoraphobia, and . . . you end up here, in a missile bunker."

"But one with great amenities."

"Exactly." He smiled, but it was weary and small, and she took his hand in hers. "Ah. I guess this is one of the guest rooms."

It was labeled that way, with a simple black nameplate, and a write-on/wipe-off board below that. Bryn wrote her name on the board and opened the door. She was expecting the basics—a plain bed, maybe a desk, a simple shower. But the room was lushly carpeted, with a broad king-sized bed, nightstand, work desk, art . . . and a modern full-sized bath. Suddenly, Bryn craved every single bit of that with an intensity that made her shake.

She looked wordlessly at Patrick, and he read it in her. He leaned in and kissed her gently. "Go catch a shower and rest," he said. "We can talk later."

What he wasn't saying was that they *needed* to talk later, but she understood. It didn't matter just now. She was far too sore, too exhausted, too dirty to care, and she closed and thumb-locked the door, stripped off her bloody clothes down to the skin, and was in the shower and shampooing her hair before she remembered she hadn't thought to go to the wardrobe room. *Damn.*

That, she decided, was a problem she'd face later. Half an hour of hot water later, she toweled her hair dry and crawled naked between the sheets, and was asleep within seconds of hitting the dimmer switch by the bed.

She probably could have slept the clock round, but six hours later, a doorbell she didn't know she had rang a soft chime, and the room's lights automatically brightened themselves to a soft shimmer, enough to let her make her way to the door. She remembered she was naked about two seconds before opening it, and hunted in the closet to find—*yes!*—a fluffy white bathrobe that enveloped her in sandalwood-scented luxury.

She found Liam standing on the other side of the door when she opened it. He was holding a set of hangers, and bowed slightly as he handed them over. "I took the liberty," he said. "Patrick thought you might need something, considering how damaged your clothing was. He didn't think you had the energy to go shopping."

Liam had also freshened up; the jeans and checked shirt he wore weren't his usual dapper style, but he still looked starched, somehow. She took the clothes and smiled back at him. "Thanks, Liam. Um . . . I didn't have time to ask, but . . . are the dogs okay . . . ?" Because one thing the two of them shared was a love of dogs. His were the various hounds that lived at the McCallister estate; hers was a bulldog that had gotten caught up in the recent chaos. And she'd missed him badly.

"I made sure we recovered them outside of Pharmadene, including Mr. French," he said. "I had the opportunity to board them before we came for you. I'm afraid anything we left in the estate is probably going to be seized, at best, and I was afraid to leave the dogs to their tender mercies."

It hurt her to think of her adorable bulldog, Mr. French, in some boarding cage, but she couldn't do anything for him just now—and besides, knowing Liam, it would be the cushiest pet spa of all, and Mr. French wouldn't want for a thing. Right now, she needed her dog's unquestioning love more than he needed hers.

Her world had narrowed down into the single goal of kill or be killed, and her sweet pet didn't have any place in that. And she wasn't cruel enough to pretend he did.

Even if she wanted to.

"May I ask you something?" he said, and she blinked and focused back on Liam. "Your . . . new biological status. How dangerous are you, Bryn? Really?"

"Not dangerous to you or Patrick," she said. "Maybe a little, to my sister, because she's already got the nanites. These upgrades can't infect regular people, only those brought back with Returné."

His smile didn't waver as he said, "You wouldn't be lying to me about that, would you?"

"I wouldn't, Liam."

"I'd fully understand if you felt the need," he said. "But it would be a rather massive mistake to give in to the temptation."

She nodded, just a little, and didn't break eye contact. "You'd kill to protect him," she said. "I know that."

"Specifically, I would kill *you* to protect him," Liam said. "If you posed a clear and present danger. But I will take your word for it that you don't." The unspoken part of that was *for now*, and Bryn clearly understood it, and acknowledged it. "Dinner is being served. I thought you might be hungry."

She was, she realized. Very. Which was upsetting and worrisome. Bryn clutched the clothes to her chest, closed the door and dressed very quickly; it all fit, more or less, and as she came out of the room she saw her sister waiting in the hallway.

Annie looked pale and drawn, and when she saw Bryn, her eyes filled with tears. She came over, and they hugged silently for a long, long moment. "I was so worried about you," Annie whispered. "God, Bryn. You okay?"

"Yeah, I'm fine," Bryn said, and patted Annie's back. "Not like we haven't been through worse, right?"

"That is way too right to be funny anymore. Oh God, I guess we're going to have to call the fam pretty soon and lie to them, aren't we? Just so they don't freak out and do something stupid like call the cops and file missing persons on us."

That was an excellent point, and Bryn was a little startled that she hadn't thought of it. "God, you're right. We had to ditch the cell phones, after all. They might think we've been—"

"Abducted," Annie said, and burst into strange, borderline-hysterical laughter. "Funny, isn't it?"

The laughter was infectious, and Bryn felt it bubbling its way up out of her too—not humor, exactly, but a black kind of amusement liberally mixed with despair. She clung to Annie, and Annie held on to her, and they laughed it out until they finally got enough breath to separate.

Annie wiped her eyes and said, "I guess we really should eat something, right?"

"I hope they have steak," Bryn said. "I *really* hope they have steak."

In fact, they did. Evidently, Riley and Pansy had put their heads together, and dinner was mostly available self-serve in pots and pans . . . but there were steaks, big ones, and a small stack of them were left almost raw. When Bryn took a plate, Riley—who looked rested and fresh, too—pointed her toward the meat. "Specially made," she said. "I think you'll find it's what you need. It helped me a lot."

"You already ate?"

"Had to," Riley said. That was a short answer, but it conveyed a lot, especially when she raised her eyebrows just a bit. "Pansy was kind enough to fix something."

That must have been quite the culinary conversation, Bryn thought. "Is Manny awake?"

"Oh, yes," Liam said, where he was spooning broccoli onto his plate beside a chicken breast. "Mr. Glickman woke very loudly. He is now barricaded in his room and says he will not come out until you and Riley vacate the premises and he has a chance to decontaminate the rooms."

"He'll come around," Pansy said. "It was just the shock. He'll be monitoring to make sure everything stays chill. If it does, he'll come out in a few days. You'll see."

"We don't have days," Patrick said. He and Joe already had plates and were seated at the table, and Joe was halfway through what looked like some kind of stew. Bryn plated her steak and carried it over to sit next to them. "We have *a* day, maybe, but the people behind the Fountain Group's research, whoever they are, however they intend to use all this sick technology. . . they clearly have more money than Gates. They'll find us, and as good as this place is, it has vulnerabilities—principally, it's a bunker, which means limited ways in and out. They can, and will, find a way to dig us out, and we'll have a hard time slipping by them once they settle in. So here's my thought: we let them lay siege, but some of us go on now and take the fight directly to their doorstep. We can't win this by fighting a defensive war."

"How exactly can we do that, when we have no idea where their doorstep might be?" Annie asked, as she put her food on the table and sat down beside Joe. "Other than Pharmadene, I mean. I'd rather not take the fight to them there again, please."

"The FBI will take good care of Pharmadene; trust me, they're probably not too happy that their people got subverted in the first place," Bryn said. "But we *do* know something. We know who owned the old folks' home that was our first introduction to the nanite harvesting."

"The Fountain Group," Patrick said. "Liam's doing the research. Well, he was before we had to break off and run, but I suppose membership in this fortress comes with Wi-Fi access."

"If you ask me nicely," Pansy said sunnily. "The password is randomly generated, and it changes every day. I'll let you know where to get the new codes."

"Wow," Bryn said. "Doesn't it just make you tired? All the ... security?"

"Sure," Pansy answered, and spooned up soup. "But you end up surrendering things, little by little, when your partner needs more than you do. And Manny needs it. You get used to it. It's not any different from living here when the Titan missile program was actually under way, only we have Blu-ray and surround sound."

"That's one way to look at it, I suppose. Liam?"

"I'll continue the Fountain Group investigation immediately," Liam nodded. "Of course, they will know we're onto them once I begin to dig hard."

"They can't trace it here. We use a lot of anonymizers."

"Of course you do, dear Pansy. But nevertheless, they will know someone is checking, and that will cause them to upgrade their alert status. I imagine that will make them move with a bit more speed. We should factor it in."

Bryn controlled the sudden urge to tear into her steak with her bare hands, and forced herself to use the steak knife and fork she'd brought over with her. The first bloody, juicy bite of meat made her shiver in cell-deep relief, and she closed her eyes and let out a slow sigh of a breath.

When she opened her eyes, they were all looking at her.

"Good steak," she said, and took another bite. They watched another few seconds, probably to be sure she wouldn't turn ravenous zombie on them, and went back to their own meals.

Pansy, Bryn noticed, had strapped on a sidearm, and she'd been aiming the weapon at her under the table the whole time. Now Pansy slipped it back into its holster and gave Bryn a half-apologetic lift of her shoulders. Bryn didn't really blame her. Being ready at all times to kill her, at least temporarily, was probably the bargain that Pansy had made with Manny to allow Bryn to stay—and it was good tactical sense. And for all her calm good humor, and seeming fragility, Pansy was perfectly capable of pulling the trigger when it counted. Much like Manny, although Manny was often a bit *too* eager on that score.

"Liam's right," she said, as she cut her third bite. "Once you start poking into the Fountain Group, they'll react, and if we're sending a team out of here, it needs to be away before they're parked outside our front door. The point of having a fortress is to pin our enemies down in one place and leave a strike force mobile. I say we stay the night and head out in the morning—and *then* Liam starts his Internet stalking. He can send us info as he gets it."

Nobody had any objections, except for Annie. She was glaring across the table at Bryn. "You're going to leave me stuck here, aren't you?" she asked. "Oh, come on, I know it's coming. I'm the stupid kid sister liability."

"No," Riley Block said. She'd already finished half her steak, eating quickly and quietly, but she drew all their attention now. "You're a liability for several reasons, Annie. You're not combat trained, for one thing. For another, you still require the shot daily, and that means carrying supplies that can be destroyed or lost, putting you at risk." She exchanged a glance with Bryn, and made a decision. "I didn't say it earlier because I thought it might complicate matters, but ... I don't need the shots, either. I'm upgraded. Like Bryn."

Silence around the table, and then Patrick said, tightly, "Why keep that from us?"

"Because when Manny found out *one* of us was upgraded, he shot Bryn in the head. I had good reason to think he'd take a more salt-the-earth approach if he thought it was some kind of epidemic."

Joe thought it over, and he was the first to shrug. "Fine by me," he said. "The way I see it, we're going to need advantages if we intend to have any kind of a shot at winning."

Annie licked her lips. "But—I could help, right? I could. I'm not helpless."

"There is no *but* to it," Riley said. "You're a liability, and you stay here. Manny and Pansy have all the supplies necessary to make the serum for you, and you can help them defend this place if needed. Besides, I'm sure Bryn would feel better not having to worry about losing you, again. If you were my sister, I'd want you kept as much out of danger as possible, Annie, because you're family. I'm pretty sure Bryn feels the same."

Annalie fell silent, studying Riley; it was exactly what Bryn would have said, but somehow, it was going down much better coming from an impartial third party. And incredibly, Annie nodded. "Okay," she said. "I admit, that makes sense. But I hate being the one who isn't, you know, up to it."

"The best people are the broken ones," Pansy said,

"because we heal stronger. Look at Manny and me. We've been shattered and glued back together, just like you. You're not fragile, Annie. You're still healing. There's a difference."

Annie took a deep breath, and nodded. She even ate some broccoli, which Bryn knew she loathed. Seemed like a good first step.

"So we rest," said Joe Fideli, "and hit the road tomorrow. Pat, me, Riley, Bryn. Liam and Annie stay here with you, Pansy. Sound right?"

"It sounds perfect. Make me a list of what you want to take with you in terms of supplies and weapons, and I'll get it together. How's the chow?"

"You should open an underground fortress restaurant and day spa," Joe said. "Maybe put in a massage therapy room, an aromatherapy pool . . ."

"You're assuming we don't already have one?"

"I'd never assume a damn thing about you, Pansy. Because I'd always be wrong."

"You say the sweetest things, Mr. Fideli. Just for that, I'll give you the half-off special on hot stone massage."

"Before you two start making small talk about rolfing, let's get serious for a moment," Patrick said. "We're going to need more than just the four of us. Does Manny have any contacts he can touch?"

"Don't *you*?"

"Yes. But I'm almost certain they'll all be tagged by now. Manny's friends, on the other hand, will be much harder to identify, locate, and hopefully to sideline."

"His friends like to be paid. They're kind of, you know, mercenary."

"We can do that," Liam said. "For a short time, anyway. I'm presuming that this is not a long-term struggle."

"If it is, we'll lose," Patrick said. "The Fountain Group is a very clear threat; they stepped in when Pharmadene folded, and they had enough influence and forward planning to infiltrate the FBI and take control of the research program—and make the upgrades. We don't know what they're planning, only that they have gone too far to stop, and they clearly don't have any kind of moral limit. We'll have the government backing us, at least the honest parts of it, for some of what we do. But if we can get to the people who run the Fountain Group, do it fast and surgically, we can break this down in a matter of days. That's our goal. Days, not weeks."

"Good, because I don't want to have my wife and kids in hiding forever," Joe said. Bryn felt a twinge of guilt for that, because it was her fault that his family had been drawn into all this, even tangentially; they were great kids, and Kylie was a lovely woman. Joe didn't deserve to have his life destroyed, but now that they were all marked for destruction, there wasn't any choice. It was fight and win, or lose everything.

Patrick caught Bryn's eye, and held it, as he said, "We're not giving up. Nobody here is giving up. It's not in our natures."

After that, it seemed as if a dark shadow had passed. Bryn and Riley finished their steaks; everybody else ate their dinners; Joe and Annie and Pansy traded friendly, snarky banter. Liam added in the occasional dry bon mot. It was . . . comfortable.

Bryn glanced up in the corner, and realized that there was a small camera installed there. She'd subconsciously been aware of it, she realized—and aware that Manny was almost certainly watching them.

She picked up her plate and silverware, walked to the sink, and washed everything before loading it in the dishwasher. Let him observe that the ravening, unpredictable zombie was being domestic. Maybe he'd change his mind, a little, if she didn't do anything to freak him out again. Pansy often referred to "talking Manny off the ledge," and sometimes she meant it literally—but his mood was more focused on homicide than suicide, Bryn thought.

She got herself a glass of wine from the common bottle, and touched Patrick on the shoulder as she passed him. "I'm going to my room," she said. "We need to talk. Come see me."

He shot her a glance, clearly assessing, and then nodded. In all the chaos and fury of their escape from Pharmadene, she hadn't had time to address the big five-hundred-pound gorilla standing between them, but tonight . . . tonight that had to change.

Tonight, they had to talk about her new status as what amounted to a full-on zombie, if mercifully free of the rotting flesh . . . and, although it might be something selfish, they also had to talk about something Patrick had chosen to hide from her.

One way or another, whatever else the conversation brought . . . they were going to talk about Jane.

Bryn waited in her room sitting at the table; she'd found a stack of books on a small shelf in the corner, and was thumbing through a pretty interesting account of an Amazon explorer when the knock came at the door.

Deep breath.

She opened it, nodded to Patrick, who nodded back, and shut the door behind him. She took the edge of the bed, and he didn't try to sit beside her; one thing about Patrick, he'd never been colorblind to nuances. He took the office chair and rolled it close, sat, and put his elbows on his knees as he leaned forward. She didn't think she'd seen him looking quite so lumberjack-casual before; the jeans and hiking boots suited him. So did the gray tee under the checked shirt. It made his late-day beard growth look comfortable and appropriate.

She had to admit it: she liked him scruffy. But she had to put that aside, in a mental closet, and lock the door on it, because this discussion wasn't going there.

At all.

"So," he said. "You're . . . the new, improved model."

"I'm still me, Pat. You know that I am. I'm just . . . tougher to hurt. Comes in handy, believe me."

"I do," he said. "But we didn't even fully understand the fallout from the original version of the drug, Bryn. And now . . . now you're carrying around something that's first-trial experimental. You have to promise me that you'll tell me if you feel something is . . . different. Anything."

"Well," she said, "I have this totally unsettling need to overeat. You know how when you're pregnant, they say you're eating for two? Well, I'm eating for about a hundred billion of these little bastards." She tried to make it sound flippant, but it scared her, and she knew he saw it.

But it was okay. It was okay to be scared, with him.

"Don't keep it from me if anything changes," he said. "Promise me."

"Yeah, speaking of that, you should have told me that your ex-wife was a psychopathic sadist killer for hire," she said. "Or, failing that, you could have at least told me you'd been married before."

"It was —" He stopped and shook his head, looking down at his boots for a moment before meeting her gaze again. "It was not something I want to look back on very much, Bryn. I was hoping you'd get that."

"You must have loved her."

"I did," he said softly. "We were young and we shared the same ideals, the same goals. I met her in the military. It's a hothouse environment, and it breeds obsessions . . . and we obsessed on each other. I admit that. But I truly thought we could make it work once we'd shipped home, and we did, for a while. But she had a dark side, darker than mine, and it just kept . . . growing. By the time she volunteered for the Pharmadene trial, when they were first testing the nanites . . . she was already a little unstable. I tried to stop her from signing up, but she just wouldn't let me."

"Jane was one of the first, then. One of the first Returné experiments."

"Yes. And she was a success. A brilliant success. She adapted so well, so quickly to the nanites that it seemed to prove everything that they'd been hoping . . . until she turned violent. It was the dark side, the one I'd been worried about. She started . . . hurting people—small stuff, at first. Then, the second mission they sent her on, she killed someone. Not just . . . killed. She killed him unnecessarily hard." He looked away. "You know what she's like now—she wasn't quite that bad then. They asked me to—to try to reach her. Bring her back from the edge. But she tried to kill me, too, Bryn. And I had to . . . I had to try to stop her. I thought she was dead—I really did. They told me she was *dead*. And the worst part of that was that I was really glad, because I knew she'd have only gotten worse."

"And she did," Bryn said. "A hell of a lot worse. I should know, Patrick. She had me strapped down at her mercy for *hours*. And she liked to hurt me. She enjoyed it as much as any serial killer ever did."

He flinched, then. "I'm sorry." He reached out for her hand, but she kept both in her lap, and he finally sat back. "You're right. I should have told you about her, but—I really thought that she was dead. I thought she was the past. I was hoping—"

"When you met me, and I was newly Revived, you thought you'd try to keep me from becoming Jane. I get that. You transferred what you felt for her to me." God, this hurt; it boiled in her guts like liquid nitrogen, achingly cold. "I can't be Jane for you, Patrick."

"You're not. God, Bryn, you are *not*. I don't know how to make you believe that, but—"

"You can't," she said. "Not right now. You should have told me. Maybe with that in the open between us, we could have found a way around it, but right now . . . right now I believe in my heart that I was a replacement, and

I don't want to be a replacement. Not for *her*. She tortured me, Pat, but finding out she was your wife . . . that really cut me, in ways I can't even explain."

He took in a sharp breath, and almost spoke, but then he stood up and rolled the office chair back to the desk. He held on to it with both hands, facing away from her, as he said, "Can you trust me enough to have your back when we leave here? Because right now, that's the most important thing. Trust. Everything else . . . everything else will take time, but we need trust now."

"I know you will do the right thing," she said. "I've always trusted you for that. You're my ally and my friend and my colleague. But that's all right now. That's all I can handle. There's too much—too much *chaos*. Because the upgrade I was given—it's what Jane had, too. It might take me down, just like it destroyed her from the inside."

"Not you," he said, and turned to face her. "I told you, Jane had a dark streak, something that the nanites just enhanced. You . . . you're different, Bryn. You're not cruel. And it won't change you, not like it changed her. I believe that."

Bryn wished she could believe it herself; she wished that with a passion that seemed all out of balance. But she understood the madness and malice in Jane in a way that she feared she'd see in herself, in the mirror; there was something about being so *capable* of violence that made it almost inevitable. When violence was such an easy answer, so effortless . . . it quickly became the only answer.

"Thank you," she said, and meant it. "I'm sorry. I wish I could—I wish I could be what you want right now. But I can't."

"You said you could still be yourself," he said. "Prove it."

"Sorry?"

"It's killing me, Bryn. Because I love you, and I get that you believe I'm using you as some . . . stand-in for my ex. I'm not. You're not her, and I've never for one moment confused the two of you. But I have to ask it straight out—do you still feel something for me? Anything?"

His directness took her breath away for a moment, and so did the steady, calm way he studied her. "I really hated you when I found out about Jane," she said. "Apart from everything else, even the horrible things that have happened to me, it felt like the only person I could trust stuck the knife in."

A shadow moved over him, and she saw his face tense, ready for the blow.

"But I still do love you," she said then, quietly. "I almost wish I didn't. I'd rather keep you at arm's length, because . . . because I'm afraid I'll hurt you, like Jane. Or lose you. And that would destroy me, too."

He looked down for a moment, and without making eye contact again, said, "Would you let me kiss you? Because I need to do that right now."

She was afraid to—not because she thought she'd hate it, but because she was afraid that it would unleash a torrent of feelings she couldn't control. Things that might sweep them both again. Of the two of them, it was *Patrick* who had a bit of darkness in him, and she couldn't let that carry him away, either.

But she came into his arms.

His lips met hers with exquisite slowness.

The warmth came first—the feeling of his skin glowing on hers before the touch, whisper-soft and then firmer, hotter, damp and smooth and rough where his beard rubbed her chin. It was a long kiss, and it tasted like dark things to her, sweet and disturbing. And it made all of her body warm and tingle and respond, and she broke free with a gasp.

"Go," she whispered, and sank down on the bed. "Please just leave. I'm sorry."

He didn't speak, and he didn't delay for more than a

few seconds; she saw him in the periphery of her vision as he moved away, walked to the door, and she heard the click of the catch as he pulled it shut behind him.

Only then did she raise her hand to her lips.

Whatever magnetism Patrick held for her, it was still there, still stronger than logic and reason. Stronger than pain and disappointment. She wanted him. Every part of her body *needed* him.

And she couldn't possibly deal with that, and the complications it represented. Not now.

She undressed, wrapped herself in sheets and blankets, and surrendered herself to the darkness, for a few precious hours of restless, nightmare-driven sleep.

It was hard to tell night from day, but evidently the lights were programmed to help—at dawn, the room lights slowly increased in intensity, and Bryn woke up feeling as if she were bathed in morning sunlight. It was a nice feeling. Calm.

And then she remembered that she was essentially buried deep, deep underground, she was essentially dead, and people really were trying to destroy everyone she loved. So that good feeling passed quickly.

She still treasured the shower; common sense told her it might be the last luxury she experienced for a while, so she made the most of the hot water, foaming soap, and floral shampoo. The fluffy robe came in handy again, and then she put on the same clothes she'd worn the night before. They felt cool and comfortable against her flushed skin. She brushed her teeth and hair, and looked in the mirror for a long, silent moment.

I should look different, she thought. When someone made you a monster—more of a monster than before—you ought to stop looking like yourself. It was confusing, and probably heartbreaking for everyone around her, that her new flesh-craving self looked so ... normal. Zombies should announce themselves with mindless ambling and snarling, at the very least. It was only decent.

A knock at the door startled her out of useless contemplation, and she opened it to find Joe Fideli standing there, fully kitted out in street clothes, with a bulky black duffel bag slung over his shoulder. He rubbed his shaved head and gave her an impartial smile. "Morning," he said. "Time to pack up, Bryn."

"Yeah, I figured," she said, and shut the door behind her as she stepped out in the hall with him. "You're already geared up?"

"I like to shop before the stores get busy," he said. "Plus, I admit it, I wanted my pick of the good stuff. Don't worry, I don't wear your size."

She gave him an eye roll and an air kiss, and he nudged her with an elbow in reply. She and Joe were comfortable together—had been almost from the start. He was just . . . a real guy. A good man. No sparks between them, but genuine comfort. "How heavy are we packing?"

"Can't afford to get caught with anything technically illegal, so I kept it to the legal carry weapons, plus a couple of bonuses we'll have to not show unless we mean to use them. Easiest way for our enemies to take us out is to trap us and call the cops on us. We end up in cells, easy pickings. So we do everything legal and aboveboard, until we don't. Right?"

"Right," she agreed. "But I actually meant, how many days of clothes did you bring?"

"I'm a guy, Bryn. It ain't like I'm going to need a lot of variety."

They had reached the end of the hall, and he led her down a set of metal spiral steps to the next level down. A door with a biometric lock on it was labeled ARMORY, but they bypassed that for the moment, and went into one called WARDROBE.

It was like a mini-mall. There were even signs on the

walls calling out sections for men, women, and children.
At the back, there was a mini–shoe store. Bryn checked
the racks, and found more practical outfits for herself —
shirts, pants, nothing fancy and nothing that would get
her noticed in a crowd. She added a light jacket and
a thick coat, because she wasn't sure where they'd end
up, and a pair of boots in addition to the athletic shoes
she was already wearing. Underwear. The bras were all
stretchy sports models, which were practical to cut down
on the sizing choices.

She finished in fifteen minutes, and loaded everything
into another duffel (suitcases and bags were in the far
corner). Hers was navy blue, and once she'd packed it,
she hefted it over her shoulder and nodded. "Next," she
said. Joe took her out of the wardrobe room, and to the
armory.

She wasn't surprised, by that point, that the armory
was the size of a small-town gun show, ranked neatly
from revolvers to semiautomatic handguns to shotguns,
and all the varying types of rifles (sniper, hunting, military assault). Manny showed a little bit of a predisposi-
tion toward American made, but it was a veritable U.N.
of killing power — Israeli, Russian, German, Swiss, Bel-
gian, Chinese. Bryn whistled. "Gives new meaning to the
term *stockpile*," she said. "Does the ATF know about
this?"

"Hell, those guys probably helped him get half this
stuff. The feds love Manny," Joe said.

Bryn picked her favorite handgun from the rack — a
Glock 23, with the standard thirteen round clip. The extended clips added more rounds but jutted from the butt
of the gun and threw off the weight, at least in her opinion. It was a solid weapon, favored by various US agen-
cies, including the FBI, and it had the reputation of being
one of the most reliable, even in rapid-fire situations.

Shotguns were heavy weight, but they were decisive
in close quarters, and after consulting with Joe about his

choices, she added a Winchester of her own, and then chose an FN PS90, the civilian version of the selective-fire P90. She'd always felt comfortable with them, and from her army experience, they were sturdy and accurate.

Ammunition took up the rest of the space in her bag, and when she hefted it, it was about as much weight as she felt comfortable carrying. "Where's the checkout?" she asked, and Joe grinned.

"I'm guessing that the scanners in here tote it all up, and Manny will bill us later," he said. "He's not a giver, really."

That was very true. Manny had, from the beginning, made it very clear that his help came with a price, and a hefty one. Bryn respected that. She also knew he'd never bargained for this much trouble, either, and she wondered if Patrick had thought about what to do if Manny ever decided to switch teams on them. He could, any time. Pansy would try to stop him, that was certain, but Manny didn't always listen to her, especially when it came to personal security issues.

Bryn knew she'd tested the limits of his tolerance, and probably shattered them, and he was certainly not happy with the current situation. The only thing stopping him from selling them out would be the certainty that if he did, the Fountain Group would never let him live with as much as he knew about their business.

Self-interest would keep him on their side, at least.

They met Riley and Patrick upstairs again, near the elevators. Riley handed Bryn a backpack, which she found upon inspection to be full of high-protein bars, stacks of cash, and airplane-style toiletry kits. "The essentials," Riley said. "I don't know about you, but I don't want to be stuck hungry or broke in our current situation . . . and I hate not having a toothbrush."

"Amen, sister," Joe said, and accepted his own backpack. "Sweet. Now all we need is a deck of cards."

"I thought you'd be more of a chess man, somehow."

"Hard to bet on chess," he said. "Harder to bluff. Okay, then, let's hit it."

"I need to say good-bye to my—" Bryn began, but before she could finish, Annalie stepped out of her room, still dressed in a fluffy robe and slippers, and hurried toward them. She breathlessly threw her arms around Bryn, and Bryn hugged her back, hard. "—sister. Hey, Annie."

"Hey, stupid," Annie said. "I can't believe you're leaving me behind."

"I can't believe I'm going. Crazy, huh?"

"Pretty crazy." Annie pushed back to arm's length, but held on to Bryn's hands. "You be careful, okay? I mean it. *Careful.*"

"I will. And you, stay out of trouble. Do what Manny and Pansy tell you." Bryn kissed her cheek and hugged her again. "I love you, brat."

"Love you, too." Annie forced a smile, though tears shone in her eyes. "Some reunion we've had, huh?"

"I don't know. We've had worse. Remember that time at Cousin Bernard's, and the stories about the aunt with four thumbs?"

"And the roadkill stew," Annie said. "Oh yeah, I remember. You're right. This doesn't really even make the top five."

Patrick tapped Bryn on the shoulder, and it was definitely time to go. Like it or not. One more hug, and Annie stepped back, crossing her arms across her chest. Not defensively, but in a way that suggested she wanted to hold that last hug very, very close.

The elevator doors opened, and Bryn stepped in, followed by the others. They arranged themselves at equal distances, the way people did in elevators, and so Bryn had a clear view of Annie standing there in her disheveled, just-out-of-bed glory one more time.

Annie raised her hand and waved.

Bryn waved back, and then the doors shut, and they left the security of what might have passed for normal life.

"Before we hit the surface, let's make sure we all understand procedure," Patrick said. "Pansy's given us a hardened SUV from the motor pool; it's registered to a shell company out of Belize, so it shouldn't trip any alerts. We get on the road, and Pansy's going to feed us intel as we drive. Within a few hours, she says she will break down the firewalls on their servers and start feeding us names and locations of people in the top ranks of the Fountain Group, or near it. We take out as many as we can, as fast as we can. If we run into trouble while we're out of the vehicle, we run and stay in contact. Burner phones are in your packs. Do *not* engage in a firefight unless you've got no choice, understand?"

"Yep," Bryn said. "And stay off the police radar."

"They'll probably have some kind of alerts out for us, and we can't always avoid facial recognition; too many street cameras. But we should try to stay out of metro areas as much as possible. Anything else?"

Riley said, "I've got a friend who can help us. His name is Jonas. He's retired Bureau—honest as they come. And he runs his own show now, mostly doing contract work in war zones."

"I've heard of him," Joe said. "Good man, by all accounts."

"No," Patrick said. "Nobody else unless we get in over our heads. We've dragged down enough good people."

He wasn't wrong, Bryn thought, but neither was Riley; it was good to have options, and there would inevitably come a time when they'd need someone to help who wasn't already flagged. Maybe Patrick was thinking it, too, but the expression on his face said that there wouldn't be any discussion on the subject.

Riley shrugged and let it go as the doors opened on the ground floor level. This exit had four security stops, and they passed through them all. As they entered the last room, a light flashed red and Manny's voice came over an invisible intercom.

"As of now, your security creds are burned here," he said. "Try to get in, and you'll trigger the countermeasures. Trust me—you won't like the countermeasures, and you won't survive them. From this point on, it's one way only: straight out the door. Understand me?"

"Manny—"

"Don't, Patrick. You screwed me, you and your little girlfriend. I want the Zombie Apocalypse outside, not in here. Get it? So don't come back. Ever."

"What about my sister?" Bryn asked. "What about Liam?"

Silence, and then finally Manny said, "I'll look out for them, because they had no choice. But not for you. As of right now, the store's closed."

The thick blast-proof outer door buzzed and winched itself open, and strobe lights flashed yellow. A recorded voice came on, advising them that they had thirty seconds to exit the room before countermeasures were employed.

They got out, and watched the blast door swing shut. Then, with a heavy crunch of gears, it locked.

"Right," Patrick said. He sounded resigned, and a little bit bleak. "Let's get moving."

Chapter 3

Info came in an hour down the road, in the form of a text to Patrick's phone from Pansy. It didn't say much, but it did give them an address in Kansas City. Bryn sighed when she saw it, because it meant a long, boring drive . . . if they were lucky, of course. And for the first few hours, they were; they managed to stay at a constant, legal speed, and no one seemed to notice them. "It's a little late to ask, but are we sure the anti-tracking shot worked?" she said. Riley glanced up from whatever she was doing on her phone, and nodded.

"I double-checked," she said. "We're dead air. Nobody's tracking us."

That was a relief, because Bryn was fairly sure that without Pansy's countermeasure they'd have already been under attack. Jane wouldn't be messing around, and she'd be investigating any avenue to finding them. Including, of course, going after their friends and family.

Her own family, in fact. The only saving grace to that was her family, with the exception of Annie, who'd gotten caught up in the madness, had no idea what was going on. Sometimes, dysfunction was good for something after all. She didn't know about Riley, but she hoped

Joe's family was somewhere very, very safe. He had a lot of precious people he could lose.

It was too late to warn them or try to get them to safety—not that her family, never all that close, would have listened to what she had to say in any case. Certainly not to the extent of pulling up stakes and running away. It would be far, far better just to stay away from them. Any contact could put them in greater danger.

"We're staying on I-40 all the way to Oklahoma City," Joe said, "and then switching to 35. I figure we'll need a gas and rest break in about thirty minutes. Sound okay?"

"Find someplace with lots of traffic," Patrick said. "The more people that pass through, the better; major truck stop, preferably. Crowds are good cover. If that looks iffy, go for someplace off the beaten path with old pumps. If they haven't upgraded those, chances are they won't have state-of-the-art surveillance, either."

"You're really worried, aren't you?" Bryn asked him. Patrick looked at her for a few seconds, and then nodded.

"I'm worried," he agreed. "The Fountain Group hasn't exactly been idle this whole time while we thought the government was in charge of Pharmadene's research programs; they've been carrying things forward, and they've got Jane on their payroll. I know Jane. We both understand what she's capable of doing, but more than that, I understand how tactical she is. She'll be casting as wide a net as possible. For all I know, she might have already pinpointed every one of Manny's secured bolt-holes, which means she might be satellite-tracking us right now; I don't doubt the Fountain Group has that capability, or can buy it from those who do. So any stops we make are risky, and potentially deadly. We need to bear it in mind."

"And I was looking forward to scoring some beef jerky and beer for the road," Joe said. "You really know how to kill a good time, man."

"Let's hope I'm wrong."

He seemed to be, at least for the first portion of the trip. Joe picked a huge truck stop, one with at least fifty cars, trucks, and vans crowding the lot, and dozens more giant tractor trailers. Joe pulled up to a pump, and the other three bailed out to head inside to the store. Even if they'd been willing to forego the magic lure of beef jerky and candy bars, Bryn needed to pee, and she knew she'd better grab the chance while it was available. The line was—inevitably—longer than she would have liked, and she felt tremendously vulnerable standing in one place ... but the bathroom break passed without incident, other than a squalling two-year-old throwing a fit at the counter.

She bought a not-entirely-unflattering hat to shade her face from the cameras, and some candy bars, and was in the van before anyone else except Joe.

Odd. She'd thought Riley would have made it back first, since she'd been ahead of her in the bathroom line. Or Patrick. He didn't strike her as much of a convenience store browser.

Bryn passed Joe a Snickers bar, and he unwrapped it and ate half. She had taken over the shotgun passenger seat, and they sat in chocolate-medicated silence for a full minute, but she didn't stop watching their surroundings, and neither did Joe.

Patrick returned, bearing bottles of water and a ridiculously large coffee, which explained his delay.

But Riley was missing.

Joe finished his candy and said, "Bryn."

"I'm on it," she said, and bailed out to go back inside. The ever-shifting crowd had a certain weird sameness ... mostly overweight bodies not flattered by baggy cargo shorts and overly patriotic T-shirts, with a few holding-their-noses sleek-looking elites scattered in for diversity, getting their chic diet water before climbing back into their high-dollar cars. She wasn't sure how she fit in here, or anywhere. But one thing was certain: Riley wasn't anywhere in sight.

Bryn checked the restroom. Nothing. She was on the point of calling an alert when she finally spotted Riley outside the windows, pacing back and forth at the side of the building. She was on the phone, and she closed the call just as Bryn headed toward her.

"What are you doing?"

"Hedging our bets," the other woman said. She'd also invested in a hat, a khaki boonie-style thing that was oddly cute on her. "It isn't that I don't trust Pansy, but I want to be sure we have some options and backup."

"You called your friend Jonas, didn't you? Patrick said—"

"Nobody elected him Commander in Chief," Riley said. "And trust me, we're going to need help."

She was, of course, right about that. They did, and Bryn finally shook her head and said, "Fine, I won't tell him. But we need to get going. By the way, I bought Snickers. What've you got?"

"Hair dye," Riley said. "And scissors. We're both getting makeovers."

They had one more stop before night closed in around them, and after some discussion Joe and Patrick decided to choose a motel for the night. No-tell roadside inns were plentiful, at least; the pink stucco place that Joe picked seemed likely to have been in business since the 1950s at least. It catered to kitsch, but it was definitely not much in terms of technology. Flat screen televisions still only existed in the realm of science fiction, and air-conditioning was a leaky window unit. At least it was clean, and quiet, and the hot water worked.

Bryn cut her hair short, and applied the hair dye, which turned her from dark blond to a brunette. Riley, on the other hand, elected to go punk—shaggy hair with purple streaks, and a black dog collar with spikes.

"That's not regulation FBI. I'm pretty sure," Bryn said, as Riley fluffed her hair into a spiky shag.

"Good," she said. "If we get time, I'll get some nose studs and a low-cut top. The less they look at my face, the better."

They had an uneasy night's sleep—and a short one. Bryn ate protein bars every few hours, and it seemed to help assuage the anxious feeling of hunger . . . not completely erasing it, but pacifying it. *We still need meat,* she thought. She wondered if she could convince her friends to find a diner for breakfast that didn't mind serving an almost-raw steak. The very thought made her mouth water.

She was on her way to the van when she noticed how *quiet* it was. Yes, it was a rural area, off the freeway's constant hum, but there seemed to be such a deep well of stillness in the early morning that it keyed her instincts up to alert.

Bryn changed directions and went to Patrick's door, and rapped softly. He took only a couple of seconds to open it, and she stepped in and shut it behind her. "Trouble," she said. She wasn't sure, but she also wasn't willing to be gratuitously stupid.

Patrick didn't doubt her, or even take a glance outside. As she dumped her kit on the floor and opened it to remove the PS90, he did the same, only he took out his shotgun. It was a good choice, she thought. They also silently separated out their ammunition on the bed, ready for reloading.

Patrick paused in the act of reaching for another shotgun shell as a voice called out from beyond the window. "Hello, honey, I'm home!" It was Jane. Bryn couldn't possibly forget that voice, and she saw Patrick close his eyes briefly in a storm of emotion that probably wasn't love and relief. It lasted only a second before he gathered himself, slammed the shell home, and pumped the shotgun.

"They'll already have us boxed," he said. "She wouldn't announce anything until she was sure of her position. She thinks she's got us cold."

"Maybe she does," Bryn said.

"We'll make it a fight unless she's got more upgraded models with her like you and Riley, which I doubt; Jane always did want to be the strongest person in the room. She won't want anyone who's in danger of upstaging her. If she's got an Achilles' heel, it's her ego."

He was talking calmly, but quickly, and he took up a position to the right of the curtained plate glass window. Bryn took the left side. She knew, from her own reconnaissance of her room, that the bathroom's high, narrow, barred window wasn't so much of a threat. It'd take time and energy for an enemy to get through, and it would be noisy as fuck.

No, Jane would favor the frontal assault, as usual. Patrick was right, Jane needed to show them who was boss. Especially Patrick. *Especially* Bryn.

"We're screwed, aren't we?" she asked Patrick, without really looking at him.

He didn't look back, either. "Probably." She saw a ghost of a smile in her peripheral vision. "Let's make the bitch pay for the privilege of killing us."

They didn't actually have the chance, because right about then, there was the sound of a helicopter. No, not just one—*lots* of helicopters. The dull chopping sound got loud, crisper, until it was an overhead drone.

Bryn swept the curtain aside to look, and saw ten military helicopters hovering over the little motel—fully armed and armored, state-of-the-art death from the air. They were in perfect formation, tightly grouped, and the threat could not have been clearer. They didn't even make any announcements.

"Right," Patrick said softly. "That's it, then." And he was right. If Jane had managed to summon up that kind of firepower, they had nothing to match it. Their armory—

however good it might be for a running operation—
wouldn't stand for long against rockets and high-capacity
aerial machine guns.

But then something very odd happened, because the
helicopters didn't attack; they just hung there in the sky.
It didn't look like the formation was aimed at *them* at all.

It was, she realized, aimed straight at *Jane*. Patrick's
ex—tall, strong, and crazy—was standing beside a fleet
of five converted Humvees, and even if she was trying
not to look intimidated, her posse with her wasn't doing
the look so well, staring up at the hovering ceiling of
doom. Big guys, heavily armed and Kevlared, but as nervous as mice in a field with a hawk soaring overhead.
They were disciplined enough to hold their ground until
she gave the signal, at least, but once it was given, the
retreat was decidedly not casual.

"Did you expect this?" Bryn asked. Patrick gave her
a curt shake of his head. "Are we in bigger trouble?"

This time, the skin around his eyes crinkled in what
was almost a smile. "You know, I've learned not to assume anything," he said. "Let's wait and see."

Jane was the last to retreat. She was holding an assault
rifle—hard to see what it was, but it looked deadly
enough—and she lifted it and aimed it at the window.
Bryn stepped back, out of sheer instinct, but Patrick—
Patrick didn't move. He was a clear, easy target if Jane
decided she didn't care about the consequences.

But she did after all, because she laughed, lowered the
weapon, and got in the Humvee. As soon as her ass was
in the seat, it did a fast U-turn and sped away, all the others falling into formation behind it. Three of the helicopters split off, following, but the trucks distributed their
retreat, too, and the remaining formation shifted. Bryn
couldn't understand what was happening at first, but
then she saw it—*more* helicopters coming, from the direction to which the Humvees had fled. Not as many in

this formation, but enough to make it an *Apocalypse Now* kind of fight.

The two formations settled into a hovering standoff, each protecting their own forces.

"Jane has air support, too," Patrick said. He sounded a little numbed, which was pretty much how Bryn was feeling about things as well. "Christ. *We've* got air support. What the hell is happening?"

"I think ours came from Riley," Bryn said. "She made a call yesterday, to her friend Jonas. I'm guessing he pulled in some favors, just in case. I didn't tell you because I knew you wouldn't take it so well."

"I'd have been angry about it," he acknowledged. "And we'd all be dead because of me being too low-profile. I expected her to bring a small strike force, not the frigging armored division."

"She knows what you expect. Which is why we can't let you run the strategy against her, Patrick. You know her, she knows you, and you can't get out of each other's way. Let Riley run it. Jane won't see that coming—just like she didn't expect this." Bryn gestured at the helicopters. One was dropping out of formation, graceful as a falling leaf, toward an open spot in the sparsely occupied parking lot. It touched down, rotors still at speed, and a tall man disembarked. Like Jane's people, he'd come prepared for war, with body armor and fearsome personal weaponry. At his side was another man, shorter and wider, who was wearing what looked to Bryn's eyes like the uniform of an army major.

Riley stepped out of her room, and a second later, Joe Fideli followed her. He had his own PS90 with him, but carried at port arms—a friendly but cautious gesture. There was no question he had Riley's back.

Bryn and Patrick exited, too, and reached the two newcomers about the same time as Riley and Joe.

"Brick," Riley said, and extended her hand to the

man who wasn't in uniform. He ignored it and pulled her into a hug. "Ooof. Been working out, madman?"

"Yep, little bit, here and there. Looks like you were right about the trouble, Riley," Brick said. He let Riley go, and his lively dark gaze fixed first on Joe, then Bryn, then Patrick. "I'm Jonas Wall. Brick, to my friends. Riley says you'll fall into that category. Hope she's right, because I just put my ass on the line for you."

"You're not the only one," Riley said, and extended her hand to the man standing next to Brick. "Major Plummer. Been a while. How much trouble are you in right now?"

He shrugged; it was impressive he *could* shrug, given the amount of muscle he packed on those shoulders. Definitely a bodybuilder. "We're conducting maneuvers," he said. "Way I see it, I have less to explain than our opposite numbers across the way. I've got authorizations. They're black ops-ing it in a very public way, and I promise you that right now there are some scrambles going on to cover asses. But Agent Block, you've got a problem, too. A big one."

She laughed. "You mean, in addition to the people who almost mowed down the entire motel?"

"Yeah. I've already gotten countermand from up high, so I have to pull out and head back to base. I'm doing that at a leisurely pace, because we're having mechanical problems, as you can see." His pilot leaned out of the helicopter and held up a wrench. "Very serious issues. He'll be a while fixing that, for safety. My point is, these jackholes may be conducting their own off-the-books operation, but they've got coverage somewhere in the Pentagon. Maybe elsewhere on Capitol Hill, too. You need to be careful. This is some political shit."

Brick nodded. "They've already gone to work inside the FBI, too; way I hear it, higher ups are saying you went off the reservation, bribes might have been involved. It's a tangled mess, and the gods on high are going to be wading through it for a while, but until they do I doubt you can count on much in the way of official government support. Pharmadene was enough of a black eye all by itself. It's now officially an embarrassing clusterfuck, and nobody wants to be caught in charge of it."

"I don't care about politics," Riley said. "Major, I know you have to withdraw; I owe you a favor for riding to our rescue in the first place. I never expected you to bring quite this much . . . thunder."

"Better too much than too little," he said, and bared his teeth in a smile. They were big teeth, and very white. "If you get in over your head, yell. I'll do what I can. So will some of my brothers and sisters, to the best of their ability. But you're in good hands with Brick."

He shook hands all around, and he was good at it—a firm, dry hand, good eye contact. Then he was in his helicopter and they were rising up into the air, an eerie combination of brute effort and mechanical grace.

"Plummer will give us maybe fifteen minutes," Brick shouted over the dull, rolling chop of blades that hovered over them. "Get moving. I'll escort you where we're going."

"Where *are* we going?" Bryn asked, and got a full, assessing look from the man. He was . . . intense, she had to admit. Intense in a good way—like Joe, he preferred a shaved head, which added to the richness of his brown eyes and dark skin. The goatee framed a mouth that seemed, even now, to be just on the edge of a smile.

"Classified," he told her, and winked. "Trust me. I know where you need to get, and I'll make sure you travel safe. That's my job. Logistics and protection."

"Brick owns a private security company," Riley said. "Trust me. He's a friend."

"Does he understand what he's getting into?" Patrick asked. "Brick, the people looking for us mean to kill us, and they don't care who they have to go through to do it. They may not quite be ready for a missile battle in the skies on sovereign soil, but they're not far from it. Are you prepared for that?"

Brick gave him a slow, wide smile. "Prepared for it, staffed for it, used to it. Mount up, kids. We're rolling."

He walked away as a black SUV—not too dissimilar from their own, actually—pulled up, and Bryn noticed for the first time as he climbed in that he moved a little stiffly. It wasn't terribly noticeable, until he stepped up in the cab. The way he moved his right leg seemed . . . off.

Riley noticed, too. "Brick lost a leg in Iraq," she said. "Took shrapnel to the head, too. They said it was a miracle he survived. He decided to put it to good use."

"You trust him? With your life?" Patrick asked.

"Yes," Riley said. "With all our lives. Come on."

With that, they were on their way to their own SUV, and in less than a minute, they were on the road, surrounded by flanking vehicles, with a cloud of air support blocking the sun as they headed northeast.

Major Plummer's helicopters peeled off half an hour later and beat the skies toward home base, which left them cruising along at a steady sixty-five miles an hour in a box formation, which rarely had to break up for traffic—wrong time of day, and wrong part of the country, although there were plenty of tractor trailers on the road. Bryn didn't feel safe, but she also felt a whole lot less vulnerable than before. Jonas Wall—Brick—had a confidence that seemed utterly warranted. Even against Jane and her thugs.

Of course, he probably hadn't seen what she and Riley could do, under pressure. Or Jane. *How many of us are there?* She hadn't stopped wondering about that . . . because it terrified her. The whole operation that had been under way at the nursing home, colonizing the helpless bodies of the elderly in the locked facility, had been about breeding more of the nanites and siphoning them off for later implantation. Had the Fountain Group actually reached the stage where they were seeding the nanites, or was that still a goal for the future? Or was Pharmadene the only pilot program running?

She knew that with ten soldiers equipped like herself, she could have taken on a hundred men, easily. Maybe ten times as many. It was an advantage as lopsided as machine guns against Stone Age clubs. Give those same upgraded soldiers advanced weaponry, and . . . her mind just balked. Better not to imagine what could happen.

"We'll be in Wichita soon," Joe Fideli said. "As pimpin' awesome as the fleet is, are they really going to stick with us in the city, too?"

"They'll flank us and shadow, but they won't be right on our bumpers," Riley said. "Once we leave Wichita we'll re-form the group until Topeka. Brick will have replacements ready to meet us there, so these will peel off and head in for relief."

"Damn," Joe said. "Maybe I need to work for this guy. I love organization, and you don't get it too often in private security. And Bryn, love you, but so far my association with you hasn't exactly paid my mortgage, much less put my kids through college."

"I thought you were doing it because you loved me, Joe."

"Well, that, too. But the hazard pay invoice is going to be a bitch." Joe grinned a little madly. "Bet Manny's saying that, too."

She could only imagine. The rental on his bulletproof SUV alone would run into the tens of thousands. "Dude, I already gave you a job at my funeral home." A funeral home she had owned and operated, albeit under government control and funding—because they needed to track the progress of those being administered the Returné drug, like Riley and others who'd been illegally brought back by Mr. Fairview, who'd once owned the place. She'd been in charge, more or less, of taking care of those who'd survived the revival process—and making

sure they took their shots, stayed sane, and didn't attract
too much attention. It had been part of the deal.

Now she guessed all that was over, which was sad,
because she'd been . . . happy. As happy as a dead woman
could be, she supposed. She'd liked the work, the calm,
steady, useful work of caring for those who were gone —
and those who'd been returned against their will through
the magic of super-science. She'd been den mother and
counselor to many of those who'd been addicted, against
their will, to Returné. She'd seen some adapt, and some
give up.

The consequences of giving up were pretty horrific,
because the drug was designed to keep you going at any
cost, and as its nanites lost efficiency, you simply . . .
decomposed. But stayed alive and aware until the bitter
end.

I'm not going out that way, she promised herself. If
necessary, she'd make Patrick or Joe swear to load her
into a crematory oven and burn her to ashes. It would be
awful, but relatively fast, at least.

Second thought, maybe she should ask Riley to do it,
and they could make a mutual destruction pact. Riley
would understand.

Riley's cell phone rang, and she answered it, listened,
and made a monosyllabic response. Then she hung up
and said, "Heads up. We've got word of some kind of
intercept being planned. Brick's on it, but keep your eyes
open —" It was prime territory for it, Bryn thought; the
narrowing road out here in the country meant that their
escort stayed ahead and behind, but couldn't fully box
them in.

But the flat Kansas fields didn't seem to offer any
kind of obvious threat, either.

They watched tensely for anything big enough to
present a threat, and for miles — almost fifty miles — they
saw nothing, unless the enemy had taken to recruiting
thermal-surfing hawks overhead as surveillance.

Up ahead, Brick's SUV flashed its lights, and took an exit, heading for the access road. Bryn wondered why, but then she caught a look at Joe's gas gauge—they were running low, too. And the sign they passed said LAST GAS FOR 150 MILES, so she supposed it was sensible enough. The Shell station up ahead looked ancient and deserted, and it was on the other side of a train track.

She was looking out for everything, but somehow, she forgot to watch out for roadside IEDs.

Bryn saw the car abandoned by the side of the road, half in the ditch about twenty-five feet from the tracks, and even with her experiences in Iraq, her *personal* experience at being nastily surprised by such things, she didn't immediately key in on it as a threat. It was positioned crookedly, one tire off, and there was one of those Day-Glo stickers on it that showed the local police had tagged it for towing. Entirely normal, and any other time and day in the USA, entirely safe.

But not today.

She didn't even see it go up; her head was turned away, checking the other side of the road. She didn't hear it, either, because before the sound reached her and rolled over her like a tank, the impact had already thrown the SUV up in the air and flipped it partly over, and her body was too busy trying to sort out all of the unnatural inputs—sound, light, heat, gravity twisting out of shape, pressure, pain.

And then the SUV landed on its side with a boom like cannon fire—tinny in her shocked ears—and rolled over on its top in a gritty chorus of bulletproof glass warping and cracking. It didn't have enough momentum to keep tumbling, so it rocked to a stop, and for a second Bryn held still, waiting for her body to tell her its status.

Good to go, apparently. Aches and pains that she'd have normally felt faded under adrenaline, and besides, the nanites were good for one thing, and that was healing damage.

The cabin was full of smoke, and she heard coughing. "Patrick?" Her fingers scrabbled for the seat belt release, and she found it and pressed. That dropped her onto her neck and shoulder, and she slithered around over the broken glass to ease the strain. "Joe? Riley?"

"Riley's good," came the agent's voice, and then Riley's body slipped out of the upside-down restraints and rolled next to her.

"Joe here," Fideli said, and coughed again. "Fuck. Hey, Pat, you sleeping in? Because we're in some trouble here." While he talked, he was working the release on his seat belt. It was stuck, but in seconds he had a combat knife out of its sheath and was slicing through the thick fabric like silk. Riley squirmed back to give him room to drop; he did it more elegantly than either she or Bryn had done, but then, he'd probably had more practice.

Patrick didn't answer. He was hanging limp, bloodied arms dangling. Joe cursed under his breath, rose to his knees, and cut the man free. Bryn, without prompting, helped ease him down. Behind her, she heard more glass breaking, and metal groaning; Riley was forcing open the driver's side door with muscular kicks.

There was a firefight going on outside the toppled SUV, a thundering chatter of bullets punctuated by a low rumble and a loud blatting horn, and what the *hell was that . . . ?*

Joe had taken hold of Patrick beneath the arms and was crab-walking backward, dragging the other man with him. Bryn shook the lingering fog out of her head and turned to the cracked window next to her. Impossible to see what was going on, so she smashed it out with a flurry of quick punches. Cuts and breaks didn't matter.

There was a spotlight rushing toward them, and the sound of metallic screeching pierced the noise of combat, and Bryn had time to realize that the vibration was coming from the railroad tracks, the railroad tracks *underneath the SUV that she was in*, and the headlight was from a black locomotive rushing toward them with the pulping force of God's biggest hammer.

Riley realized it, too, and from the other side of the SUV she grabbed Joe and heaved, hauling him *and* Patrick out with one bone-shaking pull and dragging them at an angle backward to a ditch.

Bryn bailed out of the window she'd broken, hit the hard, vibrating metal of the tracks, and didn't have time to get out of the way . . . just enough time to roll off the metal and onto the wood and gravel in the center.

The train went over her like a storm, a roaring black hurricane of steel and smoke, burning metal and sparks. She was facedown, cheek pressed onto the sharp chunks of rock, and the smell of burning oil overwhelmed her.

She didn't hear the train hit the SUV, but it must have, because it kept moving, thundering over her and gradually easing to a stop still parked on top of her.

She made sure it was stable, then shakily crawled out between the smoking wheels, slithered down the embankment and rolled into a weed-filled ditch that was smoldering with pieces of the exploded car.

The battle was in full force up on the road.

Half the escorting SUVs were trapped on the other side of the tracks, barred from them by the train; Brick's two other teams were still in the game and laying down hot fire to keep the attackers—from the goddamn *train* now—from firing down on Riley, Pat, and Joe, who needed cover badly. Bryn took only a couple of seconds to take the situation in, and focused on the body-armored assault team in the boxcars of the freight train, who'd slid aside the doors and were pouring semiauto fire at the guardian SUVs, trying to take them out first.

Bryn lunged back up out of the ditch, grabbed hold of the back passenger door of their wrecked, mangled, chopped-in-half SUV, and braced herself. *All about leverage,* she told herself. The door was twisted and hanging loose anyway. *Go.*

She yanked, and metal groaned and shook, but the door held.

One of their attackers turned his fire on her. She felt the bullets striking but ignored them; pain was pain, the nanites would fix it. Her world narrowed to the door.

She yanked violently, twisting down, and the one remaining hinge snapped at its stress point, leaving her holding a thick armored door.

She picked it up and ran to the opposite side, around the still-smoking SUV, and rolled into the ditch that held Joe, Patrick, and Riley. She and Riley got the door up and above them, protecting the two men, seconds before the concentrated fire bore down.

"Ladies," Joe said between gasps for breath, "you're making me feel kinda useless here."

"You're the only one who can shoot right now," Bryn panted. "How's that for feeling useful?"

He grinned. He was bloody from a cut on his head, and his smile looked wild and warlike. He still had his sidearm, though Bryn hadn't had time to grab her weapons bag, and he crawled to the edge of the sheltering door. "Go," he said, and they shifted it a few inches down his body. He fired six shots in about three seconds, moving his aim with tiny, precise ticks. "Clear." They moved the door back to cover him—and the answering fire was less—a lot less. "Got five out of six. Last bastard twitched."

"Vest shots?" Riley asked.

"What am I, an amateur? Head shots, thank you very much." He took a couple of deep, pumping breaths, and nodded. "Go."

They repeated the maneuver, and he did six more shots. When he signaled clear again, there was only a desultory rattle of fire on the steel, and then silence.

They were retreating.

Joe wasn't assuming anything, though. He ejected his clip, slapped in a new one, and racked the slide so fast that it was one blur of motion. Ten seconds passed. Fifteen. Twenty. Bryn's arms were starting to burn under the strain, and she could see that Riley's were shaking, too.

Then she heard a shout from behind her, and saw that one of Brick's men was gesturing at them from his bullet-pocked SUV. "Guys, I think we're leaving," she said. "Joe, can you carry Patrick?"

"Better if I drag him," he said, and holstered his weapon to take hold of the still-unconscious Patrick beneath his arms. "On three?"

They counted down, and as Joe pulled, Riley and Bryn kept the shield over their heads as they moved toward the waiting SUV. From there, Brick's surviving men—there were at least two down on the road—loaded Patrick in, and then Joe, Riley, and Bryn. One of them tried to hold up the door as a shield, and looked comically surprised when he realized how heavy it was.

Bryn found it funnier than she should have and had to suppress panic giggles. She swallowed them as the remaining mercenaries piled in with them, and pressed her fingers to Patrick's throat. His pulse was steady and strong, but he had a wicked blow to the head, and plenty of cuts.

"He alive?" the man in charge asked. He resembled Brick a little, but in miniature—small, muscular, and a man who'd clearly been given quality training in mayhem; he was in the shotgun role, and before they could answer he fired out the window of the SUV at the remaining members of the assaulting team. One went down. The others broke for cover.

"He'll be okay," Joe said. "Could be a concussion. Hopefully his skull didn't get fracked."

"We've got a portable med unit I can roll to us," the man said. "Anybody else got holes in them?"

"Nothing that won't fix itself," Bryn said. She wasn't being flip; she knew she'd taken five or six rounds, but the wounds had already closed, and the bullets had been pushed out. She was, if not healed, well on the way to healing. Efficient things, the nanites. She could almost like the little bastards, except for the side effects.

Like looking at the blood on Joe's face and having an almost irresistible desire to lick it off and bite into that soft, tender flesh. . . .

She looked away and squeezed her eyes closed. "Riley," she said.

"Yeah," Riley said. "I know. Hang in there."

"Trouble?" the driver asked. He jammed the SUV into reverse, expertly steering around the abandoned vehicle in the way—from the way the engine was smoking, it wasn't drivable—and hit the gas.

"Nothing you can fix," Riley said. "What's the plan?"

The truck was rocketing backward at a terrifying speed—Bryn couldn't imagine driving that fast in reverse, but the man behind the wheel looked perfectly comfortable with the whole thing. She decided the best thing to do was to not watch, and instead focused on the man in the passenger seat, who was changing out the clip on his military-grade selectable full-auto P90. "We get the fuck out of this killbox and regroup," he said. "I've been around, but I've never seen that much firepower to kill four people, outside of diplomats or drug dealers. Jesus, who'd you folks piss off?"

"Better you don't know," Riley said. "Classified. What's your name, soldier?"

"You can call me Harm," he said. "Everybody does."

"Seriously?"

He laughed a little, but it was humorless. "Harmon Strang the Third. Harm, for short. Ain't no brag, ma'am."

"I don't think you go in for bragging, Harm," Bryn said. "Guys like you don't need it."

"You say the sweetest things. I almost don't mind getting shot up for you." The sarcasm was scorching, and so was the bleak look in his dark eyes. "Can't say the same for the two men I lost back there."

"I'm sorry," Bryn said. "Friends?"

"Coworkers," he said. "Risk is part of the job. I'm pretty sure they never thought they'd be bleeding out on a side road in Kansas, though. Seems like a fucking waste."

He wasn't wrong about that.

The driver got to a wider spot in the road, and performed a bootlegger turn that made a scream of panic rise in Bryn's throat, but she braced herself and swallowed it, somehow. She could tell Riley was feeling some of that, too, in the glance they exchanged.

Joe, grinning, looked like he was having the time of his life. Adrenaline junkie. He'd probably have a hard comedown later, but for now he'd go off a cliff, screaming defiance and shooting people on the way down. A genuine to-the-bone soldier.

They sped down the access road, did a shrieking sharp turn to get back on the freeway, and rocketed over the arching bridge, beneath which lay the train, the remains of the train-bisected SUV Bryn and her friends had been inside, the exploded car, and the bullet-disabled second escort vehicle. She could see, from this vantage point, the bodies scattered like broken toys. There were a lot more than the two they'd lost. On the other side of the train, the other two SUVs—Brick's—were off the road and shielded behind the concrete of the gas station—which, Bryn realized, was abandoned and closed. The whole thing had been a setup.

And a well-thought-out one, too.

Brick's SUVs started their engines and sped out to join them on the freeway . . . and then they were on the road, and accelerating; their convoy was two vehicles lighter, but going a whole lot faster. Harm got on the cell phone to his boss. "Don't like this road, Brick, it's too straight and not enough cover. Got any options?"

"Not much," Brick's voice came back over the speaker. "Got reinforcements rolling, but you're right, this whole damn section is all grids. No way to get anywhere out of sight. Everybody good there?"

"McCallister's down, but not out. Rest of 'em look fight-ready."

"You keep 'em that way," Brick said, "because I got the feeling this isn't over yet."

Brick was right, and if they hadn't had qualified combat drivers, all four SUVs might have been junk on the side of the highway, because they hadn't gotten more than a few miles before two eighteen-wheeler trucks tried to run them off the road. It was almost as hard to negotiate with semitrucks as it had been with the train, but the SUVs had the advantage of speed and maneuverability over momentum, and at least one of the men in Brick's SUV was a crack shot, taking out one driver within thirty seconds, and putting the other truck out of commission with well-placed bullets to the engine block.

"Brick," Harm said, as they sped away from the rapidly dwindling shape of the last attack truck, "we're running on fumes, man. Give me some good news."

"Refueling stop coming up," Brick said. "Stay tight on my bumper. We're about to test the off-road claims on these bastards."

In half a mile, his driver took a drastic slide off the road and into the soft dirt, and then a sharp right . . . into a cornfield. "Well, shit," Harm said, and braced himself on the dashboard. "Hope to hell he knows what he's doing."

Brick's SUV was taking the brunt of mowing down the crops, so the rest of them were able to keep right with it, traveling through a newly plowed tunnel in the tall, summer-blown corn. It smelled like dirt and mashed plants—something like mown grass, which was funny when you looked at the size of the stalks being cut down.

It didn't last long, because the lead truck burst through the corn and onto a narrow dirt path, thick with sun-dried ruts that the farmer and his employees must have used. They took it way too fast for the terrain, sending up a smoke signal that shimmered in the dry, hot air like the finger of God, pointing straight to them. So much for stealth.

"Where are we going?" Joe asked. "Because I'm not loving this plan if it involves some pissed corn farmers with sawed-offs."

"Relax," Brick said over the cell. "It's a safe house."

And it was.

The farmhouse—typically Kansan, with whitewashed board walls and neat russet trim—sat in a cleared square mile next to a big red barn and a shiny metal tower that could have been feed storage or water; Bryn was no specialist in that. It looked well cared for, and utterly normal.

At least, until the doors of the barn opened with hydraulic smoothness, and proved to be as thick as the doors of Manny's Titan missile complex. Brick drove in and came to a fast stop, and the SUV Bryn was in veered around and parked with military precision next in line. In ten seconds, they were all in place, and the doors were cranking shut behind them.

"Hands up," said an amplified male voice from somewhere outside their truck. "Everybody. We're looking with thermal, and we'll see if you're not in compliance."

Bryn raised her hands, and so did all the others, except Patrick, who was still cold unconscious. That took some explaining to the disembodied voice, but finally, they were all told to exit the vehicles and line up along the wall, hands still raised.

"I don't like this," Riley said, and Bryn caught that shine in her eyes—the unsettling gleam of savagery, the same hungry, ferocious burn she felt in her own stomach. "I thought it was a *safe* house."

"He never said it was ours," Harm said, and led the way out. He took his place at the wall, and Bryn joined him, reluctantly. She felt exposed and angry, and as Joe stood next to her, he sent her a concerned glance.

"Hold together," he told her.

Do I look that bad? She must have. Bryn took a deep breath and concentrated on the wood pattern of the boards in front of her. At least, it looked like wood—but it probably wasn't, given the reinforced front doors.

Brick didn't join them at the wall. She glanced over her shoulder and saw him in hushed, urgent conversation with two people who'd emerged from what looked like a control room, from the angled view she had of the consoles and switches inside. She couldn't hear the conversation from where she stood, but Riley frowned and half turned toward Harm.

"Are they speaking Russian?"

He shrugged. "It's a multicultural world."

"Is this a *Russian agent* safe house?"

"Why? You got a problem?"

"Besides the fact that I am an agent of the FBI, you mean?"

"We're all friends now, last I heard," he said, with a smile that was far from innocent. "Cold War's over. Besides, what the holy hell would Russian spies be doing holed up in a farmhouse in Kansas?"

She glared at him hard enough that Bryn thought it might leave marks . . . but before she could answer, if she intended to do so, Brick came striding over. "Put your hands down," he said. "But keep them in plain sight. They're going to refuel the vehicles, and then we'll be on our way."

"Brick, what the hell is—"

Joe Fideli shook his head, stopping Riley midsentence. "Look, kiddo, I respect that you've got loyalty oaths and all, but me, Brick, and Harm all share a couple of things. First, we aren't government employees. Second, we all *used* to be, and we haven't forgotten that. So regardless what the hell all this is, it isn't being used to

hurt the government or people of the United States, and
I suggest you let it slide, because without them, we're
dead on the side of the road."

Riley didn't like it, and neither did Bryn, but she had
to acknowledge the wisdom of what he was saying. She
trusted Joe, and she believed him when he said he
wouldn't have let it go himself if he thought it was a
threat. She didn't know Brick or Harm so well, but she
thought that they had the same post-military sensibility
that Joe did . . . and she did, for that matter.

So she nodded. Riley didn't.

"I need to know what's going on," she said.

"Then ask Brick—he's your friend."

"I mean it, Joe. I can't just shut my eyes to this—"

"You have to," he said flatly. "Literally, close your
eyes and pretend to be somewhere else if you have to,
but if you screw this up, Riley, you'll get us all killed.
What happens if you get us in a firefight and they find
out how *well trained* you and Bryn are? You think they
won't want to break off a piece of that knowledge?" He
leaned significantly on the two words, and raised his eyebrows.

That gave Riley pause, and evidently shook her out of
her role as FBI agent . . . and into her bigger, scarier role
as a prized lab rat. She'd been caged before, Bryn
thought. She wouldn't want to be in a Russian lab, under-
going the same horrors.

Of course, the fact that Bryn's clothes had bullet holes
and blood, but no matching wounds, might be something
of interest . . . but luckily, after the explosion and the
ditch, her clothes were filthy enough that the blood and
tears were nothing special to pick out.

Riley finally not so much agreed as just stopped disagreeing . . . which was good enough. They stood in tight
silence as Brick and his men backed each of the vehicles
to the gas pump located outside, and the Russians—if
that's what they really were, a man and woman who

looked very much middle-American—waited as well. Their gazes were not fixed, they were active and mobile, observing everything, judging everyone.

When Patrick groaned and stirred a little, the strange woman exchanged a glance with her significant other and broke off to come to them. She crouched down next to him as his eyelids fluttered, and he groaned again. She probed his head injury carefully, then nodded.

"No fracture I can determine, but there could be swelling," she said, "and almost certainly a major concussion. You should take him to a hospital as soon as possible to rule out any permanent damage. He has been unconscious for too long for it not to be serious." Her American accent was, of course, flawless.

"Thanks, Doctor, but we've got this," Bryn said. She was guessing, but the woman's brisk, calm manner was something that seemed very familiar to her. Not that she had any fondness now for the medical professions. "He'll be fine."

The woman raised an eyebrow, shrugged, and went back to her cold-war spouse. It was good of her to have made the overture, though; she didn't have to, by the letter of her verbal agreement with Brick.

Bryn knelt down next to Patrick as his eyelids fluttered again. He wasn't quite out of it, and wasn't quite in it, either. She checked his pupils. They were equal, which was good news, but the Russian doc had been right; he needed to be seen by someone qualified to check him over in detail. Field medicine could do only so much, and then it got its patient killed from the myriad of deeper complications that weren't immediately obvious.

"Ready," Brick said, and she glanced up to see that all the cars had been backed out of the barn and into the gravel yard. "Get him in—we'll rendezvous with the med team in half an hour."

"How exactly are we going to do that with Jane on our tail?" Joe asked.

"You let me worry about that," Brick said. "Let's roll."

"A moment," the Russian woman said, and stepped forward again, frowning. "You've been wounded."

She said it to Bryn, and her gaze was fixed on the barely visible blood beneath the grass and mud stains on her shirt. Bryn froze a second, darting a glance at Joe, and knew he was on high alert, too.

"Not my blood," she said, and smiled just a little. "I'm fine, thanks for asking. Joe, help me get Patrick in the truck, will you?"

Joe didn't hesitate. He dragged Pat up, and Bryn took his feet—not that Joe couldn't do it all by himself, but she needed an excuse to get away from further scrutiny. Together, they carried him to the SUV, easing him into a seat. Riley went around to the other side and got in as well. Brick took the driver's seat, and Bryn backed up toward the passenger side.

"A moment," the Russian doctor said again, insistently. "You've been hit, or you stripped a corpse that was shot. There is no other explanation for—"

Brick calmly pulled a sawed-off shotgun out from under his seat and pointed it right at the two Russians, and said, "And we were all getting along so well. Guess détente never lasts, right? Leave the girl alone, unless you want to hear the bad things that happened to her while she was being held naked in a warehouse until we rescued her. Yeah, she stripped a corpse. Killed him her own damn self. You wouldn't?"

His flat delivery, and the forbidding look in his eyes, reinforced the threat of the shotgun, and although the Russians didn't raise their hands in surrender, they didn't give them any more trouble or ask any more questions. Brick handed the shotgun to Joe, who stepped in and took the back passenger seat behind him, keeping the aim steady on the other two.

"Thanks for the hospitality, folks," he said. "Let's do lunch sometime, eh? Vodka and borscht on me."

Brick backed the truck out in one smooth, fast motion, and led the convoy out of the farm, back on the service road. This time, they didn't take the corn shortcut, but followed the grids of dirt roads all the way back to the freeway.

Joe rolled up the window and said, "Nice gun. Can I keep it?"

"Hell no," Brick said, and held his hand up. "Family heirloom—man, get your own."

"I had some nice stuff, but it got run over by a friggin' train."

"Sounds like the start of a pretty good country song." Brick grinned, and handed the shotgun back to him. "You can keep it warm for me."

"Careful, that's how I married my wife."

The banter eased some of the coiled tension in Bryn's stomach, but she wasn't sure they were out of the woods—or the tall corn—quite yet. "How did you know about this place, Brick?"

"Did some work for those folks a while back. We were friendly. As friendly as people like us get, anyway. They're all right. A little tense, but ain't we all just now."

"They're Russian spies," Riley said. "They ought to be tense, operating on American soil."

"They'll pull up stakes and be in the wind by the time you report 'em," Brick said. "Which is too bad, because they had a nice setup out here in the big nowhere. Not like they were hiding nukes or anything."

"Then what *are* they doing?"

"Providing a way station," he said. "Food, clothing, shelter, medical assistance, communication, that sort of stuff. You know. The CIA has similar places all over Europe, and in Russia, too. Part of the game, lady."

"I don't think it's a game."

"Your mistake. It is, and it never ends, and it never has a winner. You score points, you lose points, players and sides come and go, but the game itself never stops. Hasn't

since the first nations in the world started talking instead
of fighting. Spycraft's the world's second oldest profession. Has a lot in common with the first oldest, too, only
you're doing it for your country."

Bryn wasn't sure whether that was depressing or inspiring, but she was more concerned with Patrick, who
was definitely waking up now—and from the shallow,
rapid breathing when he opened his eyes, was also fighting back some extreme disorientation and nausea.

"Patrick?" She took his hand and held it, and after a
blank few seconds, he turned his head to look at her.
"Patrick, how's the head?"

"I think I'd like to have your nanites right now," he
said, and tried for a smile but didn't quite make it. "What
the hell happened?"

"IED in the car on the side of the road, we rolled, you
hit your head, full-on firefight. We even got hit by a
train," Bryn said. "Sorry you missed it. It was pretty epic.
Also, there were Russian spies."

"You're making this up."

"You'd think so, wouldn't you?"

"Jesus. Where's Jane?"

"I don't know exactly, but I expect she'll be coming
for us again soon. We're meeting up with a medical team;
they'll check you out."

"Not necessary," Patrick said, but she didn't like his
pallor, and she thought his pupils were looking a little
strange. "Just give me a weapon."

"I'm not giving up my sweet heirloom shotgun," Joe
said. "I just got it. Rest, Pat. We're good for now." His
tone was light, but he shot a glance back over the head-
rest, and Bryn could tell that he was concerned as well.
"Brick, how far to that rendezvous?"

"Fifteen minutes once we make the highway."

Joe didn't say *go faster,* but Brick got the message, and
the SUV accelerated as fast as the rutted dirt road would
allow. Patrick hung on grimly to his seat belt, looking

green and agonized, and whatever disrepair the freeway was in when they finally bumped up onto its hard surface, it felt like silk under the wheels, and Patrick (and all of them) breathed a sigh of relief. The flanking trucks closed in around them on the two-lane surface—not quite a box, but as close as it could get for the conditions. And Brick opened the throttle even more, blowing past speed limits to the point that the blur of corn and wheat outside the window became a disorienting kaleidoscope.

Patrick shut his eyes again, and she felt his grip on her hand tighten. "Are you okay?" she asked, and got no response. Dread gathered in her chest, smothering her. "Patrick!"

His hand slowly loosened, but his eyes didn't open again. He didn't respond when she called his name again, either.

"Brick!" she called, and heard the sharp edge of panic in her voice. "Brick, he's out again!" She knew that was a bad sign, and rubbed her knuckles on his sternum—a painful sensation, one that would bring most people around.

But he stayed limp. He was breathing, though, and when she checked his pulse, it remained fast, but steady.

"Five minutes," he said. "Can't cut it down more than that."

She knew he was right, but it still felt like an eternity. She kept her fingers pressed to his neck, feeling his pulse, and she thought his skin felt clammy. Shock, probably. They needed to get him warm before his blood pressure fell too far.

She was so intent on Patrick that it came as a surprise when the SUV braked, and she looked up to see that the lead truck was making a sharp left turn—again, an unmarked dirt road. This time, it wasn't quite as rutted, or as long, and they pulled to a stop in a cleared area next to what looked like some kind of abandoned pumping station.

An unmarked black tractor trailer was parked there, and as the fleet of SUVs came to a halt, the back doors of the trailer opened, and three people bailed out, plainclothes but carrying red medical bags. From there, it all went very fast—they had Patrick on a gurney and into the trailer, which turned out to be a well-equipped medical bay, in minutes. There wasn't room to observe, so Bryn was left outside, with the others, as they triaged his condition.

It took fifteen minutes for the man in charge—or at least, Bryn assumed he was the head doctor—to come back to report. "Pretty bad concussion," he said. "No skull fracture, but there is bruising and swelling of the brain. We're going to keep him here and run more tests; he needs rest and quiet, and it's pretty obvious he won't get it on the road with you. You want to stay with him?"

She did. Desperately. But that wouldn't help—it would only hurt, in fact, and Patrick would be the first to tell her she needed to continue the mission and finish this, or it would all be for nothing. By staying with him, she might lead Jane to Patrick, when he was next to helpless.

So she swallowed and said, "No. I'll check in on him, but I can't stay."

The doctor seemed unsurprised, and handed her a blank white business card with a phone number handwritten on it. "Here's the number," he said. "If he's anything like our usual patients, he'll try checking himself out of our care way too soon, but we'll make sure he's out of danger before we let him go. Anything else we should know?"

"We have heat all over us," Brick said. "A shit ton of it, and some of it may spill onto you, so be prepared. Get somewhere safe and locked down."

"Will do, sir." The doc was definitely a veteran of combat, Bryn thought; he took the news with total calm, and climbed back into the trailer to give orders to his people. They shut up the trailer, and the drivers—whom Bryn assumed were combat trained—started up the truck and headed off down the dirt road in the opposite direction from the freeway behind them. Evidently, they had a different destination in mind.

Brick's radio cracked as they headed for their own transportation, and he answered. "Go."

"Sir, we've got some activity to the northeast."

"Helicopters?"

"No, sir, looks like it could be a drone. I don't like it, sir. You need to get under cover immediately."

"What's our window?"

"Ten minutes at best."

"Jesus, son, we're in fucking Kansas—you know that? It's as flat as a table, and we can't outrun a drone. What assets do we have to kill it?"

"Nothing in the air right now, sir. I'm reaching out to our nearest air force friend, but I have the feeling they'll want to stay out of it before shooting down their own expensive toys, even unmanned ones."

Bryn grabbed for her phone and checked their location on the map. *Close. Very close.* Brick and his men were still talking, and Joe was tossing in suggestions, but Bryn leaned forward and held out her phone. "Here," she said. "Go here. Haul ass and max the engines. It's our only option."

"Go," Brick said to Joe, and got on the radio to deliver the orders. To his credit, he didn't even ask where they were going; Bryn supposed it didn't much matter to him. She thought, *Wait until I tell Annie about this*, because it was Annie's teenage obsession with kitschy roadside attractions that had rung a bell for her, out here in the middle of nowhere.

They were heading to the salt mines.

Chapter 4

"Here," Riley said, and pressed a protein bar into her hands; Bryn wasn't even really aware of her hunger, except as a gnawing constant, but she realized that she'd been staring fixedly at Brick's neck, and that probably wasn't a good thing. She licked her lips and tasted salt, and nodded to Riley as she unwrapped the foil from the food.

It tasted like sawdust, sweet glue, and fake chocolate, but it did, surprisingly, help—not as much as a thick, bloody steak would have done, but it made her less likely to imitate a raving zombie in the close confines of the truck. That would be inadvisable, not to mention messy.

She ate three of the bars ... and so did Riley, which meant that the other woman was just as protein-challenged as she was. That was inherently dangerous, but at least they were still thinking, still understanding that the cliff was ahead of them, and taking action to change course.

But the cliff ... well, the cliff was always there, and she knew Riley was acutely aware of it, too.

"Highway 50," she said, and pointed at the off-ramp. The convoy took it at a speed just under insane, and she held on for dear life. "Head west and floor it. We're heading for the Kansas Underground Salt Museum."

"Wait, a *museum*?" Brick said. "You understand that this drone could be set to bomb the holy shit out of—"

"It's a mine," she said. "And it has a secured slant-drilled shaft they use to ferry heavy equipment in and out, which means we can drive our own vehicles inside—instant cover. The mine itself is about seventy miles of tunnels under solid rock, and a block of salt so hard you can't even drive nails into it. The drone won't be able to blow through that."

"We going to have to worry about civilian casualties?" Brick asked, which was a reasonable question, and Bryn had already checked it on her phone.

"They're closed Mondays, so I think we're good," she said. "It isn't like they're overstaffed. Our enemies might send in a team, but it'll be damn hard for them to get to us. If we lock off the elevator and secure the vehicle exit, it's a long way down—six hundred fifty feet of narrow stairs. I'm pretty sure they wouldn't risk it, because just one of us could hold that forever."

"Not ideal, but it'll do," Brick said. "They can't keep the drone up there long; people get the idea that they're conducting military drone ops on American soil, and it gets ugly. They were hoping for a quick, fatal strike in the middle of nowhere. Taking out a tourist attraction won't have nearly so much appeal. They ain't that desperate."

"Yet," Riley said.

He didn't argue. They all rode in silence as the engine of the SUV roared, and Kansas miles disappeared under the whining tires. It felt effortless, the way momentum always did, but it wasn't. Bryn was acutely aware of the drone somewhere out there in the cloud-clotted sky, making its way to them with equally ruthless efficiency. She wouldn't even know it when it happened, most likely. The weapons the drone carried would make the trucks infernos, and she doubted the nanites, no matter how upgraded, could survive a direct strike like that.

Good way to go, some traitorous part of her said. *Maybe it would be for the best if it ended right here, right now. Before I do things I can't take back.*

But if she gave up now, there was nothing to stop the Fountain Group—and their agenda was something they were willing to do horrible, ruthless things to accomplish. They didn't have pity, or mercy, or second thoughts. And she needed to stay alive and stay fighting if she wanted to have even an outside chance of stopping them.

So tempting as that fireball would be, she knew they needed to *win* this one.

The sign for the Underground Salt Museum flashed past, signaling they were coming up on it soon, and Brick activated his radio. "Hard right coming up, guys—be ready. What's the ETA on our little friend?"

"Getting ready to say howdy," his man said. "About one minute out. Going to be close, boss."

The drone wasn't, strictly speaking, just an automated killing machine; drones could be used for all kinds of purposes from simple reconnaissance and supply delivery all the way up to bomb-dropping, and they were always piloted—remotely—by highly trained teams. That was part of why the damn things were so effective—they were flexible, and they could react to new information at a moment's notice. This one didn't *have* to be on a WMD mission, but it was safer to assume that it would be if the opportunity presented itself. In the wide Kansas countryside, it sure wasn't coming in to map unfamiliar territory or track down the Taliban.

Bryn found herself trying to look for it in the sky, but that was useless; drones were hard to spot even when you knew the exact trajectory. She grabbed for the panic strap as the SUV, true to Brick's warning, began the precarious hard right. The left side wheels left the ground, but they didn't quite topple, and they also didn't slow down, at least enough to matter.

They hit the low parking lot barrier hard enough to shatter it open and throw bits of chain into the air like hard confetti. Ahead, in a modest-sized car lot, was a rounded blue building, but that wasn't where they needed to go. Bryn pulled up the aerial map and zoomed in. "Back of the building," she said. "You'll see a chain-link fence with a gate. Go through the gate and straight—the ramp down will be about a hundred feet in. Once we're under the concrete, the drone will lose us, but they could go ahead with the missiles in hopes of collapsing the place on top of us before we go deep. So don't let off on the speed."

She was hoping, desperately, that the Salt Museum wouldn't have state-of-the-art surveillance or security; she also hoped that the drone operators would hesitate to throw heavy weapons around at a public attraction, on American soil, without a clear target. If the drone was military—and they were all *supposed* to be—then even if the particular op was run by someone friendly to their enemies, there would be dissension in the ranks, chains of command, lots of places for the op to get hung up and fail.

If it was private security who'd gotten their hands on the same tech, and had nothing but dollars at stake, then all bets were off.

Brick's driver was good, *really* good. They smashed the chain-link gate open at the back of the building without slowing, and in less than ten seconds the concrete box that overhung the ramp loomed up, a square of darkness that looked, for a heart-stopping second—like a solid barrier . . . and then they were hurtling down a ramp in the dark, blowing through another chain-link gate along the way. He'd flipped on the lights, and by the time she caught her breath, they were roaring at the same speed, angling down, through a narrow tunnel.

The other SUVs were right on their rear bumper.

Bryn was waiting for the explosion, braced for it with every muscle twitching and tight, but it never came. The driver slacked off on the speed after another twenty seconds, and the four-truck convoy coasted down the incline, deeper and deeper. The bedrock walls of the tunnel changed to what looked like limestone—aquifer level—and then took on a gray, diamondlike shine.

Salt.

They'd made it.

The oppressive darkness made it feel as if the shimmering walls were pressing in, but then the headlight beams suddenly seemed to dim. . . . No, not dim—*spread*. They'd reached the end of the ramp, and coasted out into a large open space—round and cluttered. Definitely not the public areas of the museum's tunnels; this was some kind of storage area for equipment using for tunneling and maintenance. They also bumped over a large iron grate, like a cattle guard. A water diversion, Bryn realized, like a sewer grate, designed to drain off any rain that rolled down the ramp. Couldn't have the rain soaking into the salt, or the entire place might dissolve. She shuddered to think about that.

The four SUVs pulled into a line and shut off their engines, and Bryn got out and looked around at the walls. She found an electrical box, opened it, and pulled the switch, and overhead work lights popped on.

It was a grayish fairyland of glitter, streaked here and there with muted browns from minerals trapped in the salt. She ran her fingers over the surface. The crystals felt hard as steel, and sharp enough to cut if you weren't careful. She licked her finger, ran it over the surface, and tasted. There was something miraculous about the fact that the walls were . . . edible. Just bizarre.

Which reminded her that she was hungry, again.

"We're out of the drone's target zone," Brick said from behind her, "but we're gonna need a strategy for extraction. It'll take time for them to get boots on the ground for a strike team, but they'll be coming, and I don't want to be here when they are. My job is to get you people where you're going, and I'd sure as hell like to deliver you to Kansas City without losing any more of my own people. After that, fair warning, I'm out. This has turned out to be a whole lot more expensive and nasty than anybody thought."

He was standing with Joe Fideli and Riley Block, and Bryn went back to join them. She missed Patrick's calm, solid presence. Badly. "What if we split up?" she asked. "The three of us can go on foot through the tunnels, find the public museum area, and get out that way while your team goes out the way we came in. This tunnel is a work space, so it ought to be clearly marked and lit, and it ought to dump right into the public spaces. Your four cars hit the freeway and split up, we go on foot and meet up with one SUV down the road. Divide and conquer. They've only got one drone, and they can't keep it out for long."

He thought it over, and nodded. "All right," he said. "Harm, you take one vehicle, assign drivers to the other two. We're going to sit tight for twenty minutes, then bug out."

"You should give it more time," Riley said. "Drones have plenty of fuel capacity. They could circle it a long time."

"They could," he agreed. "But they won't."

"Because?"

He grinned. It was intimidating. "Because we've already worked back channels, and the drone ops is off book. Chains of command are being informed, and trust me, in twenty minutes it'll be shut down, recalled to the barn, and the operators won't even remember they ever flew their toys over Kansas. Those who do remember will be seeing Leavenworth real close. There are some rogue commanders out there that Jane's paying, but none of them want to get court-martialed over it. Knowledge is on our side, not theirs. So far, anyway."

"Don't get cocky," Joe said. "But if we've got the chance, we need to take it. No room for hesitation in this game."

"Agreed," Riley said. "Let's do it, people. Narrow window, if the drone's off the table for them as an option. They'll be fielding a team, but we can get out before they arrive if we hustle."

"Take go-bags," Brick said, and nodded at Harm, who jogged off to the nearest SUV and came back with four camo backpacks. "We kicked in some Glocks and extra clips. Sorry I can't give you anything with more firepower, but we're running a little short, and we like to keep it street legal for anybody who isn't on the payroll."

"It's good," Bryn said. She took the Glock out of her backpack, loaded it, and clipped the holster to her waistband at an easy draw angle. "Ready?"

Joe Fideli threw the backpack over his shoulder. He was still carrying a shotgun, liberated from Brick's stores most likely, and Riley, like Bryn, had taken out a handgun.

They set off toward the clearly marked tunnel that said HARDHAT AREA. There was a map in a lighted case next to the entrance, and Bryn checked it quickly. The tunnel they were entering led straight and true through to an area shaded in light green—the public area. There was some sort of train, though that didn't seem like a great idea to use for the three of them, and also something labeled CARTS.

"Outstanding," she said. "This way."

Jogging felt good. Her body liked movement, and her muscles were grateful for the chance to stretch. Riley easily paced her, and Joe ran behind—not nanite-enhanced, but pretty fit nonetheless. His endurance wouldn't be equal to theirs, of course, but they didn't have that far to travel. It was about a half mile down the tunnel, and then there was a steel door—locked, but between the two of them, Riley and Bryn's enhanced strength shattered the mechanism enough to let them swing open the bent door.

The problem was that the lights on the other side were on a different circuit, and it was like stepping into space.

Joe already had an LED flashlight out, and as the door swung shut behind them he lit up the walls of the vast chamber. The same salt made up the entire surface, and the floor was smooth and gritty with it. He swept the light around, spotted another junction box, and went over to open it and flip the switches.

The overheads—more finished-looking than those in the parking area where they'd started out—marched on in ranks, illuminating a huge open space with a low ceiling, ten feet or so, enough to feel oppressive. The air was fresh, at least. This area seemed to be part of the tourist experience, and there were ranks of electric trams plugged in and ready to go. Bryn headed for one and disconnected it from the plug, and Riley and Bryn boarded behind her as she started it up. There was an old early-twentieth-century train that was clearly only for historical display—boxcars and wooden boxes labeled DYNAMITE that hadn't seen real explosives in a hundred years. Bryn pressed the accelerator, and with a hum, the cart rolled forward. She floored it—after all, they didn't need to worry about visitors—and sped past offshoot tunnels, dark and blocked off. It'd be easy to get lost in here, if you wandered off the public paths.

There were signs posted—new restrooms, apparently, plus an event area . . . and film storage. She supposed this would be a perfect environment for rare films—dry, cool, unlikely to burn.

Too bad they didn't have time to sightsee. She kind of loved history.

But survival had to come first.

The ride was smooth and flat, and she followed signs

down the wide arched tunnels, with their sparkling, striated gray walls and ceilings, until it opened into a huge domed area. A sign called it the Great Room, and she had to agree. Pretty great.

"Elevator," Riley said, and pointed to a large industry cage at the far end. Bryn headed for it, and braked just a few feet away. She bailed out and reached to press the CALL button. . . .

But before she touched it, a rattle from above sounded.

Bryn backed off and cast Riley and Joe a glance. "That wasn't me," she said. "Someone's coming down."

"Shit," Joe said. "How long?"

"This depth? About ninety seconds," Riley said. "We need cover."

Their advantage, Bryn thought, was that whoever was on the way down would be pinned inside the elevator. Sitting ducks. And it wasn't a closed steel structure; it had open grating, which wouldn't be much, if any, protection.

She felt a little sick at the idea of what was going to happen, but she also knew better than to regret it. If it was Jane, or Jane's people, there would be no hesitation, and no mercy asked or given. "Scatter," Bryn said. She broke for a large, square block of salt, one of the tactile exhibits, and as good as a steel barrier for bullets. Riley went for a support column, and Joe went for a free-standing informational board.

It was a long ninety seconds, listening to the clattering lurch of the descending elevator. And Bryn double-checked her Glock, wiped her palm, and braced herself against the salt block, aim sure and steady as she glimpsed the first signs of movement. The cage had come down in darkness, so she had no visual on who was within it, or how many, and she took a deep breath as the metal door slid aside.

With a cold start, she took her finger off the trigger. *Security guards.* Two of them, uniformed—one young

and fit, one overweight and graying. They had pistols—
revolvers—but they didn't look particularly dangerous.
Just nervous. Of *course* the place would have security. . . .
She remembered that there was film storage, probably
rare material. There was always a market for rarity.
They'd probably have silent alarms to protect that stuff,
at the very least.

That was the problem with having to make snap decisions and no time to research. You missed the obvious.

The two men stepped out and did a quick visual
check, but missed Bryn, who was pretty much in plain
view. It didn't say a lot for their abilities.

"Probably nothing," the younger one said. "I'm telling
you, we get those motion detector alarms all the time.
Usually it's just some kind of animal. They don't hang
around. Nothing in here for 'em."

"Did a stray cat turn on the lights, too?" So, the brains
of the operation was the older man. He also was the first
to really focus on Bryn, and the weapon she had aimed
at them. His flinch was visible, but he didn't dive for
cover, he just shifted his aim back at her. "Drop it, miss!
Drop it now!"

"Can't do that," she said. "Sir, you're covered from
two other angles. Please drop your weapons and lie
down flat on the ground."

"You're bluffing," the younger man said, and grinned
as he brought his own weapon to bear on her. "We
caught a thief, Bud."

Bud didn't seem so convinced of that. Her confidence
had caught him off balance. That was good. She definitely did not want to hurt these men.

"She's not bluffing," Riley called from her cover, and
edged around to point her weapon at the two men.

"Shotgun trumps revolver," Joe said, stepping out
from behind the information board. "It's like rock-paper-
scissors, but with more pellets."

That did it. The older man made an instant, smart decision to drop his weapon to the ground, while the younger one was still staring wide-eyed at the newcomers. Four seconds later, with his partner (or boss) already spread facedown on the ground, the kid realized that he was about to get himself shot, and threw the gun away in a panic, thrusting his hands straight up in the air. More like he was planning a high dive than surrender.

"Down, son," Joe said, and gestured with the barrel of the shotgun. "Just like your friend there." The young man dropped to his knees, arms still up, then looked confused about what to do next. Joe sighed. "You can use your hands to lower yourself."

"Thanks," he mumbled, and stretched out.

Riley, who had the most experience in this kind of thing, given that she was FBI, took charge with calm efficiency, zip-tying their wrists and confiscating the weapons, which she added to her backpack. "Right," she said, and patted Bud on the shoulder. "The alarms. Did they go straight to the police, too?"

"Yes," he said. "They'll be here in about two minutes. So you'd better clear out, fast." He sounded confident, and Bryn would have bought it, except she—like Riley—was watching the younger man. He seemed confused.

"Yeah, nice try," Riley said. "Bryn, the alarms are local only. We're fine for now. Tell you what, we're going to call it in for you on the way out, so you don't have to worry about being stuck here like this for long." She rose to her feet, and walked into the elevator, and Joe and Bryn joined her. Bryn slid the gate closed, and the second she did, the elevator began to rise.

"Did you press the button?" she asked Riley, who was next to the control panel. The elevator rose past the ceiling level, and the light from the cavern cut out, leaving them in pitch darkness in the popping, groaning metal of the elevator. A dark ride, for sure. It felt claustrophobic and rickety, and Bryn had to take in slow, deep breaths to stop herself from feeling so trapped.

"No, I didn't press anything," Riley's voice finally said, flat and calm. "I'm pretty sure we're going to have company up top, and they won't be rent-a-cops."

"On the plus side, they might assume that we are, at least for a second," Bryn said. "If they know that security's on the premises and just descended."

"You think it'll slow them down any? Because if it's Jane's people, they're not worried about innocent bystander breakage."

That was true. Worryingly true. Bryn counted the seconds, and when she reached seventy she quietly said, "Get ready. Stay against the sides."

Joe and Riley took the left, and Bryn took the right, and as the light spilled into the elevator's cab through the grate, so did a rattle of noise, and the smell of gunfire. *Worstcasescenario,* Bryn thought in a burst of adrenaline, and time seemed to slow down.

She moved faster.

Opening the grate was too slow; they'd be hit multiple times, probably in the head, before that could happen. So she simply took hold of the grate and shoved, popping it loose from its moorings, and the heavy thing toppled fast and heavy—landing on and smashing two of their attackers to the floor of the lobby. Bryn didn't pause; she jumped out, aimed, and it seemed almost as if she were laser-targeting each gunman with split-second accuracy.

Seven shots, delivered as fast she could pull the trigger, and seven people went down, hard. Riley was shoulder to shoulder with her, also firing, and before Joe had even moved out of the elevator, the lobby was silent, save for twitches from the fallen bodies. The smell of blood and relaxing bladders and bowels mixed with that of the gunpowder.

Jane's people, but Jane wasn't with them. And none of these, as far as Bryn could tell, were Revived; at the very least, the head shots had put them down and out for now. Bryn bent and scooped up two assault rifles; she tossed one to Riley and slung the other over her chest, and looked around the place. It was small. There was a gift shop off to the left that sold T-shirts, hoodies, and—inevitably—salt-related items such as lamps and table condiments. She was more interested in the small food counter that was next to it, though, and vaulted the counter and through the swinging doors to the back, where the refrigerator was kept. They did simple food here, like burgers—sure enough, the raw materials were in place. Bryn grabbed several tubular packs of raw ground beef, and shoved them in her pack.

Riley knew what she was doing, even if Joe wouldn't have; they exchanged nods, and Joe went on checking their downed enemies for pulses. He looked up when he reached the last one and shook his head. "Okay, officially it's a bloodbath, and ladies, I am a little creeped out," he said. "Time to get the hell on the road. We've just become public enemies."

Bryn agreed. There were two menacing-looking trucks outside belonging to Jane's people, but she had no doubt they'd be jacked up with GPS; stealing them was a nonstarter, unless she wanted to lead Jane right to them. "Let's go."

On the way out, though, she picked up the phone and dialed 911. "Seven gunmen dead at the Underground Salt Museum," she said. "Two security guards alive but in need of assistance below." She hung up as soon as she was sure the operator had gotten the information, and joined Riley and Joe, already halfway across the parking lot.

They headed out on foot.

There was no real cover out here, but they used what there was—trees, mostly, and some ditches. They intersected the main road, and looking back toward the museum, Bryn spotted a black SUV heading toward them at high speed. The timing was nearly perfect.

The SUV barely hit the brakes long enough for the three of them to pile in.

Brick looked up from his map as Bryn slammed the door shut, and the truck accelerated smoothly forward. "Any problems?"

"Nothing we couldn't handle," Riley said. Joe didn't say anything, but there was a tight muscle in his jaw. He hadn't liked any of that, but he was professional enough to keep it to himself. "Any sign of pursuit?"

"Jane's people are converging," Brick said, "but they split up chasing the other vehicles. The ones you killed back at the museum would have been in charge of this side of the box."

So, he knew there had been trouble, and the question had just been to establish how fast they'd lie to him. A test they'd failed, of course. Riley's gaze brushed over Bryn's, and she saw the FBI agent was aware of that, too. "Sorry," Riley said. "But I meant what I said. We handled it."

"You're leaving a messy trail of bodies," he pointed out. "And some of them were back at that train, and might point straight to me. So excuse me if I'm not feeling the love and trust right now."

"Are we breaking up, Brick? Because I'd like to keep my engagement shotgun," Joe said. He sounded flippant, but he wasn't. The atmosphere inside the truck was grim and tense, and there was a moment when it felt like things might come to violence.

And then Brick smiled. A false smile, but a signal he was willing to let it go. "Date night's not over yet, Joe," he said. "I'll let you hang on to it for a while. But fair warning: don't you ever lie to me again, any of you, or this ride ends. Got me?"

"Yes, sir," Bryn said. Riley was a little late, but she nodded, and so did Joe. "Sorry. It's been a little bit more than we bargained for, and we thought we knew what we were getting."

"No plan ever survives the first engagement," Joe said. "The great ones are the ones who can change the plan and keep moving toward the objective. We're doing it, Bryn. Chin up."

She forced a smile, one she didn't much feel, and closed her eyes for a while, as the SUV rocketed toward the next destination.

Surprisingly—and menacingly—there were no further attacks on them, all the way to Wichita, and then to Kansas City. No one mentioned it, but they all took it for an ominous sign. Still, maybe it meant that lack of military support had knocked the props from under Jane's response plans, and losing so many foot soldiers so early had forced her to reassess her strategy.

Bryn hoped for that, anyway. But she didn't count on it.

Brick's SUV made some turns once they'd entered suburbia, and pulled into an industrial area—aging, mostly deserted, filled with unrentable factory space and weeds. There was another SUV waiting there, engine idling.

"Right," Brick said. "It's been nice, but this concludes our business arrangement. Riley, love you—don't call me again. It ain't worth it."

"I owe you for the SUV," Riley said, and offered her hand. He shook it, and smiled.

"You owe me a lot more than that, and it'll be on the bill," he said. "Vehicle's fully stocked, clean, can't be traced back to any of you. It's got a laptop in it that's clean, too. If you need more than what's there, I hope you're as resourceful as you are lucky." He offered his hand to Joe next, and they shook solemnly. "Job offer's open anytime, man."

Joe nodded. "Good to work with you."

Last, he focused on Bryn, and she said, "You won't sell us out, will you?"

He laughed, but oddly enough, he didn't take offense. "I get bought, I stay bought," he said. "If somebody hires me to take you out in a year, that's a different thing, but I'm not going to change into the other team's jersey right now. And I promise, nobody in my organization will sell you out."

"Okay," she said, and took a deep breath. "One more thing. Could you check on my family? I'm worried Jane might come after them as leverage. I'll pay."

His eyebrows twitched, just a little, and he was silent for a minute, then said, "Your relatives are just normal folks?"

"Normal is a stretch. I have an aunt with four thumbs. But they're not involved in any of this, and I'd like to keep it that way if I could."

He thought about it for a moment, then said, "I'll look into it. Fair warning: I may not take the job. But I'll consider it, and if I don't, I will let you know what's happening with them. Deal?"

"Deal," she said, and they shook on it. "Thank you, Brick. I'm sorry we met like this."

"Yeah, me too. I might like you otherwise, sunshine."

She nodded, grabbed the backpack he'd given them before, and bailed out. As she, Riley, and Joe walked toward the other vehicle, the driver of it got out and crossed in the opposite direction, like a prisoner exchange. It was all done silently and efficiently, and by the time Joe had taken his place behind the wheel, and Bryn in the front passenger seat, Brick's vehicle was already cruising smoothly out of the parking lot. One quick turn, and it vanished.

"Suddenly I feel jilted," Joe said, and put the truck in drive. "Strap in, ladies. Bumpy ride ahead. Bryn, navigate me."

She'd already found the address that Pansy had sent, and punched it into the truck's GPS positioning system. "It's five miles away," she said.

"Outstanding. We don't have to wonder long what kind of reception we'll get."

He pulled the truck out to the street and followed the map's glowing directions. Bryn took deep breaths and looked out; it was late afternoon, sliding toward evening, and traffic was light in this area even during rush hour—whatever rush hour meant, in Kansas City. Around them, people were living normal lives, even if normal life here in this part of town involved pushing a rusty shopping cart and scavenging from trash cans.

Speaking of that ... Bryn hated to do it, but she grabbed her backpack, unzipped it, and took out one of the tubes of lukewarm hamburger meat. "We'd better power up," she said to Riley, who nodded. Riley sliced open the tube with a knife, and took a handful of the raw beef. Bryn made a face and plunged her own fingers in; it felt ... gross. But the smell hit her in a wave, and woke an insane tsunami of red-hot hunger that made her jaw ache, and suddenly, she was shoveling the slippery meat into her mouth and chewing, and the taste was like ambrosia and honey, like the best and rightest food in the world.

She ate four handfuls of it, then forced herself to stop. Riley took an extra. There wasn't much left in the tube.

Bryn wiped her mouth and sat back, and caught Joe staring at them. The expression on his face wiped out to impartiality, but there was no doubt that he'd found what he'd just seen disturbing, at the very least.

"Sorry," she said, and swallowed the taste of iron and meat. "Better to go in full strength."

"Copy that," he said, and put the truck in gear without another word.

The elation the meat brought with it was unsettling. Despite that, Bryn felt sad and disoriented, and realized that it wasn't so much for herself—she'd given up hope that she'd come out of this in any way normal—but for the world around her that had no idea it was on the verge of change. Because change it would; it wouldn't have a choice. Whatever happened, even if they miraculously stopped the Fountain Group dead in its tracks, word about Returné would begin to creep out. People would seek it out of desperation and pain and anguish. And someone, somewhere would meet that need.

It would turn clinging to life into a drug-addicted plague.

She blinked as Joe steered the truck to a stop, and looked around. "We're here," he said, and nodded ahead. "See that building? That's the address. Call me crazy, but it doesn't exactly look like the high-dollar establishment I was expecting from these guys."

It was a clinic. A free clinic, one of those charity operations that served the down and out and disenfranchised. Bryn felt a sudden sweep of chill, as she thought about the sick, old people who'd been used so cruelly at their supposedly safe memory care unit by the Fountain Group. "They like to pick off the weak," she said. "Use them. This is a place they might find attractive."

"Or maybe it's a person we're looking for," Riley said, leaning forward. "Call Pansy."

Bryn dialed the burner phone, and it rang three times before Pansy picked up, sounding breathless. "If you're calling to offer me low rates on my credit card, it's not a good time," she said.

"It's me," Bryn said. "Everything all right?"

"That all depends on your definitions," Pansy said. "Manny's come out of his bunker, so that's good. Your sister is bored out of her skull, which is bad. Liam is making amazing meals out of our food stores, and did you know he could cook? I think we might keep him. Oh, and we're completely surrounded, and Jane's people are trying to dig us out."

Bryn took in a sharp breath and looked at Joe. "Are you going to be all right?"

"Sure. Nothing we can't handle," Pansy said. "Not if you can do your job and get this thing resolved within the next week, anyway. That's about how long it'll take them to break in, we think. What do you need?"

"We've reached the address you sent us to. What are we looking for?"

"All I was able to get was a last name: Ziegler. He, or she, was specifically named in Fountain Group comm that we decrypted. But I don't know what role this person plays, only that he seems highly involved." There was a shout on Pansy's end of the phone, and her sunny tone grew brisk. "Okay, Manny's calling, gotta run. Good luck, Bryn."

"You too," she said, but Pansy was already gone. Bryn shook her head, folded the phone, and relayed the information to her two remaining allies.

"Well," Riley said, "I'm the logical choice to go collect intel. My new look fits in."

She was right; the punk esthetic she'd put on would probably blend better than either Joe or Bryn could. "Keep your phone on," Joe said. "We'll be fifteen seconds away."

Riley nodded, concealed the handgun under her shirt at the back of her pants, and bailed out of the van. She walked the short block, hands in the pockets of her jacket and head down, with slow, wandering steps.

If Bryn hadn't known who she was, she'd have missed her altogether. "She's good," she said.

"Surprised?"

"A little."

"By the time she reaches the door, she'll already have a backstory worked out for her character, and she'll have some specific medical problem that fits in with what they normally see."

"But she won't be sick."

"Doesn't matter. A lot of people coming into these places aren't, they just want drugs. It's pretty much foolproof," Joe said. Just then, Bryn's phone rang, and she put it on the console between them and pressed the speaker button. "Riley, you're on, we're here."

Riley must have been holding the phone to ear while

standing at some sort of reception desk, because she said, "Hold on," and then, "Yeah, I need to see a doc. My back hurts real bad."

The receptionist sounded muffled and world-weary, but clear enough. "Fill in these forms here. Have you been before?"

"Yeah, I saw Doc—um, Ziegler, maybe?"

"Dr. Ziegler's here," the receptionist said. "Take a seat. We'll call you."

Riley's clothes rustled, and then she said in a low voice, "I'm on the list. Will redial when they call me back."

"Riley, no, don't hang up—" But it was too late, and Bryn was talking to a dial tone. "Dammit."

"She's trying to save on battery power," Joe said. "It's a clinic. Could be an hour before she sees anybody but homeless dudes and crying kids."

"It could be seconds before they drag her off, if Ziegler was a hot name," Bryn said. "Right?"

"Not arguing that, but we have to let this play out. It ain't Riley's first prom."

"Maybe not, but this is the Fountain Group, and they're not playing, Joe."

He thought about it for a second, then sighed and nodded. "Okay, you win. Check that first aid kit there for bandages."

"Uh—okay?" She opened the kit built into the wheel well and pulled out a roll of gauze. "This?"

"Yep, that'll do. Spool some off and get ready."

"For what?"

"This," he said, and pulled out his combat knife from a wrist sheath. Before she could ask what he was about to do, he sliced a cut in his forehead, above the eyebrow. It was about half an inch long, but the blood immediately sheeted out down his face in a shiny red stream, pooling around his eyes, snaking down his chin and pattering in thick drops on his shirt. It kept coming, a steady red rain, and she was mesmerized by it. *Glad I ate,* she thought, because the smell of the blood tantalized.

"Old fighter trick," he said. "You can give me the gauze now."

She blinked, flinched, and handed it over with guilty haste. He pressed it to his forehead and said, "How do I look?"

"Gruesome," she said.

"Excellent. I'm just going to lurk. This cut'll seal itself in about thirty minutes; all I need is a couple of butterfly bandages and a cleanup, but it gives me an excuse to sit and watch Riley."

"Be careful," she said.

"My phone will be on," he said. "You hear me say the word *wife,* get your ass in there, because something will be on fire. Probably me."

She nodded, and then Joe got out and walked toward the clinic. Like Riley, he did a good job of selling his distress, but instead of looking like someone in need of a fix, he walked fast, a little unsteadily, like a man urgently in need of help.

Her phone rang when he was still outside the door, and when she put it on speaker he said, "Going in, radio silence."

She listened as he did the same exchange with the receptionist, who sounded just as disinterested with a bloody man as she did with drug-seekers, though at least she asked him a few more triage questions. He sold it just enough to need to see a doctor but not enough to be rushed through to the front of the line, and Bryn heard him settle into a chair. "In place," he said in a low voice. "Riley's secure. . . . Wait one."

In the distance, Bryn heard a voice calling a name she didn't recognize, but Joe muttered, "She's going back. Hang on. Stepping it up."

He must have stood up, because she heard him say, in

a louder voice, "Hey, can I get some help here? I feel kinda—"

And then there was a loud, concussive thud, as if he'd keeled over and hit the floor.

Bryn resisted the urge to speak, but she quickly armed herself with a handgun and extra ammo, and got out of the vehicle. She took the keys with her, and locked it, since there were weapons inside she didn't want to see walking away in the hands of scavengers. Then she faded into the shadows of a doorway, well out of range of the fading daylight, and watched the clinic's brightly lit entrance.

She heard sounds and mumbling that signaled Joe being escorted to the treatment area, she guessed; within about thirty seconds he was professing that he was fine, and they must have left him alone because he muttered, "In the back. Riley's got a bed across from me, but she's curtained off. Will try to get a look."

"Careful," she whispered back, but she wasn't sure he could hear her, and it was superfluous advice, anyway. He rose, and she heard the scrape of curtain rings as he exited his treatment area, then another similar sound as he entered Riley's.

And then he said, in a slurred, confused voice, "Wait'll I tell my wife about this!"

Wife.

She gasped in a breath and burst from cover, crossing the thirty feet to the clinic in seconds. The swinging door slammed open under the force of her outstretched arm, and she vaulted over the reception desk feet first, sending the openmouthed lady sitting there over backward in her rolling chair.

Bryn didn't stop for more than an instant to get her bearings, and didn't need to, because she could hear the sounds of things falling and breaking from her left. She charged that way, just in time to catch Joe as he staggered backward down the hall. His head wound was still bleeding, but he was now also sliced down the arm, and it looked deep. She steadied him and pushed him behind her, and took in what was in front of her.

It wasn't good.

Riley was pinned down in her bed by a man in a lab coat armed with a scalpel. He was an older man, maybe in his early fifties, with a graying fringe of hair that clung to the curve of his skull and desperate dark eyes shining behind wire-frame glasses.

The scalpel was at Riley's neck, pressing hard enough to draw a red bubble that burst and ran threads down her pale skin. She was absolutely still, but her eyes were open and burning.

"I may not be able to get her head completely off before you stop me, but I'll do a fair job of trying," the doctor said to Bryn. There was a glittering mist of sweat on his brow, but his surgical hand was absolutely steady. "A blade this sharp will make the soft tissue part like silk. Back off."

"Riley?" she asked.

"Dr. Ziegler, I presume," Riley said, and Ziegler looked down at her with an almost comical surprise. "You're coming with us."

He got in one slice that sent a fountain of blood rushing for the ceiling, but Riley had hold of his wrist by then, and she was rolling him off the bed and to the floor, and Bryn joined her fast. Together, they wrestled the scalpel away from him, and Riley sat back against the tile wall, gagging and holding a hand to her sliced throat.

"She's dead," Ziegler said, and bared his teeth. "And you won't get anything from me!"

"Who exactly do you think we are?" Bryn asked him. "Riley?"

Riley gave her a silent, shaky thumbs up. Ziegler did a double take that was just about priceless in its sincerity, and watched as Riley's arterial blood loss lessened, then stopped.

Healing.

"Oh God," he whispered. "Oh *God*."

"Not hardly," Bryn said. "Up. We're going."

She grabbed a stitching kit and bandages on the way out, not for Riley, but for Joe, who was looking legitimately green now. He took the medical supplies and led the way out. Bryn had the doctor in an armlock, and hustled him out as fast as possible. The people in the waiting room had either vanished, or were trying to be invisible, like the receptionist, who was crouched down on the floor looking terrified.

Riley was right behind them.

It was a long hundred feet to the SUV, and Bryn handed the doctor over to Riley as she dug the keys from her pocket and unlocked it; Ziegler went into the backseat with Riley and Joe, and Bryn took the driver's position. She peeled out fast, checking for any police lights, but nothing popped in the mirrors.

Apparently, responding to an altercation at the free clinic wasn't a hot priority. Thankfully.

"Hey, Doc," Joe said. "Whatever happened to *first, do no harm*? Isn't that still a thing?"

"Screw you, you freaks—" Dr. Ziegler's voice faded as he looked at Joe more closely. "You're not healing."

"Yeah, no shit."

"You're not one of them?"

"I'm not even sure who *them* is right now."

Ziegler looked confused now. And scared. "You— you're not with that psychopath Jane?"

"Definitely not," Bryn said. "But you've definitely got my interest, Doctor. Please, go on."

"Your friend needs attention."

"Then do it. There's a suture kit right there, and Betadine here in the first aid kit on the seat. But talk while you work. We may not have long."

The doctor didn't fuss about it; with Riley's silent help, he opened the suture kit, gloved up and threaded the needle, then washed Joe's arm slash with Betadine before he began the handiwork. "Sorry about the pain," he said. "No local."

"It's cool," Joe said. "One thing I love about docs— they might slice you up, but they sew you back together afterward."

"You've lost a fairly significant amount of blood. You'll want to rest."

"Does that really look likely to you?" Bryn said, and got silence in response. "Doctor, we got your name from decrypted Fountain Group materials. What is it exactly that has you involved with them?"

"Research," he said, and wiped his forehead with his sleeve, then continued to stitch. Bryn tried to hold the truck steady, and Riley focused a flashlight on Joe's arm as the doctor worked. "I've been involved in the program for years. But I got out."

"Let's get specific," Bryn said. "Tell me about the Fountain Group. Names, places, details."

"I can't," he said. "They'll kill me. They'll kill my family. They'll kill everyone I ever *met*."

Riley must have recovered enough to speak, because she said, "Too late, Doctor. They'll know we have you, and that makes you toxic already." Her voice had a hideous hoarseness to it, and that leant a scary conviction to her words. "It was only a matter of time, wasn't it? That's why you were hiding out at the free clinic. I can't imagine it's your usual digs."

He shuddered and avoided her stare, preferring to talk to Joe's surgical fix, apparently. "I was out of work. Fountain Group recruited me for a new program."

"And exactly what were you doing?"

"Research!"

"Don't be a dick, Doc," Joe said. "You know what she's asking you."

"I'm not answering any more of your questions," Ziegler said, and tied off his stitches—which, from Bryn's seat up front, looked surprisingly expert. "Just let me out."

"No," Riley said, and the word was as rough as gravel in a blender. She didn't look in a forgiving mood, and as blood-drenched as she was, she looked more dead than alive. "You're telling us everything you know. One way or another. So just say it now, and save yourself the pain."

Bryn was almost sure that was an empty threat, but it didn't sound that way, and Ziegler seemed to take it very seriously. Riley took the rest of the suture kit away from him, and he folded his hands in his lap and looked scared and miserable.

Too bad. Bryn couldn't summon up much sympathy.

"My name isn't Ziegler," he said softly. "It's Calvin Thorpe. I was in charge of the Revival team at Pharmadene Pharmaceuticals before I—before things went wrong and I left."

"Left," Bryn said. "You mean ran. They didn't let anyone leave alive if they could help it."

He nodded, eyes still fixed on his gloved hands. "Someone helped me out. A friend inside the company. He—helped me fake my death. I changed my name and tried to find work, but Fountain Group found me first. I didn't want to do it anymore. I didn't want to have anything to do with the filthy process of bringing back those abominations." He hesitated, and then said in an unconvinced voice, "No offense."

"None taken," Bryn said in the same tone. "You're a specialist in reviving the dead during the administration of the nanite drug—do I have that right?"

"I administer the drugs, measure the results, do the follow-ups. I was the first to raise the issue of . . . maladjustments."

"What kind of maladjustments?"

"Like that psychopath Jane," he said. "I nearly succeeded in killing her. If they'd let me finish my work, I would have done it."

Bryn braked and steered the truck to the curb, because her heart had started racing, and she was no longer sure she had the attention span for driving while talking. "Killed her," she repeated. "You mean, before she took on the upgrades?"

He gave her a frowning glance, then looked away as if she was something too horrible to behold full-on. "I mean that I tried to kill her *last month*," he said. "Upgrades and all. And I could have done it if they hadn't spotted me. I had to go under again. I was hoping to try again soon."

There was a heavy moment of silence, and then Joe said, "Doc, exactly how do you plan on killing Jane? Because I thought that was a pretty tall order."

"It is," he said, and for the first time, Bryn saw the arrogance of one of the men who'd decided to play God with human lives. "But essentially, what runs her—all of them—is just a biomechanical program. It can be disrupted. And it can be killed. And I know how to do it."

"Who else knows?"

"No one," Thorpe said, and glared at Joe. "Which is why you'd better not threaten me again, if you plan to take that bitch down. I'm your only hope."

Chapter 5

"We need a safe house," Riley croaked out. "Right now. We can't take a chance keeping him out in the open like this. What the hell were you doing, out in public? Don't you know how hard they'll kill you?"

"Of course I know!" Thorpe shot back, and clenched his fists on his thighs. "But I can't hide in a hole. While I'm alive, I'll help the living. That's all I can do to make up for—for what I've done, helping release this terrible plague."

"It's not a plague," Bryn said. "It's not contagious."

He laughed hollowly, and when he met her eyes in the mirror, his were haunted and more than a touch insane. "No?" he asked softly. "You don't think so? Because it's just a matter of time. A few mods. And then we're all just . . . lost. I helped make that happen. I *deserve* to die. But not yet. Not until I take Jane with me, and as many of them"—his glance included Bryn and Riley in that—"as I can."

"Yeah, that's real noble," Joe said, "but you're not going to do it from the inside of a plastic bag in a landfill, so let's get you under cover."

"I'm open to suggestions!" Bryn said. "Driving aimlessly probably isn't the best solution."

Joe took out his phone—Bryn realized he still had it on—and hung up the call, then dialed again. "Yo, lady," he said. "How's tricks? Yeah, still alive. We have Ziegler. Well, Dr. Calvin Thorpe, turns out, so look into that for me. But more to the point, we'd like to please not get hate-murdered out here by Jane, if she's sniffing around after us, so . . . any suggestions?"

He listened, covered the phone's speaker, and said, "She says glad you're still alive, and also, they have another place here in KC. Hasn't used it for years, but it should still be operational." He gave her the address. "She says she can unlock it remotely for us. It isn't as impressive as her digs, but it'll do in a pinch."

For all his cheerful, casual tone, Joe was deliberately not dropping any names—in case, Bryn assumed, that Calvin Thorpe turned out to be a liability, or sold information on. He was right. The last thing any of them wanted was to compromise Manny any further.

Though Manny would almost certainly burn this place to the ground and salt the earth after they sheltered there. As far as levels of trust went, Bryn figured they were well into negative numbers.

Traffic had thickened, hardening the city's main arteries, but she used the GPS to find side streets; the last thing they needed was to be stuck in traffic, sitting ducks. And Manny's bolt-hole was in—surprise—a decaying industrial area, which made things easier . . . at least until they came face-to face with the massive iron gate.

Which was closed.

"And . . . ?" Bryn asked, but just as she did, a buzzer sounded, and the gate rumbled back on tracks. She drove in, and before her back wheels were through the gap, the gap began closing. "Is she watching us on satellite?"

"I think it's safe to say she could nuke us from orbit," Joe said. "Go straight into the underground parking. From there, she'll open the elevator for us."

The setup here was much the same as what Bryn had

seen before, but smaller—the elevator was more claustrophobic, and when it opened up top, the lab was bare,
dusty and pocked with—bullet holes? Something epic
had gone on here, once. There were stains on the concrete that might have been blood.

But the important thing was that it was secure.

Bryn fired up the lights, and with them came a bank
of security monitors, which was handy. "Dr. Thorpe,
come with me," she said. "Let's find you a private room."
One with a locking door. She did find one, toward the
back; it had the dimensions of a storeroom, but nothing
in it but a cot, toilet, and sink. Perfect.

Dr. Thorpe sank down on the bed and stared at her
with grim fury. "I'm your prisoner, then?"

"Let's just say we don't trust you with scalpels. Or
anything sharp," she said. "Get some rest. I'll be back
with something for you to eat."

"I'd rather talk to the other one."

"Riley? Not sure she's up to talking, since you cut her—"

"The man," he interrupted. "The *human*. I don't want
anything to do with you, or her."

Bryn raised her eyebrows, returned his bitter stare
calmly, and said, "I'm really not sure you're likely to get
a choice, but I'll do what I can to accommodate your . . .
preferences." She shut the door, and found that it locked
automatically. Glancing up, she found the small glittering lens of a camera pointed down at her, and waved to
Pansy.

Good to have friends in high places.

With him secured, Bryn wandered the place. It was a
short tour—empty lab tables, a giant walk-in pantry with
canned food and bottled water, basic medical supplies,
nothing in the fridge. There was a surprisingly lush bed,
sofa, and entertainment center, though. Joe had already
claimed the recliner, and Bryn heard water running
somewhere from the right—Riley, in the bathroom,
showering off the blood.

"Doc all squared away?" Joe asked, and Bryn nodded. "I'm not wild about the guy, Bryn. Of course, I'm not crazy about anybody who opens his negotiations by throat-slashing."

"Maybe he knew she'd heal."

"He didn't know I would when he came at me with the scalpel," he pointed out. "And I don't like anybody who judges by group, not by individual. Which, you'll notice, he does. Watch your back, Bryn. He gets half a shot, he'll put you down."

"If he can."

"Isn't that why we're keeping him? Because he says he can?"

Joe had a hell of a good point. Bryn shook her head and wandered a little more, looking for a computer station—and when she checked the elevator again, saw another button that did nothing when she pressed it.

The speaker came on below the keypad. "Bryn?"

"Pansy?" Bryn looked up. Sure enough, surveillance stared back. "Just looking around. Is there a secure computer I can use here?"

"No," she said. "Sorry, we stripped things out that could be traced back, or had personal intel on them. It's pretty much just what you see. At least I left sheets on the beds and guest towels."

"You're nothing if not a great host," Bryn agreed. "What's the extra floor?"

Silence. A long one. And then, Pansy said, "It's private. And besides, there's nothing left up there of interest to you. It's mostly cold case files from Manny's lab days. Things he was playing around with, trying to unearth evidence. And he'd kill me if I gave you access to any of that."

"Okay. So ... what now? We have Thorpe. He says he's got a way to kill Jane—so that means kill me and Riley, too. That's a good thing, and a scary thing. What do you want me to do?"

"Nothing," Pansy said. "Sit tight where you are."

"Pansy, I can't." Bryn lowered her voice, hoping it didn't carry through the echo chamber of the lab. "Riley and I need meat. I've got enough to get us through for now, but after that, we're going to get hungry. When we get hungry, things are going to get ugly if we're still locked in here. Understand? We can't just—wait for some indefinite period. Not without some supplies."

"Yeah, I get it. There's a motorcycle stored in a locked closet downstairs in the parking area; it ought to be ready to ride. You can use it to go on a grocery run, but be careful, and stay away from facial recognition if you can. Oh—and there's cash in the safe in the bedroom, behind the abstract on the wall. I'll open it for you."

Bryn took a deep breath and nodded. "Keep an eye on everyone while I'm gone?"

"Always," Pansy said, and gave a warm, disembodied chuckle. "Just call me HAL."

"Ha," Bryn said sourly. She pressed the button to open the elevator doors.

They didn't open.

"I can't do that, Bryn," Pansy said.

She sighed. "So not funny."

"C'mon, it's a *little* funny."

Chapter 6

Bryn put out the raw meat, which was turning bad fast, and let Joe and Riley—fresh from the shower now, hair spiked and fierce, and hoarseness all but gone from her voice—know that she'd be making a grocery run. Joe ordered beer, which she ignored, and after retrieving cash from the safe—really, Pansy and Manny were taking paranoid preparedness to Zombie Apocalypse levels—she went down to find the motorcycle.

It was a simple black Honda, nothing fancy, with a simple black helmet; somehow, Bryn had been prepared for something space-age and expensive, but Pansy had clearly chosen function over form. Bryn checked the fuel gauge, and as Pansy had promised, it was still full. The battery had been taken out and connected to a charger, and it was the work of a few minutes to reinstall it, and then Bryn put the empty backpack on her shoulders, the helmet on her head, and kicked the cycle to life.

It felt pleasantly relaxing to ride again—she'd been checked out on motorcycles when she was a teen, and again in the army, but she hadn't been on one in a while. Kansas City wasn't nearly as much of a danger zone as most places she'd been, and she enjoyed zipping through side streets, looking for the nearest hole-in-the-wall butcher shop she could find. The town was big on meat, so it wasn't too difficult to find one, and she bought as much as she could carry—hamburger, steaks, and salami. The salami, fully cooked, could be carried with them easily enough even when they didn't have a home to return to.

All in all, it filled the backpack to its max, and cost her a significant chunk of cash.

Just in case—and because she'd gotten lessons in paranoia from Manny—she took loops and circles, heading back at oblique angles to the safe house . . . and that was how she noticed the helicopter overhead.

In a city this size, seeing whirlybirds wasn't unusual; they were part of the urban landscape, usually doing traffic reports or providing air support for police and fire. There would be a few private sightseeing operations around, too, though the area wasn't the most scenic.

What alerted her, though, was that this one seemed to stay if not on top of her, at least in line of sight. It seemed unlikely that the butcher shop would have had plugged-in surveillance and facial recognition; it seemed equally unlikely that their enemies could have been watching every meat vendor in the entire city, on the off chance of spotting one of them.

Bryn sped away on an entirely random track, heading for the countryside. The vibration of the motorcycle jolted through her, brutal and yet somehow soothing, and she watched the helicopter in the mirror. It tacked after her, swinging on a course that would pace her as she headed away from the safe house.

Dammit.

She was going to have to ditch the surveillance, if that was possible—and that meant ditching the ride.

If you want to hide a tree, you go to the forest . . . and hiding a motorcycle was relatively easy if you picked a big, well-populated biker bar.

Luckily, Kansas City wasn't short on them, especially

on the outskirts of town. A little investigative riding, and she caught sight of an old-school biker dude in a battered leather vest and bucket helmet, riding his Harley. She gunned up next to him, pacing him, and shouted a cordial howdy; he nodded, and when she asked about a bar, he pointed and told her to follow.

He led her to the mother of all bars. The thing was like a shopping mall, with more neon than Vegas, and the ranks of bikes parked there warmed her heart.

Perfect.

She ranked her ride in next to his and gave him a smile, and he offered to buy her a beer, which she accepted, because ... why not? She needed the helicopter to circle for a while, waiting in frustration.

She drank her beer sparingly, crushed the biker's hopes as gently as she could, and fended off overtures from a dozen others. A trip to the bathroom took her toward the back, and from there, it was a quick, stealthy trip to the employees' lounge. Nobody was inside, which was lucky, but then they were pretty busy. She rifled quickly through lockers, and found a set of car keys.

She left the rest of the cash she'd taken from Manny's safe — about a thousand — stuffed in the locker, as a dollar sign apology, and went out the back door.

The key fit a battered Ford, which was probably worth about what she'd left in the locker. Bryn had taken the precaution of throwing on a stolen jacket over her clothes, putting the backpack in a big trash bag, and tying her hair back in a ponytail; she didn't think anyone would be able to pick her out easily, and she made sure to keep her face turned away from the still-circling helicopter.

When she drove away, the helicopter didn't follow.

Once she was safely away, Bryn drove fast. She ditched the hot car a mile from the safe house, wiped it down to remove any prints, and jogged the rest of the way back.

So far . . . so good. She hoped.

Once back inside, thanks to Pansy's remote control of the gates and elevators, Bryn dumped the supplies in the refrigerator, then went to find Joe and Riley. Riley was sound asleep on the sofa, wrapped in a fluffy blanket; Joe was in the kitchen, making something out of canned foods. "You took your time," he said, and stirred something that looked like baked beans. "Trouble?"

"A little," she said. "I had eyes on me from the sky. Helicopter."

He froze for a few seconds, then continued stirring. "So, that's not so good."

"The thing is, they couldn't have picked me up coming out of here unless they had a way to track us, Joe."

"You think the van's compromised?"

"I think we have a bug, but it's not on us. We know the Fountain Group had found Ziegler, because we got that intel out of their files. But if they'd found him, why hadn't they grabbed him?"

"Shit," he said. "Because they bugged him, goddammit. I didn't check him. I patted him for weapons, but—" He turned the burners off on the stove and followed her to the bedroom area; the closets still had a few clothes on hangers, plain things for both men and women. He grabbed the essentials, and he and Bryn headed for Thorpe's cell.

Pansy opened it without comment. She'd heard everything, of course; this wouldn't be enhancing their already rocky relationship with Manny, and Bryn felt the cameras on them like lasers. As the door swung open, Bryn stood guard while Joe went in with the clothes. "Strip," he told Thorpe, who looked at him warily. "Down to your skin, including your glasses. Put this on."

"I need my glasses."

"You can have them back once we check them out."

"You think I'm *bugged*?" Thorpe looked outraged, then color drained from his face, and he yanked his glasses off to stare at them. When Joe extended his hand, Thorpe surrendered them, then stood and began to unbutton his shirt.

Bryn turned slightly away, giving him privacy. It didn't take long. Joe tapped her on the shoulder and handed her the discards as Thorpe fastened the new pants (a size too big, but acceptable). "Burn them," he said. "I'd be real surprised if Manny didn't have some kind of incinerator around here."

"Back left—" Pansy said, but Bryn cut her off.

"No."

Joe paused, watching her. "No?"

"If there's a bug, they've already got us. What we need to do is throw them off track, and the only way to do that is to lead them somewhere else. Pansy, is there underground access out of here?" Silence. Bryn sharpened her tone. "Pansy, *we don't have time!* Is there underground access? We need to get this thing out without being spotted!"

"I can't—"

Suddenly, the link went dead.

Everything went dead. The lights went off—the air conditioner fluttered to a stop. After a second, a constellation of red strobe lights began silently flashing overhead.

"Shit," Joe said. "I was really looking forward to those beans. C'mon, sunshine, let's move." He grabbed Thorpe by the collar and propelled him out the open door, where Bryn took the doctor by the arm. She dumped the clothes on the floor, and the glasses as well.

"Get Riley," she said, but she didn't need to; Riley was already there, looking pale and focused as she put on her shoulder holster and snugged a leather jacket over it. She'd put the spiked dog collar back on, too—it covered a barely visible pink line where Thorpe's slice had healed. "Riley, grab the backpack in the fridge. That's food."

She nodded and headed that way. Bryn checked the elevator, but the power was dead, the cage locked down.

"Here's hoping emergency exits still work," she said, and followed the flashing red exit signs to a small hallway and a thick steel door. It had a keypad and an alarm sign next to it, but it also had a push bar, and when she hit it, it creaked open onto a dark, steep stairwell.

More bullet holes in the wall here, she noticed. And more blood on the stairs. None of it looked fresh, at least; that was some comfort—but it was yet more evidence, if she'd needed any, that Manny and Pansy had reasons for their security. "Down," she snapped at Thorpe, when he hesitated. The emergency lighting had kicked in, and the red strobes gave the place a nightmarish horror-movie vibe, but she managed to pull him down the steps to the first landing, then the second. There was a door there with another push bar, and she almost hit it . . . and then glanced back to the concrete underpinning the stairs.

There was another door there. It was subtle and recessed, but there.

Bryn tried the handle. It had probably been electronically locked, but since the power had been cut, it also sighed open . . . on utter darkness. No emergency lighting here. It smelled damp and earthy, but there was a fresh quality to the air, and she felt a faint breeze. "This way," she said. She hesitated until she saw Joe at the top of the steps, and pointed; he nodded and tossed her a flashlight.

"I'll get the go-bags," he said. "Got a weapon?"

She shook her head. He dropped down his Glock, and she shoved it in the back of her pants, grateful for the solid weight of it. Thirteen shots. Not enough, but a start.

The flashlight showed them a tunnel—concrete, round as an oversized piece of sewer pipe. A thin depression in the middle channeled a muddy stream of water, and stains waist-high on the walls showed that it had gotten flooded at least once . . . but thankfully, not today. Today, in the faint distance, the sun was shining beyond a rusty slanted grating.

Joe and Riley caught up to them halfway down the tunnel, and Riley took charge of Thorpe as Bryn put on a burst of speed and arrived at the grating first. She gestured for them to stay back in the shadows, and carefully assessed the view.

It was a view of a dingy culvert, weed-grown and with a lifeless stream that had turned a peculiar shade of poison green. No signs of life except insects, though from the beer bottles and condoms she was fairly sure people weren't strangers here. What *kind* of people would find this romantic, she wasn't sure she wanted to imagine, though.

The grating looked rusted in place, but that was camouflage; it was hinged, and after she popped the catch on the inside, it swung smoothly open without so much as a squeak.

Bryn stepped out and waited. No sounds except traffic somewhere close by. No helicopter hovering. She gestured for the others, and they moved out in a tight, fast group down the culvert, which turned into a ditch.... Choked with trash and rusting metal, it became impassible after about half a mile, and Bryn scrambled up the side, using tough, spiny weeds as handholds, to peer up at ground level.

They were in the clear. Twenty feet away lay the rusty chain link back fence of a busy shipping operation, with teams loading boxes onto semitrucks. When Bryn looked back the way they'd come, though, she saw flashing lights. Police, or at least, something official. Manny's Kansas City hiding place was definitely blown wide-open now.

Her cell phone rang as she offered a hand to Thorpe, who was boosted up by Riley, and she answered it as she gave Riley an assist after him. Joe waved her off. "Hello?"

"You made it?" Pansy asked.

"Looks good so far," she said. "We found the tunnel. We're about to find ourselves some transportation, but you've done enough. Don't get involved any more than you have to."

"I can't help any more," Pansy admitted. "Manny's blowing fuses right and left, and I have to shut down. One last thing, though—I've got the name of someone high up in the Fountain Group. If you want to take the fight to them, it's probably a good place to start, especially if Thorpe can really do what you think he can."

"Yeah, jury's still out on that, but we'll see. Give me the address."

"I don't have it. The best I can do is tell you it's in Northern California."

"Shit."

"I know. I wish I could give you more. The name is Martin Damien Reynolds. Ignore all the false trails, there are a ton of them. Look for him in California. . . . Bryn, take care. I'm so sorry." Pansy clicked off, and Bryn had the feeling that if she tried redialing, she'd get voice mail, at best. Probably a message that the number was out of service. When Manny cut ties, he burned them, too.

"Let me guess," Joe said. "We've been dropped."

"Like the proverbial hot potato," Bryn said. "Maybe we can stow away on one of these trucks."

"Maybe," he said doubtfully. "They're pretty busy, and with four of us it's tougher. Probably a better bet to boost a car from the employee lot."

"I'd just like to get our faces out of sight on the way out of town," Riley said. "They've been all over us, and we need to break the trail clean."

Bryn considered that for a few long seconds, watching the trucks, then nodded. "Follow me," she said. "I think I've got this one."

Joe wasn't a fan of her plan, but he went along with it anyway. They cut across industrial lots and empty, weed-choked areas, down a couple of ditches, and came up near the access road leading from the busy shipping company. Bryn timed the trucks. They were leaving at the rate of one every ten minutes or so.

She positioned herself behind a scrub tree, and waited until she heard the grumble of an approaching engine. The truck was coming over a slight hill, coasting down to the stop sign, where it would turn right onto a road that led it to the nearest freeway.

She counted down, and at the last possible second, stepped out in front of him.

The visceral need to run was almost impossible to overcome, but somehow, she managed to root her feet to the pavement, and turn to face the onrushing grill of the truck. She had a two-second glimpse of the face of the driver, going from bored to shocked to horrified, and heard the chatter of the air brakes . . .

. . . And then the truck hit her hard enough to throw her twenty feet down the road. She landed with enough force to snap several bones, and smash the back of her skull against the tarred surface. Red-hot agony blitzed through her, knocking out sensation and sense alike, until she rolled to a stop in a limp, broken heap. A rush of heat flared, then, and she distantly recognized it. Her trusty little zombie invaders, rushing to her rescue . . . assessing the damage, knitting together smashed cells. It would all take time, but she'd live. Of course.

She might hate it, but the little bastards came in handy sometimes. Like now, as the truck slid to a stop, and the driver hastily dismounted and rushed to her, pulling out his cell along the way.

Joe stepped out from cover, calmly plucked the phone away, and said, "Please get back in the truck, sir. We're going to be joining you."

"But—she's hurt! She needs—"

"She'll be fine, believe me." Joe pulled his sidearm and held it steadily on the driver. "In the truck. Please. Now."

The driver did it without any further protests, though he did look scared to death—and even more frightened as Riley picked up Bryn (a process that was beyond painful, from Bryn's broken perspective) and carried her to the cab of the truck, where Joe pulled her in and laid her down on the narrow bunk in the back. Riley sat in the back with her, along with Thorpe, and Joe took the literal shotgun seat, with his weapon held with casual competence on the driver. "What's your name, sir?" Joe asked.

"Um—Lonnie. Lonnie Brinks." He looked scared out of his mind. "Please don't kill me, man, I got kids."

"Me too. And I love them, just like you do," Joe said. "Relax. We just need a ride. Nobody's going to hurt you. Where you heading?"

"Long haul to San Francisco," he said. "Where do you want to go?"

"San Francisco," Joe said.

"Uh—that lady—she's gonna die, man."

"No," Bryn said blearily. "I might look like it, but I won't. Promise."

Lonnie looked frankly shocked that she could talk at all, and when he looked back, she gave him a shaky thumbs-up. He stared at her blankly, then at the rest of them. "Who the hell *are* you people?"

"People who need your help, if we're ever going to see our families again, Lonnie," Joe said, and the sincerity and warmth that radiated out of him washed away whatever fear Lonnie still held. "I swear on my kids that you're gonna walk away from this alive, and maybe with some cash, too. You don't have to do anything except drive."

He was bluffing about the cash, Bryn thought; she'd left the rest of it in that locker, in compensation for the stolen car. Pansy was right—life on the run was expensive. Joe sold it, though—sold it so well that the driver Lonnie sighed, nodded, and put the engine in gear. "Okay," he said. "But don't get me fired. I need this job."

"Worst case, you're under duress," Joe said. "I figure either way you come out of this a winner—especially if you deliver your load on time, right?"

Lonnie looked considerably more cheerful after that.

Joe had a way of making just about anybody relax and feel normal in the most abnormal of situations. It was one of the key reasons Bryn liked him so much.

He was just a genuinely nice guy.

Bryn's healing continued, snaps and pops of pain as bones pulled into alignment and muscles knitted themselves together. She'd gotten used to the sensations, but that didn't make them any less awful. *I'm going to get PTSD*, she thought. Maybe that was part of what made Jane who she was—the trauma. The unending prospect of pain. Eventually, though, the worst of it passed, and she was just raw and aching, and that didn't matter as much. Riley helped her clean up from the bloody impact. Nothing to be done about the stains and rips on her clothes, but Riley assured her they made her look tough and travel-worn. Bryn had to laugh at that. Even wearing army fatigues, she'd never looked tough, exactly.

But at least she'd *been* tough. And still was.

The beef in the bag was thawed, but it'd be edible for a while yet—and Bryn had to admit, she wasn't sure that her nanites wouldn't find rotting meat just as attractive. The thought took away her appetite for it, and she choked down two protein bars to help satisfy the nanites' cravings. Thorpe ate in silence; he was watching them all with wary attention. He found a dog-eared paperback that Lonnie must have been reading, and contented himself with that.

As Joe and Lonnie—increasingly the best of friends—chatted away the miles, Bryn and Riley rested silently. Slept. Ate.

Thorpe kept to his corner, reading and rereading the battered novel with single-minded intensity. He clearly didn't want to get to know any of them, and Bryn decided she was perfectly fine with that.

It was a surprisingly restorative journey. For the first time in days, Bryn felt free of the oppressive burden of being hunted, tracked, watched.

And by the time the sun had fallen below the horizon, and the road was a space-black ribbon lit by the head-lights of fellow travelers, Bryn's phone rang.

It wasn't Pansy's number.

Bryn felt a surge of paranoid fear that shattered the fragile bubble of well-being, and exchanged a look with Riley, then Joe, before she answered. "Hello?"

"I'll keep it short," said Brick, on the other end. "Hope you're doing all right. Just wanted to report that your friend's head wound wasn't serious, so he checked himself out against my people's medical advice. I guess he's out there looking for you."

Patrick. Bryn felt a surge of mixed relief and guilt. She hadn't tried to find out how he was doing, for his own protection, but she ought to have been worrying more, she realized now. "You let him leave."

"Hit the brakes, he didn't exactly ask me nicely. He pulled a gun from one of my guys and told the med team he was going, and they decided they didn't want to see how far he'd take it. They get paid to take damage from the enemies of the clients, not the clients. That's just screwed up." Brick sounded calm and amused. "He's all right, and since he stole one of our best trucks, he's mo-bile and well equipped, if you know what I mean. So I'd be on the lookout."

"We will," Bryn said. "Thanks. I mean it. Especially for taking care of him; I know that was above and be-yond."

"I get the feeling you folks are going to be repeat cus-tomers," he said. "And you know what they say—the customer's always right."

"I thought you said never to call you again."

"Well, your friend Pansy airlifted me a pallet full of money, so I'm rethinking it. Also, took a look at your folks. They seem okay. We'll keep watch. Take care."

"You too." She hung up and tried to dial Patrick's phone, but got nothing but voice mail. Her own device was dangerously low on charge, and she didn't have anything to power it with—but Joe did, stuffed in one of his many pockets.

He also didn't think Patrick not answering was a problem. "If he got separated from his power supply, then he's out of juice," Joe pointed out. "Pat's been in lots worse situations—trust me. He'll get us a message, and he'll rendezvous down the road with us. Good to know his head's in one piece, though."

Lonnie was, by this time, studying Bryn in the rearview mirror. "Why is hers?" he asked. "I saw how hard I hit her, man. She ought to be dead."

"Stuntwoman," Joe said. "Trained professional at bouncing off of moving vehicles."

Lonnie considered that, and seemed to accept it—mainly, Bryn thought, because it was too weird to accept the alternative. "How does that pay, anyway? You work on movies and shit?"

"Yeah, we do," she lied smoothly. "And yeah, it does. See, you're doing us a huge favor. You're helping us get to a gig—we're working on a film with Spielberg."

"Really?" His eyes rounded, and his face lit up. "I *love* the movies, man. Hey, why didn't you just fly?"

Joe stuck a thumb at Riley. "She's on a no-fly list." She did, Bryn had to admit, look it, with her shag-cut punk-spiked hair and dog collar. Riley shot him the finger, just to sell it.

"Could have rented a car, right?"

"Yeah, if we'd had a credit card," Joe said. He'd long ago put the gun away. "We got robbed, man. Suitcases, clothes, wallets, everything. We've got some cash, but that's it. So it was stop you, or steal somebody's car."

Again, Bryn thought but didn't say.

Lonnie accepted that and went back to the shiny object. "What movie are you making?"

Bryn made up something out of whole cloth, an alien invasion of San Francisco, and Lonnie was rapt. She cast the thing with big-name stars, just for the hell of it, and promised Lonnie a photo op with Johnny Depp.

As long as it kept him driving.

Joe was—probably not surprisingly—a qualified and licensed semitruck driver, so Lonnie let him take shifts while Lonnie crashed in the bunk. Dr. Thorpe, who'd so far been dangerously quiet, took the opportunity while Lonnie snored to say, "If you let me go at the next rest stop, I promise, I won't say a word. I'll just disappear."

"Why would we want that, Doc?" Joe asked him. "We're just getting to know you. And also, you claim to be able to stop Jane and the upgrades, and believe me, we need that right now. What is it, some kind of device? A shot?"

"I'm not telling you anything," Thorpe said, and clenched his jaw in a way that he probably thought made him look determined. It actually made him look constipated. "You've got no reason to keep me alive if I show you what I know."

"Actually," Riley said in a low, silky voice, hanging right over his shoulder, "you've got that backward. We've got no reason to keep you alive if you *don't*. Because if you're not an ally, you're a liability or an enemy. Which would you rather be?"

He flinched. "You wouldn't hurt me. You've got no reason to—"

"I've got the same upgrades as Jane," Riley said. "Try again."

That shut him up, and made his face grow a shade or two more pale. He believed her. He would, Bryn thought, believe absolutely anything of someone like them—of the Revived. In any society, there are people accepting of difference—like Joe and Patrick—and people terrified of it, like Thorpe. That didn't make her any more fond of him.

At least, until he said, with great reluctance, "I suppose I have to be an ally, then. You don't give me much choice."

"There's always a choice," Riley said. "Just not a very good one. What do you need to make it happen?"

He *really* didn't want to tell them, that much was obvious, but after a long, long silence, he finally said, "I just need a phone."

They all looked at him. Thorpe's face reddened.

"I have it stored in a safe place," he said. "And I can get it for you if you let me make a phone call."

"How about we make it for you?" Riley asked, and readied her dialing finger. He shook his head.

"I'm not giving that up," he said. "You buy me an untraceable phone at the next place we stop, I will make a call, arrange for delivery, and destroy the SIM card so you can't trace where it's being held. Understand?"

Joe shrugged. "I'm okay. Bryn?"

"Not until I know what it is that's being delivered to him," she said, and Riley nodded. "You understand, Riley and I have something of an investment in this mutual trust thing."

Thorpe sighed, clearly frustrated, and considered for another torturously long moment before he said, "It's a vaccine. It contains another strain of engineered nanites whose sole purpose is to attack and destroy their opposite numbers."

"I thought that was impossible," Riley said. "Since they'd have to be programmed with the exact sequence codes for the existing nanites, and those get rewritten based on genetic structure."

"Yes, yes, that's true, but the genius of it—if I may say so—is that it uses the exact same replication technology in writing its own code. It fills in the gaps, so to speak. But of course, the shot can only be used once, for one person. The cure for one can't be passed along the way that the upgraded nanites can be. One shot, one cure."

"And how many shots do you have?" Bryn asked.

"One," he said. "Just one. I had three, but I used two in the testing process. I was saving this one for replication in a neutral growth medium."

"One?" Joe shook his head and exchanged glances with Bryn and Riley. "Fucking useless. If you use it, how long to develop more?"

"Days," Thorpe said in a precise, clipped voice. "At a minimum days, and that's if you have all the right equipment in place. If I use the last dose as you suggest, on Jane, then I waste it by downing one insignificant part of the Fountain Group's army. She might be a general, but generals can be replaced, if you take my meaning."

"Then why did you use your other doses?"

"The first one, for proof of efficacy. The second because I had no choice," he said, and—for the first time—bared his teeth in a humorless smile. It was surprisingly unsettling. "They'd turned my colleague, you see. And it was her job to destroy me and take the antidote to her superiors. They want a way to control their own creations; that was why they allowed me to develop it in the first place. I thought I was acting for myself, when in reality, I was just another of their pawns. Like all of you."

"How exactly are we pawns, genius?" Riley asked, and shoved him back against the shivering steel wall of the truck. "We're the ones who found you. We're the ones the Fountain Group has been moving heaven and earth to stop."

"You think so? Then you're more stupid than I thought. If they really wanted you dead, you'd already be buried in a ditch. Well, not the two of you. You'd be cremated like the rest of their failed experiments. But they've let you run. And that means you serve their purposes, somehow. I hate to explain this to you, but you're nothing but meat puppets, and just because you can't feel the strings doesn't mean someone isn't pulling them."

"He's insane," Riley said to Bryn, and Bryn was inclined to agree. There was a deeply weird glow in the man's eyes, a paranoia dialed up to eleven. But still, the old saying was right: you're not paranoid if they really are out to get you. "If he's our best hope, then in my professional opinion . . ."

"We're screwed," Joe finished flatly. "Well, hell, been there so often I ought to have my mail forwarded. C'mon, Riley. Buck up."

She shot him an entirely unhappy grin. "Look, if he's right, we're done. If he's wrong, then we're stuck with a paranoid—"

"Genius who may or may not help us? I'd say we're familiar with that scenario, too," Bryn said. She looked straight at Riley. "Stop at the next truck stop and buy the phone."

"No," Riley shot back. "I'm telling you, it's too big a risk."

Maybe it was, but after considering for a few silent moments, Joe nodded. "Maybe risky, but we're not exactly in the business of safe choices right now," he said. "Yo, Lonnie, up and at 'em. Need you to take the wheel. Pull in at the next convenience store you spot."

It took a while longer, but they found a store and a disposable cell. Once it was acquired and activated, Lonnie got the truck moving again, and Bryn got in the back with Thorpe. "Dial," she said, and handed over the phone. She pulled her sidearm and held it loosely at her side, and lowered her voice to a level Lonnie wouldn't overhear. "Say one word I think is questionable, and I'll kill you. No negotiation."

He stared at her for a second, expressionless, and then nodded. He dialed, held the phone to his ear, and waited. Then he said two words.

"Drop three."

"That's it?" Bryn asked as he cut the call and handed back the device.

"That's it."

"You didn't tell them where to bring it."

"I told them which drop site to use," he said. "We have to go get it."

"How far is it?"

"From here?" He shrugged. "Couple of hundred miles across the border in California. I chose the one in the direction you're heading."

Bryn signaled to Joe, and he joined them in the back, switching seats with Riley. She repeated the information, and Joe sighed. "I hate this cloak-and-dagger bullshit," he said. "Just give me the fucking address already."

Thorpe did. It didn't mean anything to Bryn, so she left Joe to work it out. Bryn broke down the cell phone, pulled out the chip, and smashed it, then threw all the pieces out the window; she was thorough about it, just for safety's sake. With nothing left to do, she stretched out on the small, thin bed that Lonnie used for his home away from home. It smelled like a man, with a dark tint of sweat and body odor. He'd taped up a centerfold on the ceiling, staring down at him with inviting eyes and open legs. Great. Now she needed a shower. Again.

God, she missed Patrick. *I left him. We all left him. He's all alone out there.* It made her short of breath, the idea that he was wandering out there, potentially at Jane's mercy, and wounded. *I should have stayed with him. Protected him.*

"Still worried about Pat?"

She opened her eyes to see Joe watching her, with a gentle concern on his face, and she forced a smile. "Brick said he checked out against medical advice, so he's not — not at a hundred percent. He's out there, trying to catch up, but I have no idea how he's going to do that. He's on his own, Joe. Against *Jane*."

He shifted a little, looked away, and said, "Yeah, about that. He can find us."

That got absolutely everyone's attention, including Riley's, who went very still. "Excuse me?"

"Burst transmitter," Joe said. "One use only, untraceable. I send, he receives. It gives him the GPS locator. We've done this before, Bryn; it ain't our first rodeo. He's okay. He'll keep his head down, and make his way to us on his own."

She blinked at him, unable to process it for a few seconds, and then relief spread sweet and warm through her veins. *He's okay. He'll be okay.* She couldn't bear the thought of Jane on his trail, but this—this was much better. If Joe had faith, then she could, too.

She spent the next two hours catnapping, and she suspected that Joe did as well, while Riley stayed awake and alert to any moves that Thorpe might have dared to try. He played nice, though, and Lonnie seemed cheerful. She was even getting used to his choice of music—he veered between funky jazz and a strange kind of wired-up country. It seemed oddly soothing, after a while, and the road vibration was a constant, gentle massage up and down her spine. *Massage.* That was a fantasy life, right there, ever being able to look forward to something so simple and sensual as having an hour when people weren't trying to destroy her. An hour to let her guard down, utterly, and put herself in the healing hands of someone else.

Yeah, that was fantasy. This—half sleeping, always tense somewhere underneath, ready for anything—this was real life now.

But the fantasy of that massage was so real, it almost made her weep with longing.

"Wakey wakey," Joe said, and touched her shoulder, bringing her out of what she supposed must have been a wary doze, instantly and painfully alert. "We're here. Gear up—we'll need the guns."

She shot an alarmed look at Lonnie, but Lonnie gave her a broad smile. "Yeah, I kind of figured out you weren't just regular folks about two hundred miles ago," he said. "Spies, right? Some kind of black ops thing?

That's cool. I won't blow your cover. Most excitement I've had in years."

That was . . . worrying. But Bryn didn't see any way around it; Lonnie was bound to make assumptions, and there was no way they wouldn't end up confirming them, or besting them. So she threw a shrug to Joe, who said; "Yeah, man, busted. What we're doing is eyes only clearance, so I can't tell you much, but I promise you, what you're doing is vital to our national security."

"Cool," Lonnie said. "Are you going to give me a gun, then?"

"No," Riley said. She was already checking her ammunition, looking competent and deadly as ever, and Bryn quickly followed suit. "You do exactly what we say, when we say it, and keep your head down, Lonnie. Let the professionals work."

"Yes, ma'am." He sketched a sloppy salute that didn't go with the eager smile.

God, Bryn hoped they didn't get him killed.

"Getting close," Joe said. Lonnie slowed the truck down, and Joe turned toward Thorpe. "What exactly are we looking for?"

"There's a billboard to the right. What we're looking for will be duct-taped to one of the posts."

"Anybody waiting?"

"No. It's a dead drop."

Bryn knew it was a technical term, but that didn't mean it wasn't ominous. Out of the truck they were exposed and vulnerable.

"Thorpe," she said. He looked at her with a frown grooved into his brow, and there was fright in his eyes, as well as distaste. "You'll go out with me to retrieve it. Riley and Joe stay here to cover us and make sure Lonnie is safe." What she really meant was *make sure Lonnie doesn't run out on us*, but the other way sounded better.

Thorpe looked momentarily very unhappy with this proposal, but she thought it was mainly because he was being paired up with *her*. He preferred to hang out with Joe Fideli. She understood that. Hell, she preferred to hang out with Joe, too. But he was going to have to suck up his prejudices and deal with it for five minutes. God only knew, she'd had to put her own preferences on hold for . . . what seemed like forever.

"Don't I get a weapon?" he asked plaintively, as she checked her sidearm. She gave him a lifted eyebrow for answer, and threw open the door to jump down to the ground. Solid, unmoving ground. That was a cell-deep relief, just to be *still* for a moment, after that eternity of driving, but she couldn't stand in place, either. She grabbed Thorpe and pulled him next to her, then thrust him toward the billboard that gently swayed and creaked in the breeze. The air felt clean and fresh to her, with the scent of sage mixed in with the hot metal and grease of the truck. As they stepped away from the cab, the industrial stench faded, and left the much nicer smell of blooming herbs and brush.

Thorpe must have decided he didn't like being exposed, because he rushed forward toward the billboard's base. There were four heavy posts driven into the ground, and between them were drifts of trash and tangled spiderwebs.

But the one on the end was cleaned of all that. There was a dried-up stack of weeds packed in there, but it looked constructed, not natural.

Thorpe shoved at the weeds, and revealed a shiny gray oblong of duct tape, lumpy in the middle. He stepped forward and reached out for it . . . and Bryn heard a very clear, crisp *click*. A sound she knew all too well. It sent a bolt of cold through her, and as Thorpe looked down, probably wondering if he'd stepped on a twig, she grabbed him and said, "Hold still."

"Why? What in the world—"

"Just don't move," she said, and dropped to her knees next to him. The dry, sandy soil had blown away a little and revealed the curved dull gray side of the top plate of the bomb. She blew away more of the sand, careful not to touch anything. It wasn't military-issue, more of an IED-type device, though she couldn't be sure of anything without a better look at it.

A look she wasn't likely to get, considering that Thorpe was resting his full weight on it. But she had dealt with enough of these types of bombs, and bomb makers, to know that the point wouldn't be flash and show—not like a movie explosion, all flame and smoke. This would be a dirty, hard sort of bomb, one packed with shrapnel that would rip Thorpe and her apart, and probably severely injure everybody in the truck, too. Shrapnel was cheap and easy and utterly, horribly effective.

It was all going to depend on the structure, and there was simply no way, and no time, to do an effective analysis of it. Thorpe was screwed. He didn't have the discipline to hold perfectly still for hours on end, and even if he did, they couldn't possibly stay here. The very existence of the trap meant they were blown.

He knew all that, too. She saw it go over his face in waves of emotion that finally settled into a pale, still mask.

"Listen," Thorpe said. He licked his lips, and his eyelids fluttered shut briefly, and then he looked straight into her eyes. "If you use this on Jane, you won't have anything left to use on anyone else—nothing to backward engineer. A weapon doesn't do you any good if you don't have the ability to reproduce it."

"We may not have a choice. If she comes at us before we can get the cure to our scientists . . . I promise, we won't use it unless we have to."

"Not good enough," he said. "Redundancy is everything, Bryn. I lied to you. There's one more dose, the prototype. I sent it as far away as I could with someone I trusted. You—you might need it. More than that, you need to keep it out of *her* hands."

"Who has it? Thorpe, you're out of time!"

"I know." He smiled sadly, palely, and nodded just a little. "Her name is Kiera Johannsen, and she's a climatologist living in a remote research station outside of Barrow, Alaska. She doesn't know what she has. I told her it was just a failed formula I wanted to keep on hand for research purposes, and asked her to store it for me. She agreed. Try to protect her, if you can."

"I will," Bryn said. Suddenly, all his bullshit and prejudice and annoying little quirks didn't seem to matter all that much. This was a man on the edge of eternity, and he knew it. "I'm sorry."

"Not your fault." He took in another deep breath. "The person I called sold us out. It probably doesn't matter now, but it's my brother-in-law, Jason Grant. Jane probably got to him, and he's probably dead. Everyone I knew is probably dead, but they might not know about Kiera. Not yet." He gave her a sudden, cynical grin. "You ever been blown up?"

"No," she said. "Shot, stabbed, fallen from a height, several inventive things that Jane cooked up, but not completely blown up. Are you asking if it will hurt?"

"I'm fairly sure I won't feel much," he said. "Please ask them to move the truck back."

Bryn nodded, opened her phone, and called Joe. He answered before it even rang. "The fuck?"

"IED," she said. "Get the truck back. Way back. It's going to go off."

"Then get your ass back here and we'll go."

She took a step back, and then hesitated. "No," Bryn said, without taking her eyes from Thorpe's. "No, I think there's something I can do here that's more useful."

"Die?"

"We both know it won't kill me."

"How the hell do you know?"

"It's worth the risk," she said. "Just do it, Joe."

He cursed some, but then he hung up, and in the next

ten seconds Lonnie was backing the truck up the road, over the curve of the hill. Putting solid earth between them and the explosion.

When Bryn couldn't see it anymore, she tossed the phone on the other side of the road, into the ditch, and then nodded to Dr. Thorpe.

"Here goes nothing," he said. "You know what I want you to do?"

"Yes," she said. "Good luck, Calvin."

"My friends call me Cal," he said. "See you."

Then he took a deep breath, reached out, and ripped the duct-taped item from the rough board of the billboard's supporting column.

Bryn saw it in high-definition slow motion—him turning, tossing the silvery mass of tape toward her, her hand grabbing it from the air. She was already turning away from him by that time, with the grace and efficiency of a dancer, not a motion or muscle wasted, and then she was running, great long leaps powered by adrenaline and the extra boost of the nanites, and she made it almost halfway across the road before the wave of the blast hit her.

It picked her up in a shimmer of superheated air and threw her, ripped her, punched through her in a nail of white-hot shrapnel, and she rolled, shredded, into the ditch with just enough instinct left to clutch the ducttape ball to the core of her body. She screwed her eyes shut against a flare of intense bright light.

The sound hit her a second later, rippling in a physical wave that shattered eardrums, and as the brutal glow still shimmered in the air, Bryn Davis's shredded body died.

Her last thought was incoherent and strange.

I miss you.

She saw Patrick's face, just a flash, and then it was all gone.

Again.

Chapter 7

Coming back wasn't fun. Bryn hadn't expected it to be; she'd gone into this on instinct, and instinct had a fatalistic sort of acceptance to the pain that she'd earned. At first, it was all instinct – whimpering, twitching, just an overwhelming sense of the world rushing over her, sweeping her back into a bloody swirl of agony and fury, and it took time for her conscious mind to fight its way to the front and be able to begin to analyze the inputs.

There were a lot. And they weren't good news.

Sight came online before hearing. She knew they were speaking to her, but she couldn't lip-read; it was simply too much effort. Instead, she watched Joe's face for clues about how bad this was going to be.

He was pale, and his face was set into a hard mask. So, presumably not very good at all. Riley was on her other side. She became aware that her bones were resetting, slowly. Usually they snapped together like Legos, but this was more of a . . . bending, a slow knitting that felt torturously deliberate. Her lungs were full of blood that was being pushed up, out through her mouth. Muscles twitched and convulsed as they repaired themselves.

The nanites had a lot to do. But, incredibly, they were *doing it*. She'd given herself only about a twenty percent chance, tops, of surviving the blast, but damned if the little monsters weren't pulling it off. She could almost like them, in that moment.

Almost.

She coughed out a massive amount of blood that left Riley and Joe exchanging horrified looks, but Riley toweled her face and hair clean. The water on her burning skin felt as good as paradise. *Running a fever,* she thought, and almost laughed, because a little cold was the least of her problems, wasn't it? She coughed again, and this time managed to drag in some sweet, life-giving air.

Riley patted her shoulder in congratulations. When Bryn concentrated on the movement of her lips, she thought she was saying, *Good, Bryn, just breathe*. One thing was for sure: if Riley Block looked shaken, Bryn had truly been on the edge of permanent, gruesome death.

She wasn't sure she ought to find it quite as oddly funny as she did, that deep concern on Riley's face. But hysteria was probably about as good a way to deal with this horror as screaming, and a lot more fun. *There's that PTSD,* she thought, and was instantly sobered up. Dying over and over was bound to have a cost—mental, if not physical. What had Patrick said about Jane? She hadn't been the cruel bitch she was now, not at first. It took time.

It took agony, and the wearing away of sanity against the hard rocks of immortality.

Her eardrums healed, finally, and sound crashed in raw and hard, and she almost cried out just from the shock of it. Everything sounded wrong, and too loud, and vertigo hit her, hard, even though she was flat on her back on the ground. She gulped in tearful breaths, heard the uneven, too-fast beat of her heart, and felt the last important, load-bearing bones seal together. Just ribs and fingers and toes left now. They'd heal up in a bit.

"Do you have it?" she said. Her voice sounded raw and garbled, and she tried again, and again, until finally Riley got the message and held up something bloody, wrapped in duct tape.

"This?" she asked. Bryn nodded. It probably looked like a convulsion. Felt a little like one, too. "It survived, Bryn. You did it."

Bryn shook free of Joe's hand and rolled over on her side, then shakily pushed herself up to a sitting position. That was hard. It was only then that she realized she was lying on the hard shoulder of the road, surrounded by blood like one of those old-time tape outlines from old cop shows. Blood dripped from her hair, from her clothes, and she smelled the hot coppery tang of it everywhere.

Then she smelled the smoke, because what was left of the billboard—a couple of ragged poles and collapsed wreckage—was burning with furnace-level intensity. It looked ghastly. She didn't see any sign of Calvin Thorpe, but she expected that if she searched around, she'd find pieces of him, here and there. Not big ones.

He was right. It had probably been very quick.

Riley said something to Joe, and he jogged back to the truck, which was idling nearby; he came back with a stack of fresh clothes and a big jug of water. Bryn, with Riley's help, stripped off the tattered rags of her clothes and stood in her burned and shredded panties and bra to pour the water over herself, washing off the worst of the blood and grit before she threw on the loose jeans and blue work shirt. Her shoes were mostly intact.

There were a lot of small, round metal objects on the road. Larger than shotgun pellets. *Ball bearings.* There were also nails, bent and broken and scorched, littering the road as well. They'd built a first-class dirty IED, all right.

It made her light-headed to think about all of that shrapnel tearing through her flesh and bone, turning her into a shredded bag of meat. What the concussion didn't rupture in the first place. God, she *hated* bombs.

"You okay?" Riley asked, and then gave her a very pale imitation of a smile. "As much as possible, I mean."

"Yeah," she said. "Let's go." Her voice still sounded as if she'd gargled with those nails, and she hoped it would get better. The nanites were focusing on the important things first, and being comfortable didn't really figure into their priorities.

The first hunger pangs hit her after she took three steps, and doubled her over like a cast-iron fist in the guts. Bryn stumbled, choking, and felt something feral clawing its way out from inside her. The nanites needed fuel. They were overheating, operating beyond their capacity.

Food. Now. NOW.

Joe stepped down out of the cab of the truck, and before she could think what she was doing, before she could even *try* to think, she was lunging at him.

Riley got in the way. Thank God. Bryn fought her, hard and violently, trying to get not to *Joe* but to the *fuel* that Joe represented—the raw energy stored in that fat and blood and muscle and tissue.

Riley wrestled her down to the road and held her there, and after a few minutes, forced something into her open mouth.

Meat. Sweet, salty meat, tough and chewy ... salami from the meat store in Kansas City. She chewed and swallowed with mechanical intensity until it was all gone, and the red eased its grip on her just a bit, until she could signal to Riley that she was back in control.

Riley didn't trust that, and kept hold of her, but let her have another big chunk of the salami. She chewed and swallowed again, a process that had nothing of pleasure to it and everything of desperation. She ate at least three huge hunks of the stuff before suddenly the need just ... switched off, like a circuit being cut.

She burped, mumbled an apology, and handed the rest back to Riley, who offered her—incongruously—a napkin. Bryn used it to wipe the greasy residue from her mouth and hands.

"Sexy," Riley deadpanned. "Better?"

Bryn nodded. The taste of meat was metallic and sweet in her mouth, and she wasn't sure she could bring herself to give an actual answer in words. She was still shaking, but that was terror, not hunger.

She hoped she'd never get the two of those confused. The idea of hurting Joe Fideli brought tears to her eyes, and she couldn't look at him as, with Riley's help, she walked to the truck and climbed inside.

Lonnie wasn't looking too happy anymore. He seemed scared, flinching from meeting her eyes, and he was only too happy to put the truck in gear as Joe settled in next to him while Bryn and Riley sat on the bunk behind them. "You—you were *dead*," he said. "Not just wounded. I saw you, lady—you were *fucked*."

Bryn didn't have the energy to try to convince him otherwise. He'd seen it, he knew it, and it terrified him. Fair enough. It had spooked Joe, too; she saw it in the wary way he studied her, as if he was waiting for her to turn feral again. She gave him a shaky, apologetic *sorry*, and he nodded. Not like he quite trusted her, but as if he understood she was trying.

Lonnie's wide brown eyes were staring at her from the rearview mirror. He looked away when she glanced his way. She knew she ought to feel something about that—feel sorry, maybe, that he saw her as such a monster. But truthfully, it didn't matter anymore. Nothing mattered that much.

Nothing except that blood-smeared syringe in its nest of duct tape, that Riley was still holding.

Joe said, quietly, "Lonnie, focus. You're nearly done with us—I promise you that. We just need you to take us the rest of the way and we're done. Another two hours, tops." He patted Lonnie on the shoulder, brother to brother, and Lonnie didn't flinch from *him*, at least. Though he did shoot him a doubting look.

"You—you're going to let me go, like you promised, right?"

"Absolutely," Joe said. "And I want you to do me a favor, man, I want you to call in a 911 on the fire when we're pulling away, okay? Just tell them the billboard's on fire and you're not sure what happened. You would normally call a thing like that in, right?"

"Right," Lonnie agreed. He took a deep breath, and nodded. "Okay. Okay, we can do this."

"Bet your ass," Joe said. "Now let's roll."

Lonnie engaged the gears, and the truck growled forward. The blood-angel that Bryn had left on the road surface disappeared under the tires, and then they were past the smoke, to the clear air beyond. The truck was moving at decent speed by the time they crested the next hill, and beyond it was . . . a normal world. Hawks soared the skies, planes skimmed the roof of the world, and on the ground it was just blank, empty road and country-side, with some scrub houses in the distance. They'd probably have seen the smoke, Bryn thought. Maybe even the explosion.

Lonnie made his emergency call, and reported it as simply as possible; his voice was shaking, but that probably wasn't too unusual for someone calling in a thing like that, especially on a long-haul drive. He looked relieved when it was over, she thought, and settled in behind the wheel to drive.

She dismissed him as unimportant, at least for now, and focused herself on more important things. *Who the fuck are these people?* She was shaken, she had to admit it. Somehow, while they'd been driving, the Fountain Group had found out who Thorpe was, tracked down his allegedly foolproof contact, and probably tortured and killed him. . . . Then, instead of sending an assault force (since the last overwhelming onslaught hadn't gone so well for them) they'd done something incredibly smart—they'd gone unmanned low-tech. There'd been some surveillance, most likely remote-piloted, but they'd thought that they'd be able to take out Thorpe, his weapon, and (as a bonus) at least one of them, too.

And they nearly had, with something as simple as a pressure bomb. Something you could build from plans on the fucking *Internet*.

Whoever was running this—and Bryn was now sure it wasn't Jane, Jane wasn't sane enough, or flexible enough, to plan this way—it was someone capable of making cold-bloodedly rational decisions. Losses and gains, offset by risks. Varying tactics. That wasn't Jane; she was smart, and brutal, but she wasn't a fantastic tactician.

Bypassing Jane and getting to the brains of the operation would stop this, stop it dead and cold. *Then* she could destroy Jane, but it was important just now to learn something from her enemy—to change tactics.

"We need to get out," Bryn said.

Lonnie sent her a startled, scared look, and then Joe turned and frowned at her. "What?"

"Just trust me on this," she said. "We get the hell out of this truck, and head out on foot. Then we split up, and you give me Patrick's burst transmitter. You and Riley, you get back to whatever hole Manny is hiding in. Please, Joe. You know me. You know I'm right."

"Right about *what*?" Riley asked sharply. "We're two hours from our goal. If we ditch our transportation, we add a day of hard hiking. Besides, do you think you can run off on your own, without backup, and get anything accomplished? *Jane* is out there. And she can call on half the military and, for all we know, half the law enforcement in this country. She's rich in resources, and we're not. Don't throw away what little we've got."

Joe was watching her without replying. She felt closer to him than to Riley, even now—even after both of them had experienced the infection of the nanite upgrades. Joe was basic version 1.0 human, and he had always had her back. Always. Even when he couldn't trust her not to turn flesh-eating monster on him, which was . . . quite a lot of trust.

"Yeah, I get it," he said after a long moment. "Lonnie, stop the truck."

Lonnie clearly didn't want to, but he hit the air brakes, and the truck sighed to a halt on the road's shoulder.

"You can't let her do this," Riley said, and put a hand on Bryn's shoulder as she tried to get up. "No. Just—no, Bryn. This is the wrong move; I know it. I'm telling you, just *stay*. We need to stay in the truck."

Bryn looked at her for a long moment, and then shook her head. "We can't," she said, and moved Riley's hand away. "I see something. You don't. You take that vaccine to Manny and get him to start making more. I think we're going to need it. Badly. We have no idea how far the Fountain Group has taken this—how many upgraded foot soldiers they have besides Jane." She nodded at the duct taped syringe.

Riley pulled her sidearm. She did it in a motion so fast Bryn hardly even saw it; the muzzle of the gun stopped with perfect precision in line with Bryn's eyes. Close range. Messy. "I have no idea what you think you're doing, but you're going to get yourself killed," Riley said. "Stay with us, and help us get this to Manny. This is precious. It's more important than you or me or any of us or all of us. It can *stop them*."

"Riley—we don't even know if it works," Bryn said. "The Fountain Group had access to that syringe before we did; they could have swapped out the drug with saline, for all we know. If they did, if they've got the genuine cure and we don't . . . *they* can take *us* out, and we've got nothing. Thorpe told me something important, and I need to follow it up."

Riley didn't move, and didn't holster her weapon,

either. "So you want to leave our transportation and just . . . go. Where?"

"We have the lead Pansy gave me."

"What, somewhere in Northern California? In case you hadn't noticed, it's a big area. That's insane. You're just asking Jane to kill you."

"Maybe," Bryn said. "But if you don't make it back to Manny, or if that syringe is useless, we might lose our only solid lead. So we need to follow both tracks, don't we? I'll go. You two go the other way. I'll see you again."

"Are you sure?" Joe asked her.

"Yes."

"Good enough for me," Joe said. "Ease off, Riley."

"No."

"Jesus," Joe sighed, annoyed, and drew his own gun. He wasn't as fast a draw as Riley, but he didn't need to be, because they both knew he was probably just as good a shot. He aimed straight for her, two-handed. "Back the fuck off. Bryn's right. We get out now, and split up. Lonnie, you're welcome to come with us if you want."

"Uh . . . no, thanks. I'll . . . stay here," Lonnie said. He looked rigid, hands locked to the steering wheel, and his eyes were about to bug right out of his sockets. His blood pressure must have been through the roof. "Thanks . . . ?" That last came faintly, almost as a question.

Joe didn't take his eyes off of Riley as he said, "Okay then. Sorry, man. About everything. You didn't deserve any of this, and I wish I could change it."

"No, it's okay, it's okay. I won't say a thing, really."

Lonnie thought Joe was going to shoot him, and Bryn thought he was probably right. . . . But then Joe shook his head, opened the passenger door, and descended from the truck. "Bryn," he said. "You next."

She cocked an eyebrow at Riley. "You going to shoot me?"

"Probably not."

Bryn took her at her word, and eased backward out

the door, hopping down onto the pavement and standing next to Joe. Riley followed, smooth as a snake, landing flat-footed and absolutely steady with her aim on Joe. "Are we done with this bullshit?" she asked.

"Guess so," he said, and holstered his sidearm, apparently unconcerned with what she would do. Bryn watched her—not the eyes, because it wasn't the eyes that betrayed people, it was the micro-twitches in the hands.

But Riley simply put her gun away, too, and the standoff was over. "Hold this, Joe," she said, and gave him the syringe. "I'm going back for supplies before Lonnie rabbits it out of here." She disappeared back into the truck, and emerged about fifteen seconds later with backpacks, which she tossed to each of them. Bryn strapped hers on, and the weight settled in nicely. One thing about being in the infantry, you never forgot the feel of a kit on your back. Like riding a bike. Or at least, like going on twenty-mile hikes carrying half your weight.

By unspoken consent, they moved away from the truck and into the shelter of a big, low-spreading tree — the kind of landscape people called trash trees, Bryn recalled, short-lived and strong-willed. Lonnie wasted no time in laying the hammer down, and he was over the horizon in less time than it took Bryn to get her directional bearings.

"You're sure about splitting up?" Joe asked. "Because I get where you're going, but I'm not sure you'll make it."

"Riley's right about the formula," Bryn said. "It needs to get back to Manny; that's vital. If this is the answer, he's the only one we can trust to analyze and—hopefully—reproduce it."

"You really think he's going to let us back inside? He seemed a little, I don't know, paranoid."

"Pansy will make him." Bryn tried to sound sure of that, but in truth, she wasn't sure; no one could be sure of what Manny would do. But she hoped she was right, anyway. "And this plays into his paranoia, because he'll be the only one with the cure. Then it'll be up to you to pry it out of his hands, of course, but one step at a time. I love the guy, but he's definitely Handle With Care." She turned her attention on Riley. "Unless you think you're going to take it and give it to your bosses."

Riley cocked an eyebrow. "I never made any secret of the fact that I work for the FBI. I never said I quit. And it doesn't matter, because in this, the federal government and our little rogue op have exactly the same goals: stop the spread of infection, and stop the Fountain Group. Manny's our best option."

"Are you under orders right now?" Joe asked. It sounded like a casual question, and it would have been easy to mistake him for relaxed, standing here under the gently rustling leaves of the trash tree, with the sun beating down. But he wasn't.

"Not as such," Riley said, and tilted her head just a little. Her eyes narrowed. "You think they surveilled us. Satellite?"

"Wouldn't put that shit past them," Joe said. "We already know they're into the air force's command and control; all it would really take would be a drone flyover. Could have been slipped in without anybody noticing at all. But yeah, if they were sharp enough to set the trap, they're sharp enough to watch and see who walks away from it. We stay in the truck, we're marked, at best. Or we're—"

"Dead," Bryn finished softly. She looked after the truck, but it was lost to view now, heading fast down the road. "You made the offer, Joe. Whatever happens now, you made the offer to him."

"Look, let's not kid ourselves, the best thing that guy has to look forward to now is torture and death, or—if he's really damn lucky—they'll just bomb the shit out of the truck and kill him that way. But he's not walking away unscathed. We all know that." Joe was expressionless, but there was a glitter in his eyes, something sharp and angry. "We owe it to him to not fail, you understand. We don't owe Thorpe; he started this—fuck him. We owe *Lonnie*. We owe the Lonnies of this world who get caught in the middle."

Bryn was caught by surprise, but she slowly nodded. So did Riley. "I was Lonnie once, too," she said. "I walked into this. I was just—taking a job. I went in the wrong door at the wrong time. And you're right. But I can't forget that we got Lonnie into this—not our enemies."

"Innocent people are going to die in this," Joe said. "Don't like it, but I have to accept it. Innocents are who we're fighting for. Not ourselves, not the government, not the military, just . . . the ones who don't even see this coming."

It was almost as if they'd made some kind of pact, and Bryn supposed they had—a quiet, unspoken sort of promise that didn't need handshakes or salutes. Just nods.

Joe dug in his pocket and handed over what looked like—lipstick? No, it was the same general cylindrical shape, but when he pulled the cap off, there was a round black button on it. "You get where you're safe, you push this," he said, and recapped the thing. "Patrick will read the coordinates and come to you. But make sure you're someplace you can wait for him. Like I said: one use only."

"Got it," she said, and zipped it into a pocket on her pants. One thing she was hoping not to lose this time: her pants.

"Want to tell us where you're heading?" Riley asked.

Bryn slowly shook her head, still watching the horizon. "No," she said. "I don't."

"Probably not wrong," Joe Fideli said. He hugged her hard, and she hugged him back, suddenly shaky inside because, although she didn't particularly mind splitting from Riley, Joe was . . . different. And he must have known that, because he kissed her lightly on the forehead. "Want to know a secret, kid?"

"Sure."

"If I wasn't already married . . ."

"Tease." She kissed him back on the cheek, and stepped away, and got a real, and very sweet, smile from him. "Take care of yourselves."

Riley didn't hug. She settled for a nod, and then Bryn set out at a run, heading west.

When she looked back, they were gone.

Chapter 8

It was a risk—a big one—to hitchhike. . . . Not for the obvious personal dangers that the post-1970s generations took for granted, but because Bryn knew that she'd be exposing those drivers—innocent, like Lonnie—to the possibility of torture and death, and she didn't intend for that to happen again. Not unless she didn't have another option. She resorted to her old trick—jumping on the back of the cabs of random tractor trailers when they paused for the merge at the next northward freeway. Then it was just a matter of balance and endurance. It wasn't too bad, though; the roads were mostly smooth, the wind buffeting manageable, though she had to shield her eyes to avoid drying them out. She was noticed a few times by passing cars, and as soon as she spotted the driver's or passenger's jaw-dropped expressions, she found a place to exit with relative safety, and catch another ride. The best she found was lying flat atop a monumental RV, big enough to qualify for a housing grant. She actually fell asleep for a while, drowsing in the hot sun, but dreams woke her. Bad, wrong dreams.

Slipping off the roof of the RV at a busy truck stop, she finally felt safe enough to activate the tracker. Pressing the button felt like a commitment, but she chased her foreboding away with a large, rare hamburger, fries, and cold drink. The food tasted unbelievably decadent. She didn't know how long she'd have to wait, so she lingered over it, careful to keep the hat she'd bought low over her eyes to hide her face from any hidden cameras. Her hair, unwashed for a while now, looked lank and tangled from the wind, and she left it that way. Better to look like a shabby traveler, though it wouldn't fool any facial recognition software if she was unlucky enough to be scanned. She'd bought a book from the handy racks in the general store part of the truck stop, and was immersing herself in epic fantasy when a man slid into the booth across from her.

For a split second she didn't recognize him, and her instincts went on full alert, but then she realized it was Patrick, half-hidden under thick stubble and bruises. He looked . . . rough. It was a shock, because she'd healed up from a goddamn *IED*, and he was still fighting the damage he'd taken in their first serious fight. If she'd needed proof of just how different they were now, it was written in their bodies.

He saw it, too, even though he wouldn't know about the extent of her own sufferings, and he half smiled and shook his head. "I'm okay," he said, and leaned forward on his elbows. They had the same style of cap, she realized, only his had some sort of fish on it, and hers had a bear. It might have been a cosmic karma sort of message. She hoped not. "Funny, I'd have taken you for a spy novel kind of girl. Maybe even romance." He raised his eyebrows, and just like that, she fell in love with him, an almost physical *click*, a wave of emotion that washed through her like ice water and chemical heat and a longing so deep it brought tears to her eyes. She threw out a hand toward his, and he took it, and the warmth of his skin on hers made her shudder and lower her head, afraid she might actually cry. "Hey. You all right?"

She managed to nod. She'd kept so much down, bottled up, locked away, but all it took to shatter that wall was just a single stroke of his fingers.

He was what broke her. Every time.

"We need to go," he said. "If you're done eating."

"How about you?"

"I've got something. Come on."

She held his hand as they exited the booth; she'd already thrown cash on the table for the meal, and the coast seemed clear as they went out the side door. The place was as busy as ever, with walking-shorts-wearing travelers coming and going, some with cranky kids in tow. Professional truckers looked weary and no-nonsense, except for a few who were chatting up the lot lizard prostitutes who always seemed to find a place to stand at a place like this.

She linked her arm with Patrick's. "What happened?"

"I didn't dare stay with the medics. Good people, but too easy to find. So I checked myself out once they were sure I wasn't in any danger of keeling over, and I checked in with Manny, who wouldn't take the call. Pansy said you, Joe, and Riley had dropped off the radar." He turned his head toward her, and she felt his eyes intent on her. "Is Joe all right?"

"Joe's fine. So's Riley. We found the guy we were looking for, but it was . . . complicated." Bryn decided this wasn't the time, or the place, to have that conversation.

"So, we're not done."

"Hardly." She leaned against a wall with him, content for just this bare second to feel his fingers twined with hers, the clean air blowing in on them. "I need to head north."

"Heading for . . . ?"

"I'd rather not say out here. Let's find someplace more private." She sent him a sidelong look. "Do you have a car?"

"Nope," he said with a strange sort of cheer. "But I can get us where you need to go."

That, Bryn realized as he led her around the parking lot, was because he had a motorcycle. A Harley, and it wasn't new—battered, in fact, but well maintained. He had one helmet, which he handed her, an automatic courtesy that made her laugh, and then he checked himself and sighed. "Right. Only one of us has to worry about head injuries."

"You sure you know how to drive this beast?"

"I got it this far." He mounted the motorcycle with total assurance, keyed the ignition, and kicked it to life. It roared like a pissed-off lion. "Hop on."

She did, carefully. It felt like straddling an earthquake. She wrapped her arms around his waist, and he accelerated smoothly into a curve, looping around cars and trucks and pedestrians, to the access road. Once on there, he opened the throttle to a steady, bone-shaking growl, and she found she got used to the vibration, the noise, and the general buffeting the wind gave her. She didn't *like* it, per se, but it was an interesting way to travel as a passenger. On the whole, she liked being in control, though.

They went only about twenty miles or so before they arrived at a cluster of tourist hotels—celebrating what local attraction, Bryn couldn't imagine, but it didn't matter much. They were all low to medium rent places, and mostly half-full. Patrick picked one right in the middle and parked.

"Seriously?"

"You wanted to talk," he said. "And I don't know about you, but I need a shower and rack time. Plus, they have a bar. I could use a drink."

She couldn't argue with any of that logic.

"Hat on, head down," he told her. "These places will have surveillance."

She gave him a thumbs-up and tugged on her ball cap; he'd already pulled his from inside his jacket and fitted it low, shading his face.

Check-in was brief and uneventful, since Patrick peeled off a startling amount to put down as a cash deposit for the night, and the clerk was only too happy to pocket an extra two hundred to keep them out of the register. That won them two plastic keycards and a warm cookie, which Bryn thought was funny, but she devoured it like a savage in the elevator. Not protein, but delicious.

The room was conveniently located next to the stairs at the end of the hall—a decent escape point, if it came to that, which Bryn devoutly hoped it would not. Inside, the room was cool and dark and still, and when Patrick found the lights, it was also unexceptional.

It didn't matter. Bryn took off her hat, tossed it on the dresser, shed the backpack, and collapsed on the bed with an almost sexual moan of gratification. Patrick stretched himself out next to her, staring at her with such intensity that it made her feel odd. "What?" she asked him.

"You look different," he said. "Stronger. Sharper."

"Is that bad?"

"No," he said. "It's good. You need to be." He reached out and, very gently, ran a hand over her arm. "I'm going to take a shower. We'll talk after, yeah?"

"Yeah," she echoed, and watched as he rolled up off the mattress and began stripping off layers. The hat went on the dresser next to hers. The battered leather jacket went next, thumped on the armchair with a click of buckles; he unbuttoned the jeans, slid them off, and sat on the bed to dispose of shirt, socks and underwear.

As he stood up, she lost her breath at the sight of him . . . not for the gorgeous planes of his body, which were objectively great, but for the bruises. They were days old and fading, but he'd taken a hell of a beating in that wreck.

He'd been lucky. No, *she'd* been lucky not to lose him.

He didn't look at her, although she knew he was acutely aware of her stare; he crossed the small distance to the bathroom, closed the door, and a few seconds later she heard the hiss of the water start.

It felt like a dream, getting up and stripping off her sweaty clothes, all the way to the skin; the chill motel air made her shiver, and made her nipples stiffen and ache as she hesitated in front of the door. Then she opened it, breathed in the warm steam, and as she shut it behind her, Patrick slid back the shower door. He was shrouded in the mist and spray, slick and gleaming, and the slow warmth of his smile made her shiver.

"I was hoping you'd come."

"Haven't yet," she said, "but what the hell, we can start slow."

She stepped into the stinging hot downpour and sealed the two of them in. His mouth found hers in a hungry rush, damp flesh and a dark, smoky taste that made her whimper a little against his lips. The water hardly had room to run between their pressed bodies, and it felt good, so good, to be with him, *with* him, in ways that had nothing to do with all the nightmares they'd been living. This . . . this was a dream, a sweetly seductive one, and for a long time they just held on, kissing, stroking, lazy with desire and sated by touch. He was already fully aroused, but one thing Patrick was a master at was restraint, and right now, he was in the mood to play slow, which suited her. His strong hands shampooed her hair, soaped her body, slipped into soft, dark places that made her catch her breath and arch against him.

Somehow, she expected it to end in a hot, hard pounding against the tile, but it didn't; he shut off the water and toweled her dry, head to toe, and she wiped him down slowly, pausing along the way to get him wet again, tracing her tongue along the hot velvet length of his erection. That wasn't enough, not for her, and from the groan she drew from him when her lips parted and slid down, he liked the extra attention.

He let it go on for a long few moments, leaning against

the bathroom door and taking in slow, deep, raw breaths; his eyes were half-shut, watching, and his hands caressed her damp hair, moved it back from her face as they moved together, silent and one. Then he gently pushed her back and lifted her up and kissed her again, slowly and deep and drunk on pleasure.

Then they went to bed.

It was a solid hour of lovemaking that kept the world outside the walls—Jane, the past, the future, even the nanites busily crawling inside her veins and the looming threats coming at them, somewhere. Bryn didn't care. She didn't care about anything outside of the sensations he woke in her body—tension, friction, release, pain, pleasure, sweat, tears, a thousand more exploding and mixing as he made her feel, for the first time in a long time, free.

Just . . . free.

"Easy," he said, as she arched against him, begging for him to go faster. "We have time." It was all he said, other than whispers hot in her ear and against her skin, but even he couldn't hold time back forever.

When he finally collapsed on her, sweaty and trembling and spent, she rolled him over and rested her head on his chest. He had a thick growth of hair over hard muscle, and she stroked her fingers through it. The silken tug of it felt good. Soothing.

"God," Patrick finally said, in a voice that was more than a little religious, "that felt good. Thank you."

She laughed a little, and turned her face toward him. He moved the still-damp hair out of her eyes with a gentle brush of his fingers. "Thank *me*?" she said. "I like that you're so polite, but . . ."

"Thank you for letting go," he said, and he was very serious. "Thank you for not letting my past with Jane stand between us."

Jane. Some of the warmth went out of the room with the mention of her name, but Bryn tried not to let it show. She put her hand on his cheek — prickly with stubble, he needed a shave, and she'd have friction burns all over her to prove it — and said, "Jane's not here. Let's not bring her into the bed with us."

He took in a breath, closed his eyes, and let it out. Then he nodded. "Sorry. I just — Bryn, I don't know if we're still — "

"We are," she said. "We're okay. I promise you, we're okay. It hurt, a lot, but I understand." She gave him a small, crooked smile. "I almost wish I didn't."

"I did warn you I was complicated."

"You didn't warn me you were a ball of razor wire, but that's cool, I have this special healing thing — you might have heard about it. . . ."

He put his arms around her and held her, and she knew from the slowing of his breath that he was sliding toward sleep.

She knew that one of them should stay alert, ready for trouble, but in the end, the safety and warmth overwhelmed her, and she fell with him, into the dark.

Chapter 9

What woke her was Patrick's hand touching her bare shoulder—not a caress, a deliberate tap, followed by a firm pressure. *Wake up, stay still.* Bryn came instantly and fully aware, heart racing. They were still in almost the same positions in which they'd fallen asleep, but she could see the digital clock over Patrick's shoulder, and long, much-needed hours had passed. It was almost midnight.

There was someone at the door. She heard it clearly—shuffling feet on the carpet, followed by a scraping, as if someone was inserting a key card in the door. Patrick let her go, and she rolled quietly one direction, while he went the other; they both landed near-silently on their feet and, still naked, took up posts out of the clear field of fire in case whoever was on the other side came in shooting. Bryn got closest, in the bathroom doorway; she was only an arm's length from the door, and now she heard that scrape-click again as the card was inserted.

And then, a loud bump against the wall, and a drunken voice saying, "Shit, that's not the right room. What's the room? Yo, man, what's the number?"

There were several of them in the hall, and Bryn didn't take the whole thing on first impressions; she grabbed a towel, draped it around herself, and eased the door open enough to peer outside.

Frat boys, wearing matching T-shirts, two of them still clutching open bottles of cheap liquor. God, they really did still drink schnapps.

They didn't see her. Bryn eased the door shut as they wandered off in the other direction, still arguing and bouncing shoulders off the wall as they weaved along. She let out a held breath and turned on the hall light switch. "Clear," she said, probably unnecessarily, and ran a hand over her face to hold back laughter. Patrick wasn't bothering. He sat down on the bed, head in his hands to muffle the chuckles. She took a spot beside him, and they leaned together a moment. "Well, I don't know about you, but I'm awake," she said. "And we need to talk, don't we?"

"Do we?" The laughter faded fast, and when he looked up, he was tense and ready for some kind of blow.

"Not about us." She sent him a warm smile, and his tension eased. "Work. We need to talk about what we're going to do next. If everything worked, Joe and Riley should be making their way back to the bunker with a sample of Thorpe's formula—the stuff that kills the nanites. The advanced models. Best case—we're a distraction, until they can mass-produce the equalizer."

"Worst case, they don't make it," he said. "And we're all there is."

"I didn't like splitting us up, but we had a better shot that way. If Jane has to divide her attention and second-guess two groups . . ."

"Three. Manny will have a completely separate plan in motion, guaranteed. And she'd better be worried. She might be able to guess what I will do, but she's a hell of a lot less conversant with you, Joe, or Manny. Joe will make it. He's made it through—" An odd look crossed Patrick's face, and then he shook his head. "I was about to say he's made it through worse, but I'm actually not sure that's true anymore. We're into whole new levels of worse."

"Then I hate to lay this on top, but we're going to have to risk being spotted," Bryn said. "Because we need to do some research. I have a name from Thorpe of someone on the Fountain Group board, but I don't know how to get to him."

"If you think we're going to get anywhere using a Google search, I think you're wrong," Patrick said. "But you're right, anyone we reach out to is an exposure, and it locks down a point of data against us. But we can't just sit here, nice as that would be." He thought for a few seconds, and then nodded again. "I think I've got a guy. Get dressed."

"Are we leaving?"

"Didn't you say you wanted a drink?"

Chapter 10

The bar he took her to was not in the hotel. In fact, it was nowhere nearby, and from the gradual scuffing-up of the scenery as they drove, it also wasn't in what she'd term a better part of town. Just one of those places you'd ignore driving by, in fact, a black-painted concrete building without windows, a flickering neon sign, and sparse parking.

Inside, the place was something out of a bad movie, Bryn thought, as they walked through the swinging doors and into a dim interior. The smell of old booze and sweat hit her first, followed almost immediately by the sound of music. The place had an old west saloon vibe, so the music seemed oddly off; no tinkly piano or western honky-tonk, but a smoky torch song better suited to a wine bar.

The place was a relatively small square, and booths lined the walls, with the equally square four-sided bar in the center. The man behind it was about six feet tall, blond, in black leather with tattoos crawling up and down both arms.

The booths were mostly occupied by men. No, not mostly . . . Bryn realized that she was the only woman in the entire place.

And from the bartender's look, not very welcome, either.

"Sorry," he said. "You're probably looking for the place next door, sweetheart."

"She's not," Patrick said, and eased onto a barstool in front of the man. "I'm here to see Brent."

"Don't know him."

"Yes, you do. He's in that booth right there, with the curtains closed. I want you to walk over and tell him that Patrick is here to see him."

The bartender's face settled into a scowl. "He knows you; you know where he is. Why put me in the middle?"

"Because we both know if someone opens that curtain without the right signal, bad things happen to them," Patrick said. His voice was still calm and pleasant, but there was something different in his body language. "Get your ass over there and introduce me."

The place had gone almost silent, except for the time-worn whisper of the singer. . . . Everyone was looking at them, and the pressure of the stares made Bryn's muscles go tense. This place—she couldn't get a good read on it. Not at all.

"Anything else?" the bartender asked sarcastically. Patrick smiled and dug two tens out of his pocket to lay them on the wood.

"I'll have a scotch, neat. Bryn?"

"Tequila," she said. "You can skip the lime and salt. That's for *turistas*."

That got the bartender to reappraise her, and she saw a flash of humor in those cold blue eyes. "True enough," he agreed, and poured the drinks. "Be right back."

The money disappeared into the till, and he didn't offer change. Then he flipped up the pass-through on the bar, walked to the booth with the closed curtain, and rapped with both hands on the wood on either side. Then he slid the curtain over about an inch and murmured something.

The curtain slid back on its rod with a hiss of metal rings, and the bartender beckoned to them.

"Right. We're up," Patrick said, and grabbed his drink. "Follow my lead, Bryn."

She drained her tequila in one burning gulp, put the empty glass down, and trailed him to the booth.

Inside, it was even more dim than at the bar, and as Bryn slid into the wooden seat next to Patrick, she tried to get a sense of the man across from them. Older, fit, tough, with a military haircut and bearing.

"Major," Patrick said, and nodded. The man didn't nod back. He didn't, Bryn thought, look especially happy to see them. "Came to cash in a favor."

"McCallister." The voice was gravelly—so much so that it seemed like one that had suffered serious damage at some point. "I don't think so. You've got nothing I want. Who's the bitch?"

"The bitch," Bryn said, "is sitting right here, and she's someone who could break your kneecaps in about five seconds. Sir."

"Name."

"If you called me a bitch, you don't really care too much."

She surprised a smile out of him, but that wasn't an improvement, not at all. He was . . . creepy. He didn't respond, just turned his attention back to Patrick. "Not going to defend the little lady, McCallister?"

"I don't need to defend what's secure," he said. "Buy you a drink, sir?"

The man—Brent?—looked at him with empty eyes for a long few seconds, then said, "Bourbon. A double."

Patrick gestured at the bartender, but he was already pouring, as if he knew the order, which he probably did. Once he'd delivered the glass, Brent, without a word, swept the curtain closed.

The space felt claustrophobic with the three of them. Bryn tried to keep her breathing slow and steady, and her eyes on the man on the other side. He needed watching; there was no doubt about that. He was armed, and very dangerous.

Patrick seemed as relaxed as she'd ever seen him. He silently toasted their host—captor?—and took a sip of his scotch. Brent picked up his bourbon and drank off half of it in a gulp.

"Favor," Brent said then, and turned the glass in a slow circle on the table as if he intended to grind it into the wood. "I'm out of that business. It's strictly cash these days."

"Then let's call it what it is: a debt. You owe me. And I want payment. Not in cash. In action."

"You're fucking crazy, coming in here to tell me that. The fuck you think you are, you little shit?" The words were aggressive, but oddly, the tone sounded almost … tolerant. At least as much as Bryn could hear through the rough, scarred blurring.

"I think I'm the man who saved your son, sir," Patrick said. "And I think we should just stop posturing before one of us gets carried away."

"You think you scare me?"

"I think it's mutually assured destruction, and I brought my girlfriend," Patrick said, and smiled. "So one of us is more confident."

"Or more stupid."

Patrick just waited. He sipped scotch. Brent didn't sip, but he gulped the rest of his bourbon, and after a solid minute of silence, said, "I don't deny you did my son right. Favor's owed to you by him, not by me."

"He isn't here. You are. I think it's more a family debt."

"Case could be made," Brent acknowledged, and then sat back and pushed away his empty glass. Bryn tensed, because it was the kind of move a man made before going for a weapon. Not this man, though. He stayed still, waiting to see what they'd do, and when neither she nor Patrick reacted, he nodded. "Tell me what you want."

"I need to know where to find a man, and I need you to take the news we were here to your goddamn grave, sir. Deep black. You get me?"

"I get you. What's the name?"

Patrick hadn't ever asked, and now he looked at Bryn. She resisted the urge to nervously clear her throat, and said, in a gratifyingly calm voice, "Martin Damien Reynolds."

"Shit," Brent said. "You people."

"You know him?" Patrick asked, and now there was a little trace of a frown on his face. If Brent did know the man, that would, Bryn realized, be a terrible complication. This was a world of favors, and if Brent owed a bigger one to Reynolds . . .

"I know *of* him," Brent said, which was a relief. "What if I told you that bastard was in Paris?"

"What if I told you I've noticed that people who phrase things that way are full of bullshit?" Bryn asked. "He's not in Paris. He's not anywhere but in Northern California, so let's try this again."

That got her the second smile of the meeting from Brent. She didn't like that one any better than the first. "Where the hell did McCallister dig you up, cupcake?"

That made her almost laugh, in a sweep of bleak humor. *Dig you up*, indeed. McCallister cut her off, though, by saying, "She's ex-army, so knock it off or she'll knock something off of you, Major. And she's right. Stop fucking around."

"Buy me another round."

Patrick's frustration showed in the way he yanked the curtain back and signaled the bartender, but not in his expression as he turned back. "Well?"

Brent drew it out as long as he could, waiting until the drink was delivered, then slow-gulping the first half before nodding. "You're lucky," he said. "Could have been in Paris. Could have been in fucking Afghanistan, for that matter. But the guy you're looking for is up north."

"Address."

"You think I memorized it? Give me a break. It's going to take a minute."

"We'll wait."

"You'll fucking wait *out there*, McCallister. And this info pays all debts, you understand? I never want to see you again."

Patrick nodded, and Bryn slid out of the booth.

He didn't. He asked, in a very different, almost gentle tone of voice, "How is he?"

There was a heavy silence, and then Brent said, "Don't know. My boy doesn't talk to me. He's alive, though. Alive and well. Got married, I hear. Probably got some kids he won't tell me about until I'm too feeble to care. If you ever see him, tell him—" Brent went silent for a second, face set in a blank mask, and then continued, "Hell. Just tell him you saw me and I asked after him. That'll do."

Patrick nodded assent, and got out of the booth. He pulled the curtain behind him and walked Bryn to the bar, where he ordered them both drinks and paid the tab.

"Who the hell *is* he?" she asked, as her tequila shot was deposited on the bar in front of her.

"One tough, slippery son of a bitch," Patrick said. "Could have been a general if he'd kept his mouth shut, but he isn't built that way. These days, he runs people like Brick, and a lot of other shit that isn't so nice. You want things done, no matter how messy, you find Brent."

"And he seems like such a nice guy."

Patrick snorted in amusement, then took a long sip of his scotch. "I liked his son."

"And you saved his life?"

"He took some pretty bad hits. I got him to cover and did first aid until they could evac him. Head injury. I never saw him again, but he wrote to me, after. Told me they'd discharged him and he was doing better. Considering they didn't think he'd make it off the battlefield, I thought that was a pretty good outcome."

There was a *but* in there, she sensed. "And?"

He drank the rest of the scotch in a rush. "He lost both his legs."

She nodded. She knew plenty of guys like that—legs or arms blown off, replaced by impressively crafted replacements. "Lucky," she said.

"Let's hope we are, too."

The curtain on Brent's booth slid open, and the man beckoned to them. Bryn swallowed her tequila before she went and nodded to the bartender, who nodded back, cautiously polite this time.

"Don't sit," Brent said when they came to the booth. "Here. Take it and get out. I don't know what you're into, and I don't want to know." He slid a folded piece of paper across the table, and Bryn took it. Their fingers touched, and the man drew back fast.

"Brent," Patrick said. "I can't lie. There could be blowback from this. Watch your ass."

That made the older man—Bryn couldn't think of him as *old*, even though objectively he probably was—laugh. It sounded like a gravel crusher loaded with broken glass. "Son," he said. "You think I do anything *but*? Fuck off. I'm done." He slid the curtain closed with a brisk whip of his wrist, and Bryn unfolded the paper. On it was a two-line address. The city was Paradise, California.

Ironic.

As they walked away from the bar, she looked over at Patrick and said, "How do you know he won't turn around and sell us out?"

"He won't," Patrick said. "He may be a hard bastard, but he's loyal. And like it or not, he did owe me. He'll die before he tells them a damn thing."

She hoped he was right.

Chapter 11

San Francisco was about an hour away, but they only skirted it; in Oakland, they found a long-term parking garage thanks to Google, which was exactly what they needed. The place was staffed, but with lackluster, disinterested employees who were just holding space until it was time to clock out. No problem to shop the available selection and choose the best without anyone noticing, especially since Patrick spotted and disabled the cameras first.

Then it was just a matter of waiting until the attendant went for a restroom break, then picking the lock on the booth to retrieve the key, conveniently labeled by space number. Patrick even logged the car out on the computer, since the attendant had left it running without password protection, and they'd started it and driven off the lot before he ever made it back.

Patrick even put the cameras back into working order on the way out. With even average luck, they had a clean car, one the police wouldn't flag for days, maybe even months.

Plus, it was a pretty sweet ride . . . some kind of BMW, one of the luxury models with all the bells and whistles. Patrick tried to take the first shift driving, but Bryn sensibly pointed out that he was still healing, and she wasn't, so a nap would do him good. In true military fashion, he took about two minutes to sack out in the embrace of the butter-soft leather upholstery. Driving in Cali wasn't exactly a hardship, and Bryn enjoyed feeling in control, for once — even in a minor way, by controlling speed and direction of her forward motion. And this time, there *was* forward motion. A Fountain Group member, on their radar. Finally.

The miles passed fast and effortlessly; the BMW was a gas sipper, not a gulper, so she had to pull in to fill up only once along the way. At the stop, Patrick woke up, visited the men's room, and demanded to take a turn at the wheel. Despite the cups of coffee that Bryn bought, and the fact that she drank all of hers, she was asleep in minutes once they were on the road again, seduced by the faint, low rumble of the road beneath their wheels.

But she woke up instantly when she felt the speed of the car change, and opened her eyes to see that they were taking an exit from the freeway ... toward Chico. Paradise, according to the map, was just a few miles from that medium-sized metropolis ... a sparse community, looked like, scraping out a living in tough country. "We're close," he said. "We're going to need to do some reconnaissance."

"How about a blatant drive-by?" she asked. "Nobody's looking for us. Not here."

"You hope," he said, but it was an absent-minded, reflexive sort of pessimism — well earned, these days. "Keep your hat on."

She slid on sunglasses as well — the car's owner was female, and had helpfully included some sweet designer frames. "How's that?"

"Spyworthy," he said. "Keep watch. You see anything suspicious, we abort and go at this another way."

But they didn't spot anything. Chico was a nice town, nobody looked at them twice, and by the time they were out heading for Paradise, they were almost alone on the road, except for the ever-present truckers. The hills were rugged, but the BMW handled them with style, and they made good time.

The built-in satnav led them through the small downtown of Paradise—pretty, neat, perched up above the coast's fog and away from the hot zones. It looked, Bryn thought, like the kind of place she'd enjoy staying—something that might actually live up to the name, if you enjoyed the rustic comforts.

They didn't stop. The navigation system led them outside of town, up into the hills, and indicated a dirt-road turnoff that looked isolated and private.

"Drive-by isn't going to work," she said, and Patrick nodded. "So, this is a job for the infantry. Want to let me out?"

"I'm not letting you go on your own," he said, and went another mile or two before pulling the BMW into a scenic overlook spot. It had some deserted picnic tables, so it probably got some traffic; the car wouldn't attract too much attention, provided it didn't stay for long. "One sec." He pulled the chip out of the navigation system and pocketed it. "Just in case."

They locked the car, and Bryn hoped they'd see it again; she'd miss her backpack, badly. The meat had no doubt gone rancid by now, and even though she could almost certainly still eat it—with nauseating pleasure—her conscious mind had enough decency left to object unless there was no other choice. She needed to find something less perishable—maybe beef jerky, by the pound. That thought made her stomach growl, again. *Oh, relax,* she told the nanites, annoyed. *You're not exactly working hard.*

The hike was a little strenuous but it felt good, stretching those muscles, and it had been too long since Bryn had been in the trees, enjoying the fresh breezes and the dappled sun. Patrick spotted animals better than she did, and pointed out a deer watching them from a thicket, motionless and wary; as soon as she looked, it bounded away with hardly a rustle of brush.

Within half a mile, they came upon the fence. It was, at first glance, not much of a thing . . . more an annoyance than a barrier. But they both paused and took a closer look. It was for show, of course; the real security came from proximity sensors that would feed directly into the house's security. There were probably motion-activated cameras, too.

Patrick took her hand in a very natural sort of motion, and they strolled a little ways down the fence line to a clearing, where he pressed her against a tree and kissed her. That was nice. More than nice, actually. She had a sudden fantasy of sex in the soft grass, but she knew what he was doing . . . creating a plausible show for the cameras. "So," he said, as he kissed her neck. She didn't have any difficulty showing enthusiasm for that move. "Recon is probably a bust, unless you want to spend a couple of days camping out and watching the comings and goings."

"That's a no. It just gives them more time to trace us."

"Then we just go?"

"We just go," she said.

"Now?"

"Dark won't help." These days, the serious security had night vision cameras, and motion sensors never slept. Without tech help, they wouldn't be able to overcome it anyway.

What they had left was pure ferocity and nerve. Unknown odds, unknown conditions, and they didn't even know if their target was on-site.

"I love you," he murmured, and kissed her again, with real heat. "Let's go."

She felt her adrenaline surge, and a smile form without any direction from her conscious brain. And then, without more than a breath to prepare, they both turned, leaped the fence, and began running for their target.

There was no outcry, no barking dogs or sirens to give alarm. The two of them were fast, and Bryn faster than Patrick, although he worked hard to catch up when he could. The uphill course crossed a couple of small streams flowing the other way, and she leaped them easily without much of a pause. It felt good, this run. This *hunt*. It felt like she'd been born for it. Engineered for it, at the very least.

When she flushed a rabbit out of her path, the urge to chase it down and feast was strong, insanely so, and she had to struggle to tamp it down. The distraction allowed Patrick to catch and pass her, and she took a deep breath to center herself again.

Then they both reached the top of the ridge together, shaded and concealed by the tree line, and looked down on a steep slope that led to a pasture. A large one, marked by a genuinely serious fence that marked this as an estate, and maybe a compound. The pasture was a glass-smooth expanse of lush green, no cover, no protection. The wall was eight feet high and reinforced with razor wire at the top.

"Shit," Patrick said, which pretty much summed it up. "We can't wait. They'll know we're coming."

Maybe they did, but if so, there wasn't the response that Bryn would have expected to see—no boiling-up of security personnel, no vehicles, no dogs. Nothing. She didn't see a thing moving, anywhere.

"You getting a bad feeling?" she asked him. Patrick didn't take his eyes off the scene lying before them.

"Yeah. Either this guy is supremely confident his fence will keep us out, he's got something in place we can't see that he knows will kill us, or . . ."

". . . or there's something very wrong here," Bryn finished. He nodded. "Well. Only one way to find out. You stay behind me, no matter what."

He drew his sidearm and nodded; no macho arguments, which was a relief. He knew she could take the abuse.

She jumped out onto the downslope and ran down, hearing a tumble of rocks and soil behind her. As soon as she cleared the tree line she felt exposed and cold, despite the warm morning sun. Any second, she expected to feel bullets striking, followed by the time-delayed chatter of a machine pistol . . . but she reached the fence easily, without any kind of attack or alarm.

Patrick said, "Bryn! On your nine!" She turned left, expecting to see an enemy, but there was nothing but fence, and . . . and a gate.

And the gate was a whole lot easier to scale than the wall itself.

Bryn climbed, slipped down the other side, and unlocked it to swing it open for Patrick, who eased in with his eyes darting from one side of the interior pasture area to the other. Nothing to see, not even a dog or a gardener. Eerily quiet.

"Maybe he's gone," she said. "This may not be his full-time home."

"You know us rich people with our vagabond ways," Patrick said, but he wasn't disagreeing. "Go. I'll cover you."

There wasn't any need. There were no booby traps, no ambushes, no hidden deadly enemies. They simply ran— and then walked—right up to the front door.

The mansion was big, and conventionally built for this part of the country. . . . It was what the well-to-do thought of as "rustic" despite being completely modern, just with rougher log finish. All the lights were on inside. Bryn thought about opening the door, but then, on a whim, decided to just . . . knock.

The door was answered by a boy.

Bryn blinked. Yes, that was a boy, all right, about ten years old, brown hair, a coffee-and-cream skin tone, eyes so darkly colored it was hard to tell iris from pupil. He stared at her for a second, then turned and yelled at ear-piercing volume, "Dad! They're here!"

Bryn looked over her shoulder at Patrick, who seemed just as stunned. He quietly holstered his gun. So did she. Bryn had time to mouth, *what the fuck?* and then the boy moved aside, and a man stepped up into the doorway in his place.

He was medium height, a little plump and straining the buttons on his button-down shirt. Well-worn jeans and battered work boots.

"Ah," he said. "Come in. I've been expecting you; I don't think there's anything I can add to what you already know, but I'll certainly try. Can I offer you a drink? Iced tea, maybe?"

"Sure," Bryn said. She wasn't at all sure what the hell was going on, and from his expression, neither was Patrick. "That'd be fine. Excuse me, but you *are* Martin Reynolds?"

"All day long," the man said. "And you're here about the Fountain Group. Aaron, go play with your sister. Stay out of here until I call you—understand?"

The boy looked up at his father and frowned. "Why can't I stay?"

"Boring stuff," Reynolds said. "Go. Scoot." As his son ran off through the large, comfortable living room and turned to the right, Reynolds watched him with a soft, loving smile. "Good kid." He turned and met Bryn's gaze with surprising directness. "Come on. Let's get you that tea and sort all this out."

Chapter 12

Bryn had to wonder whether Patrick found this as surreal as she did—sitting at the breakfast table in the big granite-countered kitchen while the man they'd been dead set on capturing made them iced tea. With freshly sliced lemons. "I saw you on the security cameras," he said. "I'd have gone out to let you in, but I was afraid you'd think that was confrontational."

He set Bryn's iced tea in front of her, then Patrick's. She gave Patrick a little shake of her head to tell him not to drink yet, and took a deep mouthful. Cold, tangy, and good. She waited for any ill effects, but nothing came.

"So—you're on the board of the Fountain Group."

"Yes." He put his glass down, and his easy expression shifted to something serious. "At least I was, until very recently. Until I discovered exactly what they were doing in their . . . processing centers. I've resigned now, and I can assure you, I had absolutely no idea of the cost overruns associated with the research. If I'd known, I'd have taken aggressive action to rein in that kind of reckless behavior."

The stunning *cluelessness* of it made Bryn sit there, staring at him, unable to think how to even begin. Finally she said, "You were concerned about the *costs*," she repeated. "What about the—ethics of what you were doing?"

"Ethics?" He said it as if the word were untranslatable. Maybe it was, in his world. "Look, this is about budgets, isn't it? I told you, when the true costs were uncovered, I just found it all unacceptable, and I simply could not sign off on the expense of turning it into the expanded program. That's all. I know you're here from the auditors, but—"

"Auditors," Patrick said, and pulled his sidearm. He put it on the table between them with a heavy *thunk* on the wood. "You really think we're auditors."

Bryn watched his eyes go blank and wide, and his knuckles whiten around his glass. He didn't make a move. Finally, he licked his lips and said, "What is this?"

"It's a gun," Bryn said. "I can give you make and model, if that's what you're asking. But I think we need to rewind this conversation again. Why *exactly* did you quit?"

"I—I told you! I found out there were significant costs that weren't being accounted for, and it was bound to come out. I wanted to be on record as having nothing to do with it. . . . What's going on? Why are you carrying a gun?"

"More than one," Bryn said, and showed him hers, concealed under the jacket. "You're talking about numbers. We're talking about *lives*. The Fountain Group is killing people, Mr. Reynolds."

"Dr. Reynolds," he said, in an automatic sort of way as if he corrected people all the time. He did strike her as an academic more than a businessman, she thought. Someone with his head in the ivory-tower clouds. "I have no idea why you would say a thing like that, Miss Davis."

"Bryn," she said. "Since we're all friendly, Dr. Reynolds. And I say that because I've seen it. I've seen the experiments. I've seen the damage. I've seen the death.

And you were part of it." His clueless confusion was making anger knot tight inside her guts. How could he—how *dare* he sit there with his iced tea in his smug little mountain getaway and tell her that *he had no idea*? She had a sudden, unsettling impulse to grab him by the throat and squeeze, out of blind fury.

"I have no idea what you're talking about," he said, and slowly rose to his feet. "I think you'd better leave."

"I think you'd better sit your ass down," Bryn snapped. "Anyone else in the house besides your kids?"

"No. My wife is traveling. She's—" He sank back in the chair, even though she hadn't made a move for the gun. "Are you going to kill me? Please, not my kids, please—"

"We're not here to kill anybody," Patrick broke in. *Speak for yourself,* Bryn thought. "Dr. Reynolds, you must have been aware of the pharmaceutical research being conducted under the Fountain Group's direction."

"Of course I was. The research is vital to national defense. But I didn't know the *cost.* . . ."

"You mean, in helpless dementia patients being used as human petri dishes to grow nanites?" Bryn said. "The entire staff of Pharmadene killed and revived to ensure corporate loyalty? *That* cost?"

She expected him to get more upset, but oddly enough, he relaxed. He sat back in the chair, sighed, looked down, and shook his head. "I only learned about Pharmadene after the fact, and that had nothing to do with us, nothing at all. We were merely investors in the project. Once Pharmadene imploded, we took over the intellectual property, and it immediately became clear the potential was vast, so we made arrangements with the military to continue the technology in a very tightly controlled manner. There's nothing wrong with what we did."

They all sat in silence for a moment. Bryn couldn't come up with a reply, not one that didn't involve physical force. It took Patrick to say, in a tight but calm voice,

"You mean you see nothing wrong with conducting illegal experiments on nonconsenting patients. Or destroying them when you're done."

"You fail to see the bigger picture." Dr. Reynolds leaned forward now, earnest and eager. "Those people were dying in a horribly useless way; I know, my own father suffered from Alzheimer's. But this drug, our drug—it gave them a chance to be useful."

"Useful," Bryn repeated. Her throat was so tight it hurt. "They were *incubators*. I was there. When you were finished with them, you *dumped them in incinerators*. Don't you get it?"

He flinched and looked away. "You just don't understand the potential," he said, but his voice was fainter now. Less certain. "We can *cure everything* with this, ultimately. We can stop the suffering of billions. Wipe out disease completely in our lifetimes."

"You can create a sterilized crop of controllable creatures who aren't human any longer. Want to see what you've accomplished, doctor?" Bryn's hand blurred to the side, and she picked up the gun and aimed it at Reynolds before Patrick could stop her. "Want to *really* see what you've made? Because I can show you. I can show you, your kids, and any other living thing in this house. And you will *not* enjoy it."

"Bryn."

She knew Patrick had said her name, but it only registered as a blip, a vague shadow. Her focus was a needle-sharp arrow pointed right at Reynolds. He seemed to be the only thing she *could* focus on.

A predator's instinct.

"*Bryn.* Enough." This time, Patrick's voice, and his hand on her wrist, broke through. She blinked and sat back, but she didn't give up the weapon. "Take a good look, Doctor. This woman was murdered by people associated with Pharmadene; she was brought back. Doesn't she seem grateful?"

"But hasn't it made you better?" Reynolds asked urgently. "You won't get sick. You can't be injured badly, or for long. You can't be killed except by . . . extreme measures. It's what humanity has always wanted—health and survival, a guarantee in a hostile world."

"You have kids," Bryn said. "Two kids."

"Yes."

"Well, I won't," she said. "Ever. I always wanted kids—two, maybe three. I always wanted a daughter, especially. And you know what I have now? *Nothing.* A future of survival. Of being twisted into some shape that isn't human anymore, because you wanted to *play God.* You want that for them? Don't you want them to have a life, not a . . . a living *death*?"

"I want them to be safe," he said. "That's what any parent wants for their children. They should become adults first, of course; they have to reach full maturity or the nanites will simply repair them to a permanent childhood. But yes, that's what I want for them. A future without disease and decay and death. And you know what? Ask any parent who's watched a child suffer, and they will agree with me."

How in the hell could a man look so reasonable, so compassionate, and be so *wrong*? He was endorsing torture and murder, and he didn't seem to *get it.*

She wanted to force him to face it, in all the wrong, bloody ways that the nanites seemed to foster. It was all she could do not to pull the trigger and shatter his skull all over the nice, clean kitchen.

And then eat his brain, some part of her whispered, and she gagged on that image.

"You're going to help us stop it," Patrick said.

"I won't."

"You don't have a fucking choice, Doctor." He took the gun from Bryn's hand and stood up. "Thanks for the tea. Now you're going to show us to your office, where you'll give us all the information you have on the Foun-

tain Group, who's involved, where they are, and anything
else you can think of mentioning."

"Or what?" Reynolds actually *crossed his legs* and
settled back in his chair, and sipped his tea. As if he
didn't have a care in the world. "Or you'll kill me?"

"Yes," he said, very calmly. "I'll kill you quietly, and
bury you somewhere your kids won't see. You'll just . . .
vanish. Maybe the cops will find your rotting corpse,
maybe not, but either way, your big, fancy dream ends
here, today. You can end with it, or live to see your kids
grow up. Your choice."

"You wouldn't."

Patrick gave him a long, still very calm look, and
Reynolds flinched and set down his tea. No longer looking all that confident. "Let's go to your office," he said. "I
really don't want your kids to be involved, and neither
do you. Right?"

When Reynolds didn't get up immediately, Bryn
helped him with a hand under his arm. His muscles
tensed, and for half a second he must have thought about
trying to yank free, but then good sense prevailed. She
walked him—with his tea—out to the wide living room
that had a breathtaking view through the windows of a
tree-filled valley and river.

"It's upstairs," he said. The three of them went up as
a tight group, and just before they made the turn Bryn
saw the kids' door open up, and a small face peer out in
worry.

"Everything's okay," she told the boy, and smiled.
"Your dad's just helping us for a minute. You just stay in
there, okay?"

He nodded and shut the door. She hoped he wasn't—
as she would have been at that age—curious enough to
try to sneak up and observe what was going on. *Better
keep an eye out,* she thought.

Reynolds kept his study locked up, which was probably wise, and it required a key code to get in. No way to

know if what he punched in was the real number, or a secret alert code that would sound alarms yet stay silent in the house . . . probably the latter. She knew Patrick would think of it, too, so she didn't bother to say it.

"You go with him," she told Patrick. "I'll stay out here and keep watch."

He nodded, probably also understanding that Reynolds' smug, brazen attitude made her want to rip his throat out—and that was something she was more than capable of doing, even at the best of times now. Reynolds wasn't inspiring her better angels, not at all. Better if she worked off her tension by watching for unwelcome visitors, and keeping the kids from snooping.

At least we're remote out here, Bryn thought. She took a moment to look around the house, and something struck her as odd. It was . . . perfect. Movie-set perfect. In fact, even the books seemed artificial, like the sort of things bought by the yard by a set designer, not things people chose for their own reasons. Normally, looking at someone's bookshelf could give you a sense of who they were, what they believed in . . . even if the person was widely read, there was still some sort of a core to it.

But this . . . It was random books, shelved for appearance and not content.

Bryn left the hallway and went into the first upstairs bedroom. It held a bed, all the normal furniture one would expect, and even a bathrobe draped over the bedpost . . . but when she checked the closet, the clothes were the same as the books—mismatched and not even the same sizes.

The drawers in the bathroom were all empty.

It *was* a movie set. There were only things set out in plain view.

And these people . . . these people were *actors*.

Bryn caught her breath on a gasp, whirled, and ran to the kids' room. She tried the knob. It was locked. She shattered that with a kick.

No kids. There was a room that looked like a department-store illustration of a room a kid would like, with two twin beds.

The window was open. The kids were gone.

Jane stepped out from behind the closet door, smiling. She looked great, in her serial-killer-crazy kind of way.... Her smile was lovely, but her eyes were almost totally blank. "If you're looking for the Stock Theater Kids, we've taken them offstage," she said. "Welcome to the show, Bryn. You're a natural. You played your part perfectly."

She was holding a military-quality MP5, a Heckler & Koch machine pistol that Bryn knew would cut her in half at this distance. Wouldn't kill her, most likely, but it would damn sure put her down for the fight. Jane wasn't pointing it, but it was an easy swing up and left on the strap, and boom.

So she stayed very still. "Using kids," she said. "That's low, Jane. Even for you."

Jane shrugged. "They're Revived," she said. "Not really much risk for them, even if you went Cannibal Queen on them."

That shook Bryn, deep down, the idea that someone, somewhere, had decided to Revive *children*. But then, of all the situations where desperate, bereaved people would have paid to have their loved ones brought back, children were the most probable.

And the most awful, because those children would never progress beyond that age. Ten years old, forever. Their brains and bodies were developmentally stalled, and before too long, the child inside would stagnate, twist, become something else, like fruit left too long canned on a shelf. Her revulsion must have shown, because Jane laughed. A hollow kind of a sound, one without any real humor. "Weird that we agree," she said. "I wouldn't have done it, either. And we both know there's not much I won't do, right? But even for me, there are limits. I might kill a kid, but I wouldn't be that cruel to one." Bryn must have twitched, or looked as if she was thinking about killing Jane bare-handed, because Jane's right hand moved and brought the machine pistol up to a dead aim. "Ah, ah, let's not fight, sweetheart. I'm enjoying the moment."

"Where's Reynolds?"

"Oh, that's really him upstairs," Jane said. "He volunteered—of course, we told him it really was all about internal matters, hence his audit spiel. Didn't see any reason to alarm him with the full details. He set up this place a long time ago, on the off chance Calvin Thorpe decided to turn on us . . . and it's his only known address, these days, though of course he doesn't live here. We caught you on facial recognition in California, and an alarm tripped when someone started looking for an address—not either of you. Nice subcontracting, by the way. But still, two and two equals four in this world."

"Is Reynolds one of the Revived?" Bryn asked. Jane cocked her head a little and raised her eyebrows. "Just wondering."

"Most of the Fountain Group have taken the treatment."

"That what they're calling having a plastic bag over your head and suffocating to death, then crawling out of hell?"

"Well, you know the medical profession. They never tell you the nasty stuff about the procedures ahead of time." Jane leaned against the wall and gave the room a quick, unimpressed look. "Looks like catalogs had an orgy in here, don't you think?"

She did. That was actually almost funny, and Bryn had to suppress the smile, but she knew Jane would see the impulse, the micro-twitch at the corners of her mouth. And that made her angry. She did not want Jane to make her laugh. That was more of a violation than Jane making her bleed. "So," Bryn said. "What now?"

"Now, kiddo, I kill you—temporarily, of course—and go upstairs to get Patrick. If I can take him alive, I will. If not . . . hope you had Paris. Ah, ah, don't do that. Just don't." Jane's eyes sharpened focus, and the tremor of Bryn's hand toward her pistol was the focus. "Go for that gun and all this goes south very fast."

"You just said you were going to kill Patrick."

"Of course I will, but I'm not cruel. I'd put him into the Revival program. And unlike you, he'd get the right dose of nanite programming, so he'd stay . . . compliant."

"And me?" Bryn asked. "Because you damn sure know I won't be *compliant.*"

"Yeah, I damn sure do," Jane agreed. "Tell me, have you felt the hunger yet? Gotten your teeth into living skin? Felt the rush of the hunt?" Bryn was silent, and Jane gave her a slow, intimate, greasy smile. "I see you have. Impressive, isn't it? That human beings could engineer that kind of savagery in, and call it *progress.* But then, we've always been capable of that kind of cognitive dissonance. Killing for God, for the master race, always some kind of bullshit to ease our consciences. Sit down, Bryn. Right there on that model-home bed. Then take your weapons out, two-finger touch—you know the drill. Kick them over to me."

Jane could ramble, but she was never distracted, and Bryn knew it was a fool's errand to assume differently. She walked to the bed, sat down, and took off her jacket. Then she pulled the sidearm from its concealment, using two fingers, and dropped it to the primary-colored throw rug. After a second's hesitation, she added the knife from the small of her back, too. Then she kicked them both across the room toward Jane's booted feet. She was hoping Jane would take a split-second's attention from her to pick them up, but Pat's ex was wiser than that; she just kicked them onward, toward the far wall. "Facedown on the bed," Jane said. "Hands laced on your head, ankles crossed. Any struggle, and you get a bullet in the skull."

There wasn't much choice. Jane was too good to make a careless mistake. She'd chosen the bed instead of the floor to avoid having to alter her center of gravity so much, and to make it that much harder for Bryn to react fast; mattresses and springs were designed for comfort, not for precise motion. Any attack she'd try to mount would flounder, and she would die.

So Bryn, seething with fury, silently got on the bed, turned facedown, laced her fingers together on the back of her head, and crossed her ankles. Only when she was still did Jane approach and dig a knee painfully into her back, then drag her wrists down and zip-tie them firmly.

The bony knee went away, thankfully. "Up," Jane said. "Slow."

It wasn't as easy with her hands pinned, but Bryn rolled over and put her legs out, and leveraged her way to a sitting position on the edge of the bed. "What now?" Bryn asked, without getting up. "You march me into an oven somewhere? Problem solved?"

"You're the kind of problem that doesn't get solved any other way," Jane said. "Take that as a compliment. Up."

Bryn shook her head. "Why should I?"

"Bitch—" Jane checked herself as she started to take a step closer, and a slow, demented smile spread across her lips. "You're buying time for Patrick. You think he's going to figure it out."

"Why not? I did."

That wiped the smile from Jane's lips, and she activated a hands-free radio with a tap on the choke-band around her neck. "Who's got eyes on McCallister and Reynolds?" She continued to stare straight at Bryn as she listened to the reply. "How do you know they're still there? . . . Shit. Get somebody in here to watch this bitch."

That sounded promising. Bryn kept her attention close on Jane, but there wasn't any kind of a slip she could take advantage of.... Jane stayed very still until another soldier—dressed in the same nonuniform rugged clothing that Jane favored—came in the door and took up a position with his MP4 at the ready and trained on Bryn.

"Watch her," Jane said. "She makes a move, even a wiggle, you shoot her in the fucking head a whole lot, understand? Bryn, you play nice, now. I'm going to see what my beloved hubby's up to."

"News flash, you're still divorced!" Bryn called after her. "And he still hates you!" She gave the soldier guarding her a full-on eye roll, bringing him into it with the motion. "Bet he's not the only one in this house. So do you hate her guts or are you just terrified of her? You can pick both."

"We're not chatting," the guard said. He was handsome, in a vacant kind of way—close-cropped brown hair, steady dark eyes, a square, strong chin, and some impressive cheekbones.

We already are chatting, Bryn thought. "Suit yourself," she said aloud. "But she is *such* a bitch. You really can't deny that."

He didn't, and she saw a little bit of a relaxing of his shoulders.

"Are you, you know . . ." She lifted her eyebrows. He frowned at her. "Revived?"

"Shut up," he said. "I told you, we're not chatting."

"I only ask because she's got a bad habit of killing people and bringing them back, for fun. I know. She did it to me about"—Bryn thought for a second—"ten times, more or less, in the space of about a day. That's not counting the torture. There was a lot of that. Have you noticed? She's got a taste for it."

"Shut *up*." She'd rattled him; she saw it in the muscle jumping in his jaw. Jane spooked him. Not surprising; she spooked everybody, sooner or later, or at least Bryn would assume she did.

There was a thump, a loud one, on the wood above their heads. Her guard glanced up, a single involuntary movement, and Bryn didn't, because she'd been pretty sure that would happen.

She launched herself at him in a blur of speed, crashed into him in a crush of flesh, bone, and spraying blood from where her skull met his nose, and the two of them rolled to the floor, tangled up in a messy knot. His gun went off in a roaring burst, and the bullets tore by close enough to leave heat trails and powder burns on her skin, but somehow, she was able to keep the barrel off target just enough to matter.

Just enough to roll them over to where Jane had kicked her knife. No easy job of it, but she nicked the plastic zip tie enough to make it possible to pull her hands apart with one violent tug. She picked up the knife on the next roll over it and jammed it straight into the guard's chest.

His eyes went wide and blank, as if he were struggling to understand, and she twisted, ripping his heart wide-open.

Game over, at least for a while. She was hurt too — strains, a broken rib or two, and her head hurt like mad from the impact with the guard's skull — but she'd live. She controlled her impulse to groan and roll away, and instead tugged the knife free and gave him a few more fatal wounds to worry about, including leaving the knife buried in his eye socket. Sawing through bone with this particular knife would be time-consuming, and she couldn't afford the effort — but the knife in the brain would keep his nanites plenty busy, particularly if the knife was still in place.

More thumping from upstairs.

Bryn rolled to her feet, staggered, pushed away the damage, and ran for the stairs.

Chapter 13

She was halfway up the steps when Jane's limp body came crashing through the door, sending it spinning off its hinges. Jane hit the railing and spun like a rag doll, folding over the barrier and sliding off and down to plummet to the floor. She landed on her neck with a crack that sounded like a stiff branch being broken.

Good.

"Patrick?" Bryn raced the rest of the way, hardly feeling the steps, and stopped fast when she ran into the still-hot muzzle of a gun. Jane's. It was in Patrick's hands, and his eyes were wide and a little wild, but he took a deep breath, lowered the weapon, and nodded to her.

"Are you hurt?" she asked breathlessly. There was blood on his face, and after a second she spotted the cut on his head. It looked gruesome, but it probably wasn't as bad as it seemed. He wiped at the mess impatiently to get his vision clear.

"I'm fine," he said. "Is she down?"

"For now. I need to go put her down for longer. Are you sure—"

"Fine," he said again, so flatly she wasn't at all sure that he meant it in the least. "Check Reynolds."

Reynolds—and there was no reason for Jane to have

lied about it being the real man, not a double — was cowering in the corner. Broken arm, she noted without any sympathy; as a Revived, he'd heal. He just wasn't enjoying himself. He curled in on himself defensively when she approached him, but she struck aside his flailing keep-away hand and checked the pulse on his neck. "He's fine," she said, and grabbed the man by his collar. "Get up." She put the MP4 at his back to encourage it, and he practically sprang to his feet in a convulsive leap.

"You're crazy," he blurted. He looked scared, all right, scared and sweating and thoroughly convinced she'd shoot. "You're all *crazy*. They'll kill you. Don't you get it? You're surrounded. There's no way out!"

He may have been right, but Bryn wasn't convinced, not without some first-person recon. She pushed Reynolds back to Patrick, who took him in a hold that must have really hurt that broken arm more than a little. *Good.* Without any words exchanged, Bryn took the lead on the way down. One good thing about an open-plan modern house — there were very few blind corners or places to hide.

Jane was still down and motionless on the floor, but they'd have very little time before the rest of her team descended. . . . Bryn could hear them outside, running feet on stone and grass. "Knife!" she said to Patrick and he tossed her his; she plucked it out of the air and, in the same motion, slammed it down and into Jane's left eye. The corpse jerked just a little bit in reaction. Maybe she'd only been playing dead. That would have been typical.

This time, she pulled the knife out and started grimly sawing through the skin, muscle, gristle, and bone to separate Jane's head from her body.

"No time," Patrick snapped. "Leave it."

"I can't. We have to finish her!"

"They'll finish us first."

He took the knife away and slammed it back into

Jane's already-healing eye, and hauled Bryn up by the elbow. She regretted losing not one but two knives in rapid succession, but he was right—they couldn't wait, not even another breath. Speed and ruthlessness were their only allies right now. Reynolds didn't look as if he was inclined to give them trouble, but he wasn't helping, either. Her brain clicked through plans, rejecting each one. . . . The front was obviously out, the side where Jane had come in would be covered, and the back of the house . . .

Bryn took a single breath to consider it—those giant plate glass windows showed off the house's best feature: its view of a sharp drop to the valley, and the glittering ribbon of the river. She didn't ask Patrick. There wasn't time for debate.

Instead, she grabbed one of the end tables—a blocky, heavy, square affair, very new modern—and whirled, lifting as she put her momentum into it. Then she let go.

The table sailed through the air as if on wings, hit the glass with one of those sharp edges forward, and thick as it was, the glass frosted with cracks and then shattered in a mighty crash. The end table sailed out into the void and took a comet-trail of glass shards with it. But that didn't clear the window fully; there were still jagged blades sticking out. Bryn grabbed the fireplace poker on the fly and held it like a sword as she leaped closer; she broke the worst of it out and turned as Patrick joined her.

"This is crazy," he told her. "That's a hell of a drop. One of us isn't really up to it. By that I mean me."

Shit. In her rush, she'd somehow forgotten—forgotten!—that Patrick wasn't capable of the same feats she was. Reynolds was Revived; he hardly mattered. But Patrick . . .

Bryn took hold of Reynolds and pulled him from Patrick's grip. "How's the arm?" she asked him. There would be flash-bangs deployed behind them in seconds, and then Jane's shock troops would be inside, spraying the house with bullets and taking down anything that moved.

"Hurts," he said.

"Good." She threw him out the window, just like the table.

Then she wrapped her arms around Patrick and pulled him out held tight to her body.

Chapter 14

She landed awkwardly and very painfully on her back. That was what she'd meant to do, and it served to take the brunt of the bare-rock impact away from Patrick, whom she held in a rock-hard grip against her chest all the way down. His body weight was solid and muscular, and it did the rest of the job that her own momentum hadn't. She felt a lot of bones cracking, a few more shattering, and if she'd been normal and human, she'd have been concussed and probably dying from skull fractures. The concussion still occurred, but though she felt woozy and unfocused, her little nanite helpers kept her moving. That was the military upgrade. Damage was registered, but it mostly wouldn't keep her down, or not for long.

God, she hated the busy little bastards. But she also had to admit that at moments like these, they were all that kept her alive. Her, and Patrick, too.

Patrick grunted in pain and rolled off of her. He shook his head to clear it, and then took a good look at her. "Bryn?" His expression went grim and furious. "What the hell was that?"

"Got you out, didn't it?" she shot back breathlessly. It was hard to talk. Shattered ribs stabbed at her with every move. If she'd been standard human normal, she'd have been terrified that she'd have shredded her lungs and drowned in her own blood. Amazing how free you could feel when you just no longer worried about those kinds of considerations. "Come on, we're clear targets." She got up—with his help—and tried a step. At least she hadn't landed feetfirst; that would have resulted in disabling damage that would have taken time to heal. This was all heal-on-the-move stuff.

But . . . Reynolds hadn't been so lucky. They found him off to the right, crawling for the trees. His right leg was folded the wrong way, and if his arm had been broken before, it was worse now. He was sobbing and babbling under his breath, and under most circumstances Bryn would have been stricken with guilt for what she'd done to him. But then, Reynolds would heal up, and a little pain, for what he'd done, for what he thought was right to do . . . that didn't bother her much at all.

"Let me go," he panted as she grabbed him by the unbroken arm and hauled him up. He hopped on his one good leg, and groaned and almost dropped from the pain. "Oh God, oh God . . ."

"Suck it up, Doctor," Bryn said. "Pat, can you—?" He took the doctor's other side, and together they half pulled, half led Reynolds into the woods.

Just in time, too, because she heard shouting behind them, and peering back, she saw Jane's men at the window, looking for them. One of them decided to try a random spray of bullets, which ended up hitting well away from them, but it was proof that they didn't much care about hitting Dr. Reynolds if it meant stopping the two of them.

"We have to make it to the river," Bryn said. "It's too deserted up here, and we're at a disadvantage."

"Agreed," Patrick said. He checked his clip and extra ammo, and shared some with her. "He's going to take some time to heal. About, what, a couple of hours to get that leg straight again?"

The one time it might have been useful to be contagious, Bryn thought ... But her upgraded nanites had a cooking time, and they weren't done yet. Even if she bit Reynolds, all she'd leave was bite marks.

Which reminded her, forcefully, that she was hungry. Seriously, awfully hungry, a sudden emptiness in the pit of her stomach that made her wince and stagger a little—enough that Patrick put a hand on her shoulder.

She heard him ask if she was okay, but all she could see, all she could focus on was his hand. On the thin skin of his wrist. On the blood and veins and muscle and protein that represented.

She closed her eyes in a sudden, sane fit of nausea, and said, "I'm fine. Gotta move, now."

They did, in grim silence, except for Reynolds; she'd have loved to have silenced him, but a dead (if healing) body would have been even less use than a half-cooperative one. They just kept moving. The hill was granite, with pines stubbornly clinging to the rock and shedding dry needles as they moved beneath them. It smelled lush, but the drought had hit hard up here, and these pines were far from healthy.

If Jane was awake and in charge, Bryn had a terrible premonition of how she'd handle this situation. And she would be awake and back in charge, soon. They'd de-knife her first thing, and while the brain would be a few minutes healing, it wouldn't keep her unconscious for long.

Jane was a practical sort of ruthless, and she'd want to drive Bryn and Patrick out in the open, out of the trees. She could do that by a huge, expensive deployment of her troops, and risk them being picked off in the dimness, or ...

... Or, she could just use nature to do it for her.

"Faster," Bryn said breathlessly. Patrick nodded. He didn't even have the wind to reply, at this point. His head wound was still steadily bleeding, but he wasn't making a big deal out of it at all. His footing was sure, and he was holding up Reynolds just as solidly as ever—but she didn't like the tense set of his jaw, or the blank look in his eyes. He was tapping reserves that no one should go for unless they're down to empty.

They were halfway down the slope, with the glitter of the river distantly in sight, when a five-point buck burst from the trees, running fast. It almost crashed into them, but it veered hard and just brushed Bryn on the way by—graceful and fast and undeniably panicked.

Because behind it, the trees were burning.

A whole row of pines behind the house was on fire—tall, surreal matchsticks burning with an unholy glow even in the afternoon sun. As Bryn watched, the flames jumped from one dry branch to another, creating a solid line of fury.

And it was moving with the wind.

Toward them.

The smell was, incongruously, like warm memories of home, logs on the fire, warm cocoa, safety.

"Jesus," Patrick said, and dragged Reynolds faster. "Move it!"

The smoke flooded them maybe two minutes later. It wasn't a gradual thing, though the smell of the fire was already strong. The smoke came in a thick, choking blanket, rolling like fog down the slope, and in seconds their visibility was reduced to hazy, indistinct outlines. Patrick coughed as the ash began to swirl around them. It was hot already, but Bryn felt pinpricks of hellfire where the cinders began to settle on her.

Still at least half a mile to the river. It was impossible to make good time on the rocky, jagged ground, especially with the decreased field of vision, and she began to realize, horribly, that Jane had outmaneuvered her, again. They weren't going to make it.

She'd died a lot of ways in the past few months—enough to earn herself permanent psych ward status, anyway—but burning . . . burning had a special horror to it. That was how they disposed of the Revived in the end—burning long enough, hot enough would disable the nanites and ultimately end all their lives, even the upgraded ones.

Patrick didn't even have that to look forward to. He would suffocate in the smoke.

"Go!" Bryn yelled at him. She took all of Reynolds' weight. "Just run, Patrick—go! You can make it! I'll follow!"

He was coughing too hard to argue, and she shoved him, hard, in the direction of the downslope. At least they wouldn't get too far lost. . . . It was obvious which way was down, if nothing else.

Patrick disappeared ahead of them, gone in three steps.

She could hear the roar of the trees behind them now, like rabid animals on their heels. The world shrank to steps, fast and deliberate. Her muscles screamed in pain, her still-healing bones shifted and ripped and pierced, but she didn't care, didn't care at all.

Reynolds screamed, snapping her from her trance, and she realized that his shirt was smoking. So was hers.

But they were close. She could see the water. A hundred yards, maybe a hundred and fifty.

All they had to do was make it just a little farther.

She saw Patrick at the edge of the tree line, and he spotted them; he started to run toward them, but she shouted at him to get back, get back, and as Reynolds stumbled and dragged her down, his shirt bursting into open flame, she let him go. She kicked him into a rolling, messy tumble down the slope toward where Patrick anxiously waited. Stop, drop and roll, she thought, and an insane giggle tickled the back of her throat. She swallowed it, because there were things to do. Serious things.

She risked a look at the fire, and froze.

It was . . . terrifying. And beautiful. A monster the size

of a building, moving with easy grace and fluid speed. Trees were combusting so fast that their trunks exploded as sap boiled. Animals raced around her—mice, rabbits, what looked like a fox but it was hard to spot in the thick, curling smoke.

Her shirt was on fire now. So was her hair.

No. *God.* The nanites would keep her hideously alive, of course—hideously alive as the flames burned through skin and muscle and fat. At some point, there wouldn't be enough of them left, and they'd shut down, but the last of them, the very last, would keep her brain sending and receiving signals while the rest of her burned away. She'd know. She'd know every single second of the agony.

There was no way out, because the flames had caught her now.

The pain was enormous. Mind-melting. She knew she was screaming, and she couldn't stop, couldn't begin to think how to stop, and the flames were alive, alive and eating her alive, eating her like a lion with a wounded gazelle. She could feel its eagerness, its hot-breath hunger, and she snarled out a challenge as she felt her skin sizzle and pop, and she turned and ran blindly through smoke, flames, past blazing torches of pines. A bear was running with her, its fur on fire, making grunting howls of pain. They trailed smoke and tongues of yellow and red like streamers, and suddenly someone was there, a shadow, and she felt a crack that hardly registered over the fury consuming her body and soul, and then . . .

Then she ran headlong into one of Jane's soldiers, who had just shot her. More than once, she supposed; she couldn't feel it. Couldn't feel much of anything, as her nerves shorted and fried from the overwhelming assault.

She hit him as a fireball and took him to the ground, and as they rolled over and over down the rocky slope, they hit damp, sandy ground, and the motion smothered most of the flames, and then they rolled into the river itself, and steam exploded up in a cloud as the last of the fire went out on her body and clothing.

She dragged him underwater. He was struggling, panicked, and she saw the wide, white-rimmed flare of his eyes as she dragged him deeper. It didn't take long before the last silvery bubbles burst out of his mouth, and his eyes took on the dull, flat look of death.

His blood was a rusty cloud in the water, and she needed it. Needed it so badly.

She was on him like a shark in the next, breathless second. She needed to breathe, but she didn't care except to note it as additional things to heal.

For healing, she needed . . .

. . . She only needed.

No thought.

Just flesh.

Chapter 15

She crawled out of the water and lay facedown on the riverbank, gasping for air. Pain had come back—and come back way too fast for any kind of sanity—and she shuddered all over, unable to move now, pinned under the weight of the agony. She felt someone taking her under the shoulders and dragging her. Jane's people, maybe. She no longer knew, or cared.

Death would have been a blessing.

She didn't get it.

The nanites must have been merciful, at some point, or her brain simply blotted out the worst of it, because the next time Bryn opened her eyes, she was lying in the backseat of a car, with the road vibration steady beneath her back.

I was dying, she thought. *Burning alive.*

But when she looked down at herself, she seemed better. Her skin looked angry and fragile, but it was healing. Her clothing must have been a total loss, because she was naked, wrapped in a blanket that was soaked through with blood. It smelled like smoke and disease, and even with the windows down in the car, the stench lingered.

"Patrick?" she whispered.

The speed of the car slowed dramatically, and she felt

it veer over to the side and come to a stop. Ten seconds later, the door opened at her head, and she saw him leaning over her, upside down. The setting sun haloed him like a smoke-stained, bloodied angel. "Bryn? Stay still. You're still healing."

She didn't feel inclined to move now, now that she knew he was safe. She held out her hand, which shook, and he took it in both of his. He pressed the back of her fingers to his lips, very gently. There was a terribly haunted look in his eyes.

She wasn't the only one with permanent PTSD. The people around her, the ones who had to watch what happened to her—it was just as bad for them. And maybe worse.

"Reynolds?" Her throat rasped, and when she swallowed she tasted greasy smoke. Barbecue. Ugh.

"He's fine. He's tied up in the trunk," Patrick said. "I need to buy you clothes."

"Car?"

"Stolen from a campsite," he said. "Nobody there. Some hikers are going to have a bad day. Bryn—"

"Am okay," she said, and attempted a smile. It must not have been convincing. "Drive."

He nodded. "We need to get the fuck out of here and someplace safe."

She had no idea where that would be, now. They were far from Manny's bunker. They'd lost their allies. They'd even lost Thorpe, ripped apart in an instant. Reynolds was all they had, and Jane was not going to let them have him. Not without one hell of a fight.

It didn't look good.

Luckily, she was too exhausted to fully enjoy the landscape of how much their situation sucked.

She left it to Patrick to fully consider it, and fell back into a deep, dreamless rest, broken by flashes of pain, fire, and blood.

What had she done, there in the water?

She could only remember it in nightmares, after.

Chapter 16

They bought her clothing at an ancient camping stop up in the mountains; she'd managed to tell him to head north, and that took them farther into the wilderness. The clothes weren't exactly stylish, but they were tough — granny panties and sports bras, flannel shirts and thick khaki pants. Her boots had survived, somehow, though she traded out for fresh socks that hadn't been through a day of exertion and a dunking in the river.

Her skin looked pink now, more like a sunburn. It hurt all over but at least it was intact. The hair, on the other hand, was an unmitigated disaster.

It looked like someone had taken a blowtorch to her head. Some of it was completely gone, down to the pink, unnaturally healing scalp; some of it was still there, but charred. She asked Patrick for a razor and, using the bathroom's sink and soap, hacked off what remained, then gave herself a smooth shave.

The result was appalling, but she topped it with a 1950s-era scarf Patrick had bought, and a big pair of sunglasses. Retro chic. The hair would grow back, but not quickly; she had to be prepared to rock the bald look for at least a few days, and then a super-short cut after that, for weeks most likely. Hair was something that didn't regenerate so fast. Nonessential, according to the nanite programming.

Well, she thought, I'd wanted to change my look. That made her want to laugh, in a dark kind of way. She somehow choked it back, just barely.

Then it was Patrick's turn. He'd escaped direct contact with the flames, but his clothing was saturated with smoke, and that definitely wouldn't do; if it came to stealth, the smell of him would announce his presence far too well. He shopped the men's aisle, and when he was changed he could have posed for an L.L. Bean catalog photo, except for the scabbed wound on his head up close to the hairline, and the bruises. They were turning sickly yellow now, but she had no doubt he had a lot more under the clothing. Fresh ones. New wounds.

"Feeling okay?" he asked her, and took a moment to really look at her. She nodded slowly. She did, and she knew it was because—because of what she'd done. A thing she couldn't even look closely into, for fear of what she'd see looking back. Water and blood. Thrashing. Food.

"We need to get back on the road," Bryn said. "Did you get camping gear?"

"We're set," he said. "I'll pay. You go on to the car. He didn't see you."

He meaning the proprietor, an ancient man who had decorated his store in American flags and signs. There was a sticker on the door for the John Birch Society, and a Tea Party symbol, and she had the distinct impression that the crusty old man wouldn't give information about anybody who shopped here to anyone he perceived as government.

Bad luck for Jane, since she was going to look like his worst black helicopter nightmares come to life. If she managed to trace them this far, Bryn doubted that it would get her too much.

Once Patrick was in the car, they headed up a winding mountain road, and he took a turn to the east, veering off.

"Where are we going?" she asked him. She was in the front passenger seat now.

"Someplace you won't like much," Patrick said, "but I've got a cover there, from way back. Just play along with me, whatever I do. It's our best possible chance to make this work and get resupplied."

"Is it worse than a Russian spy station?"

"It isn't better."

Lovely. She sighed, relaxed, and looked out the window. At least she was fairly certain Jane would be furious over the way things had gone; she'd brought her A game, had set a very good trap, and still, they'd managed to wiggle out of it (not without leaving skin behind) and taken the bait with them, to add insult to injury. "I hate to say it, but you know what? Stabbing your ex felt really good, Pat."

"I was thinking the same thing about kicking her ass over the railing," he said, and smiled. He reached for her hand and held it. "That makes us sound less than well adjusted."

"Well, in the words of *Chicago*, she had it coming."

"Pretty sure that doesn't make us sound any more stable, Bryn." He got sober fast, and sent her a glance so quick she wasn't even sure she'd seen it. "You took a ton of damage back there. Do you need to eat?"

"I ate," she said dully, and shut her eyes. When she swallowed, she could still taste the blood rusting her mouth, even though she'd brushed her teeth, rinsed, spit a dozen times, and used up half a bottle of mouthwash.

"Bryn—"

"Leave it."

He did. She wondered exactly what he'd seen. Exactly what he thought. He didn't let go of her hand, that was something; she hadn't known she needed that until she'd felt the warmth of the grip, holding her in place. She felt like she'd spin off the edge of the earth if he let her go.

There was a thump from the trunk. "Reynolds is awake," she observed. "Is it too hot for him in there?"

"I punched air holes in the top and made sure there wasn't any carbon monoxide problem. It won't be comfortable, but he's got bottles of water, and he'll live. I'm not too concerned about his bruises."

"Maybe he needs a bathroom break."

"I'd rather steam clean the trunk later."

She had a sudden, horrifyingly clear thought. "He's Revived, right? He's chipped. They're tracking him!"

"Relax. I had one last shot Manny had given me just in case, and I gave it to Reynolds before I stuck him in the trunk. It's loaded with tracking inhibitors. He's off their radar, for now anyway."

"You're sure you got rid of anything that might be bugged?"

"Stripped him, threw him in the river, soaked him, and gave him the hikers' clothes to put on," he confirmed. "This isn't new to me, Bryn. Relax. We're okay."

She didn't think so.

She didn't think she'd ever feel okay again, honestly. But the miles disappeared under the humming tires, and the beauty of the mountain scenery lulled her into what was probably a false sense of peace. Somewhere, Joe and Riley were fighting to get to Manny, if Manny and Pansy still held their bunker secure. Somewhere, Jane was kicking walls and thinking about how hard she was going to torture them when she got her hands on them.

Somewhere, the rest of the Fountain Group, learning of Reynolds' disappearance, might be starting to sweat. She hoped so.

Night fell, and he kept driving, taking roads that seemed sketchy at best, until she'd thoroughly lost her sense of direction; navigating by the stars was a skill she'd developed back in Iraq, but you could actually *see* stars in the desert. Here, smothered by the trees, she could see only thin strips of inky sky, with hard chips of stars shimmering through. Not enough to place herself.

"We're here," he said, and slowed the sedan to a crawl

as he made a last turn. Ahead, there was a clearing in the trees, and a fence that wouldn't have been out of place in a prison—fifteen foot walls topped by razor wire, turreted guard posts, and blazing security lights that popped on when they came close enough. The glare blinded them, and Patrick brought the car to a stop and put it in gear.

"Get out and keep your hands up," he said. "Do what they say."

"Where the hell did you bring me?"

"Just don't talk if you can help it."

She had to settle for that, because an amplified voice was telling her to do exactly what he'd just instructed—out of the car, hands up. Patrick complied, and she did, too, though she didn't feel too good about it. The road was sharp gravel, and it dug into her knees as she followed instructions to kneel, hands on head.

Moving figures emerged from the blinding glare, and though she could have reacted—violently—she didn't, because Patrick didn't. The shapes resolved into armed, burly men, none of them too clean, who pushed the two of them facedown and handcuffed their wrists behind their backs. Bryn's tender new skin protested at the harsh handling, but she didn't complain. Ten seconds later, she was on her feet and shoved shoulder to shoulder with Patrick.

"We safe?" she asked softly. He nodded, but his slitted eyes were searching the glare for something.

She saw him relax when he found it: another shape heading toward them. As he reached them, the blinding halogens turned off, leaving only general illumination, which seemed like pitch darkness after that scorching of her eyeballs. When she blinked away the afterimages, she saw a medium-sized man standing there, staring at Patrick. He had a narrow face, narrow dark eyes, lank shoulder-length brown hair, and he looked hardened and sunbaked, like the rest of them.

"Son of a bitch," he said. "Look who's come home."

Then he pulled out a vicious-looking bowie knife and held it point-up under Patrick's chin. The point dented the flesh, and blood welled and ran down the steel.

"Walt," Patrick said. "Been a while. You mad?"

"What gives you that idea?" The knife stayed where it was. Walt's mouth stretched in a smile, but it wasn't much of a reassurance. "Who's the bitch?"

"Mine," Patrick said. "Hands off."

"We'll see."

"You going to slit my throat or kiss me?" Patrick asked.

"Well, now, I was considering that first thing, but if you want kissing I'll see if I can find a couple of volunteers. You left some bad feelings behind in here. Why come back?"

"Had to," Patrick said. "I've got heat on me."

"And you bring it here?"

"I bring it to the man who can handle it."

That made Walt smile again, a dark, angry sort of thing that made a shiver run up Bryn's back. "Get them and the car inside," Walt said. "Sweep everything. Don't want no federal ears in here."

"Fair warning," Patrick said. "I have a man tied up in the trunk. He could be dead. Or not."

That brought . . . utter silence. And then Walt laughed, and took the knife away from his throat. "That's what I always liked about you, Vaughn. You are utterly fucked up." He turned and waved at his men. One slid behind the wheel of the sedan, and the others crowded around Patrick and Bryn and hustled them in through the parting gates. It was an efficient operation, maybe thirty seconds between gates opening and closing, and then they were inside the compound—she couldn't think of it any other way—which was a tidily maintained, almost military style design. Barracks surrounded by neatly raked gravel. Their sedan was driven to an area that served as a motor pool, mostly populated by old, solid Humvees and four-wheelers, along with some pickups. A flagpole—empty at the moment—stood tall sentry in the center. Toward the center of the place there was something out of place—a square building with playground equipment such as swings, teeter-totters, and slides, all in camouflage colors.

Children. There were children here.

Their captors pushed them down to a cross-legged sitting position by the flagpole and withdrew to convenient shooting distance. They had a firing squad of four, which would be plenty to kill Patrick, but not enough to take Bryn if she needed to move. Of course, they couldn't know that.

Yet.

"Who the hell are these guys?" she whispered to him. He tilted his head toward her, just a little, but he didn't take his eyes off their guards.

"Well, that's Mel there on your end. He's got a mean streak, so watch him closely. Next to him is some new blood—don't recognize him. Third one is Paul, and then Queeg—he's Walt's best buddy. Kind of the second in command around here, or was, anyway. I've been gone a few years."

"I meant *who are they in general?*"

"I know," he whispered. "Short answer is militia. But it's complicated."

"Uncomplicate it!"

Even if he could have, or wanted to try, he didn't have the chance, because one of the men—Queeg, wasn't *that* cute—gave them a menacing glare and growled, "Shut up before I break your jaws."

Patrick sighed and put his head back against the flagpole, closed his eyes, and just . . . relaxed. Bryn tried, but her brain was firing too fast, running on constant adrenaline and paranoia now. She counted at least thirty armed men, and she supposed most of them wouldn't be

outside and visible at this hour; the windows on the barracks and small houses glowed warm and bright, and for
most people it was bound to be dinner hour. One reason
their guards looked so grim, she supposed. Taking away
dinner in a place like this, where dinner might be just
about all you looked forward to, was probably a firing
squad offense.

One thing: some of these men carried themselves
with that unmistakable posture you earned from long
hours in the military. Bryn knew she had it; she'd learned
to recognize it at a glance, in others. These men were a
long way from any army or marine base, but they still
had the look.

Militias did tend to draw in the fringes of ex-military.
So she knew they couldn't afford to underestimate the
danger.

Patrick had been here *undercover.* That was interesting and significant; she knew about his military service,
but not anything law enforcement–related. If it was that
at all. It could easily have been a black ops mission, she
supposed, highly illegally conducted on American soil.

Walt reappeared, coming back from the motor pool
with a pack of his men. Two of them were half-carrying
Reynolds, who'd been dressed in a greasy-looking blue
jumpsuit—air force surplus, from the look of it. He filled
it out a little too much around the middle.

And he was talking. "—have to let me go. I'm telling
you, these people kidnapped me! Right from my own
house! Please, you need to call my people. They'll pay
you a handsome fee for rescuing me. . . ."

"Shut up," Walt said in a pleasant kind of tone as he
paused about three feet out of any reasonable lunging
distance from Patrick and Bryn. "So, *friend,* you want to
explain to me why you have a black man in your trunk?"

"I told you, they kidnapped me!" Reynolds blurted.
One of his guards shook him, hard enough to make his
teeth clack.

"I didn't ask you," Walt said without looking at him. "Well, Vaughn? Not going to ask you again."

"He's not lying," Patrick/Vaughn said, and grinned. He looked different, suddenly, as if another person inhabited his skin. Creepy. "Son of a bitch screwed me on a deal. I grabbed him and took him for a ride. Just wanted to teach him a valuable life lesson."

"You kidnapped this prick and brought him here? To *my* house?"

"He screwed you, too, Walt," Patrick said. "That's the beauty of it. Remember that shipment of Stingers that you paid for and didn't get? Well, meet the man responsible. He jacked it and sold it to the Taliban."

Walt looked away from Patrick this time, to study Reynolds, who was looking shocked now. "I—I don't know anything about this!" he said. "This man *kidnapped me* and if you just call my people—"

"Hang on a second. My friend here just told me that you sold my Stinger missiles to the Taliban, so they could shoot down American planes. You don't think we should discuss that just a little bit first?"

Reynolds wet his lips. He looked sweaty and scared, and Bryn knew that would probably, in the eyes of Walt and his men, translate into guilt. "I don't know what he's talking about."

"He's talking about me paying somebody half a million dollars and getting two of my men arrested when they went to pick up the goods, and getting no product. You the man? You the one who was behind the jack?"

"I've got nothing to do with weapons! Nothing!"

"He's right," Patrick said. "He's a middleman who sells whatever people want. Drugs, weapons, hell, pirated DVDs for all I know. Doesn't matter. He's the one. He pocketed the cash and called the feds and walked away clean as a whistle. Until I found him."

"He's lying!" Reynolds was trying his best to look sincere now, but he wasn't doing a very good job of it; too scared, and too confused. "I told you, I'll give you money. What did you say, half a million? I'll double it. A million dollars to call my people and let me go."

"Good offer," Walt said, and nodded. The men on either side let Reynolds go. He looked relieved, and straightened up as much as he could in the too-small jumpsuit. "Too bad I don't believe you."

He raised his gun and shot Reynolds straight between the eyes. Large caliber round. It left a significant hole in the front, and though Bryn couldn't see much of it from where she sat, there wouldn't have been a lot of skull left around the exit wound. A gout of blood sprayed a few feet from the back of Reynolds' head, and his eyes rolled up to show the whites, and . . . he was down. Crumpled like a dropped toy.

The sound of the shot echoed sharply from the surrounding mountains, but nobody reacted in any way. Not even a twitch.

"Right," Walt said. "Get him out of here."

"That was stupid," Patrick said. "You could've gotten paid."

"I did get paid," Walt replied. "That why you left? Looking for him?"

"One of the reasons," Patrick said. He stretched his legs out in front of him and crossed them at the ankles, very much at ease even with his hands still pinned behind him. "Couldn't stand looking at Queeg's ugly face anymore, either."

Queeg showed teeth, and Bryn had to admit, he didn't look like something she'd want to wake up to, either. "Fuck you," he growled.

Patrick puckered lips in a silent kiss. "Missed you, too, Queeg. What are you going to do with him?" Meaning Reynolds, who was being dragged off by Walt's men toward the darkness. Bryn was wondering, too.

"Dumping him in a ditch for the night," Walt said. "We'll take him out and bury him good and deep tomorrow."

It was a deadly shot, of course, but there was every chance that Reynolds would recover in a matter of an hour or two, and if he was just dumped in a ditch, he'd be off and running. Even out here, eventually he'd run into a hiker or hunter or ranger with a cell phone.

They could *not* let him get away now. Not now.

Walt was gesturing to his men again, but this time, they hauled her and Patrick up to their feet, turned them around, and released the handcuffs. She automatically rubbed at the sore places the metal had left on her wrists, but she was thinking fast, and she knew Patrick was doing the same. She locked eyes with him as she turned, and before he could speak, she said, "You let him kill our payday? You *asshole*! I needed my share!"

He got it, instantly, and shoved her backward. "Stow it, bitch. You'll get paid when I say you get paid."

"I didn't sign up for this cracker militia shit, and your *friends* just put a bullet in the skull of the man I found for you. You think that isn't going to ruin my life just a little bit? You burned me, Vaughn. I'm not going to forget it."

Patrick looked at her with the deadest eyes she'd ever seen in him, an absolute zero of emotion, and in one smooth motion reached sideways, took Walt's gun, and aimed it at her heart.

"Fuck you," he said, and pulled the trigger.

She felt it. Not an instant death, not quite; there was time for the shock to travel to her brain, for her heart to struggle to beat and fail and fibrillate, for shock and panic to set in. Her mouth worked, opening and closing for breath she couldn't seem to pull into her lungs. The pain was sudden and shocking, but brief.

She saw red, and then she saw black, and then she was just . . . gone.

Chapter 17

She'd counted on Walt's men to be economical, and she woke up right—they'd simply dumped her limp, dead body on top of Reynolds' in the ditch at the edge of camp. In fact, she woke up with her head pillowed on his fat-soft stomach.

For a long moment she didn't move or react. Patrick had gone for the shortest-term kill wound he could; nanites rushed to repair heart damage, and it was much less complex than a brain repair, like what Reynolds' little beasts were dealing with right now. He'd fixed it so she'd wake first . . . and she had.

No way to tell how much time had passed, but it was quiet now, except for the rustle of wind in trees and the normal sounds of crickets and nocturnal creatures. Bryn carefully rolled herself off. The ditch was damp and muddy, but generally free of less pleasant things. At least it wasn't a latrine. At moments like this, she'd learned to count her blessings.

She sat there, trying to breathe slowly and calmly. Her newly repaired heart kept pounding, pounding, pounding, and she was filled with a furious, trembling rage. *So tired of this,* she thought. *I don't want to keep dying. Nobody should have to do this.*

But she'd managed to stay with Reynolds, she was unbound, and Patrick's actions had ensured that Walt believed him completely. Nobody could say he was a federal agent, not after watching him shoot his own girlfriend.

He'd sold it even to her. The lightless look in his eyes haunted her. Was that who Patrick really was, down deep? Someone with no soul, no compass?

Isn't that what you are? a piece of her whispered. *Aren't you just like Jane? Remember what you did back at the river. Remember how good it felt.*

She didn't want to remember. Because remembering left her feeling not nauseated, but . . . *hungry*. Especially with Reynolds' still body lying next to her in the ditch.

Easy pickings. And something in her, something frighteningly cold and logical, was telling her that if she ate a couple of pieces, they'd heal, wouldn't they? She needed the protein.

Besides, he deserved it.

She stomped that part of her down, bolted it under steel, but it took a lot of effort, and it left her shaking. She heard crunching footsteps nearby—patrols, walking the gravel. They'd have to be quiet. Very quiet.

The fence was reinforced cement, and as far as she could see, there was no way underneath it. . . . They were diligent about their security, which was too bad, really. She remembered the motion lights, too. No going out the front, for certain. Maybe they'd neglected to put the same system on the side of the compound, since it faced only the forest, but she had to assume that Walt's paranoia would have won out, even if all the security ever revealed were startled deer and the occasional wandering bear.

There had to be another way out. Walt was one of those men who never had just one entrance and exit. He'd have something else, something concealed, probably under the camp, where he could evacuate his people in a crisis. At the very least, he'd have a defensible bunker. . . .

No. She thought it through, and the post-death fog finally lifted. The correct answer—the only answer—was to stay dead.

She eased herself down into position. There was light on the eastern horizon, so dawn wouldn't be far away.

Just in case, though, she quietly leaned her weight on Reynolds' unresisting throat, and smashed his hyoid bone. Something else for his nanites to work on, and something to keep him out. . . . Having him wake up hysterical wouldn't do, not now.

Not yet.

The men arrived, grumbling, before dawn even blushed; there were four of them, and the first two climbed in, grabbed Bryn's wrists and ankles, and slung her out to roll bonelessly across the gravel, where she was picked up by the other two. They didn't make any comments. She was just a job to them, something to be finished before breakfast.

The other two grunted and struggled getting Reynolds out, but soon they were moving. Bryn kept limp, though it was an uncomfortable position for her head hanging backward. She hoped the dim light would disguise the beating pulse that was probably visible on the exposed skin.

Still, they had absolutely no reason to check her, or even look at her for long. She was dead. And they just wanted to be rid of her before she started to make a mess.

The men carrying her went in silence, and they moved with assurance. At least one of them was wearing night vision; had to be, from the general speed at which they went down the hill.

One of them stopped, putting a strain on her feet, and Bryn resisted the urge to react. "Wait," he said. "Where are you going?"

"Gully," the other one said. "Come on."

"We're supposed to bury them, Walt said."

"Hard work to bury them. We toss 'em over, they get broken up in the fall. Come winter, nothing left but bones anyway. Nobody's gonna find 'em down there except the bugs, and even if somebody does, there won't be enough left to identify. Save us a couple of hours, too."

"I don't know. Seems— "

"Move it," the first man said, and his voice had gone hard. "I ain't tramping around here for my health, and I ain't digging graves for these two assholes. You want to pray over 'em, pray over the gully that they get eaten quick."

The second man shut up, and started following the first man's lead. *The gully.* Bryn hoped it was a long way off, but she didn't expect it would be. These didn't seem like men who wanted to go to a whole lot of trouble for a body dump.

She was right. They slowed and stopped after about five minutes more, and she heard the men with Reynolds' body pausing nearby.

"Jesus, this guy's heavy," one of them said, and groaned. "Ate his weight in cheeseburgers or something."

"I could kill a cheeseburger right now. Maybe two."

"Shut up and get him over the edge, and we can get chow," snapped the man standing over Bryn. "Unless you're so attached you want to take him back and play house."

"Fuck you, you're the one with the cute bald chick."

"Cute and fucking dead."

"Hot, though."

"Shut up, you freak—"

And right then, Reynolds woke up, with a vengeance. And a shriek like a devil coming straight up out of hell with a pitchfork up his ass.

There was a chorus of alarm from the body disposal unit—hers and Reynolds alike. She heard his body fall with a thump to the ground, and she was dropped just a second later. She opened her eyes.

All four of the men had backed off and were staring with understandable horror at the dead man flailing and screaming on the ground.

She rolled to her feet, stepped up behind one of them, and pulled his sidearm from the holster he wore in the small of his back. She pressed it to the base of his skull and said, "Boo."

He yelped and flinched, but he didn't try to move away. His buddies did, retreating another couple of steps in a triangle that put her and Reynolds' still-twitching not-quite-corpse on the other three points. Sticking together for safety. One of them pulled his gun, but he couldn't quite decide what to do with it, especially when Bryn put her arm around their comrade's throat, yanked him off balance, and aimed over his shoulder at the ones still free. "Drop them," she said. "Or I start making corpses. And I can promise you, that gully's still a valid destination. Just not for me."

"Kill this bitch!" said the one she had choked out. She grinned. It probably looked as savage as she felt.

"Yeah, please do," she said. "In case you haven't noticed, killing me doesn't really help. Thanks for getting us outside the gates, boys."

That spooked them enough that they pulled out their weapons and tossed them, which was exactly what she wanted. Reynolds had stopped screaming, but he lay on his side, sobbing. She knew how it felt. The headache alone would disable him for a while, much less the overwhelming shock of what had happened to him.

"Right," she said. "Let's do this."

She didn't know anything about these men, but they'd been party to two murders that she knew of, and found body disposal boring work. That didn't mean they deserved to die, but she didn't have much choice. Not if she wanted to preserve Patrick's life.

She snapped the neck of the one she was holding. It wasn't easy; he was a big man, but she had leverage and strength, and she felt it when the bone shifted and his spinal cord severed. Shots carried in these hills. She was going to have to do this quietly.

She expected it to be difficult. She *wanted* it to be. But the adrenaline that flooded her made it seem effortless as she shoved the dead man aside and leaped for the group. She hit hard, dead center, and they tumbled like bowling pins. She took hold of the center man as they rolled. He was pulling a knife, which she recognized with a pleased jolt; she needed it. So Bryn took it, by breaking his fingers, and then buried the knife twice in his chest, twisting to be sure he was down. Blood bathed her, but she was already moving on, licking the iron tang from her lips as she ducked a thrown fist, rushed in, and delivered four fast, accurate stabs, severing vital organs and arteries.

The third was running, and that triggered something awful and feral in her. She took him down ten feet away, and severed his spine with a single, sharp cut. Clean, this time. Simple.

She rose, breathing hard, fighting back the urge to rip into the corpses. She thought about cold water, icy rivers rushing over her and washing away the blood and fear and fury.

By the time she opened her eyes, Dr. Reynolds had stopped groaning, and had made it, swaying, to his knees. Behind him, the dawn was glowing gold and pink.

It was going to be a beautiful day.

He didn't resist as she pulled him to his feet.

"Where are we going?" he asked dully. Still in shock. Good. That made him easier to handle. "What just happened?"

"I saved your ass," she said. "Walk and shut up, Doctor."

He did.

Chapter 18

The compound was just coming awake by the time they'd made it to the tree line near the fence; roosters were crowing, people were chattering, and Bryn heard the laughter of kids as they ran close to the ditch where she and Reynolds had spent the night dead.

She wondered if they were used to seeing bodies there. She hoped not. She hoped that was why their surly body-disposal team had been up so early, to avoid letting the kids see that ugly truth.

But she wasn't really sure Walt would have even taken that into consideration. He was probably of the "they have to grow up sometime" school.

She had no way of knowing whether Patrick was okay inside those walls, or what his plan was to try to get out . . . at least, until the front gate opened, and a dusty, mud-stained black pickup rumbled out. Walt was in the driver's seat, and next to him . . .

Next to him was Patrick.

Patrick seemed perfectly at ease. They were laughing together. Walt shook a cigarette out of a pack, and Patrick took it and lit up with casual competence. *I didn't know he smoked,* she thought. Not that it mattered. Patrick didn't smoke; the role he was playing did. Even the little motions—the way he sat, the tilt of his head—those were alien to her from the way Patrick normally moved. She'd never realized he was such an expert chameleon.

Funny how that seemed such a betrayal just now.

"Come on," Bryn said, and grabbed hold of Reynolds' arm. He was feeling better now, and from the look he shot her, he was starting to think about resisting. She twisted the arm up behind his back and stepped in close. "I'm not feeling like putting up with this, so let's not dance, all right? Just move."

"You won't kill me. You need me."

"That's true," she said. "But I have a really sharp knife, and I promise you, regenerating things that have been cut off is painful and slow. Think about all the things you could lose. I'll be nice. I'll just start with an ear."

That got him moving, willingly. He kept up with her when she settled into a run, though he was out of shape— she wondered how that worked. Did the nanites see his extra pounds as being normal? That would suck. It meant no matter how much he dieted or exercised, he'd never permanently lose a pound. They'd just find a way to put it back on. Another way that medical miracles could screw someone, she thought, and almost laughed. Almost. Luckily, she didn't really have the breath.

The vehicle trail was full of switchbacks, to avoid too steep a grade for safe braking, but Bryn plunged straight down the slope, with Reynolds running beside her. He wasn't too sure-footed, but he grimly kept pace until she slowed about halfway down to check their progress. Good. They'd pulled ahead of the truck, and the farther they went, the easier the footing . . . but then, the vegetation was growing more dense as the elevation fell. More brambles, thicker trees. She cut right, trying to keep the switchback road in sight as they ran.

By the time they'd forced their way through the thickest mass at the very bottom of the slope, she was exhausted, and Reynolds was gasping for breath like a man about to expire of a heart attack. He wouldn't, of course, but he definitely wasn't looking too good. Was his skin just a little gray, beneath the brown? She thought it might be. And his eyes had dulled, too.

He'd been Revived, not upgraded, like her. The nanites were starting to lose their ability to heal him completely, and unlike her, his couldn't be recharged through proteins. They were starting to break down into waste products in his blood.

He was in the early stages of decomp. She saw it in the clumsy way he folded up when they reached the edge of the road, clinging to a tree. There wasn't much time to get what they needed out of him, not without another shot of Returné on hand.

She almost, almost felt sorry for him.

"Please," he whimpered. "Please let me rest."

"Soon," she said. "Just stay put."

He didn't have the energy to bolt, even if he had the will, so it wasn't much of a risk leaving him there. She readied the knife, and watched as the truck made the last set of turns on the access road and stopped.

This was the moment. She had no idea where Walt was heading. . . . If he was going toward civilization, he'd probably go left, and pass near her. If not, he'd go right, and she might miss her chance.

But she saw Patrick point, and the knot in her chest eased. They were turning toward her.

One . . . two . . . on three, she bolted from cover and jumped onto the running board of the truck. Walt reacted exactly the way most people would have, with an instinctive flinch away from her, and so he didn't see Patrick making a lightning-fast grab for the knife in Walt's belt holster.

She didn't have to make a move. Walt slammed on the brakes and skidded to a stop, and Patrick jammed the knife into the flesh at the base of his throat—almost exactly the same spot Walt had selected when they were in opposite positions. It wasn't, Bryn felt, an accident.

"Well, shit, Vaughn," Walt said. "What kind of special-effects dickery is your dead girlfriend?"

"No CGIs were hurt," Bryn said. She opened the door and stepped down from the running board as she did. Patrick unlocked Walt's seat belt—she was mildly surprised a rebel like him was bothering to wear one—and Walt, upon some gentle knife-related urging, eased his way out of the cab. Bryn watched carefully, waiting for the tensing of muscles she knew would come; the second it did, she added her own knife, pressing in just over his kidneys. "This doesn't have to go badly for you, Walt. Just relax."

"What happened to my men?"

"Sorry." She wasn't. He turned his head just enough that she saw the hateful gleam in his eyes. "Didn't have much of a choice. They weren't going to just let us go."

"You were dead. I know you were...." Walt's voice trailed off, because he'd caught sight of Reynolds clinging to the tree. His mouth opened, as if he intended to say something, but nothing came out.

"Yeah, we were," Bryn said. "Call it a miracle."

"Not from any god I'd worship."

"I'd be surprised if you ever worshipped any god except your own ambition," Patrick said. He was no longer being Vaughn, and the cigarette was gone, stamped out on the road. He looked taller now, and straighter. "Taking the truck, Walt. Do you want to live to make it back to your compound?"

"If you're offering."

"I am," he said. "But you have to make me a promise."

"Why the hell would I do that? *Vaughn?*"

"Because I know how much you hate governments and corporations and rich fat cats," Patrick said. "And we've got all three of those things looking for us now. They're going to find their way to you, eventually, and I need you to do exactly what comes naturally—put up a fight. I'm not asking you to fall on any swords, but just don't help them. Not right away. If you could forget about the truck, I'd owe you."

"Owe me what?"

"That half a million you lost on the Stinger deal," Patrick said. "By the way, that was me. I took it and I burned your weapons contact. Sorry. The job was to close off the dealer, and I did it. And I wasn't too wild about someone like you having the missiles, either, to be honest. But if you do this for me, I'll get you the half million back, in cash, untraceable bills."

"Not enough," Walt said. "I want a full million. Interest."

"For doing exactly what you always do, fight whatever comes at you? No."

"A million, or I pick up the phone and call the cops to tell them my truck's been stolen."

"We could just kill him," Bryn said. Her voice sounded light and cold, and utterly at odds with the beautiful sunrise and the twittering birds in the trees. "Kill him and dump his body in the ditch. Seems like karma."

"It does," Patrick said, but he sent her a glance that let her know he was worried by what she'd said. And the way she'd said it. It worried her a little, too, but in a distant, arctic-ice-locked way. "But I think Walt understands there's a better outcome to be had."

"There is if there's a million on the table," Walt said. Bryn had to admit that she would not have been that calm in his situation, with a knife at his throat and another at his back, and a woman who was evidently capable of resurrection calmly threatening to slice.

Patrick knew when he was beaten, even with the upper hand, and he shook his head a little and said, "All right. One million. Deal?"

"Why would you believe a thing I said? Considering how long you've been lying to me."

"I just do," Patrick said. "Because I've lived behind those walls, and I know you care about those people. And I know you keep your word."

Walt hesitated, then said, "All right. My word on it. You take the truck, and you get me the million. I won't tell whoever comes calling."

"It may take a while on the million. Seeing as we're on the run right now."

Walt grinned. It looked maniacal. "I trust you, brother. Tell your bitch to stop poking that in my back unless she wants to buy me dinner first."

Bryn thought about pushing the knife home. Thought about it a lot. But she saw the clear warning in Patrick's expression, and finally took a deep breath and stepped back. "I think this is a mistake," she said, "but if you want to trust him, it's on you."

"Then it's on me," Patrick said. "Let him go, Bryn."

Walt gave her a second, very long look. "Bryn. You don't look much like a Bryn to me."

"What do I look like?"

"A dead woman," he said. "Because I don't forget."

She laughed. It sounded crazy.

The hackles raised on the back of her neck as she thought, *I sound like Jane.*

Patrick grabbed the shaking, exhausted Reynolds and shoved him into the truck, then took the passenger seat next to him. "You drive," he said to Bryn. He nodded to Walt as she took her spot behind the wheel, with Reynolds sandwiched in the middle. "Good luck, brother."

"Be seeing you, *Bryn*," Walt said, and aimed a finger gun at her. She managed not to bite it off. Just barely.

"I liked it better when he called me bitch," she said, and threw the truck into gear.

They left him, and his compound of maybe-crazies, behind in a veil of dust.

Patrick said, very quietly, "Are you all right?"

"Sure," she said. "Shot in the heart by the man I love,

thrown in a ditch, dragged to the edge of a cliff for disposal, forced to kill four guys to cover our escape. It's Thursday, isn't it? Typical Thursday."

He didn't laugh. He was watching her; she could sense it without glancing in his direction. "I'm sorry," he said. "It was the only thing I could think to do."

"It was the right play for the right time. I'm fine."

"Bryn—"

"I'm fine. How about you, Mr. Reynolds? Catching your breath?"

He had at least enough to say shakily, "Fuck you."

She tried to laugh, but it turned to a cough. Her throat felt very dry. Dry as the dusty road. "Pat?"

In her peripheral vision, she saw him turn his head away. "You're right. Typical Thursday," he said.

And that was the last of their conversation for a while.

Chapter 19

The truck was good for about two hundred miles before the tank signaled it was about to give out; it was good timing, because they were running on fumes when the first gas station appeared on the horizon. It was miraculously in business, and Bryn used the last of the cash Patrick had on him (and the last of what Reynolds had in his pockets when they searched him) to pay for the gas and the entire jar of Slim Jims, plus a jug of drinking water. The attendant didn't seem to think that was strange at all, but then, he was in a part of the country where it was probably survival instinct to aggressively mind your own business. Once they were fueled, they got off the main road again and angled for another freeway, where the nondescript truck joined convoys of tractor trailers heading north.

"It's probably time to get some answers," Patrick said, and shook Reynolds by the shoulder. The man was dozing. He didn't look any better than before; in fact, he looked worse, which didn't surprise Bryn in the least. When the nanites started dying, there was no recovery without more Returné, and it wasn't exactly going to appear on a convenience store shelf.

Reynolds was going to suffer, and he was going to rot,

slowly. Bryn supposed she ought to feel worse than she did about that, but honestly, she didn't really care. Fuck him. Fuck him and his feverish, dishonest greed. He hadn't cared about how many died in horrible agony; he ought to have a chance to live through it himself.

But first, he needed to *talk*. He'd been stubborn so far, but with the right pressure . . . the right tools . . .

You're becoming her, a still voice inside her whispered. *You're becoming Jane. Listen to yourself.*

She pushed it aside, because another thought struck, one that rang inside her head like a tuning fork. Returné. He was on *Returné*, not on the upgrades.

She didn't think there was a chance in hell that it would work, but on the off chance that hell had rolled snake eyes just this once, she said, "Condition sapphire."

Patrick sat bolt upright, as if she'd hit him with a cattle prod. "Can't be," he said. "Didn't they factor the command sequences out of the batch of drugs they gave their executives?"

"They lost their best scientists," she pointed out. "Maybe they couldn't. Maybe they didn't bother, because *these* men—these men would believe they were invincible, wouldn't they?"

He shook his head. "I think you're dreaming."

"We'll see. Hand me a Slim Jim, Reynolds."

Reynolds, without hesitation, reached for the jar wedged into the narrow opening between his feet and Patrick's, and took one out. He extended it to her.

"Unwrap it," she said. He did, and held out the raw jerky stick. "Now eat it."

He did, expressionless, chewing like a machine and swallowing until it was all gone.

"Good. Now eat the wrapper," she said.

He raised it to his mouth. His dulled eyes looked terrified, but he was doing it. He was really doing it. The wrapper crinkled and buckled as it hit his lips, but his fingers continued their relentless progress to shove it in.

"Bryn," Patrick snapped. "Stop him."

Reynolds had jammed most of the plastic into his mouth. She was tempted to tell him to swallow, just for the hell of it, just to watch him choke, but the anger in Patrick's voice penetrated the lazy fog of cruelty. It was misty red, that fog. Like an aerosolized spray of blood.

"Stop," she said. "Take the plastic out of your mouth and drop it on the floor, Reynolds."

He did, and, lacking instructions, folded his hands and just sat. Waiting.

Waiting for her orders.

It had worked. Condition Sapphire, the hidden feature that made Returné victims into slaves . . . it was still encoded in the nanites. Into these nanites, at least. It rendered Dr. Reynolds completely, utterly helpless and at her mercy.

She thought about what she was going to do with him. All the terrible and wonderful and horrifying things.

And then it all collapsed inside her into a black hole of pain and anguish and horror.

Bryn pulled over to the side of the road with a sudden jerk of the wheel, spewing gravel and bringing the truck to a juddering halt. She bent forward and rested her forehead on the steering wheel, gasping for breath, gagging for it. The wheel was gritty on her skin, coated with the sweaty, oily deposits of those who'd driven it before. It stank of strangers, and she thought of her own skin rubbing off, joining this horrible anonymous mixture of castoff. Thought about rolling down that hillside, ripping into the flesh of a man she'd never seen before. Thought of snapping necks and slicing flesh and the joy, the unclean joy of it made her stomach suddenly twist and try to escape.

"Drink."

Patrick's hand on the back of her head, gentle and steady. His other holding the gallon of water, uncapped and ready. She took it and gulped, gulped, trying to wash the taste of all of that away.

All of *her* away.

The water tasted like tears.

She sat back, taking deep breaths, and said, "Dr. Reynolds, we need to know where to find the rest of the Fountain Group. Please tell us where they are."

He turned that terribly dull look to her, and she saw him in there, trapped. Maybe not a good man. Maybe a man who deserved every wretched and awful thing that was going to happen to him. But, like Thorpe, she couldn't look into his eyes and not see herself . . . not understand that human spirit, however twisted, however flawed. He was staring into eternity, and she knew how that felt.

She knew how it *would* feel, when she arrived there. It was something every single human, even those like her, would eventually face.

She couldn't look at eternity and not feel small, and frail, and alone. She had to reach out.

"I'm sorry, Martin," she said, and took his hand. His fingers were limp and cool against hers. Not damp quite yet. The skin still felt firm. A near-perfect simulation of life. "I'm so very sorry. Please. Please tell us before it's too late. You know what's going to happen to you. You know how horrible it is. You don't want that for your children, too. The Fountain Group—what they're doing is evil. You know that. Somewhere deep inside, you *know*. Listen to it."

"Bryn," Patrick said, and his warm hand cupped the back of her neck for a moment. "He's conditioned to respond. You don't have to convince him."

"I know," she whispered. Tears blurred her vision. "I *want* to convince him."

Reynolds let his breath out in a slow, rattling breath. It smelled of slow death and sickness. "I don't know where they all are," he said. "I'm sorry."

"Do you know where *any* of them are?"

"Yes," Reynolds said. And that was the moment when she knew she'd reached him, because even as she started to ask for the necessary clarification the conditioning required ... he went on. "Most of them are going to be gathering in the Trigon offices in San Francisco in a few days. All the ones that matter will be there. The others— the others are like Thorpe. They don't agree with the program. They were outvoted." He swallowed. She heard the wet, thick sound, and she remembered how that felt, dissolving inside. Coming to pieces in slow, dreadful motion. "If you want to stop it, stop them. They can give you everything."

She nodded. "We will."

He held her gaze very steadily, and said, "Will you kill me now?"

The awful thing was, some part of her was still eager for it. Still hungry for pain and blood and flesh and screaming.

"Do you want me to?"

"No," he said. "I'd rather live."

Still. Even now.

How very ... human.

"Then we'll find a way to keep you alive," she told him, and locked gazes with Patrick on his other side. "Somehow."

She put the truck in gear and sprayed gravel again merging back into the sparse traffic. It was colder up here, and the skies were gloomier. Thick silver-edged clouds threatened rain, or snow, or worse.

"Bryn?" Patrick said. "San Francisco is the other way."

"I know," she said. "But we have to go somewhere else first."

"Where?"

"Alaska."

He didn't even ask if she was crazy.

The perfect definition of love.

Chapter 20

They traded the truck for tickets aboard a sightseeing vessel from Seattle to Anchorage. Reynolds' deteriorating condition was disguised by use of a wheelchair, oxygen tank, and blanket over his lap. Bryn was surprised to see how many similarly impaired people were traveling by water. . . . It didn't seem like a great idea for people who, by definition, couldn't swim worth a damn. Still, Bryn had to admit, the cabin they shared wasn't bad, and neither was the food—open buffet, and she went back for about five helpings of the rare roast beef, every meal. The ship's store took care of her clothing and toiletry needs, and by the time they disembarked in Anchorage, she looked and felt . . . normal. Patrick looked stronger, too. By avoiding the Canadian borders, they hadn't had to produce passports, which would have been . . . well, impossible. Patrick's contacts had gotten them past the necessary ID checkpoints for the ship, on and off—but that was all they could promise.

Turned out they didn't need to worry, because when they docked, sitting at the exit to the ship terminal was a big black limousine, and it had a sign that read DR. REYNOLDS & PARTY.

Bryn looked at Patrick, and then at the driver. He was

a tall, good-looking young man with a military buzz cut;
his livery uniform fit well.

He turned over the sign. It read COURTESY OF PANSY.

Bryn almost laughed. She steered the wheelchair in
that direction, and the driver smiled and opened the
back door. "Allow me, ma'am," he said. He had a pleasant Southern twang, long vowels and musical lifts. He
helped her lift Reynolds out of the chair and into the
easiest accessible seat. As he straightened, he handed
her a slim cell phone. "Miss Pansy would like you to call
her when you have a chance."

Bryn blinked at him, nodded, and pocketed the device. She and Patrick slid in the other side of the limo,
and sank into the luxuriously soft leather upholstery. The
driver loaded the wheelchair, and they were on the road
in under a minute.

"I know I'm going to be stating the obvious when I
say this, but . . . what the hell?" Patrick said. "A limousine. Really."

Bryn shrugged. "It got our attention, didn't it?" She
took the phone out and scrolled through the address
book. One number in it. She dialed it as the limo
crunched through snow—snow, already—and headed in
toward Anchorage proper. The sun was out, glittering on
glass and steel and thin patches of snow, turning everything into fairyland.

Until it turned into an ice palace, at least.

"Bryn?" It was Pansy who picked up on the other end.
She sounded breathless, but it was definitely her, and the
sound of her familiar voice made Bryn suddenly feel
shaky inside. "You're okay?"

"Relatively," she managed to say, and cleared a throat
that was suddenly too tight, stuffed with emotion. "How
are you and Manny? Is my sister okay?"

"Yeah, everybody's fine. We've run through just about
our entire DVD collection, though. We may be facing a
serious rerun problem."

"Joe and Riley?"

"Yeah . . . They made it to us. We have them locked down in a separate wing, though, because Manny—well. You know. But he's working on the formula they brought. Pretty scary stuff."

"How did you know—"

"Hang on. I'll conference."

There was a click, and then Joe's warm baritone said, "Sorry, that was me. We were pretty desperate to keep track of you. I know most of Patrick's contacts, so I focused on the ones closest to where we lost you guys. That led us to the shoot-out up in Paradise at Dr. Reynolds' place, and I thought about Walt as a possible place for Patrick to go."

"You called *Walt*? And he just . . . told you where we were going?"

"Nope. Never talked to him. But he's on some federal lists, and there's an eye in the sky that takes a look at his compound twice a day. We saw—well, I'm not going to sugarcoat it, we saw your body in a ditch. Pansy was pretty upset."

"Not you? Joe. I'm crushed."

"I've got more faith," he said. "But yeah. It was unsettling. We tracked the truck from the compound. When it was obvious where you were going, Pansy hired the driver."

"I'm guessing the driver isn't just a standard wheelman?"

Patrick was gesturing for the phone. She handed it over. "Hey, Joe. I'm assuming this is a secure line. . . . Yeah, of course. I want you to double-check on your family and move them somewhere double secure. No, nothing specific. It's just that I know Jane, and we've kicked her ass twice in a row now when she expected it to be a walkover—three times, if she runs right into the Walt buzz saw. She'll go for the throat now, and that means what's close to us."

His glance went to her, and she swallowed, suddenly catching his unease. Her sister was safe, and she had assurances from Brick that he was on guard for her mom and other brothers and sisters. But that didn't mean they wouldn't get hurt. Jane would . . .

Jane would do anything to hurt her. Bryn felt a shiver of dread pass over her like falling silk, and then it was burned off by anger. *Then we have to keep her busy,* she thought. *We have to keep her focused on us, not on our families.*

Patrick finished up and handed the phone back. It was Pansy again. "Well, this is just getting cheerier," Pansy said. "I'm starting to think Manny has the right idea about living in a perpetual state of paranoia. Gotta love a man who sticks to his principles. How are you feeling?"

"Good," Bryn said. It wasn't a lie. Physically, she was fine—better than she had been in a while. Mentally . . . well. Better to avoid that topic. "I need to take more cruises."

"Words to live by, lady. The driver's one of Joe's guys; he'll take care of you. He's also got supplies for you. Um . . . can I ask where you're heading? Because Anchorage isn't on our radar as a Fountain Group hotbed of activity."

"We're not staying here," Bryn said. "We're going to Barrow."

"Wow. Barrow. As in . . . are you renting a dogsled, too?"

"I have no idea," Bryn said. "But I need to get there and get back, and fast. We have to make it to San Francisco in time for a meeting of the Trigon board of directors."

"I—wow. Okay. So, you need one puddle jumper to Barrow. Let me . . . get on that. Bryn? Are you sure you're—"

"I'm sure," she said. "Thanks, Pansy. Tell my sister I love her."

"I will. Be careful."

"Am I ever?"

Pansy laughed, but it sounded hollow. Bryn missed her voice on the line when it was gone, and for a moment she just sat, hand gripping Patrick's. Then she said, "You were serious? About Joe's family?"

"Yes," Patrick said. "Jane won't flinch."

No. Jane wouldn't. Bryn knew that from terrifying close experience. "And . . . my family . . ."

He was quiet for a few seconds, then lifted her hand to press a kiss on the back of it. "Brick's people are watching them."

"It was just a precaution before. Now it might save their lives," she finished. She wasn't really close to her other brothers and sister; they'd all gone very different ways in their lives. Her mother . . . Well. They'd never been exactly Norman Rockwell portrait material. But that didn't mean she didn't love them, didn't worry.

And her nieces and nephews didn't deserve any part of this horror. *If I'd known what was coming,* she thought with a wave of dull, black despair, *I'd have let Jane feed me to the incinerator.* Except that would not have saved anyone else, ultimately.

The only thing that would save people, really save them, would be the destruction of the Fountain Group itself.

But first, she had to finish Jane. And for that . . . for that, she needed to get to the unlikely place of Barrow, Alaska.

The driver turned and rolled down the window up front. "Ma'am? I've been told to take you and Mr. Mc-Callister to the airport. Your friend there . . . He doesn't look so good. What would you like me to do with him?"

Reynolds. Bryn looked at the man; he was silent, eyes shut. His skin was starting to lose its elasticity now, and take on that muddy color of decomposition. Still days away from dissolution, but he was going.

"Once we're in the air, take him somewhere nice," she said. "He's dying. When I come back—when I come back, we'll figure something out."

Reynolds roused at that, and looked at her. His lips moved in what might have been intended as a smile. It looked ghastly. "Something fast," he whispered. "Please."

"Yes," she said. "I promise."

He settled back with a sigh, and closed those cloudy eyes again.

"You should stay with him," she said to Patrick. "They might still try to get him back, although I doubt it. They probably considered him a lost cause when we took him. One thing these people don't seem big on is loyalty."

"I'm coming with you," Patrick said.

"I don't need you for—"

"I'm coming," he said. It was flat, and hard as steel, and she smiled, a little.

"I love it when you get all forceful," she said. "All right. But don't blame me if you get eaten by polar bears. It's already snow season there."

"I love the cold," he said, and gave her a crooked smile that warmed her nicely. "And I trust you to take care of the polar bears."

Chapter 21

Bryn expected the driver to take them to the main terminal, where Alaska Airlines was, not surprisingly, the biggest business, but the driver went a different way ... to an access gate that led to the extensive private plane section. "I thought we were taking a commercial flight," she said. "Where are we going?"

"The supplies I brought are something you don't want to carry in through security," he said. "My instructions are to take you this way."

They passed rows of small single-engine planes and moved on to glossier, more advanced models ... and then to the private jets. The limo parked near something that had to be worth a million or more, a sleek needle of a plane that looked as if it might be equipped to go not to Barrow, but to Mars. The ladder was down, and as the driver opened the door for them, Bryn saw a familiar friend coming down to greet them.

"Joe?" she said blankly. "How—I just—"

It didn't matter, suddenly. She flew at him and got a great big warm hug in response, one that lifted her right off her feet. When he let her go, Patrick was next—back slapping included, as per the Man Code. "Inside," Joe said as he stepped back. After the limo driver opened the trunk, Joe grabbed a couple of olive-drab duffels and tossed them to Bryn and Patrick. She was surprised at the weight of them. "We probably don't have too long. You know what to do?" He directed that last at the driver, who nodded and helped Reynolds out of the limo and into his wheelchair. That wheelchair was loaded on a standard handicap-accessible lift on what was, to Bryn's eyes, a standard, well-used airport vehicle—something no one would glance at twice here. The limo driver exchanged jackets and hats with another man waiting on the tarmac. The limo quickly cruised on, heading somewhere . . . else, and the airport van moved off to blend in with the general flow of secured traffic.

"All aboard," Joe said. "We're ready to roll."

It was . . . quite the plane. Bryn had never been in anything like it—rich wood paneling, thick carpets, plush seats, and tables. Like an upper-class social club, only in the air.

And on the plane were Manny, Pansy, Liam, Riley, and Annie. The full complement from the supposedly impenetrable missile base.

Annie practically leaped on Bryn, all babbles and hugs and more hugs, and Bryn clung to her, tears burning and breaking loose as she buried her face in her sister's hair. She didn't even hear what was said. It didn't matter. She understood. And she never wanted to let go, except that Joe touched her shoulder and said, apologetically, "Strapping in time, ladies."

"Right," Bryn said, and pulled back with a deep breath. She held on to Annie's hand a moment more, then went to the empty seat next to Patrick and secured the safety belt. "Somebody want to tell me exactly what's going on here? Because I'm a little—"

"Confused? Good," Manny said. He was sitting calmly, working a crossword puzzle and wearing square reading glasses, which looked oddly delicate on him. "If you are, then I'm hoping the Fountain Group is a whole lot more baffled."

"I—how did you—"

"You don't really think that I ever stay someplace that doesn't have a secret way out, do you? And when I say secret, I mean not even Pansy knows, until we're ready to use it. Sorry, sweetheart. But you know."

"I do," Pansy said, and put her head on his shoulder. "Long story short, the Fountain Group's hired guns are still watching the complex, and there's enough activity going on to keep them very interested. They've made at least a dozen attempts at cracking it, but they're still— what's that word we like so much, Manny?"

"Stymied," he said with more than a little relish. "Stymied, exactly." He filled in another word on his puzzle. In ink, of course. "Everybody knows I'm a paranoid freakazoid who likes to hole up in bunkers against the end of the world. It's useful."

"You *are* a paranoid freakazoid who likes to hole up in bunkers. I've been to your . . . houses," Joe said.

"I'm perfectly capable of adapting when I need to," Manny said. "We routed all the communications back through the bunker, of course. Everything's programmed to make them believe we're still in place there. We even made it look as if Riley and Joe fought their way into the bunker."

"You didn't?" Bryn asked. Joe, seated across from her, shook his head.

"Never got that far," he said. "We got a message on paper to wait in a parking lot for a ride. Next thing I knew, we were on this plane headed somewhere completely new."

"And . . . where was that?"

"You don't need to know," Manny said, "because we won't be going back. I just needed the lab for a while."

"Did you synthesize the shutdown drug?" Bryn asked.

"I have the analysis under way," he said. "I think

there's another way to take it than what Thorpe did. If it works, it could change everything."

"You think it'll be ready in time?"

"That," he said without taking his attention from his crossword, "is a good question. No idea."

She wasn't sure that she should believe him; Manny's paranoia might be a convenient disguise some of the time, but it was also a fundamental truth about who he really was. It was important to never forget that if he thought it was prudent to lie to her, he'd lie without a qualm. He'd want a holdback weapon against her.

And he was probably right about that, given what she'd become on this trip. What she'd done. What she was capable of doing.

She didn't press him, just nodded and settled back for takeoff.

That was when she heard a bark and a scrabble of claws, and her gorgeous pet bulldog Mr. French appeared at her feet, panting and gazing up at her with big, dark, adoring eyes. She picked him up and cuddled him as he wiggled and whined and licked tears from her face. "How—?"

"You keep asking that question," Manny said. He sounded amused. "Ask the butler."

"I am not a butler," Liam said, but he sounded more resigned than offended. "I thought you might want to see him, Bryn. And I was a bit afraid that Jane . . . Well, you understand. The rest of the estate dogs were moved to a new kennel, but Mr. French seemed to be missing you quite a bit. I thought it was worth bringing him. He'll stay on the plane, of course."

"Did you have to put down a pet deposit?" she asked, and laughed through her tears. "Oh God, thank you, Liam. Thank you. I—I really needed him." Because Mr. French's unwavering love was one thing that hadn't become complicated, although she knew that he could tell she was . . . different. But he was sensitive to her, and she knew that he was an excellent judge of character—her character. If she found him looking at her with doubt, she would need to check herself.

And if he growled . . . she'd need to stop.

"Stupid dog," she whispered, and rubbed his ears. He made a contented sound in the back of his throat, almost like a purr, and flopped limply across her lap. "God, I missed you, mutt."

He opened one eye to look at her, as if to say that he hadn't missed her at all.

Liar.

The takeoff was bumpy, but once the plane was in the air the ride was smooth as glass. Below, the late-summer landscape of Anchorage still looked clear, but as the plane moved north, snow appeared—patchy at first, and then solid, then hardpacked. Not winter yet, but winter was coming fast, and in this part of the world, coming with an iron, icy fist to smash all the unprepared fools who tried to cross it.

Like her.

This will be fast, she told herself. *We land; I find this scientist; I grab the stored sample; we're gone and headed for San Francisco.* She had no doubt that Manny was right that his trail was clear—he was a past master of evasion and misinformation—but they'd left Reynolds behind, and Reynolds could be a fatal problem.

"Patrick," she said, "Dr. Reynolds . . . we should have brought him with us. Just in case. He's a liability."

He gave her a long, unreadable look, and then put his head back against the seat and sighed. "Do you want me to say it?" he asked. "All right. I gave the order. I didn't want you to be responsible for it. You . . . bonded with him; I could see that. You felt sorry for him, and I understand that. But I couldn't leave him there, with all the knowledge he'd gained from us along the way."

She sat upright, pulling against the seat belt. Mr.

French huffed in agitation and had to adjust his comfortable slouch on her lap. "What did you do? Patrick?"

"What you would have done if you'd been thinking
straight," he said. "The driver has what he needs."

"You had him *killed*?" She didn't know why that felt
so wrong, or like such a betrayal; it shouldn't have, really.
She'd meant to do the same on returning; it was exactly
what she knew Reynolds wanted. What he'd asked for.
But somehow, having it taken out of her hands enraged
her, and she glared at him with so much fury that she felt
Mr. French stir in her lap and put his paw on her hand,
clearly trying to get her attention. She patted him, and
felt some of the fury recede. "Patrick, why didn't you—"

"You think I had him killed? Why would you think
that?" he asked her, and gave her a very strange look. "I
made sure the driver had a supply of Returné and took
him to a secured lockdown. Nobody's going to hurt him.
We might need his information about the San Francisco
meeting. What I meant was that I arranged for him to
live."

He was right, of course, and in retrospect she couldn't
understand why she'd thought so intensely about ending
his pain, instead of getting him a palliative treatment—
another shot of Returné. It wasn't a cure, but it would
stop his suffering.

But she knew that just delayed it, and that was the
problem. It felt . . . futile. Useless. Another day of staving
off the inevitable.

"I just wanted it to be over," she confessed, and concentrated on petting Mr. French's warm, short fur. "For
him."

"Don't you mean for you?" Patrick's voice had turned
gentle and soft, and was almost lost in the sound of the
plane's engines. He took her other hand. "Bryn . . ."

"Maybe," she whispered. "Maybe I did mean that. I
just—it's so much. At first it's adrenaline; it's determina-

tion; then it just becomes adaptation, I suppose. But then you get this moment, this moment where you see it all clearly, your future, what you're going to become, and . . . I don't want to be that. I love you, but I *can't* be that. We're fooling ourselves that this is some kind of . . . disease that can be managed. Death isn't a disease, Pat. It's what cures it."

He'd paled during that short speech, and his hand had tightened on hers. "Don't," he said. "Please don't."

"I'm not going to get better, Pat," she said. "I wish I could, but we both know how this will end. It isn't just the PTSD that accumulates from all this . . . resurrection. It's more. It's worse. It . . . twists what I am, inside. Like it did Jane. Promise me—"

"No."

"Promise me that if—"

"I said no, Bryn. I mean it." He did. She could see the haunted look even in her peripheral vision, feel his distress like heat against her skin.

She never, ever wanted to hurt him, but she knew . . . she knew that she would. Eventually. Just like Jane. She could remember that cold, detached feeling inside her—the sense that she was standing apart from the world, from people. That none of it really meant anything.

That detachment wasn't distance, it was sociopathy, and she was slowly, surely contracting it. What would happen when she couldn't connect anymore? When Patrick's feelings didn't matter? When even the trusting sweetness of Mr. French no longer had any impact? It would mean the end of her as a person. Worse, it would be the beginning of her as a monster. She already ate flesh, when desperate. If she tipped over the edge, lost everything that had ever mattered . . . then hunger would be all that was left. Not Bryn.

He didn't understand that being that . . . being so empty . . . would be worse than dying.

Fine. She couldn't ask Patrick to do it, then, but Manny

wouldn't hesitate. He was ruthless enough, and he'd understand why she asked. He'd seen all this as an abomination from the beginning—a great scientific achievement, but nonetheless, something to be feared, not praised. Pansy might object, but in the end . . . in the end, she'd understand, too. Even Joe would.

Not Annie, though. Even now, not her sister.

Bryn closed her eyes against a sudden shudder of turbulence, and concentrated on the gentle, warm weight of Mr. French in her lap until she drifted off to sleep.

She woke up with the extremely sharp-edged alertness that comes with too many crises, and found, to her shock, that what she'd felt was the plane touching down on the icy runway.

They'd made it to Barrow.

And now she had to find Thorpe's mysterious scientist and grab that last sample of the cure . . . before Jane got it first.

Chapter 22

A public access computer terminal in the airport's private lounge turned up a Kiera Johannsen's blog. She had about fifty followers, and she generally talked about dense science that Bryn didn't even attempt to follow. The photo on the blog showed a fortysomething woman with close-cropped red hair and a ready smile; she had the tan of someone who enjoyed the outdoors, and a hiker's lean build. Not pretty, but she had an attractive strength in her face. Compelling, Bryn thought.

She didn't look like someone who'd give up without a fight.

Kiera Johannsen's research station was more of a cabin, and global positioning showed it was pretty much out on the fringes of everything . . . which was evidently where she liked to live. Getting out there was going to be a challenge; roads weren't a priority out that far, though there must have been some kind of rudimentary trail leading up to the research station. Johannsen did come into town from time to time, according to the blog; she had an addiction to mint chocolate chip ice cream, and the store in town ordered it special for her by the gallon. Couldn't be lucky enough to be a day the woman made an ice-cream run, though—and sure enough, when Bryn dropped into the small shop, asking casually after Kiera yielded a fountain of mostly useless info about the woman's habits and schedules. Mostly useless because she'd been in four days before to pick up her monthly order, and wasn't due back for a while. The clerk did point out the best way to get to the research station, though, and marked it on the map.

Back at the airport, Bryn showed it to the others, and Joe and Patrick and Riley all geared up to accompany her. "I don't think we need SEAL Team Six," she protested. "C'mon, she's a scientist. Manny could take her."

"Probably," Manny agreed. He was working another crossword—and, she realized, that was probably to deal with general anxiety. This was hard for him, being on the move without any good way to seek solid cover. Even the plane probably gave him bad feelings of exposure. But he was hanging in there, and playing it as cool as she'd ever seen him, except in the middle of a crisis. Pansy was being a helicopter girlfriend, though—hovering. Obviously worried about him, and just as obviously hoping nobody would notice.

Manny looked up over his glasses, straight at Bryn, and said, "Take the firepower, you idiot. We're not playing for pickup sticks. You know what's at stake."

She did, and she bowed her head to acknowledge it. "I rented a truck," she said. "It should get us out there and back in about two hours, maybe less. Keep the pilot close, we might have to leave fast."

"We'll be ready," Liam promised. He, she noticed, was conspicuously armed with what looked like a nine millimeter pistol tucked snugly in a shoulder harness. It gave him a dangerously piratical edge. Annie, on the other hand, was looking stormy; she was sitting on the edge of her seat, elbows on the table, and frowning. Liam, not too subtly, had his hand on her shoulder, pinning her in place. He smiled and said, "Don't worry, we won't eat all the snacks before you return."

"There were snacks? Damn," Bryn sighed, and she was only half kidding. "Okay, let's roll if we're rolling."

The SUV was a monster of a thing, not too late-model but it had the look of a truck well suited to its surroundings. If vehicles could evolve, this one definitely had, and as she set out from the airport down a partly muddy, partly snow-clogged road, it seemed to handle the terrain easily, if not comfortably. That was probably the springs in the seats, which had long ago given up the fight.

Patrick was hanging on to the strap, which was probably wise, considering the bouncing, and simultaneously studying the map she'd marked, though how he could do it and not be motion-sick she couldn't imagine. The town of Barrow fell away within minutes, and the Alaskan tundra stretched on in a blotched, mostly white expanse. "Glad it isn't winter," he said. "The snow would be impassible without plowing paths."

On Bryn's left was the distant curve of the bay, and beyond that, straight north, would be ... well, she supposed, a pole. Strange to think that this shore here was, in a way, what people liked to mark as the end of civilization ... at least until you crossed the pole and came down on the other side. She'd put on her sunglasses, so the sun's glitter on the snow wasn't as bad as it could have been, but within just a few miles she understood why it would blind people. The constant, unyielding glitter ... beautiful, but deadly.

"Slow down," Patrick finally said, and released the safety strap to point to the left. "Should be some kind of trail that way—yeah, right there. Turn."

If he hadn't directed her, she would have missed it, because it was less a road than a vague depression in the landscape. Snow had covered it for about a foot, and buried all traces it existed ... except for a snow-covered mailbox burdened by another layer of white. Beneath, it was painted a shocking Day-Glo yellow, probably because it would have otherwise been regularly missed.

Bryn slowed, and without being asked, Joe bailed out of the back, jogged over, and checked the mailbox. Empty. He got back in the SUV, and Bryn followed the barely visible curves of the trail up a hill . . . and at the top, she spotted a snowy roof.

She stopped. Joe and Riley exited to check the perimeter, and to keep watch; she and Patrick then drove the rest of the way up. The chill was penetrating through the windows, and she hadn't really noticed until now. "Is it getting colder out there?"

"Yeah," Patrick said. "Getting on toward sundown in the next couple of hours, and we need to be back in Barrow before it's dark or we'll have hell finding our way. This isn't country for tourists."

No kidding. She couldn't imagine how dark it would be out here, and how forbidding. Getting stuck or stranded could be a death sentence.

"Got an approach planned?" he asked her. Bryn shook her head and brought the SUV to a stop in the dirty packed snow of the cabin's front yard, such as it was.

"I don't think planning's going to help," she said. "I have no idea what to expect from her, so I'm going to play it by ear. And be as honest as I can. I—I think she deserves that. She's not part of this."

He nodded, whether or not he agreed with her, and it moved her to lean over and give him a very quick, but very warm, kiss. He smiled. "Be careful," he said. "I'll be out here."

"My last line of defense?"

"Something like that," he said. "Or you're mine, which is probably closer to the truth. I just *have* to love the powerful women."

"Flirt."

"Guilty."

She moved quickly up to the cabin's front door; the glow of lights in the windows guaranteed, she thought, that someone was home—and probably watching, because having a strange vehicle drop by in this remote expanse was likely worth noting.

The door opened on her knock, and she was facing the business end of a double-barreled shotgun, held very competently by a woman who'd probably grown up with it. The smile was gone, but the face was the same as the picture on the blog. Kiera Johannsen, in the flesh.

"Don't mean to be rude," Johannsen said, "but who the fuck are you, and why are you on my porch?"

Bryn slowly raised her hands. Her skin felt very exposed to the wind whipping across the snow, and she shivered as it found ways inside the neck of her sweater, under the parka she'd worn open. "Bryn Davis," she said. "You don't know me."

"Damn right I don't."

"Calvin Thorpe sent me."

That made the woman blink and take a step back. The shotgun, though, didn't come down. "Why would Cal send you? Where is he?"

"He's dead," Bryn said. "I'm sorry. He was killed in an explosion in California."

"Oh," she said blankly, as if she hadn't understood. And maybe she hadn't. "Oh." The second time had weight to it, and emotion. She sagged a little, as if she'd received a jab to the ribs and couldn't quite get her breath. But she didn't look surprised. "You came all the way here to tell me that?"

"No," Bryn said. "I came because Dr. Thorpe said I could trust you. He left something with you to hold, and I need it. It's important."

It was the wrong thing to say, because the woman's light blue eyes seemed to catch fire, and her face tightened. So did her aim. "I don't know you. You show up out of nowhere and tell me to hand something over? Why would I do that? How do I even know that Cal is really dead?"

"Ma'am, I'm sorry. I wish I had time to tell you everything, and explain all that happened, but . . . there just isn't a way I can do it. I was with him when it happened. He wanted me to do this, and I intend to do it, because it'll save lives. That's what he wanted to do, in the end. Save lives."

For a few seconds nothing changed, and then Johannsen shook her head, as if shaking off a bothersome fly. It wasn't the no that Bryn was expecting, though. "That sounds like him," she said. "He believed . . . he believed science could save everything. Everyone. I told him he was a dreamer, you know. But he said he'd proved me wrong. He said—you know, he got drunk once and said one day, he'd cure death." She shook her head again. "He was a fool sometimes. Science can repair, but it can destroy just as fast. I kept trying to make him understand that."

Bryn said nothing. After another few heartbeats, the woman backed up and lowered the shotgun. "All right," she said. "Come in. But I warn you, make a wrong move, and I'll blow you into polar bear bait."

"Yes, ma'am," Bryn said. "You need a lot of that? Polar bear bait?"

"You'd be surprised," Johannsen said. "Sit down. No, I'm not making you tea; I'm not stupid. But if you're sitting with hands flat on the table, you're not likely to make me shoot you."

Bryn moved to the small square breakfast table and sat in one of the two wooden chairs—handmade, felt like, and not entirely steady. One leg was a bit too short, and it clunked as she settled her weight. She put both hands flat on the table's surface, and waited.

She didn't have to wait long before Johannsen said, "Tell me what happened to Cal."

"You know he went on the run?" Bryn got a quick nod. "He was hiding out. We tracked him down because we needed his help."

"Why?"

"Because we're trying to stop the same things from happening that he was afraid of," Bryn said. "And they *are* happening. He agreed to help us get our hands on a sample of a drug that could change everything, but he was betrayed by his brother-in-law."

That, finally, was the right thing to say, because a spasm of dislike went across Johannsen's face. "Not hard to believe," she said. "And?"

"And his dead drop was compromised. It was a trap. We were both caught in it, but he—he sacrificed himself to save me. Before he did, he said to find you. He said you have the other sample."

"I don't—" She went perfectly still for a moment, and then continued. "I don't have anything from him."

"You do," Bryn said, with perfect confidence. "Please. I promise you, it's very important. And it will make a difference. Cal changed his mind about what he was doing, what he believed was right. He would have wanted you to know it."

For just a moment, those sharp blue eyes seemed a little less suspicious. Just for a moment. But Johannsen came right back on point. "You found me just fine," she said. "Should I be worried?"

"Probably," Bryn said. "You weren't trying to hide. And that's fine, except that the people who killed Calvin, who killed his family . . . They won't stop. They'll never stop until someone stops them. Do you understand? They'll kill you because you knew him, and you might be a loose end. I don't want that. If you give me what he left with you, we can help you get to Barrow. From there, you should get somewhere else. Don't tell me where, just . . . go. And don't come back."

"My work—"

"Your work won't matter when you're dead and this whole cabin burns to the ground. They'll probably make it look like an accident. Or maybe they'll leave the cabin, and fake a bear attack. Nobody would question it, would they?"

"Not around here," she said. "We don't have much of a CSI team." Johannsen crossed to the windows and looked out. "You have friends with you?"

"Three," Bryn said. "Two out by the mailbox, watching for any incoming traffic. One by the SUV. They're here for your protection as much as mine."

That woke a bleak, but real, smile on the other woman's face. "Bet that wouldn't be true if I blew a big ol' hole in your chest," she said. "You could have come in here guns blazing and just taken it, you know."

"I know," Bryn said. She kept her hands on the table. "I could do that right now, if I wanted."

It was a warning, but a gentle one, and she saw the recognition of it in Johannsen's face. For a long heartbeat, the woman thought about it, and then sighed and crossed the small room to open the front door. She leaned out and said, "You, by the car. It's cold out here. Come inside. I'm getting what you want."

Patrick came in with all due caution, sidearm ready, and immediately saw Bryn sitting at the table. She nodded to him, and he relaxed. But he didn't put the sidearm away, either. "Ma'am," he said to Johannsen, as she shut the door behind him. "Starting to get a little worried."

"I needed to make sure. Sit down, please. Hands flat on the table, just like your friend. I'll get what you want."

The shotgun was at port arms, not an active threat, but Bryn could see him debating the move. He finally said, "No, ma'am, if it's all the same to you, I'll go with you. Just in case of unfriendlies."

"Well, come on then, let's get this over with," she said, and led the way into the back room. Bryn rose and followed after Patrick.

Inside was an entirely different environment from the rustic little cabin's main living area; it hummed with computers and equipment Bryn couldn't immediately identify. Huge refrigerators took up most of the space—they were all labeled, but the designations didn't mean anything to Bryn. Ice cores, she supposed. Climatologists collected a lot of those, didn't they?

Johannsen passed those by and went to a smaller stand-alone fridge, one that in another household would have held beer, most likely, maybe in a game room. This one held small vials and samples, neatly racked.

From two-thirds of the way back, on the second shelf, she picked out a single vial that looked just like the others. It had a handwritten label on it that read CT INACTIVE SAMPLE DND.

"Do not destroy—that's what he told me," she explained, and handed the cool bottle over to Bryn. "That's all he gave me. I don't know anything about it; I just kept it for him. Is it—is it dangerous?"

"No," Bryn said. "It's the exact opposite of dangerous. It's a cure we need, very badly. Thank you."

Johannsen nodded. She still didn't seem certain, but she also seemed resigned, which was good. "You said others will come looking. What is this, some kind of—of big pharma espionage thing? How worried should I be?"

"How worried was Dr. Thorpe?" Patrick asked her. She met his eyes, and frowned. "You know the answer to that, and the fact is, he wasn't worried enough. So judge by that. I'm sure Bryn already warned you others will be coming, and trust me, they won't be so nice or so talkative as we are. You need to get the hell out of here, and don't come back. Travel on cash only. Hell, take a freighter to Russia—that's pretty safe, and it's a shorter trip from here. But, Doctor—don't come back. If you do, we won't be able to protect you." He glanced over at Bryn. "Is that everything you need?"

"I think so," she said, and carefully wrapped the vial

in a small square of bubble wrap she'd brought for that purpose, then folded it up and zipped it into an inner pocket of her parka. "Ready to go."

"Doctor," Patrick nodded, and backed toward the door. He still didn't have his gun raised, but he was watching hers with unnerving intensity. He covered Bryn as she left first, then stepped out the door and jerked his head to let her know she should precede him to the outer exit, which she did.

Johannsen followed, shotgun still comfortably cradled in the crook of her right arm but threatening only the floor.

"Thank you, Doctor," Bryn said. "Please get out of here. I really don't want anything to happen to you. Dr. Thorpe wouldn't have, either."

The woman inclined her head, just a tiny bit, and that was all the reassurance that Bryn thought she'd get. Then she and Patrick were heading with all due speed to the SUV, starting it up, and driving down the bumpy trail toward the mailbox.

Patrick keyed the small radio that he'd clipped to the collar of his parka. "Joe, you ready? On our way out."

"Bring coffee, it's freaking freezing out here," Joe said. "If I had to take a piss it'd probably be ice halfway down . . ." He paused, and his voice changed. Utterly. It went flat and cold and nothing like Joe at all. "Pat, we're boned. Get—" He cut off. Dead air.

"Joe?" Patrick clicked the radio again, twice, and got nothing in response. "Goddammit. Floor it."

She did, at least as much as she could, given the crappy road conditions; the SUV's treads were packed with hard snow, and as the temperature dropped, the little thawing from the sun was freezing into slick ice. She hit a patch, and the vehicle slid to the right with a lurch, just as they rounded the curve and she spotted the Day-Glo yellow mailbox up ahead.

Joe was on his knees in the middle of the road, blocking their path, with Riley right behind him. Bryn hit the brakes, and cried out as the SUV kept sliding toward them. The front tires hit a patch of raw snow, bit, and held, throwing both her and Patrick forward into their safety belts, and as Bryn took a deep breath of relief she realized that something was very, very wrong with Joe and Riley.

Joe was on his knees, hands at his sides. Riley was standing behind him, her eyes fixed on the cab of the SUV.

And she had her gun pointed right at Joe's head.

Patrick threw open his door and stepped out on the running board, drawing dead aim on her. She wasn't afraid of that, of course. She even smiled, just a little.

"Even if you get the sweet spot, I'll still pull the trigger," she told him. "Nobody has to die here, Pat. Toss the weapon and step away from the vehicle. Bryn, shut off the engine. Now."

She didn't have much choice. Going forward meant hitting Joe first. Bryn jammed the SUV in park and turned off the engine.

Patrick, after a long, torturous moment, held up both hands and tossed his sidearm into the snow ten feet away—equidistant between him and Riley. Then he jumped off the running board, shut the truck door, and knelt, hands laced behind his head.

"Bryn," Riley said. "Same thing. Toss the weapon, get out and on your knees."

"Sorry," Joe said. His voice was clipped and tight with fury. "Never saw it coming. Should have, I guess. But you get so used to your pets you forget they can bite."

"I said I was sorry," Riley said. She sounded calm and amused. "Bryn. Count of five, I'm blowing his head off, and then I shoot Patrick. If it comes down to the two of us, I'll probably still win. You know that, and you still lose these two. I don't want that, and neither do you."

Red fury rose up inside her, a hot spiral that made her

hands tingle with the need to rip into Riley's flesh. She wondered if it showed in her face; it must have, because Riley tensed and took hold of Joe's collar in a tight grip.

"Don't," she said. "Out. Do it."

Bryn popped the door, tossed her gun, and knelt down, hands behind her head. "You're working for Jane."

"Never," Riley said. "I told you, I work for the government. I always have, and I always will. This doesn't have to go badly. Just give me the formula, and I'll let you all go. You'll have to hole up with Johannsen at her cabin, but you won't freeze to death, at least. I'm sure she's got transportation to get you back to the plane once it thaws in the morning."

"Salving your conscience?" Patrick asked. "You know we need the formula to stop Jane. And we still don't know if the sample Manny has is any good."

"That's right, and this might be the last viable sample, so no offense to your personal vendetta against Jane, but your government needs it more. I'm sorry, but my mission diverged from yours. We'll take on the Fountain Group. You know we're better equipped to finish this."

"I know the government's half owned by these assholes," Joe said. "You know that, too, Riley. Jesus Christ, you were *there*. There was a whole helicopter regiment ready to blow our balls off in the middle of the Heartland. What makes you think the people you hand that over to will do the right thing?"

"He's right," Bryn said. "Riley, think. Your orders could just be the Fountain Group taking the easy way out, and getting you to do their dirty work for them."

"We're boned anyway," Joe said. "She's been making reports, which means somebody along that chain of command will have leaked it. We're just lucky they haven't killed us yet—"

"Shut up!" Riley said sharply, and yanked on his collar. "Joe, you know I like you, but you're talking bullshit.

Nobody is going to sell us out. I work for the FBI, not some banana republic Bureau of Corruption. . . ."

Bryn could have sworn that she heard something, but it probably wasn't the drone itself; those were eerily quiet. It was probably the missile it released, hissing toward its target. It was a split second of knowing, with a sinking feeling of horror, that something *wasn't right*, and then Dr. Johannsen's quiet, remote cabin exploded in a fireball that lit the snow with hot orange an instant before the concussion wave slammed into her, knocking her forward, and blew the SUV into a sideways skid. She'd fallen with her face toward it, and so she saw the windshield and windows explode like jagged safety glass confetti as it slid . . .

. . . toward Joe and Riley, who'd both been knocked over as well.

Riley had just enough time to wrap arms and legs around Joe and roll him out of the path before the heavy weight of the left front tire tore through where they'd been.

Bryn lunged for the gun she'd thrown away; she saw that Patrick was doing the same, fifteen feet away on the other side of the trail. They both came up armed at almost the same second. Riley was pinned under Joe's weight, and somehow, he'd come up with a backup weapon—a knife, which he was pressing right over her carotid artery.

Johannsen's cabin was a holocaust of flames and billowing black smoke. Bryn could feel the unnatural heat on her back, even at this distance.

"You were saying?" Joe asked Riley. It was almost his usual, good-natured voice, but the muscles in his jaw were tight, and his eyes were narrow and cold. "About how you don't work for the Federal Bureau of Corruption? I'm sorry, I might have lost the last of that in the giant fucking explosion that just killed an innocent woman."

She didn't answer. She didn't move, except to shake her head. More denial, Bryn thought, than response. Her world had just been rocked . . . or shattered.

"Come on," Patrick said, and tapped Joe's shoulder. "We have to get the hell out of here. If they've got a drone, they'll be coming back around for another pass."

"Not much use in trying to outrun it," Joe said, but he eased his weight off of Riley and yanked her up to her feet. While he held her, Patrick gave her a quick, competent pat down for weapons, then shoved her to the SUV. Joe took the backseat next to her, with his own recovered sidearm pointed at her for security. Bryn took the driver's seat, brushing the broken glass away, and started up the engine. It took a few tries, but it finally caught just as Patrick slammed his door closed and clicked his seat belt in place.

"Any suggestions on how to do this?" she asked him.

"Considering we're on flat, empty snow plains? Not a fucking clue," he said. "Small-arms fire won't help us, either. Just . . . drive. At least we'll make them work for the privilege."

It wasn't a great plan, but Bryn had to agree, it was all they really had. And, some thought, if the drone dropped another missile on them, at least they'd never know it. Even upgrades like her and Riley would be incinerated in a blast of that magnitude. The skies had been clear before, but over the past hour they'd darkened as weather moved in; the low, gray clouds made it impossible to spot any approaching threats. The ruins of the Johannsen cabin smoldered behind them, still burning and sending sullen belches of smoke to the skies, but it fell behind quickly as she edged more speed out of the SUV on the slick, uneven road. Her neck began to hurt from the strain of driving, craning to look at the skies, and the bone-shaking bounce of the SUV on the rutted track.

She realized, about the same time as Joe and Patrick

did, that they were worrying about a threat from the sky when they should have been looking out for one at ground level. As the SUV slithered over the top of a rise, and she caught a view of the town of Barrow in the distance, she also saw a glittering row of vehicles spread out in a semicircle below. Heavy SUVs, like the one she was driving. And in front of the SUVs were men, a lot of them, all armed with what looked like military assault rifles.

"Have I said we're boned already?" Joe asked.

"Twice," Patrick said. "Still true, though. Riley?"

"I wasn't told there would be backup," she said. "It was supposed to be simple. Get the formula, leave you at the cabin, and get back to Barrow."

"I'm going to hazard a wild guess and say they intended all of the rest of us to go up with Dr. Johannsen," Bryn said. "Then you'd run into this welcome party. They'd kill you, take the formula, and be out of here within the hour. Nice and clean."

"Not government," Joe said. "The drone was a timeshare, probably, but these guys? No way they're military."

"No," Patrick agreed flatly.

Bryn stopped the SUV. There was nowhere to go, really—heading out over the tundra wasn't much of an option. There would likely be dips and ruts that would bury the truck fast, or break an axle . . . and a drone still circled overhead, most likely.

"They're hers," Patrick said. He sounded . . . empty, Bryn thought. Drained of emotion. She understood that; too many shocks, too little adrenaline left. Her body simply couldn't be bothered to power up anymore.

Until she saw Jane.

Patrick's ex was standing on the running board of one of the SUVs. Her parka's hood was thrown back, and even at this distance, Bryn recognized her easily. It was something in her body language, really—a kind of infuriating confidence that made Bryn want to kick her ass, personally, never mind all the firepower.

"Well, shit," Joe said. "Riley? You want to tell us again about the pure, holy intentions of the federal government? I'm all fucking ears."

The men with rifles were closing them into a killbox. Even if the SUV had been hardened with bulletproof glass and reinforced steel, this would have been dark days, but it was a commercial model, and the blast back at the cabin had done for the glass, anyway. Freezing winds whipped blown snow through the openings and lashed at Bryn's face. She couldn't feel her ears, or her fingers. Frostbite could take hold fast, up here.

So could death.

"Options?" Joe asked.

"Don't see much," Patrick said, "unless you've got the cavalry on standby."

"Forgot to ship in the horses. My bad. Guess we're—"

"Giving up?" Patrick asked, and grinned. It was a manic, slightly insane expression, and Bryn's guts twisted with sudden worry. "You really think I'm giving up to that bitch? I'd rather die in a hail of bullets, wouldn't you?"

"Some of us don't have that option," Riley said quietly. "I'm sorry. This is—"

"Your fault? Yeah. It is. Fuck your apology," Joe said. "Okay. Plans?"

"Kill 'em," Patrick said. "What else?"

He grabbed Bryn suddenly, pulled her over, and kissed her. It was a frantic, hot, desperate kind of thing, and she knew, horribly, that it was good-bye.

That they would not walk away from this.

Then Patrick twisted away from her, raised his sidearm, and began calmly, precisely shooting the men who were advancing on the car. Bryn grabbed her own sidearm and fired through her window, counting as men fell. Her hands were shaking, from the cold and the fear, and she was dropping one only every two bullets. In the seat behind her, Joe must have armed Riley, because she, too, was shooting.

Jane's people weren't shooting back.

Fuck, she thought, in a cold moment of clarity. *They want us alive.* They were going to get the cure. One way or another, they'd get it . . . unless she hid it, fast.

She stopped shooting, unzipped her parka's inner pocket, and unrolled the small glass vial. It wasn't very big, but it was big enough to scare her.

No choice.

She put the vial in her mouth, shoved it back with her tongue, and forced herself to swallow.

The vial filled her throat, an unyielding, burning obstruction, and she panicked, thrashing. *Swallow, you stupid bitch, swallow!* She kept trying, and finally, on the fourth convulsive gulp, the glassy weight slid down.

She felt it hit her stomach, and almost vomited it up. Almost.

Jane gave a shouted order, and Patrick yelled, "Incoming!" and grabbed Bryn to yank her down under the cover of the dash—but it wasn't full grenades, it was flash-bangs that left her weak, blinded, and dizzy. She choked on what must have been tear gas, delivered along with the flash-bangs, and retched up bile and drool as it burned in her lungs.

Her instincts were to get out, fast, and she managed to claw her way free of the truck, somehow, and rolled into the cold snow. It burned on her face, but it felt good, too. So did the relatively clear air.

The stunning effects of the flash-bangs faded, but not before she felt the bite of handcuffs on her wrists, and zip-ties binding her booted ankles. She twisted and writhed, trying to break free, and as she rolled over on her back, she looked up to see Jane's smiling, hated face.

Jane wiped snot and drool from her mouth and nose

with a gloved hand and said, "Oh, Bryn. We are going to have *such* fun again, you and I. After I finish saying hello to my husband."

Bryn's voice came out ragged and rough. "Ex," she panted, and coughed from deep in her chest. "You fucking psychopath."

"It's good to get these feelings out. Feel free to cry if you need to. This is the end, Bryn. I win. *We* win. From now on, everything changes." Jane gave her a calm, crazy, saintly sort of smile, and moved on to the others. Sharing her gloating in equal measures.

Please, Bryn thought. Her stomach churned, and her brain was flashing feedback, images of the last time Jane had held her prisoner. She didn't need that. She needed to *think*. Liam and Annie, they were with Manny and Pansy. Still free. Manny's paranoia would have triggered by now, and they'd be heading for safety. He had the cure. It wasn't over.

It couldn't be *over*.

But, as Bryn was picked up and carried like a still-struggling corpse to Jane's truck, she had to admit that it felt that way.

The glass vial she'd swallowed sat heavy in her stomach. It was sealed, but the stomach acids could eat through the stopper. . . . And if they did, what then? If Thorpe was right, she'd just . . . die. Shut down.

It might not even hurt.

The guard with her was a square-jawed Hispanic man with a shaved head. He seemed too young to be doing this, but his eyes were ancient, and utterly cold as he shoved her into place in the back. She struggled, vainly. He ignored her until he'd filled a syringe from a bottle, and plunged the needle home. She felt warmth and chemical bliss spreading rapidly through her body, and tried to fight it.

Lost.

She felt cozy and calm by the time Joe was loaded in

next to her, equally drugged. Then Patrick. Riley was last, dumped across their laps in a mumbling daze.

And then Bryn faded off into a sunset distance that wasn't quite unconsciousness.

She never even felt the SUV drive away.

Chapter 23

Coming out of it was bad—nausea and a pounding headache, ashy taste in her mouth. A general feeling of overwhelming despair. That was partly chemical, of course, the despair, but the situation certainly didn't call for optimism.

She was alone, in an empty room. No windows. It was smooth concrete, with inset lighting far above protected by thick mesh. One door with no interior handle, and no hinges visible.

The only design feature was a drain about three inches across. That was chilling. She remembered being in one of these types of rooms before when she faced decomposition; the drain represented easy cleanup when all the screaming was over. The only difference was that where the Pharmadene death chambers had been white, and fitted with observation windows, this was more like . . . a tomb.

It terrified her that she didn't know where they'd taken Patrick, or Joe, or Riley. Dying was something she'd long ago accepted—however long and painfully it might come. But losing people . . . That was something she couldn't reconcile. She'd lost a sister when she was young, and had never known what had become of her.

She'd lost plenty of friends and people she trusted, since all this had turned her life into a nightmare.

But she couldn't become *used* to it. The idea of never seeing Patrick again made her black and hollow inside. The idea that Jane would be the last face he ever saw . . .

I have to kill her, Bryn thought, with razor-sharp clarity. *If I do nothing else ever again, I have to find a way to kill her.*

There weren't any weapons here. They'd stripped her and put her into a cheap paper coverall, in a deeply unflattering blue. Bare feet in paper slippers.

She stared hard at the drain. It wasn't just a hole in the ground; there was a brass perforated plate over it, probably to discourage rats from using it as a freeway entrance. No visible screws. She tried pulling it up, but got nowhere. Nails broke off, leaving her fingers bloody, but she finally managed to pry up one end, and work two fingertips beneath for leverage.

The cover snapped off. It wasn't a lot of help, even then, because it was smooth and round. The screw had broken off cleanly, and there was no digging it out of the fastening in the drain.

Bryn stared at the round shape for a few long moments, then licked the blood from her fingers, took a firm grip, and began methodically working it back and forth against the concrete floor. It would take hours to make any kind of dent in it.

She had all the time in the world.

Hours did pass, long ones; she kept grinding the drain cover down, and once she had a straight edge, she began to strop it back and forth in brisk scrapes. Her dad had favored a straight razor, and she'd often watched him sharpen the blade on the leather strop that had hung in the bathroom against the pale green tile. The same strop he'd used to whip them when they misbehaved, or when they'd gotten in trouble in school, or brought home bad grades, or . . .

All this time, Bryn had never thought about her father much. He was a hole, a shape without a face, but the action of sharpening that makeshift blade filled things in for her. He'd had Annie's eyes, the same clear color; he'd liked close shaves and sharply astringent aftershave. Clean white T-shirts under his work shirts.

The strop. The strop had disappeared, at some point. Bryn remembered that, remembered hearing an argument between her parents. It was about the same time that her sister Sharon had vanished into thin air at nineteen . . . and about the same time that Grace, then sixteen, had gotten pregnant.

It was all significant, somehow. The strop. Sharon. Grace's pregnancy. Bryn had just tried to block it all out; her father and brothers had been an angry bunch, though Tate, then just eleven, had stayed close to her.

It had been the strop that was significant, but Bryn didn't remember why. Just the argument, the indistinct screaming voices. Grace, weeping. Slamming doors.

And Sharon, just . . . gone. Gone and never coming back.

Bryn froze in the act of sharpening as she heard a sound at the door—the distinct click of a lock coming open. She sat against the far wall, knees drawn up, with the drain cover concealed in her right palm. She tested the edge with her pinkie fingertip. Not razor-sharp, but sharp enough to cut, with enough force behind it.

She knew it would be Jane, and it was.

The woman walked in and shut the door behind her, leaned against it, and crossed her arms. "Well," she said. "Look at you. Feeling better?"

"Sure," Bryn said. "Love what you've done with the place, Jane. You have such a flair for decorating."

"I do," Jane said, and gave her a slow, cat-in-the-cream smile. "You're going to die here, so I'm glad you like the accommodations. Of course, given your upgrades, it'll take . . . well, a really long time. No food, no water—that will starve them out. But our best estimates are that you'll probably last at least three or four weeks before you start losing limbs. That's how it happens, you know. The nanites begin to jettison excess baggage to preserve core systems, so they shut off the extremities. Legs first, one at a time. Then arms. Of course, at that point, you're just a torso and a head rolling around on the floor, screaming. I really don't know what comes after that, though; we haven't done a whole lot of research."

"Glad I can help," Bryn said. Her throat felt dry, but she still managed a smile almost as cynical as Jane's.

"Did you want to ask me anything?" Jane said.

Bryn shrugged. "Not really."

"Not even about Patrick?"

Bryn stayed quiet, eyes focused somewhere beyond Jane. It was important not to flinch just now. Not to show anything that Jane could feed from, because Jane was a bone-deep sadist.

"You'll be happy to know he was reluctant about starting things up with me again," Jane said. "Of course, that's the amazing thing about medical science. Those little blue pills don't really give a shit whether you find your partner attractive."

Bitch. She was talking about rape, Patrick's rape, and Bryn tried not to react to that in any way. "You know, I might be the first to explain this to you, but it isn't the dick that's important," she said. "It's the man."

"Wow. You're such a Girl Scout. I kind of admire that. You're not even going to ask if he's still alive?"

"Why would I make you happy?"

Jane laughed a little and shook her head. "You've certainly grown a pair since the last time we played together, Bryn. I have to give it up to you. I thought you'd go down easy. I really did. But . . . you've surprised me, and that's something I value. I hope you'll continue to be just as entertaining when you're down to a head on a torso."

Open the door, you bitch. Open it.

"We found the cure, right where you hid it," Jane said. "Just thought you should know."

The shock hit Bryn hard, and she flinched and looked up, without meaning to. Jane's smile was rich with triumph.

"So the cure still exists," she said. "Thought so. Poor Patrick spent all this time trying to sell me on the idea that it went up with the cabin, and you undid all that hard work in just one careless look. I'll let him know you fucked him. Then I'll fuck him, and then I'll come back. We'll spend some quality time while you decide to tell me where you've hidden it."

She turned and tapped on the door. The lock clicked.

Bryn tightened her grip on the brass makeshift knife she held, and watched Jane leave.

Watched the door shut again.

Killing Jane right now would feel fantastic, but it wouldn't do any good. The bitch had told her something significant, even if she didn't realize it. They'd stripped her naked and searched her—probably cavity searched them all, too. Gone over every inch of the SUV. Probably sifted through the snow near the cabin and road.

But Jane hadn't found the cure.

Bryn took in a deep breath, let it out, and unsnapped her coveralls, stepped out of them, and sat down against the wall, naked.

This was going to hurt.

She pressed the sharpened edge of the brass knife to the trembling flesh of her stomach, prayed that the nanites were still strong enough to keep her going.

Then she began to cut.

Chapter 24

Bryn passed out three times before she managed to dig the bottle out of her upper intestines. Packing her guts back in was horrifying, and she had to hold the wound closed, lying on her side, until the flesh began to knit together enough to ensure it all held together properly. She passed out with the bottle—still sealed, amazingly, though the seal showed signs of pitting from her stomach acids—clutched tight in her other hand.

Cleaning up was a challenge she decided to skip, for the most part; after the blood was dry, she put the coverall back on to disguise the worst, and spit-bathed her hands and the splashes on her visible skin. That was harder than she'd thought, simply because she'd been a long time without water, and her saliva was starting to dry up. She emptied her bladder and used the contents to scrub the blood from the floor. It was still stained, but not recognizably. If Jane asked—which she doubted—she'd tell her she'd lost control of her bowels.

Jane would find that funny.

It took another three days before her nemesis came for another gloat. Bryn had chosen her spot carefully—a corner, angled so that she could push off from the wall and reach Jane with the shortest possible path.

Jane came in with two guards—uniformed, wearing surplus military fatigues. Bryn hadn't expected that, and felt a cold chill; she didn't think she could take both armed men and still do to Jane what she'd planned. It would be too chaotic, and give Jane too much time.

But Jane had decided to up the stakes, and behind the two men came Patrick. Pale, unshaven, bruised, he walked with his gaze focused on the floor, and the curve of his shoulders . . . He looked utterly different in the way he carried himself.

He looked . . . broken.

"I brought you a friend," Jane said. "Patrick said he'd like to see you through this time of . . . challenge."

She pushed him forward, into the center of the cell. Bryn couldn't breathe, and couldn't look away from him. His hair had grown about half an inch, and it looked lank and unwashed.

He didn't meet her eyes. He just . . . stood there.

"You should be starting to feel it by now—tingles in your arms and legs. Loss of feeling in toes and fingers."

Bryn ignored her. So did Patrick, but he seemed to be walled off from the world now, as well as Jane.

Jane had expected something, she knew—some reaction from Patrick, or from her. When the silence stretched on, Jane frowned and said, "Well, I'll leave you two to get reacquainted, shall I? See you in a few days. We'll come and remove any bits that fall off. Oh, and Patrick's body, since you'll definitely end up eating most of him."

She waved her guards out first, clearly sure there was no threat now.

Patrick looked up and met Bryn's eyes, and in that moment, she saw that he'd never been broken at all.

She launched herself out of the corner. Jane was right, she felt clumsy—arms and legs growing weaker, fingers unsure around the sharpened brass weapon. But that didn't matter. Jane saw her coming and stepped back, pulling the door shut.

Patrick got there first and shot his arm out. She slammed it in the door, and Bryn heard bone crack, but he shoved it open, grabbed Jane, and dragged her inside. He flung her toward Bryn, and as Jane skidded to a stop and pulled her sidearm, Bryn's right hand moved in a precise arc, as beautifully timed as anything she had ever done in her life.

And she cut Jane's throat, laying it open through the trachea. Blood sprayed, and Jane jerked back, but Patrick had her arms, and he stripped the gun away, turned, and fired at the two guards, who had only just now realized something had gone wrong. He dropped them both.

Jane sank to her knees, both hands clutching her fountaining throat. Bryn crouched down, too, not caring about the blood hitting her, only about meeting Jane's surprised, furious eyes.

"Yeah, that won't kill you," she said. "I know. You were looking for the cure, though."

Jane bared her teeth, a cornered animal ready to bite.

"Well," Bryn said, and stripped the seal off the vial she held. "Congratulations. You found it."

She had time to savor Jane's look of incomprehension, and horror, just for a second before she forced Jane's head back with a grip on her hair and poured the serum straight down Jane's severed throat.

Then she kicked her into the corner, bleeding out, and turned to Patrick.

He was watching Jane with the coldest eyes she'd ever seen. Colder even than Jane's. But when he looked at her, the ice broke, just a little.

He held his hand out to her, and she took it. They watched for long enough to see Jane start to convulse as the cure took hold, shutting down her nanites.

Ending her.

And then they walked out. The door shut fast behind them on a peculiar whispering sound, and it took Bryn a moment to realize what it was.

Jane was trying to scream.

She supposed she ought to have felt guilty about it but in truth, she just felt relieved.

Patrick paused to strip weapons from the guards and tossed her one; she checked the clip, nodded, and fell in behind him. The paper slippers were annoying, so she kicked them off in favor of bare feet as they went down a narrow concrete hall lined with cinder-block walls. More doors, all shut. Patrick rapidly entered a code into one of the locks and opened it, and Bryn saw, over his shoulder, that Riley was lying on the floor with her arm over her eyes. She sat up quickly to stare at them. The paper jumpsuit didn't look any better on her, Bryn thought, and despite what Riley had done, what she'd cost them . . . the joy that ignited in Bryn on seeing her was undeniable.

Riley threw herself to her feet and stumbled toward them. Bryn buried her in a hug that lasted only a few seconds, then gave her a sidearm. "Good to go?" she asked.

"God, yes," Riley said, and double-checked the gun. "Where's that evil bitch?"

"Dying," Bryn said.

Riley looked up and smiled, with teeth. "Good."

Patrick had already moved off to the next cell. It was empty. So was the third.

The fourth held Joe.

"Oh Jesus," Bryn whispered, appalled. The big man was lying on his back, like Riley, but that was the only real similarity. He was black and blue, and very bloody; he was still breathing, but the sound was labored and disturbingly wet. Patrick knelt down next to him. Riley, after that first horrified glance, watched the hall, ready to shoot. "Patrick . . ."

Patrick was unsnapping Joe's paper jumpsuit, which was wet with blood, and he uncovered a gaping gut wound. A wide pool of red soaked the concrete beneath

Joe's body, and a wide stream ran toward the drain in the center of the room.

He'd been bleeding for a while—steadily, fatally bleeding. Hours. Maybe days.

His skin, beneath the bruising, was a shocking blue-white. The fact that he was still alive, still breathing was nothing short of a miracle, but . . . but it was a battle he couldn't win.

That was obvious to all of them.

"Joe," Patrick said, and put his hand on the man's forehead. "Joe, can you hear me?"

Joe's eyes fluttered open, unfocused, and he said, "Jesus, took you long enough. Bitch got me. Sorry. Kinda lost my temper."

"You? Never."

Joe's eyes slowly fixed on Patrick's. "Been friends a long time," he said. His voice was soft and lazy-slow. "Brothers."

"Brothers," Patrick agreed, and took Joe's weakly upraised hand.

"She said she was fucking you," he said. "I pretty much had to shut her up, you know?"

Patrick shut his eyes for a moment and went very still, but he somehow kept smiling. Bryn couldn't imagine the strength it took to do that. "Rest, man. We'll get you help."

"Help's not coming; we both know it. Don't fucking lie to me," Joe said. "You tell Kylie I love the hell out of her. You tell my kids the same, all right? And you take good care of them."

"I will. But you stay with me, man, stay—"

It happened just that fast, like a switch turning off. Joe went still, and a slow, uncontrolled breath bled out of his mouth. His eyes were still open, still damp, but they didn't move their focus as Patrick said his name.

He was gone. Just . . . gone.

"Fuck!" Patrick snarled, broken and angry and desperate all grinding together in that single word. "No, Joe, don't you fucking do this—"

Riley had vanished, and Bryn hadn't even noticed her departure until she came back what felt like an eternity later. She stepped into the room, crouched down, and held out a capped syringe to Pat.

"From Jane's stash in her bag down the hall," she said. "Do it. Give it to him."

It was a shot of Returné. *He wouldn't want this*, Bryn thought. *He'd want to die clean and stay that way.* She believed that, and she knew that Patrick did, too, but she also knew it was impossible just now, in this raw, painful place, to make a rational decision.

Not when there was a *chance*. That was the awful thing about the drug . . . about having a choice at all. Because, in the end, love wanted more time.

Patrick grabbed the syringe from Riley's open palm, uncapped it with his teeth, and jammed it without a pause into the motionless vein in Joe's neck. He pressed the plunger, withdrew the needle, and threw it violently away, spitting the cap after it.

Revolted by what he'd just done, but desperate for it to work, all the same.

"Come on, Joe, come on—you've never given up a fight in your whole life. . . ."

Nothing. Bryn could—on some weird meta-mechanical level—actually *feel* the nanites in Joe's blood, moving through his body, but there was something wrong. Something not quite . . . adaptive. They were going too slowly—underpowered, perhaps. Maybe the shot was flawed. Maybe the drug was too old, past its sell-by date.

But in any case, it wasn't going to work. She knew that.

From the sick despair in Patrick's eyes, he knew it, too.

Bryn felt it all spiraling up inside her, all the pain, desperation, hunger, anger, frustration, black despair, and raw, pure *anguish* of losing someone else—someone else who *did not fucking deserve it*. She was shaking, she realized. Shaking and desperate and something . . . something was driving her now, something beyond her control.

Riley had told her in the first, horrifying moments of her own infection: *The nanites are programmed for self-transfer if the host is awake and mobile. They'll transfer the excess supply to the nearest identified ally.*

What was Joe, if he wasn't her ally?

She walked over to Patrick and Joe, and that, too, was beyond her control.

"Bryn!" She heard Riley say from behind her. "Bryn—"

She felt something moving inside her, under her skin, inside her flesh, a horrifying sensation of something breaking free, splitting off, *becoming* . . . and she could not control the hands that pushed Patrick away.

She grabbed Joe's arm in one hand, raised it to her mouth, and felt a rush of heat through her blood, through her entire *body*, that seemed almost orgasmic in its intensity, though it hurt, hurt horribly . . . and she bit down, into flesh and muscle, all the way to the hard crunch of bone. She didn't have to bite to infect him, but . . . but she needed to. Some sick part of her craved it.

And the activation would be faster than simple skin-to-skin transfer.

She knew Patrick was trying to pull her away, but there was no part of her that cared about self-preservation just then; her attention was only on one thing.

This.

The nanites rushed out of her, into Joe's open wound—an army of microscopic warriors charging into a battle almost lost. It wasn't that she chose it, any more than he had asked to receive it. . . . Riley had warned her that the nanites would mature, would reproduce, and would force implantation.

But it was a small mercy that at least it was to save someone she loved.

Patrick finally succeeded in tearing her away from Joe, and he flung her into the wall hard enough to draw blood from her banged head. She didn't care. The rush left her exhausted, and she couldn't react when he hauled her upright and shook her hard enough to send blood drops flying from her head wound.

"What are you *doing*?" he was asking her, but he knew. He knew all too well. "Bryn, *Jesus . . .*"

Joe didn't move. Silence fell. No one spoke at all. The sound of a drop of Bryn's blood hitting the floor was the loudest thing in the room . . . and then Patrick let her go and collapsed on his knees at Joe's side to check his pulse.

He shook his head.

"Wait," Bryn said. She felt unnaturally calm now. It was—was almost as if she could feel those nanites that had left her body, feel them spreading and working, reviving and reinforcing the tiny army that the first shot had delivered. "Wait."

A minute passed. Riley shifted uneasily at the door. "Something's wrong—it shouldn't take this long. We have to go," she said. "Bryn—"

"Are you feeling it yet?" Bryn asked. "The compulsion to spread them?"

"No," Riley said, which didn't make sense. They were both nanite factories, both primed to infect others; Riley ought to have been ahead of her on the harvesting curve. "Guys, I'm sorry, but we *have* to get out of here."

"Wait."

"He's gone," Patrick said, and sat back. "It didn't work. He's dead."

"I've been dead," Bryn said. "Have a little faith."

They waited another full, agonizing minute before Joe's eyes opened, and he let out that horrible, mind-shattering scream—the scream of a newborn, dragged from safety and comfort into a raw, painful world.

Or the shriek of a soul dragged out of peace and into hell.

Patrick took his hand and held it tight. "Easy, Joe, easy. I'm here. We're here. Breathe. Breathe."

Joe did, big, whooping heaves of air that rattled with liquid. He coughed out blood. The next panicked set of breaths was clean.

Riley nodded and left the room.

Patrick checked his gut wound. It was still raw, but it was already better. The bleeding had stopped.

"Jesus," he said, and it was half a prayer. "I know I've seen it before, but—" He shook his head. "We have to move. Joe, can you get up?"

"Pat?" Joe blinked and, for the first time, really focused. "That bitch stabbed me, Pat. Wish I could say I got her back, but—"

"Easy, man, she's done. Come on. Get up."

Bryn helped get Joe to his feet, and after an unsteady few seconds, he started shaking in earnest. His face went pale, and his eyes ... strange. Empty and yet very focused.

He said, in a low, rough voice, "Hungry. I'm hungry."

Of course he was. Bryn realized with a jolt that he'd used up whatever energy the nanites had brought with them in this massive healing effort, and he'd need food. Fast.

Or he'd turn on Patrick, as the next available food source.

Riley had already realized that, and she came back ... dragging a body. One of the men Bryn had killed in the hallway. Jane's men.

"Oh God," Bryn murmured, but she knew there was no choice.

Riley, expressionless, ripped the sleeve from the dead

man's arm, and said, "Patrick, you'd better wait outside. Bryn—"

Bryn was only too happy to join him.

Patrick didn't say anything, but the tight expression on his face was more than enough to communicate how repulsed he was.

I did this, Bryn thought, with a wave of sick horror. *I did this to Joe.*

She tried not to listen to the sounds inside the room.

A few minutes later, Joe came to the door. He was visibly stronger. Shaken, confused, but solid on his legs. His face and hands were clean of any evidence of what he'd just consumed—that would have been Riley, and kindness. The trauma would come later for Joe, she thought—it always came, sooner or later. But for now . . . for now it was just survival.

"Good to go," he said hoarsely.

They took him at his word.

Riley took point on the hallway, all the way to the end. There was another keypad, and she eased out of the way for Patrick to work his code magic, which Bryn assumed he'd learned from watching Jane . . . and the door opened.

It also set off a shrieking alarm, and flashing strobes.

"Go!" Patrick yelled, and Bryn charged after Riley. The next hall was another cinder-block nightmare, door after door, with another code-keyed exit. He opened that, and set off more alarms.

This time, when the door opened, there was a hail of gunfire. Riley took hits, but she fired back, and Bryn stood next to her, calmly taking down three more in addition to Riley's two. These were also wearing fatigues— not official current army camo, but Desert Storm–era. No identifying marks.

Joe was trying to be himself, and he almost managed it. "Ladies and gentlemen," he said as he stripped a machine pistol from one of the fallen men, "we are officially, truly screwed if this is a military op." He spoiled it only by the trembling of his hands and the haunted shadows in his eyes.

He was right. There was a window on this hallway, neatly painted and clean, and Bryn looked out to see clear white gravel, carefully raked. Trimmed hedges. Camouflaged vehicles, and the American flag flying high.

Truly screwed just about covered it.

She looked at the four of them, in bloody jump-suits. . . . None of them looked passably military, at the moment. "Joe, Pat, they're close to your sizes—" she pointed to two of the downed soldiers, and went to strip the clothing from the smallest man. It felt horrifying; it felt dishonorable. But there wasn't any other choice. *I'm sorry,* she told his lifeless, empty corpse. *I hope you weren't innocent, just posted here on orders.*

And my God, I hope you're not actually military.

Bryn—hair just starting to emerge in a blurred fringe of pale gold around her scalp—looked like a particularly gung-ho recruit. Riley's shorter hair could at least pass muster. Nothing could be done about Patrick's messy, unshaven state, or Joe's bruising, but if they walked quickly and quietly out of the building to the vehicles, they might just manage it.

Of course, the alarms going off would be a problem—or at least, would have been, except for Joe. As doors banged open at the other end of the hallway, admitting a flood of soldiers, he bent down, grabbed one of the fallen still wearing a uniform in a collar-pull, and began towing him toward the oncoming men. "Medic!" he yelled. "We need goddamn medics in here—we've got men down!"

It was confusing enough, with the sirens and strobes, that he seemed to be on their side, and with Bryn, Riley, and Patrick all uniformed and pulling their own bodies, the crowd simply flowed around them.

Joe left his man as soon as it was clear and ran for the door. They all followed. Bryn was acutely aware that anyone could twig at any second to the thin deception, but the general chaos—and the fact that all this was undoubtedly top secret, and nobody knew what was going on, or who was supposed to be there—contributed to just enough confusion for it all to work.

They made it to the parked vehicles lining the side of the gravel, and Patrick elbowed Joe aside to take the wheel. The keys were in it, and they'd managed to get halfway to the gate—manned, of course—before the first alarm was shouted behind them.

Patrick hit the gas. Bullets started flying as they accelerated, and Bryn felt two hit her in the arm and shoulder, but then they were smashing through the barriers just before the tire shredders raised up, and taking the turn on two screaming tires to reach a main road.

When she looked back, she realized that it wasn't a genuine army base—couldn't have been. There were no signs, beyond PRIVATE PROPERTY and TRESPASSERS WILL BE SHOT. It was far, far out into what looked like . . . scrub desert.

"Where are we?" Riley asked. It damn sure wasn't Alaska; not a flake of snow in sight. The mountains in the distance were blue and more like foothills. It looked and felt like the far Southwest, but Bryn wasn't entirely sure until they took a sharp left at the next main road, heading west.

All of a sudden, the nagging familiarity fell into place.

"I know this," she said. "My God. It's El Paso. Somewhere near it, anyway."

"El Paso where?" Riley asked. "California?"

"Texas," she said. "Right at the corner of New Mexico, Texas, and Mexico."

"That wasn't Fort Bliss," Joe said. "I've been to Bliss."

"I was stationed there," Bryn nodded. "That back there is some bullshit paramilitary compound, probably one Jane bought out or took over. If we'd been at Bliss, they'd have killed us in the hallway."

"We'd have never gotten out," Joe agreed, and then, after a pause, said, "What just happened to me?"

"You know already," Riley said, quietly. "You were dying, Joe. In fact, you *did* die. Don't blame Bryn. She did it to save you."

He narrowed in on her then, and she felt a sick surge of guilt and horror. She hadn't intended any of this.

"No, you should blame me," she said. "I'm sorry. I'm so sorry, Joe. The nanites were driving me, but I still—I wanted to help you. Jane left you there to die, and I couldn't bear that. I really couldn't, for Kylie and the kids. And because you're just—better than that." She was on the verge of tears, and the guilt felt overwhelming. She knew how much she'd hated waking up to . . . that. How traumatic it was.

Joe gave her a smile. It was almost real; she had to give him credit for the effort. It was possible to see past it, to see the uncertainty and the horror and the shock, but he was holding together. *Fake it 'til you make it.* It was probably his family motto. "I'm not angry about it. Look, I want to live for them, too, even if this is not the way I expected it to come out. And let's face it: being nearly invulnerable in my line of work . . . isn't a terrible thing. I got the upgrade, right?"

"Yes," she said, and just stared at him for a while. "You're okay with that?"

"Oh *hell* no," he said, and that at least was heartfelt and honest. "I'm not okay with a lot of things. But if I was lying on the battlefield and you had to cut my leg off to save my life, I'd be okay with it because the alternative sucked worse. I'd be not so okay with all the pain and coping, but everything's a tradeoff. I'm trying to believe this is—no different."

"It—" She eye-polled the others. Riley shrugged. Regardless of what she believed, she couldn't add to Joe's general distress. He was too pale, too controlled. Let him keep his illusions, if they got him through the day. "I guess maybe it isn't."

"Then I'll whine about my awful life later," he said. "But even then, I'll be alive to whine about it. Relax, Bryn. I'm cool."

"That's why we love you," Pat said.

That was too close to real emotion for Joe to handle. Bryn saw it, and he put up the armor again. Fast. "Moving on . . . What about Jane?"

"She's dead," Bryn said. "I slashed her throat and poured Thorpe's cure right down the hole."

"Jesus!"

"She deserved it."

"Yeah, I know, but *Jesus*, Bryn. You sounded just like her for a minute; you know that?"

She did, and it made her fall utterly silent. Patrick kept them moving, speed high, until they reached another turnoff—actually he passed it, then studied that side of the road, looped around and came back.

This side road, after half a mile of badly paved road, led to something that had sometime in the seventies been a happy family mobile home community, complete with convenience store and pool and campgrounds. Today, it was polluted by crumbling ancient trailers with blacked-out windows, trash, and prowling stray dogs. The pool was empty and full of rusting junk. The convenience store had long ago been left to rot in the sun, and taggers had left their discontent all over it in primary-colored swirls of graffiti.

"What are you doing?" Riley asked. "This place looks like they might as well call it Meth Manor."

"You know what I love about meth cookers? They usually have a lot of money and drive good cars," Patrick said. "They also love weapons, and tend to not call the police when you steal from them."

"Ah," Joe said. "Supply run."

"That, and I'm pretty damn sure this truck is Lo-Jacked. So they'll be tracking us in it. On the other hand, if they come rolling hard into this place and start shoot-ing—"

"Lots of bullets come right back," Riley said, and smiled broadly.

"It's a side bonus, along with the heavy potential for explosions. Meth cooking is not exactly a low-risk busi-ness, especially when you combine it with firearms. I think it has the potential to make our friends' lives very interesting for a while."

"There," Bryn said, and pointed. In front of a particu-larly decaying trailer that had once been disco-era an-tique gold sat a new Dodge Challenger, matte black. If Batman had a casual car for running errands, that was what it would look like, she thought—and the Challeng-ers had a lot of power under that hood. Enough to get them out of a lot of trouble.

"Outstanding," Patrick said. "Riley—"

She gave him a cartoon salute, and was out of the truck the second it stopped. The Dodge was locked—not an unreasonable precaution in this neighborhood—but she took a second to search around the rocky ground near a Dumpster, and came up with a flat, thin piece of metal that she rapidly fastened into a slim jim.

"Somebody ought to tell the FBI they need to check their criminal records," Joe said. "Because she's done this before."

Fifteen seconds after Riley found the metal, she was in the car, and fifteen seconds after, she had it running, a low throb of engine that Bryn felt even through the battle-tested metal of what they were in. "Go," Patrick said, and bailed out to join Riley; Joe and Bryn were right behind him.

Bryn was still outside the car when a skinny, pale dude in smudged underwear opened the trailer's door and stepped out on the rickety front porch, mouth open in an outraged yell. His front teeth were gone.

She waved, jumped in, and Riley jammed the car into gear and smoked tires on the way out.

Joe started laughing, and the rest of them joined in, not out of any real amusement but simply because ripping off a meth cooker was probably the funniest thing that had happened to them in a long time, and it felt good to laugh

Bryn finished with a last hiccup that was almost giggles, and sagged against Joe. She put her head on his shoulder. "I'm so sorry," she said. "Really."

He shrugged a little, but he was careful not to dislodge her from that position. "I'll adjust," he said "So will Kylie. Really."

In the front seat, Patrick was quizzing Riley about her car-boosting skills; she was electing to reply with a frosty, regal silence that was funny in itself.

Jane was dead. They'd roused at least some part of the government to act directly against the Fountain Group, if Riley was to be believed. And against all odds, they were still together, still moving.

But despite all those impossible strides, she felt one thing very clearly: fear. Because while they'd been suffering in Jane's personal killing jars out here in the desert, the meeting of the Fountain Group—their opportunity to take the brains of the beast—that had happened and passed without incident.

And they didn't even have names to track.

"We're boned," she whispered, echoing Joe from before, and closed her eyes as Riley turned the Challenger on the main highway, heading east. The only thing west was Mexico, but Bryn knew that if she asked, Riley wouldn't have any sort of destination in mind except *not here*. No point in even asking about directions until they reached some point where a decision could be made . . .

which, from El Paso, would be two hundred miles at least.

They searched the car, and came up with an interesting assortment of goodies—concealed panels in the doors yielded up a couple of poorly maintained handguns and a stack of stained bills, mostly twenties and fifties. When they stopped for gas, they found the trunk was filled with stained empty cups and fast-food bags . . . but underneath, at least ten prepaid cell phones, still in the packaging.

Bryn took one out and typed in the number that they'd used to reach Manny, before—before everything had gone to hell. "Think he's still answering?" she asked.

"I think that when we didn't come back in Barrow, he folded up the tents and vanished, along with everybody else on that plane," Patrick said. "He'd have considered us dead. He'd have been perfectly right to do it."

She couldn't argue with that, but something was bothering her—something much bigger. "Patrick . . . he knows how big this is, better than any of us. He knows the risks, if the Fountain Group goes unchecked. They'll take over strategic assets, like the military, or the government itself. Once they do that, it's over for the rest of us. They want to live forever—them, and their handpicked best people. Sooner or later, they'll own us. All of us. What do you think Manny would do about that?"

"He's got the cure," Patrick said, watching the numbers roll by on the pump as the Challenger drank down the fuel. "He'll concentrate on taking it apart down to the molecules, until he understands everything about how it works. And then he'll put it back together again, synthesize it, and use it."

"He'll act."

"Yes," Patrick said. "He'll do it because it needs to be done." He frowned, shook his head, and said, "I don't know how long we were—in there. Do you?"

"Long enough," she said. "Long enough for my nanites to mature and migrate." Which made her think, suddenly, about Riley ... who hadn't shown any signs of the same impulse, though they were on the same schedule—had to be, since Riley's bite had infected her. "You're not—?"

The other woman didn't look up from where she was loading trash from the Challenger's trunk into the pumpside bin. "Jane used them," she said. "Yesterday. She brought me one of her people."

"And you upgraded him?" Patrick said. It sounded like an accusation, though he probably didn't mean it that way.

"I didn't have a choice," she snapped back. "Ask your girlfriend. Doesn't matter. He was—she doesn't like to share. She had him put down."

"Put down?" Bryn said, and went very still. "What do you mean, *put down*?"

"We can still die, Bryn. Figure it out. It isn't pretty, and it isn't easy to do, but with enough ingenuity and cruelty you can do anything." When Bryn continued to stare at her, Riley looked away. "Acid. She dissolved him. Trust me, you don't want to know the details."

"Why would she do that?"

"Because she could," Patrick said. "And because she wanted to be sure she could destroy an upgrade if she needed to do so. Research and fun: her favorite combination. I'm sorry, Riley. She found ways to hurt all of us, one way or another. That was her specialty."

Riley nodded. "At least I'm not contagious now for another thirty days. Neither is Bryn."

"I don't think we're going to make it another thirty days," Patrick said. He sounded calm, and sure, and nodded to Bryn. "Call Manny. Maybe he'll pick up. We can hope he will."

But Manny didn't pick up. The phone rang, and rang, and rang, and then a distorted recorded message reported the number had been disconnected.

Manny was gone, along with Pansy, and Liam, and Annie. They'd even taken her dog.

It was ridiculous, after all she'd been through, to want to burst into tears, but . . . suddenly, that last little piece of normality being chipped away seemed to take the last solid ground from under her feet, and Bryn had to brace herself against the Challenger's sleek fender, just to stay upright. She gently folded the phone and put it in the pocket of her fatigues.

Patrick was watching her. She couldn't afford to break down now; she couldn't let him down. The four of them — they might be all they had, now. She would *not* be the weak link.

So she simply shook her head. He didn't seem surprised. Just grim.

Fueling finished, he took a trip to the station's probably horrible restroom; Bryn used one of the smaller bills in their drug dealer's bankroll to supply them all with water and high-protein snacks, mainly for her, Riley, and Joe. She didn't know how the other two felt, but her stomach was aching with need, and Riley was probably just as starved.

After that, it was more than a hundred miles across open desert before any significant towns, broken by occasional twisted eruptions of ancient rocks and the twisted, spiked growths of Joshua trees and mesquite. Green balls of desert sage growing out of mounds of pale sand. Rotting shacks. A cloudless, bone-dry, unforgiving sky.

And nothing ahead.

They didn't talk much. She offered a phone to Joe to call his family, but he refused; Riley wanted one to call her superiors in the FBI, but that was overruled fast. "Yeah, the last time you checked in with them, they had you pull a gun on me, and then they ratted us out to Jane," Joe said. "FBI means Fucking Bastard Informants, in my book. No phone for you."

Riley glared, but she didn't ask again. Most likely, even she didn't trust her people anymore, Bryn thought. Their circle of trust was about as big as this car, now.

They were still at least fifty miles out from the next landmark—Van Horn—when Bryn's phone rang.

They all froze, staring at her as she pulled it from her pocket. The shrill ring filled the car's interior, and Patrick said, "Wrong number?"

"Wishful thinking," Bryn said. No choice, really. The caller ID was blank. She flipped it open and said, "Hello?"

There was a few second's silence, and she had an intuition of the call being forwarded through a variety of cutout points, and then Manny's voice said, "Bryn?"

"Affirmative."

He let out a slow breath. "We were pretty sure you were all—"

"We aren't," she said. "Jane is."

"You killed *Jane*."

"If Thorpe's cure worked, then she's beyond help."

"Oh, it works," he said. "Better than any of us ever expected. The nanite shutdown takes about two minutes, five at the most. And they don't come back."

"How do you know—"

"You're coming up on an exit for Highway 285. Take it northwest toward New Mexico. You'll be met."

"Manny, *wait!* Annie—"

Click, and he was gone. Dead air.

She felt short of breath. Two minutes. Five at most. *And they don't come back.*

He didn't have any guinea pigs.

Except her sister. *No, no. She doesn't have the upgrade.*

What was to stop him from giving it to her? He'd have samples, she knew that. Manny always had samples. He'd probably managed to take one from her, while she was close by.

That made her feel faint and sick, and she gripped the

phone so tightly she felt the plastic crack in her hand. *Don't you fucking hurt her. Not anymore than she's already been hurt.*

"Bryn?" Patrick asked. He sounded worried.

She swallowed and said, "Take the exit to 285 toward New Mexico."

"Why?"

"Because I don't trust Manny not to kill my sister."

Chapter 25

They never made it to anything like a destination along the narrow highway; the signs all advertised the faded glory of the Carlsbad Caverns and all its attractions, but just over the state line, Joe said, "Pat, we've got a bird coming in. Check that. Two birds, eight o'clock."

They were large helicopters, military style if not military-owned, painted in desert camouflage, and as Patrick pulled off the road, the two helicopters circled overhead in a tight spiral. One drifted down in a storm of blown dirt and tumbleweeds to settle about a hundred feet away, while the other watched from overhead.

Pansy bailed out of the helicopter's bay and ran over to the Challenger. Bryn had the door open before she reached them, and Pansy must have expected a hug, because she smiled, but the smile didn't last long as Bryn slammed her against the car. "What did that psycho do to my sister?" Bryn shouted at her over the idling roar of the bird. "What happened to Annie?"

"Bryn, let go—let *go!*" Pansy was no lightweight; she slipped out of Bryn's hold and hit her with a solid two-handed shove that sent her stumbling back two long steps. Riley, Joe, and Patrick were all out of the vehicle now. None of them intervened until Bryn reached for the sidearm that went with her uniform, and then Riley restrained her.

"Easy," Riley said. "We need to hear this."

"Thanks," Pansy said, and frowned as she rubbed her bruised arm. She looked—fine. Well fed, well rested. Tense, but otherwise completely normal. "Well, I *was* going to tell you all how excited we were you were still with us, but . . ."

"Annie," Bryn said. "I want to know what's happened to my sister."

"Annie's fine, Bryn. What did you think, that Manny—" Pansy got it, then, and covered her mouth with her hand. "No. *No.* He wouldn't do that. He's not Jane, for God's sake!"

"Then how does he know this cure is so effective?"

"Because I convinced Brick to help us out with data mining. He found another Alzheimer's facility being used as a Fountain Group farming operation," she said. "The people there couldn't be helped, Bryn. So Manny gave it to Brick, and—he tested it there. It wasn't what he wanted to do; it was what he needed to do. But it *works.* Effective on both those with the basic nanites, the ones on Returné, or those with the upgrades." Pansy glanced at the helicopter. The pilot was gesturing to her. "We need to go. Now."

Bryn was not a fan of helicopters, and this ride didn't make her feel any better about them; she clung to the hanging strap as Patrick asked more questions. She couldn't hear much over the constant noise, but he seemed satisfied enough with the answers from Pansy.

Joe silently offered her a thick piece of beef jerky. Peppered. She took it and chewed; she hadn't even realized she was hungry, but she quickly downed six pieces from his stash, to his evident amusement. Riley needed less, but she ate, too. Bryn thought about asking where they were going, but it honestly didn't make much difference, because the only alternative was a jump out the door, and from this height she didn't really look forward to the recovery.

It was a relatively short ordeal, at least, and the aircraft touched down again within an hour's flight. Still desert, so they'd likely gone west, though Bryn's sense of direction was never good in the sky. There was an excellent reason she'd never signed up for the air force.

Once they were out of the bird and on solid, sandy ground, she realized they'd been let out . . . nowhere. There was a single small concrete building, well pitted with age and wind. Big enough to be a small closet, nothing more. No windows. One thick steel door that had once been painted some color, but had now faded to a dull off-tan that matched the sand.

The helicopters weren't landing here, she realized; once the five of them were out, they immediately dusted off again and beat rotors on the sky heading east. The silence of the desert was stunning, after they'd disappeared toward the horizon. One of the quietest places in the world, she'd always thought, and it seemed even more hushed here than she expected.

Pansy said, "Welcome home." She spread her hands to indicate the expanse of nothing that surrounded them. It was inhospitable as hell, and Bryn couldn't imagine who'd *want* to call it home beyond snakes and lizards. It felt ancient here.

And it felt unwelcoming.

Pansy walked to the small concrete structure, pressed her hand flat on the center of the door, and waited. After a few seconds, the door sagged open, with an audible hiss of air.

"Hope you're all okay with stairs," she said. "It's a long way down. Watch out, it's steep."

Inside, the lighting was dim, from inset wire-covered fixtures that had a distinctly cold-war era look to them.

Concrete, and narrow, steep stairs descending. Nothing
else except a bright yellow sign, only slightly faded, that
read HIGH SECURITY AREA — KEEP ID VISIBLE AT ALL TIMES.

Bryn pulled the door shut behind her, and felt a shiver
as it locked with a heavy, forbidding *clunk*.

Then she followed the rest of them down the steps.

She counted more than a hundred before she gave up.
There were periodic flat landings, which helped them all
catch their breath, but by Bryn's estimate they went
more than six stories down ... and then arrived in a
large, bare room with nothing but another door.

This one, though, had no keypad, no sensors, no handle on the door. Pansy simply waited, face upturned to a
domed observation camera above the entrance, until it
clicked open as well.

Another missile base, Bryn thought, but it turned out
she was wrong.

"Welcome to BHC-One," Pansy said, and led them
down a clean, arcing hallway with blue carpeting. "That
stands for biohazard containment, by the way. Back in
the day, this was where the government tinkered around
with nerve gas, and then it was refitted to explore infectious agents like anthrax, botulism, lethal influenza, and
hemorrhagic fevers. Anything with a rapid infection rate
and high kill percentage ended up getting grown and
evaluated here, all the way through the late eighties," she
said. "When they mothballed the place, they disavowed
it ever existed. Most of the equipment was too expensive
to remove, and nobody wanted to take responsibility for
destroying the place, so it just ... stayed here. Manny
took it over ten years ago. It's been our home ever since."

"Home," Bryn repeated. "I thought you didn't actually have a home."

"It's where we keep what's important to us," Pansy
said; she sounded more serious than Bryn had ever
heard her. "It's our last stand. So yes. Home."

The upgrades to the facility must have been made in

the late sixties or early seventies . . . It had that vaguely futuristic, sterile, spaceship feel to the design, including the oddly shaped doorways. Everything had, no doubt, started off sleek and white, but the plastic hadn't aged well . . . most of it looked yellowed now.

"Yeah, I can see why you love it," Joe said. "Comfy."

That made Pansy finally smile, a little. "This way."

She took a turn to the right, down another weirdly curving hall, and then opened up a door on the left.

The room was circular, midcentury modern in style, and finished out the same way, with a round bed and vaguely futuristic chairs and desks. A wall-mounted flat TV didn't look out of place in all that.

Neither did Annie, who was lying on her stomach on the bed, watching *Star Wars* unfold on the plasma screen. Her wavy hair cascaded over her back, and she was wearing pale pink shorts and a white tank top, and Bryn had a flashback to seeing her in exactly this position, even to the crossed ankles and her fists wedged under her chin.

She'd been fourteen then. She looked just as young now.

"Bryn!" Annie exploded off the bed in a rush, grabbed hold, and danced Bryn around in a dizzying whirl. "Oh God God *God,* I knew you weren't dead, they told me you had to be, but I *knew it,* you bitch, how could you do that to me. . . ." Annie ran out of words and just hugged her, and Bryn hugged back.

Mr. French came charging out from under the bed, barking excitedly, jumping at their feet and shins.

Home.

It felt that way.

"She's fine," Pansy said. "I told you she was."

Bryn pushed her sister back and held her at arm's length. She looked . . . great. Not a scratch. "They haven't experimented on you?"

"Manny? No way. He just gives me the shots I need—

that's it. I talked to the fam a week ago—well, Mom and
Grace, but they'll tell everybody else. I lied. I said we
were together, and we were fine. Had to keep it short,
you know? But they're not worrying. And they're all
safe. Brick has people watching." Annie studied her face,
and Bryn saw the worry in her eyes. "You look bad,
honey. What happened to you?"

"Later," Bryn said. "As long as you're okay, I'm okay."
She turned to Pansy, who was leaning against the door.
"I assume Manny wants us."

"Manny is chewing through the straps on his strait-
jacket in his eagerness," Manny's voice said. It came
from inset speakers in the slick plastic ceiling. "Pansy,
quit playing happy families and get them up here. Now."

"Yes, o master," she said, and flipped him off.

"I saw that," he said.

"He didn't," she told them. "No cameras in the rooms.
I insisted. But come on. He needs to talk to you."

"Annie comes, too," Bryn said.

Pansy sighed. "Fine. But leave the dog."

Bryn ignored that, too. Mr. French was too excited to
be left behind, and she let him trail along after them.

There was, it seemed, an elevator after all, in the cen-
tral core; it whisked them up a couple of floors, and
Pansy got them past more security doors, into what
seemed to be . . . an office.

Manny's office.

He had a big white desk, chair, a shocking red rug, and
a few guest chairs that matched the bloody color. Modern art on the walls that seemed weirdly avant-garde for
someone like him, but Bryn had learned not to assume
anything, by now.

Liam was standing next to the desk, reading a report
from a file folder. He put it down as they filed in, and
greeted them all with a nod and smile—but no handshakes or backslaps, not now.

Manny glanced up. He was wearing the square read-

ing glasses again, punching keys on a laptop as if they'd
done him personal wrong, and he kept typing as he said,
"Never thought I'd see any of you again."

"Glad to see you, too, Manny," Patrick said. He offered Bryn a chair, but she shook her head. Annie slipped
into it instead and crossed her legs; she seemed completely at ease, but if she was, Bryn thought she was the
only one. Even Mr. French couldn't settle down, weaving
around her legs and pressing close to emphasize how
much he'd missed her. "Guess Bryn told you that Jane's
dead."

That merited another uplift of the man's attention,
and raised brows. "You can verify it?"

"I was there," Patrick said. "If the cure worked, she's
gone. But that hasn't solved anything, has it?"

"No," Manny said. "There's a reason we're in the fucking last-stand bunker. You remember your friend Major
Plummer? The one with the shiny helicopters who ran to
your rescue? Plummer reports that there's a new inocu-
lation program being implemented in select branches of
service. I think we can all guess what that might be."

"Returné," Patrick said.

"They've manufactured enough in military labs to
take care of the key areas. As far as I can tell, they're
implementing the upgrades on the elites, like the Rang-
ers, SEAL teams, and such. CIA's probably got its own
programs running. Ditto every other wannabe badass
agency with initials out there. And it's spreading. Other
countries are trying to grab samples for replication."

"What is the Fountain Group doing?"

"What they always do—profit from it," Manny said
sourly. "I know who they are. Hell, I know *where* they
are. They're the same people at the heart of everything
that cuts money out of the world and stuffs it into their
pockets. They own the factories. Right now, it's covert,
but they're protected now. The government's on board
and in bed, and making sweet nanite love. They get what

they've always gotten—power, and money. And it's done. They've won."

Bryn regretted giving up her chair to Annie, because her knees felt suddenly watery. She gripped Patrick's arm tight enough to leave a mark. "They can't. They can't win, Manny. We can't just—give up."

He studied her in silence for a moment. Studied them all. And she got the very distinct, unpleasant feeling that there was something he wasn't telling them.

"You have the solution," Patrick said. "The cure works. You said it works."

"Thorpe's cure works," Manny agreed, "but it's a losing game. No way we can get enough out there, fast enough. Worse, nobody's going to cooperate in giving it. We can't stealth-inject a hundred, or a thousand, or a million. Or a billion. And that's where it's going. Exponential growth, like a virus. Nobody wants to die, Pat. Not you, not me. It's the Achilles' heel of the human race. Our survival instinct."

"Parents will infect their children to save them," Pansy said. "Why not? Who can stand to see their children die? Or their parents, or relatives, or friends? It doesn't stop. It can't stop until we stop it." And they all knew that was true—Joe, standing there recently infected, was proof enough of that.

"You just—you just said it can't *be* stopped," Annie said. "Pansy? You're scaring me."

"Good," Manny said. "Because what I'm about to show you is fucking terrifying."

Nobody said anything to that. Liam looked down; he already knew, Bryn saw. Pansy did, too, but she just stared straight at Manny.

He said, "I didn't want this burden. You brought it to me, Pat. You made me part of this. I'm not going to make the last decision. One of you—one of you needs to do that. Because whatever you do, me and Pansy, we're going to be safe."

"Will you?" Liam asked him. "What happens when Pansy falls ill? She will. It's the human condition. She'll develop some flaw, some disease, something that will start her on a path toward the end. What will *you* do? Let her go?"

"Yes," Pansy said. "He'll let me go. Because he knows—he knows that it's the right thing to do."

"So we're all wrong, is that it?" Joe asked. "Wrong to want to fight to live?"

She shook her head to that. "I don't know. I can't answer for you, or for anybody else. Just me. And I say—I say I'd rather not be part of the next phase of humanity. I'm opting out."

"You say you can stop this," Patrick said to Manny. "Show us how."

Manny pressed keys on his computer, and behind him, the blank white wall slid aside, revealing thick, floor-to-ceiling observation glass. Beyond it was a huge array of computer servers. "The room was originally built to house those big sons of bitches they used back in the sixties," he said. "Punch cards and tape drives. It was upgraded with Crays in the eighties. What's in there now is enough computing power to make Google envious. It's running silent, but it's hooked into every single broadcast tower in the cellular networks. Every commercial television tower and satellite. Every GPS network. I've spent the time you were gone working with every major infoterrorist group in the world to get this done, so I'm not just a criminal; I'm probably on everybody's most-wanted list right now—or would be, if they knew who I was. See, Thorpe was right, but he was a doctor. He thought like a doctor, one-to-one relationship. I thought like a technician."

"Nanites are machines," Liam said. "Incredibly small, yes. Incredibly limited in some ways. But they are sensitive to certain very specific transmission signals. Thorpe's cure was the key. . . . It didn't destroy the machines; it turned them off using a code sequence."

Bryn felt cold, now, but she said what they were all thinking. "You have a remote kill code and the means to deliver it. You don't need the serum, or needles. You can kill it all, simultaneously."

"As long as it's in range of the transmission, yes," he said. "But when I said it's a kill code, it's literal. If we push it today, it kills three people in this room: Bryn, Riley, and Annie."

"Four," Joe said. Manny looked stricken. "Sorry. Meant to tell you but we haven't exactly had a chance to catch up. It was this, or being dead on a cell floor."

Manny took in a deep breath. "Four people in this room. But it's not only that. There are unknown numbers out there—the survivors from Pharmadene. The ones the Fountain Group has infected, deliberately. The ones already inoculated by other groups. I don't have any idea how many lives this will take—thousands, maybe tens of thousands. My point is this: tomorrow, it will be more. How many days can pass before none of us can justify taking action?"

The silence was profound enough that Bryn thought she could hear Patrick's heartbeat. It seemed fast to her. Hers was rushing, too, driving adrenaline into her body like shimmering waves of discomfort. *Fight or flight.* In this case, neither one would work.

"I'm not pushing the button," Manny said. "I can't. I've thought about it, every single day since you disappeared; at the time, it was a way to get back for what those bastards did. That's why I put it together—revenge. Revenge and paranoia, because you know me, I'm paranoid and I admit it. But you called. *You came back.*" He shook his head, got up, and looked out the window at the array of machines. "And I'm not a strong enough person to make this call."

"Nobody is," Riley said. "You can't. *We* can't. You're talking about playing God as much as those people are."

"It has to be done." That came from probably the

most unexpected source: Annalie. She was still sitting down in the chair, looking young and sweet and utterly vulnerable. Her clear gaze was locked on Manny like a laser. "Guys, it *has to be*. Never mind us. Never mind who else dies that doesn't deserve to. The point is, we stop it now *or it doesn't stop*. Because if we don't want to push the button on four people here, or a thousand out there . . . what happens at a million?" Her eyes filled with tears, and she blinked them away, fast. "I didn't get a choice. None of us did, really. So I say push the button."

"It's not a vote," Patrick said. "It's your sister's life, and I'm not letting that happen. I've fought too hard. I'm not going to just—give up. There's another way."

"Not one that works," Manny said. He spun the computer around. "Just press enter. It's ready to send."

On the screen was a text box, a pop-up that read simply INITIATE TRANSMISSION? Two buttons. The OK button was highlighted.

"Liam?" Manny said. The older man stood still for a moment, and Bryn saw a tremor in his fingers . . . but then he shook his head and looked away. "Patrick?"

"Fuck you," Patrick said tightly. "No."

"Pansy?"

"No," she whispered. "I'm sorry. I can't."

That left the four of them. The infected.

"No," Riley said, unprompted. "Not at that price."

"You mean, at the price of your life?"

"That's exactly what I mean," she said, and Bryn thought she saw the same flat, predatory expression in her eyes that Jane had so often flashed. *We've changed,* she thought, and felt a chill. *We'll keep changing. He's right. We might still be human, but it won't last.*

Joe just shook his head when Manny's gaze flicked to him. That left Bryn and Annie.

Bryn held out her hand. Annie took it.

"Together?" she asked.

"Bryn!" Patrick grabbed her. "No. No, you can't do this."

"Yes, I can," she said. "You don't see it. You've never seen it."

"Seen *what*?"

"The monster," she said. "And I don't want you to ever see that."

She reached for the button.

Riley hit her from behind and sent her crashing face-first onto the corner of the desk; bone shattered, blood splattered. Bryn rolled, throwing her off balance, and managed to get her arm up in time to stop Riley's knife from punching into her eye. It went through the meat of her forearm, and caught between the bones; she used that, and twisted, yanking it out of Riley's fingers. She punched Riley, punched her again, tossed her into the wall, and buried the knife in the other woman's chest, low and center, cutting her diaphragm. Riley screamed, lost air, and clawed at Bryn desperately, opening gouges and drawing blood.

"This," Bryn managed to gasp out. "This is what we are now. No future, no family, no children coming after us. Just the monsters, until we're gone, and we'll get worse. This is the future. *Push the button!*"

Patrick had forgotten her sister, riveted by the horrifying violence she and Riley were inflicting on each other.

Nobody thought to stop her as Annie, weeping, walked to the desk and pressed ENTER.

Patrick screamed out a raw, wordless scream of denial and horror and loss, but it was too late. Her hand was steady and calm, and in the aftermath, Bryn went limp and sat back, waiting. They were all waiting.

Patrick rushed to her and took her in his arms, rocking her. "No," he whispered. "No, no, God, no, don't do this, don't do this. . . ."

"I never should have come back in the first place," she said. "I'm sorry. I love you."

Annie sat down next to her and crossed her long, elegant legs, sitting Indian-style like the little girl she'd been, not so long ago. "Do you remember what happened to Sharon?" she asked Bryn.

"Sharon . . ." *She walked away from home. She never came back.*

"Brynnie, I swear—I swear it was an accident. I never meant it—we were just arguing, the way we always did. She pushed me and I was in the kitchen cutting an apple, and I fell down. Then she slipped and fell on the knife, and it cut her on the thigh, and the blood—there was so much blood. I didn't *try* to do it—I didn't. I *wouldn't.* Dad tried to save her. He used that belt, you know, the one in the bathroom? He tied it up in a tourniquet around her leg, right here." She traced the spot with her fingertips on her own leg. "But she died. And they didn't want anyone to know. Dad took her away, and Mom and I cleaned it all up. I don't know where he took her. But I'm a monster, too, Bryn. From that moment, I was a monster. I never told anybody, but—I wanted you to know before we go. I'm so sorry."

Bryn hugged her, and held on to Patrick. Riley was still bleeding, and although the wound seemed to be knitting closed, it was taking longer than usual.

Joe let out a slow, trembling sigh. "I feel—" He lurched, caught himself, and slid down into a chair. He ran both hands over his bald head. "Can I talk to Kylie and the kids?"

Pansy, tears coursing down her face, took out her cell phone and dialed a number. She held the phone up to him.

Bryn felt it, then. A lurch inside, as if something had started to glitch. A bad part in a smooth-running machine.

Annie's breath caught, as if she felt it, too. Then she let out a slow sigh, and her head slid over to rest on Bryn's shoulder.

There wasn't any pain. She was just . . . gone.

That quickly.

"It wasn't your fault," Bryn told her. It was too late, but she said it anyway. "You were just a kid, sweetie. It wasn't your fault." She glanced down. Her sister's eyes were open, and at peace.

Riley was still fighting, but it didn't last long. She couldn't speak, but the fire was there, raging and fighting, until it finally guttered out. Then she was gone, too.

Joe's low voice stopped. Bryn heard Pansy let out a low, anguished sob.

Mr. French had laid his warm weight down in her lap, and he was whimpering with distress. He knew, too. Poor thing. She put a hand on his warm head.

"You have to let me go," Bryn said to Patrick. "Please let go now. I can't be a monster. *We* can't be that."

He knew. Finally, at last, he knew. She felt it in the way he kissed her.

And that was the last thing she felt.

One last glimpse of light, one last whisper of sound. Manny's voice. *Get the . . .*

She was curious, even now. *Get what?*

But then it didn't matter, and she was gone, too.

Chapter 26

She didn't feel it, that exact moment when the world came back; it happened in slow stages. A flare of light peeking in between her fluttering eyelids. A dreadful dry taste in her mouth, like smothering on dust. The shock of nerves sparking like short circuits.

Pain. A lot of it, slow hot waves washing up and down her body like tides.

Faces.

"She's coming back," someone said. She heard the words, but she didn't understand them. Her brain felt sluggish and unresponsive, late to a party her body had already crashed. "Sinus rhythm. Oh my God."

She was so tired. Closed her eyes a moment, and opened them because someone was rubbing knuckles against her breastbone. "Ow," she whispered. Her lips felt painfully dry. As she blinked away fog, she felt the firm pressure of a straw against her lips, and automatically sucked in a mouthful of sweet, cool water. She swallowed it, took a second mouthful, and then the straw was withdrawn.

"Hey." The voice was rough and familiar, and this time, when she blinked, she saw that it was Patrick. He looked . . . different. He'd grown his hair out, hadn't he?

Thinner, too. She reached out clumsily, more of a flail than a controlled motion, and he took her hand in his and kissed the back of it.

She remembered, then. Not everything, just pieces . . . Manny. The computer. Annie's slim fingers pressing ENTER.

Going away.

"No," she whispered. "Can't—can't come back—"

"You didn't," Patrick said. His eyes were shimmering with tears, but he blinked them away and didn't let them quite fall. "Not on your own. Manny said that if you were healed well enough before the nanites died, your autonomic system might come back online. So he shocked you until your heart started beating again. It wasn't the nanites that brought you back. *We* brought you back."

She shook her head. But she had to admit, the pain she was feeling . . . That was something the nanites would have fixed. "Can't be," she said.

"Want proof?" He reached to the bedside table that held the cup, pitcher, and straw, and picked up a hand mirror. "Look."

She was a mess. Bruised. Her nose had been broken and reset, and was braced with tape and a metal band over the bridge. Her face had healing scratches, and she remembered Riley clawing at her in desperation, trying to live.

When she touched them, the bruises ached. So did her nose, with a constant dull throb.

Healing, but healing slowly. At a human rate.

And something else. A dull ache farther down, low in her torso. Familiar, but something she'd forgotten until now.

"I'm bleeding," she said, and pointed down. For some reason, it made him smile. Sure. *He* wasn't the one menstruating.

"Yes," he said. "Because you're alive, Bryn. That's the real proof."

Pain was proof. Pain and discomfort and messy, inconvenient *life*.

Bryn caught her breath on a sob. All those things she'd given up, however unwillingly—love, family, children, home—was all there again. All alive, like her, with possibilities.

"Annie?" she asked. Patrick's smile faded, and she felt tears catch fire in her throat. "Oh, no. *No.*"

"We couldn't bring her back. I'm sorry, we tried. It was—I don't know. Riley was too badly hurt, we couldn't save her, but Annie . . . Annie should have come back."

Maybe she hadn't wanted to, Bryn thought. Maybe, for Annie, she'd found what she wanted out there in the darkness beyond. Maybe she'd found Sharon.

"And Joe?"

"Home with Kylie and the kids," Patrick said. "It's over, Bryn. Most of the deaths were disconnected—rich men dying of heart attacks all over the world, or car crashes, or strokes. The Fountain Group's gone, and they're not coming back."

"Military?"

"Pentagon briefing went down yesterday. The deaths are going to be covered up; most of it was still in volunteer trials. They've destroyed whatever samples survived. It's useless, since not only do we have the kill switch, we shared it with hackers all over the world. They can't find all of us, and it's lost its strategic advantage." His hand rested warm on her forehead for a moment, and it felt so good. So *real.* "You went into a coma for five days. We didn't know if you were planning on coming back to us."

"We?" She smiled a little. "You and who else?"

"Well, Manny and Pansy and Liam, but mainly . . ." He bent over and picked up Mr. French, and the bulldog stretched out on her, staring at her with soulful eyes. He whimpered a little and licked her hand. She petted him, and he wiggled happily. "Mainly this little guy. He slept next to you the whole time."

"And so did you," she said.

He smiled, and that was enough of an answer. He stood up, stretched, and said, "I'll let everybody know you're awake. Get ready for a stampede. Kylie wants to bring the kids to see you when you're well enough."

"Not yet," she said, and took his hand. "Just you right now. Just you."

"Just us," he corrected, and kissed her.

It felt like life.

Short or long, happy or unhappy . . . it was hers.

TRACK LIST

I love my music, and I hope you enjoy checking out the musical accompaniment I had this time for *Terminated*. Remember: artists survive by your honesty. Please buy the music you love.

"My My"	Liz Phair
"Angry Johnny"	Poe
"Full of Regret"	Danko Jones
"I Got It (What You Need)"	Galactic
"Starstruck"	Robbie Williams
"Beautiful Killer"	Madonna
"Meant"	Elizaveta
"The Stations"	The Gutter Twins
"Heartbroken, In Disrepair"	Dan Auerbach
"Demons"	Imagine Dragons
"Odi et Amo"	Elizaveta
"Evil" (single version)	Matt Gross
"Darkness on the Edge of Power"	Immediate
"Satellite"	The Kills
"Mission"	Van She
"Red Eyes and Tears"	Black Rebel Motorcycle Club
"Starlight"	The Wailin' Jennys

ALSO IN THE REVIVALIST SERIES FROM

RACHEL CAINE

Two Weeks' Notice

After dying and being revived with the experimental drug Returné, Bryn Davis is theoretically free to live her unlife—with regular doses to keep her going. But Bryn knows that the government has every intention of keeping a tight lid on Pharmadene's life-altering discovery, no matter the cost.

And when some of the members of a support group for Returné addicts suddenly disappear, Bryn begins to wonder if the government is methodically removing a threat to their security, or if some unknown enemy has decided to run the zombies into the ground...

Available wherever books are sold or at penguin.com

facebook.com/AceRocBooks

R0119

Can't get enough paranormal romance?

Looking for a place to get the latest information and connect with fellow fans?

"Like" Project Paranormal on Facebook!

- Participate in author chats
- Enter book giveaways
- Learn about the latest releases
- Get book recommendations and more!

facebook.com/ProjectParanormalBooks

M883G1011